THE TIDE:

BREAKWATER

THE TIDE:

BREAKWATER

The Tide Series Volume 2

Anthony J Melchiorri
December, 2015

Sign up for Anthony's spam-free newsletter for the chance to receive free books and stories, special offers, and all the latest info on his new releases: **http://bit.ly/ajmlist**

The Tide: Breakwater

Copyright © 2015 by Anthony J. Melchiorri. All rights reserved.

First Edition: December 2015

http://AnthonyJMelchiorri.com

ISBN-13: 978-1-5228-1293-7

ISBN-10: 1-5228-1293-8

Cover Design: Eloise Knapp Design

10 9 8 7 6 5 4 3 2 1

BOOKS BY ANTHONY J MELCHIORRI

Black Market DNA Series
Fatal Injection (A Novella)
Enhancement (Book 1)
Malignant (Book 2)
Variant (Book 3)

Standalone
The Human Forged
The God Organ

The Tide Series
The Tide (Book 1)
The Tide: Breakwater (Book 2)
The Tide: Salvage (Book 3, Coming Spring 2016)

ONE

A COOL WIND LIFTED Meredith Webb's hair and tickled her skin. The crispness in the air reminded her of autumn days in decades past, when she would run along the Potomac River after her shift at the CIA headquarters in Langley. She had always thought the trees along the path looked the most beautiful when their branches were draped in the orange and red hues of a sunset. Running under the fiery colors beside the river had given her mind time to wander and her body a physical outlet to unload the day's challenges and frustrations.

That urge to run sprang up in her now—an almost imperceptible dribble slowly growing into a flood.

She needed to move. But she had nowhere to go.

Meredith touched the bandage across her forehead, the patches along her cheeks, and the gauze on her arm. Painful memories of the bus crashing and her head slamming into the wheel surged through her. All because of the Skulls. They had surrounded the bus; they'd caused the crash.

And they'd done more than that. In a matter of days, they'd brought the world to its knees. They'd left humanity begging for answers on how to stop the spread of the Oni

Agent.

The wounds beneath her bandages ached. She tried to ignore the sensation and leaned up against the gymnasium at Fort Detrick that had been converted into a temporary shelter. Within it, the military had organized a civilian triage, quarantine, and medical station in addition to the sleeping quarters.

Gunfire erupted in the distance, and she flinched. She regained her composure, and four soldiers rushed toward a gate along the north wall of the Army's medical research complex. A low explosion echoed between the buildings, and the gunfire ceased.

Across the base, the pounding of hammers against sheets of metal and planks of wood sounded. Two yellow bucket loaders toiled at one end, filling the wire-wrapped HESCO bastions with dirt to reinforce the fences around Fort Detrick's perimeter.

Meredith shook her head. The world's strongest military was resorting to makeshift privacy fences and HESCOs to barricade the base against the creatures swarming the streets outside.

From her work in biodefense, she knew Fort Detrick didn't have a mass of ordnance like some other Army installations. The base served as the center for the United States Army Medical Command and hosted civilian, federal, and military employees pursuing medical, biodefense, and health-related work, research, and training. She guessed most of the weapons and the Black Hawks sitting in the parking lots were on loan, possibly from Fort Bragg. How long would Detrick's borrowed ammunition and defenses last against the hordes of Skulls outside?

A distant howl echoed nearby. Another breeze curled past her, and the smell of smoke stung her nostrils. The lingering scent of burned flesh and decay came with it. The soldiers might be able to construct a barrier around Fort Detrick to help protect against the Skulls, but they couldn't prevent the harsh reminders of their nightmarish reality from sifting in with the wind.

A door clicked open to Meredith's right. A young woman with auburn hair stepped out, and a golden retriever followed her.

"Kara," Meredith said. "How are you?"

"All right, I think. How about you?" Kara asked as the dog circled around the grass. It favored its front leg, and Kara's makeshift splint covered the retriever's broken limb.

"I'm not even sure how to answer that question anymore." Meredith offered Kara a sympathetic smile. The golden retriever, Maggie, made her mark on the grass. She sauntered back to Kara and then lay down at her feet with a grunt. "Maggie getting by okay?"

"I don't think she has a clue what's going on. It didn't even take her long to learn how to walk with that leg." Kara folded her arms across her chest. "I wish I was like that."

A ghastly wail rose up, followed by a chorus of others outside the gates. More gunfire exploded at one end of the facility. Maggie pushed herself up with her good leg and stood protectively in front of Kara.

Kara didn't so much as flinch. The young woman had faced the Skulls, saved her neighbors, and even rescued Meredith from the beasts. And she hadn't even finished her first year at college yet. Now Meredith questioned if the girl ever would have a chance to go back to school.

The howls of the Skulls once again dissipated, and Meredith and Kara stood in silence for a while.

Kara pointed to the soldiers marching around the perimeter with rifles. One barked orders at a half-dozen men reinforcing the fence around the eastern side of the fort. "They really think that's going to keep those creatures out? If the razor wire and chain-links aren't enough, how's that going to help?"

"I think the idea is to at least provide a visual obstruction. From what your father and I learned, the Skulls hunt primarily by sight and sound."

"Guess that's true," Kara said. "So now we have a buffer against those things?"

"Right. If we're lucky, that'll keep us hidden from them." Meredith hated relying on luck, but what choice did they have?

Kara patted Maggie on the head and squinted into the distance, where smoke still billowed from downtown Frederick, Maryland. "I wonder how many normal people are still out there. What's going to happen to them?"

"I'm sure the government is planning something."

"I hope you're right."

They both stood in silence for a few moments before

Meredith spoke. "I need to meet with your father soon. Do you know where he is?"

Kara hung her head low and scratched the back of her neck. "He's telling Nina about Joe's death." She met Meredith's gaze. "I couldn't be there when he broke the news. It was too much."

Meredith had been unconscious at the time, but Dom had told her about Joe's death after the bus crash. Kara's neighbor had been a kind, courageous man, and he'd made the ultimate sacrifice to protect his family. Now his wife, Nina, and their two children would have to continue the struggle for survival without him.

"I should've been on the bus with you all," Kara continued. "Not Joe. The guy didn't even know how to work a gun until yesterday. I *did*."

"No, Kara, he didn't, but it wasn't your fault. Don't let yourself get wrapped up in the 'what ifs.' You gave him and his family a chance. You went into their home and got to them before the Skulls did. Without you, none of them would be here. Nina, her children…"

Kara didn't seem convinced. "Maybe. But now we're all stuck here, and I don't want to sit on one of those cots all day, waiting for someone to magically save the world. I can't do that."

"I've noticed." Meredith scrunched her nose. Another waft of burning Skulls drifted past. "But right now, you've got a little sister who's probably scared out of her mind."

"That's not what I meant when I said I want to be useful.

I want to actually do *something*."

"I know," Meredith said. "But that's a start. If we're going to reclaim this world from the Skulls, we've got to do it one step at time, one person at a time."

Kara's brow furrowed.

"And after that, I have a feeling there will be enough going on around here that we can find something to keep you busy. Sound reasonable?"

Kara nodded.

"So for now, do you mind taking me to your father? I think he and I need to have a long-overdue conversation with the Commander."

His SCAR-H still slung over his shoulder, Dominic Holland nodded solemnly to Nina Weaver and her children, trying to convey his sympathy for their loss in his chiseled features. The woman hugged her young son and daughter tightly as the three absorbed the news of Joe's death. Dom hated to leave them grieving, but he struggled to say anything more than the weak condolences he'd already offered.

"I'm truly sorry," he said once more before standing. He left the family amid the masses of others milling about the rows of green cots in the gymnasium. As he exited into the hall, the scene of Joe's death replayed in his mind, the Skull pouncing at him, stabbing him with its serrated claws. He'd never forget Joe's last moments. And now the haunting image of Nina's sorrowful expression was permanently etched onto his mind's eye.

Dom wondered how many other families had received news like the Weavers. And how many other families might never hear anything because there was simply no one left to hear it? How many families ate dinner together last week and were now prowling the streets as Skulls in a perpetual hunt for live flesh?

A shiver crept down his spine. They needed to act fast; they needed a vaccine, a cure, anything to stop the spread of this bioweapon.

He'd postponed his meeting with Acting Commander Shepherd so he could deliver the morbid news to Nina. Now he could focus on moving forward, and he hoped Shepherd would offer a clear path toward eradicating the Oni Agent.

His boots clicked on the tile floor as two medics rushed past with a man on a stretcher. A thick layer of gauze, already stained crimson, ringed the man's arm. His pained groans carried down the hall, and they hurried around a corner.

A door opened to the outside, and sunlight flooded through the corridor. Maggie bounded through, tail wagging, and ran to Dom. Kara chased after the dog with Meredith following.

"How'd it go?" Kara asked.

"About as hard as I thought it'd be," Dom said. "Nina's going to need some help with the kids. I'll do the best I can, but do you mind keeping an eye on them?"

"Aye, aye, Captain," Kara said, mimicking his Hunters. She led Maggie back to the makeshift civilian shelter.

Dom watched her until she left, then turned back to Meredith. He eyed her bandages but knew it was no use asking if she should be up and running about. She would go with him no matter how much he protested.

He stepped past her and opened the door to the complex. "That's the Network Enterprise Center." He gestured toward a building about a hundred yards away. "Shepherd said to meet there. Said he was also going to reestablish communications with the outside world, including the *Huntress*, from the NEC."

He and Meredith strode side by side along the sidewalk. The NEC building lay at the end of the path. Broken windows and pocks marred the side of the structure, evidence of small arms fire. Shepherd had mentioned that several of their own men and women had been victims of the Oni Agent. He had led his forces in retaking the base while preventing more Skulls from pouring into Detrick.

They neared the NEC, and the unmistakable smell of death hit Dom. Several Humvees idled in front of the building. Rifles and other weapons leaned against the brick wall. Beside them, green canvas sheets were draped over dozens of bodies laid out in the parking lot. Soldiers moved between the corpses. Some spoke into radios. Others dashed in and out of the NEC. A contingent of men and women brought empty stretchers into the front door and came back out with a body on their stretcher. Dom and Meredith moved aside when two soldiers carried one of their fallen brethren past.

A man with a dark complexion and short-cropped black hair stepped forward and offered his hand. "Dominic Holland and Meredith Webb, I presume."

Dom and Meredith shook his hand in turn.

"I'm Commander Sergeant Major Jackson." He held the door open and ushered them in. "Acting Commander Shepherd is in the middle of talks with Fort Bragg and told me to watch for you. Your comm specialist, Adam Galloway, is already here. Are we waiting on anyone else?"

"No, I don't believe so." Dom considered his crew members at the shelter. Renee had been attacked by a Skull and was still being given the chelation and antibiotic therapy that his medical team had claimed would eliminate the Oni Agent. Miguel and Hector had stayed with her and were helping the medical personnel as best they could with the other patients. And their pilot, Frank, was tending to their chopper for a return trip to the *Huntress*.

As Meredith followed Dom inside, the rattle of gunfire burst about two hundred yards away at another gate. It sounded far more substantial than the sporadic small arms fire that had thus far punctuated their time at the base.

Meredith paused at the entryway. "What the hell's going on?"

Jackson held his radio up. "South gate, Command. What's your status?"

Dom squinted at the scene as soldiers ran to the gate. The

structure hadn't yet been reinforced with the current construction efforts.

Static crackled over the radio, followed by a panicked voice. "Command, we've got contacts…breaking…overrun!"

"Shit." Jackson stepped out and called to the soldiers working around the NEC. "Stop what you're doing and head to the southern gates!"

Without delay, the men and women piled into the Humvees. The vehicles tore off across the grass between the buildings. Even from this distance, Dom could see Skulls climbing through the razor wire to get inside Detrick. The breach was only a few blocks from the gymnasium and fitness facility with the civilian shelter where Dom's Hunters and family were. He grabbed his rifle. "Let's get the hell down there!"

TWO

———◆◆◆◆———

DOM READJUSTED HIS GRIP on his rifle, anxious to get to the civilian shelter—and to his daughters.

"Private!" Jackson called into the interior corridor of the NEC. A lanky young man rushed to his side. "Let's move!"

"Yes, sir!" The private sprinted toward a jeep across the lot. He hopped inside it, and the engine revved.

Jackson picked up one of the M16s sitting outside the NEC. He offered a second to Meredith, and she accepted it. She and Dom slid in the back of the vehicle. The private punched the accelerator, and they took off.

Ahead, soldiers retreated to the cover of buildings. More Skulls poured through the breached gate. Some, freshly turned, appeared no different from normal humans. Others exhibited all the outward symptoms Dom had seen on the IBSL: arms ended in long claws, gnarled skeletal protrusions burst from their shoulder blades, spikes jutted out from their joints, and bony cages formed around their chests. Horns graced a few of their heads like morbid crowns, and fins stuck out from the spines of others. Their voices carried up in a thunderous roar of snarls and guttural screams.

A single Skull led the pack, running low with its arms outstretched. Soldiers fired frantically at the monster, and bone fragments chipped off from its organic body armor as it charged. A round finally caught the beast in its face. It crumpled forward and slid across the grass. Others jumped over its body, eager to take its place and lead the hunt.

Dom eyed the commissary near the Provost Marshall's office. The building was the only structure standing between the Skulls and the gym-turned-shelter. The beasts were closing in on it.

The jeep hit a rut, and the private struggled with the steering wheel. The vehicle bounced and twisted to the side, almost spilling Dom and Meredith. Dom tightened his grip around a rail, his knuckles turning white, and clenched his jaw. He kept his eyes on the surging wave of Skulls.

"Put us at their flank," Jackson said.

Already, more soldiers were retreating to the Provost Marshall's office. The Skulls continued to heave themselves over the gate. Some caught their legs or arms in the razor wire surrounding the entrance, but they lashed forward relentlessly. Their flesh tore and peeled as they persisted, and soon they flopped onto the grass within the fort.

"What the hell set off this attack?" Meredith asked as the jeep skidded to a stop.

"Don't know," Dom said, jumping over the side. "All it takes is one of them to get riled up." He turned to Jackson as the man leapt out. "You need to make your men understand that, Sergeant Major. Staying out of sight is key to survival."

"Our people are aware," Jackson said. "And when we kick these bastards out of here again, I'll make sure every goddamn enlisted and civvy behind our walls understands how serious this shit is."

Dom started to sprint off, and Meredith trailed behind. Jackson ran, cradling his rifle. The private lugged an M240 machine gun from the back of the jeep and followed. They slid to a stop along the side of a road behind a line of trees. The Skulls were running parallel to the street, and the brunt of Fort Detrick's defenses was firing on the creatures from the Provost Marshall's office, which kept the Skulls' attention away from Dom's group. A dozen or so men and women took positions between vehicles in the office's parking lot and let loose a vicious barrage of gunfire.

"Get ready!" Jackson ordered as he shouldered his M16.

The private dropped to a prone position and sighted up the M240 mounted on its bipod. He pressed its stock into his shoulder.

Dom traced his muzzle over the running Skulls. He kept a bead on one built like a linebacker with wide shoulders covered in yellowed plates. Its hands ended in stubby claws, and crooked spikes tore through the remnants of a suit jacket flapping around the creature's body.

"Open fire!" Jackson bellowed.

The bark of the M240's fire drowned out the blasts from the other three rifles. Dirt and grass flew up in chunks around the Skulls as the private followed them with the machine gun.

The recoil of Dom's rifle sent shockwaves through his shoulder while he poured round after round at the beasts. He took down the linebacker and then half a dozen other Skulls, but the number was paltry compared to the mass of creatures leaping over the fresh corpses with only one thing on their mind: Kill.

The majority of the Skulls still churned forward toward the Provost Marshall's office. But two, attracted by the new source of gunfire, turned and sprinted at Dom. He readjusted his aim and squeezed the trigger to take several measured shots. The two creatures spilled across the grass, blood already seeping from their cranial wounds.

The bark of the M240 continued. Rounds chewed into the Skulls' flanks. Their lives ended by the machine gun's stream of bullets, the creatures crashed to the ground, tripping up others. Skull corpses piled up along the lawn, and the flow of the beasts started to dissipate as the monsters dispersed. A few dozen still charged toward the soldiers entrenched near the gate, and another twenty or so of them turned, careening toward Dom, Meredith, Jackson, and the private.

But distance was on Dom's side. At twenty yards, the Skulls went down under a fresh barrage of bullets. One Skull limped toward them, its face caught in a malicious snarl. Its leg had been devastated by machine-gun fire. Dom caught the creature's face in his sights, pulled the trigger, and watched it fall.

He breathed a momentary sigh of relief. The rifle chatter grew more sporadic, and the distant yelling of the soldiers barricading the commissary and Provost's office seemed to quiet. But the still air was soon rent anew by howls. A fresh surge of Skulls forced themselves through the razor wire and tumbled across the asphalt and grass.

"When is this going to end?" Meredith shouted and jammed a fresh magazine into her rifle.

Dom reloaded and resumed firing, the crack of his rifle the only answer he could offer.

Weapons bristled from the windows in the buildings as soldiers took shots at the Skulls. More men and women fell back toward the commissary. But some weren't fast enough. A trio of Skulls broke through the wall of gunfire. Bullets smashed into the pavement and punched into the parked sedans and Humvees around them. Dom watched in horror. The beasts clawed and bit at the soldiers bravely defending their posts.

While the creatures rushed the buildings to the east, several dozen more rushed toward Dom's position. The rattle of the M240 suddenly ceased.

"What the hell's going on?" Jackson yelled.

Without the encumbering machine gun fire, the Skulls charged almost unhindered.

"Jam!" The private moved the safety forward, pulled up the cocking handle, and then returned it. He clicked the safety again before checking the feed pawl assembly then the feed tray. "Found it."

He fixed the ammo belt as he cleared the jam and replaced the cover assembly. He pulled the cocking handle

15

again and rode the bolt forward. The M240 burst to life, and a hail of bullets smashed against the oncoming Skulls.

But it was too late. They'd already gained too much ground.

"We've got to pull back," Dom said.

Jackson cursed and stood, picking off the closest Skulls.

They retreated to the jeep. Dom threw himself in and helped Meredith after him. The private jumped into the driver's seat, and the engine rumbled to life. The tires kicked up sod when they shot forward.

Jackson barked into his handheld radio. "All units are retreating from the breach. Warn everyone to stay indoors and out of sight. Repeat, everyone who is unarmed must stay indoors and out of sight."

"Copy that," another voice replied. Radio chatter accompanied the jeep's growling engine. They curled onto another street.

From their vantage point, Dom could see the wave of Skulls crashing against the commissary. More Humvees tore down the street behind them and from the opposite side of the base, converging on the monsters. Several Skulls clambered around the building and threw themselves at the doors and windows.

The convoy of Humvees stopped along a ridge overlooking the commissary and fitness center. Soldiers spilled out of the vehicles and took up firing positions. Yet Dom feared these reinforcements wouldn't be enough. The Skulls ignored the lead pouring down on them and continued their desperate search for a way into the building where fresh, defenseless prey awaited them.

"Where to?" The private asked.

Jackson surveyed the scene with his binos. The rattle of mounted machine guns and rifles echoed over the base. Even as Skulls fell, more seemed to take their place. A pair escaped the masses and climbed the side of the fitness center. They started heaving themselves into a skylight. A sharpshooter picked them off, but more scaled the building, whipped into a frenzy.

"The gymnasium," Dom said. "If we can't stop these things, we've got to get everyone the hell out of there."

More Skulls climbed to the top of the fitness center. Bullets smashed into the side of the building, and another voice yelled over Jackson's radio. "We've got friendlies in there. Watch your fire."

The soldiers took more careful shots, and the gunfire slowed. Their caution allowed the Skulls to continue their assault almost unimpeded.

"There's an entrance on the east side of the fitness center," Jackson said. "I've got a visual of Skulls on top and around the south and west, but fewer contacts on the east. We make our move there." He slapped the dash of the jeep. "Let's go!"

"Yes, sir!" The private slammed the gas pedal. They jolted forward and wound between the other forces converging on the area. Jackson barked into the radio to call all available personnel carriers to position themselves behind the building.

As they drew closer to the fitness facility, the unmistakable shatter of breaking glass pierced the din.

Another voice broke over the radio. "Hostiles have broken a skylight. They've breached the shelter!"

THREE

K ARA'S PULSE RACED AS RAPIDLY as the automatic gunfire outside. Two of the medics paused their work in the triage center. Their radios sprang to life with a bevy of voices. Even across the noisy room, Kara could hear the alarm and desperation in the orders transmitted across the radios. Three soldiers rushed to the doors of the gym. They clicked the heavy locks shut.

"What's going on?" Sadie asked. Kara's sister was sitting upright in her cot, Maggie at her feet. The dog cocked her head, her ears perked as if she too were asking the same question.

"I don't know," Kara said.

Seated on a neighboring cot, Nina Weaver hugged her children closer. Only a dozen soldiers were in the fitness facility, and they took positions near each of the four entrances. Several waited on the running track that overlooked the gym from the second floor.

The gunfire outside grew louder until the sound of bullets pinging against the side of the building reverberated in the large room. Whatever was happening, it was getting closer.

Kara's blood ran cold when she heard scratching above.

She stared at a skylight in the gymnasium's roof. The silhouette of a clawed figure, spikes along its back, appeared against the glass, clawing at it until its head exploded and its body went slack.

Skulls.

The creatures were in the base.

Sadie grabbed Kara's arm. Her face had gone pale. "Don't let them…"

Her voice trailed off. All around, wailing children clung to their parents, while the adults, exhausted and fearful, stared up at the roof.

Another creature crashed into the skylight above. Bullets tore into its flesh, and it lay still across the glass, its shadow looming across the people below.

"Come with me," Kara said to her sister. Sadie nodded and grabbed Maggie's collar. "Let's find Miguel."

Nina, her arms around her two children, got to her feet. "Do you see the Hunters?"

Nina and Kara stood on tiptoes. Kara tried to remain calm while they scanned the crowd. The last time she had seen the Hunters, they'd been working beside the nurses and medics to administer the chelation treatment Lauren had developed aboard the *Huntress.* The therapy seemed to be working on the people here, but it wouldn't matter anymore if the Skulls were given free rein in the gym.

She spotted a man with a ruddy complexion decked out in black combat fatigues. "Miguel!"

Miguel waved and rushed through the crowd to them.

"Good to see you all are okay." He patted Maggie's head and then led them between cots filled with the wounded to the rest of the Hunters. Kara silently repeated their names, forcing herself to remember the people she'd only just met. There was Hector Ko with his sharp jaw and his characteristic intense expression. And Renee. Dom had told her Renee was a former gymnast and fellow CIA operative.

Kara and Sadie made their way to Eric's cot. His arm was in a sling, and his face was still scrunched in lingering pain. He and his girlfriend Shauna had been saved by Meredith while hiking the Appalachian Trail. Shauna now stood by Eric, and Renee sat on the edge of a cot next to her. An IV tube led to Renee's left arm. Bandages covered half her face and her left arm, but there was still a hard, determined look in her eyes.

Hector greeted the group. "I got word from one of the Army guys that the Skulls breached one of the south gates. Something riled them up, and the defensive units couldn't beat back the surge."

More gunfire boomed outside the building, emphasizing Hector's claim.

Another two Skulls began beating on the skylights. More screams erupted from the crowd. Sadie gasped, but she didn't cry out.

Kara gave her shoulder a reassuring squeeze. "We're going to be okay."

"You know how to use a gun, right?" Miguel asked her.

Kara nodded. Thoughts of the Skulls she'd been forced to kill swam through her mind. She had hunted with her father before and had logged plenty of time at the gun range. But the Skulls had provided ample opportunity to use those skills in a manner Kara had never imagined. Aiming a firearm at a person was not something that felt good or natural to her, but the Skulls had given her no choice.

"She most definitely does, man," Eric said. "That's how she saved our asses."

Miguel unholstered his pistol. "This thing has a bit of a kick. You've used a handgun before?"

"I can handle it," Kara said.

Miguel narrowed his eyes.

"Come on," Renee said. "She's Dom's daughter. That's good enough for me."

"All right. We're desperate here." Miguel showed her how to chamber a round and change the magazine. "If shit goes down, I can trust you to use this rationally, right?"

"I promise." Kara took the handgun.

"I don't want your father to be pissed at me for giving you this."

"Got it."

"And watch your fire. This placed is filled with people."

"I know, I know." Kara held the gun at her side. She wanted to help these people. The last thing she would do was heedlessly risk their lives. "I won't take a single shot unless absolutely necessary, and only if I know I'm completely in the clear."

More gunfire sounded off outside. Several more Skulls clawed at the skylight.

"Here's the thing, if our Army friends can't hold these assholes off out there and they start dropping in on us, this is going to be a bloodbath," Hector said. "We need clear firing lanes, and we need the people somewhere we can secure easier."

"All right, see if we can get some help doing that," Miguel said.

Hector nodded and ran toward the nearest soldier with a radio. The conversation was brief, but the soldier seemed to agree with Hector's assessment. He spoke into the radio, and the soldiers started massing people near the locker room doors leading into the gymnasium.

"Sounds like the Army's getting vehicles in position for us to exit out the east side of the building," Hector said when he returned to the group. He raised his voice to be heard over the din of gunfire outside and panicked voices inside. "They're going to try and route these bastards, or at least distract them so we—"

The clatter of breaking glass exploded from above, and shards rained down from one of the skylights.

Kara stepped in front of Sadie to put herself between her sister and the busted skylight. Two Skulls fell and smashed against the polished wood floor. Their bodies crumpled with a sickening thud. More yells and cries from the civilians filled the room.

Hector and Miguel strode toward the fallen Skulls. The soldiers on the running track aimed their rifles. One of the Skulls grunted and raised its torso, pushing itself up with one twisted hand. It wore the dirty green scrubs of a nurse or doctor. But the creature no longer had any interest in saving lives. Hector ended the creature with a single shot to its head. The second made no movement. Kara figured it had died on impact.

A third and fourth landed on the others. The Skulls both picked themselves up. Mangled and broken limbs didn't seem to dissuade them from pursuing their prey. As they limped forward, Miguel and Hector again took careful shots to put them down.

Three more fell from the broken skylight. Two of the soldiers nearest the creatures' landing point shot enough rounds into the beasts to keep them down before they recovered. Everything in the gymnasium quieted for a moment. No other Skulls dropped from the ceiling. Sadie's fingers gripped the back of Kara's arm.

"We're going to be okay," Kara said.

Gunfire erupted outside, louder than before. As if someone had turned a faucet on full blast, Skulls poured through the broken skylight. The sheltered civilians' voices cried out, almost drowning out the sound of battle. Kara's hand trembled as she held the handgun. She watched Miguel and Hector lead the efforts to quell the incursion. Even Renee fired her SCAR into the pile of Skulls despite the IV tube still attached to her arm.

One of the Skulls ducked under the gunfire and charged toward the civilians. A braid of matted brown hair whipped behind its head while it ran. The soldiers ceased their firing, too afraid of hitting the people they were trying to protect. Kara sprinted at the Skull, desperate to intercept it. She unlocked her handgun's safety as she ran. Maggie started to bound after her until Sadie grabbed the dog's collar.

Throwing herself between the crowd and the Skull, Kara fired her handgun. The recoil sent the weapon high and shook her arms. The shot went wide, blasting a small hole in the cinder-block wall, and the Skull let out a shrill howl. It lunged, claws cutting the air.

Kara steadied herself and fired again. Ready for the recoil, she readjusted and let off a second and third round. This time, she hit her mark. The Skull twisted and fell with freshly formed holes in its face and shoulder. With no time to celebrate, Kara spun and fired at the next Skull bounding from the center of the gym. It slumped, and momentum carried its mutated body forward.

Miguel ran to her side. Hector and Renee stood in front of people too injured to leave their cots. With no civilians in their firing lanes, Miguel and Kara let loose.

"I got left," Kara said and aimed at one of two Skulls running on busted ankles.

Miguel nodded. He played his muzzle across the other. The creatures fell under Kara's and Miguel's fire. The soldiers on the overhead running track sprayed the mass of Skulls in the center of the gymnasium floor, and the Hunters picked off any Skulls that escaped the onslaught.

Kara's slide clicked back, and she changed to a fresh magazine. Her ears rang, muddling the intermingling sounds of enclosed gunfire and the shrieks of those she strove to protect. Each time a Skull charged and she brought it down, she grew more comfortable with her borrowed weapon, adapting quickly to its iron sights and weight.

It seemed as though the flow of Skulls was dwindling to a trickle. She glanced across the room to ensure Sadie was still safe. Her sister was kneeling behind Renee and Hector with an arm draped across Maggie. Shauna was reloading a pistol she'd been borrowing since their initial trip to Detrick, while Eric stood behind her with his arm in a sling.

Maybe it was the ringing in her ears, but it seemed to Kara that the gunfire outside had lessened. Maybe the Army had actually regained control of the base. The hot ball of adrenaline burning in her chest kept her heart racing, but a slow tingling crept through her—a spreading sense of victory. She rubbed her ears, and her hearing settled.

"Nice shooting," Miguel said. "Tell your dad I've found a replacement for him on the team."

A smile spread across her face, but it quickly dissipated when she surveyed the faces of the others behind them. Most huddled with loved ones, eyes wide, brimming with tears. Others stood frozen by shock.

Kara shuddered and strode toward Sadie to make sure she was all right. But thoughts of her own mental health flooded her mind. She recalled the first time she'd killed one of these so-called Skulls, just days ago. The guilt was overwhelming, and her stomach twisted into a painful knot as she realized how many she'd ended since then.

She paused, shivering. Miguel placed a hand on her back. It felt inhumanly cold and heavy, until she recalled he had a prosthetic limb. The artificial forearm and hand were relics of his past service. While the cost of war manifested itself physically on Miguel, she wondered what psychological scars he might carry. Would she be like him someday—seemingly unaffected by the death and destruction around them? She felt certain the damage she had accumulated from this war against the Oni Agent would run deep within her. The guilt of ending someone's life, someone who was a victim—someone like her mother. A sick, innocent person who'd been affected by a bioweapon. Someone who hadn't *chosen* to fight her.

"You all right?" Miguel asked.

Gulping, Kara managed a nod and then wrapped her arms around her sister. If bearing these weights on her conscience meant her sister lived, she would readily sacrifice her mental and physical health. The Hunters rushed about the room with the medics and nurses, ensuring no one had been injured by the Skulls or any ricocheting rounds.

Kara exhaled slowly and stared at the gaping skylight. A clear blue sky lay beyond, and sunlight poured through. Somehow, they'd done it; they'd kept the beasts from harming any of the others sheltered here. They'd been lucky the Skulls had done most of the work for them by falling three stories to the floor. If they'd broken through at ground level, Kara, the Hunters, and the rest of them might not have been so lucky.

As if on cue, the doors to the east side of the gym burst open.

27

FOUR

IN THE *HUNTRESS'S* MEDICAL BAY laboratory, Lauren Winters adjusted the stage on her light microscope. The persistent hum of the lab's ventilation system kept her company while she deposited a histology slide under the scope's lens. Peter Mikos stood beside her, anxiously awaiting their first magnified glimpse at the autopsied tissue they'd obtained from Brett Fielding's brain—the first Hunter victim of the Oni Agent. Even before they'd biopsied the tissue, they could see the empty spaces formed by the infectious proteins, the prions, that had taken residence in the gray organ.

Flicking the scope's light source on, Lauren leaned over the eyepiece. White empty spaces, voids left by the spread of the disease, made the thin slice of tissue appear like Swiss cheese. That was why prion diseases were categorized as transmissible spongiform encephalopathies—they attacked the brain, turning it into something with the texture of a sponge.

"Take a look," she said and let Peter position himself over the scope.

"Shit. This is awful. I can't believe the disease progressed this fast in such a short time."

"Bioweapon engineering at its finest," Lauren said. She

slipped another slide under the scope. "Markers of astrocytic gliosis are stained a dark brown here."

The stain indicated regions of central nervous system damage and marked the destruction of cells crucial to the health and stability of the brain. All across the sample, dark splotches littered the tissue. She flicked another switch on the scope to turn on the microscope's camera. An image of the damaged tissue stabilized on a nearby computer monitor.

"That brain tissue looks more torn up than Dresden after World War II," said Peter.

"And that might be an understatement," Lauren said. She typed a command on the keyboard and brought up the results of an earlier test. Several graphs displayed across the computer screen. "Check out these results."

"Ah, a luminescent immunoassay," Peter said. "So the more prions present, the darker the blue."

"Exactly," Lauren said. "I ran the samples in our spectrometer to assess how much light the solution absorbed." Sure enough, their tiny samples had turned the solution a deep midnight hue, and the spectrometer readings confirmed the high concentration of prions present in the samples.

"So you think we can attribute the aggression of the Skulls to these prions?"

"I think so," Lauren said, holding up one gloved hand. "Prion disease has been documented to cause confusion, hallucinations, dementia, and personality changes among other neurological alterations." She ticked off the symptoms on her fingers. "It's not farfetched to think these prions have been selected and engineered to cause extreme aggression."

"I suppose that's especially true if Chao's and Samantha's reports on the Oni Agent's early development in the Amanojaku Project are accurate."

"That's what I'd guess. If researchers have been working on this since World War II, that would explain how it does what it does so successfully."

"Just think if these people had been focused on developing treatments for diseases like cancer, malaria, or even the flu. Healing instead of killing…"

"I know," Lauren said. "What a waste of intellect and scientific progress."

"And now we're wasting our time cleaning up their mess. Instead of worrying about all the maladies Mother Nature throws at us, we also have to fight off what humans are engineering to destroy each other."

Lauren nodded, silent for a moment. "I suppose we could keep waxing philosophical about the ramifications of biological weapons, but that doesn't help us right now."

"Fair enough," Peter said. "So back to business: We can eliminate the nanobacteria that cause the extra-skeletal formations and produce the prions in the Skulls. And if we do that soon enough, we can prevent neurodegeneration and the resulting aggressive tendencies."

"Right," Lauren said. "We can even eliminate the nanobacteria in people who've been exposed to the Oni Agent for an extended period of time, but if the nanobacteria have had time to produce the prions, we have no way to reverse the damage."

Lauren turned off the microscope. She pressed a gloved hand against the window separating the lab from the isolation ward where Scott Ashworth and Ivan Price were medically sedated. Though the outward signs of their Oni Agent infections had been eliminated, their brains were still overrun with the debilitating prions left there by the nanobacteria.

"God, even if we can somehow stop the prions, we still have to find a way to restore the ravaged brain tissue," she said.

"Now we're getting ahead of ourselves."

"Can't help it," Lauren said, turning away from Scott and Ivan. She couldn't believe they might as well be as good as dead. "So let's focus on eliminating the prions." She scrolled through the research papers she'd compiled. "I found a few case studies on a small-molecule treatment used to prolong the lives of those with prion disease."

"But it doesn't cure the disease?"

Lauren shook her head. "There have been half a dozen studies using strong antibiotics, but those too simply slowed the onset of prion disease symptoms."

"I feel like we're out of our league here."

"Yeah, immunotherapy, silencing RNA, polyanionic compounds…nothing seems to do anything more than delay the inevitable."

"All these papers make it seem like a prion disease therapy might be on the cusp of scientific development, but I wouldn't know where to begin. So many different experiments to run, treatments to test…" Peter drummed his fingers along a lab bench. "And I imagine you need someone skilled in neuroscience to deal with the matters of degeneration, along with someone who knows more about drug development than we do."

"No doubt. I'm used to handling bioweapons, when we can apply existing cures and therapies to a well-characterized disease, but this is something else."

"So what do we do?"

Lauren glanced at the list of scientific papers on her monitor. Each paper had been spearheaded by different research groups in academic and medical institutions worldwide.

"What do we do?" Lauren repeated Peter's question. "We find someone who can help us."

Center for Neurodegenerative Diseases
Massachusetts General Hospital, Boston

A distant rumble shook the windows and jolted Navid Ghasemi awake. He froze at the sound, his eyes wide. The sound of the blast faded. A few ghostly howls rent the air. Then silence. He wrapped his arm tighter around Abby Martin as they lay on the hard floor. Abby continued to sleep, so Navid slowly stood, careful not to disturb her. A crick in his back hurt. He straightened his spine to assuage the slight pain.

He glanced out the window but a pervasive darkness shrouded the world. Not even the moon was visible, hidden behind a blanket of unseen clouds. *Probably better that way*, Navid thought.

He knew what it looked like in the daylight. Crazy people prowling the streets, attacking each other with all the ferocity of starving wolves, abandoned cars and the odd military vehicle, some charred. Trash strewn about and the occasional pigeon picking through the refuse of a fallen society.

Whatever it was that had spread through the people of Boston had struck with the unexpected force of a tidal wave. He rubbed his eyes as he inched past the empty desks of his colleagues. He and Abby had stayed in the graduate student office while the other researchers ran for home.

Their one-bedroom apartment was only a couple of miles away over the Charles River. Most of the time, Navid took the subway system, the so-called T, straight to work. Abby always biked. Home was so close, but he'd been too scared to risk the short journey through the madness he'd seen in the streets. Judging by the conditions of the area around the hospital, he doubted many of his colleagues had been lucky enough to take the T home to Cambridge, Fenway, or Beacon Hill.

Still, he wasn't certain he'd made the right decision to stay at Mass Gen with Abby. Trying to get home might not have been safe, but was staying in this hospital any better?

He trudged toward the office door. He and Abby had pushed a desk in front of it to create a barrier between them and what lay outside. The desk had been Brian's—another grad student. Next to the computer monitor on it sat three plush toys. Each was a cartoonish rendition, complete with eyes and a smile, of a deadly pathogen: Ebola, E. coli, and salmonella. Navid brushed the toys aside and leaned over the desk to glance through the small window in the door. The window was made of frosted glass that prevented Navid from getting a good look at what lay beyond this meager barricade. The only thing he could see was the persistent flash of the hospital's crimson emergency lights.

A dark, blotchy shape flitted in front of the window, momentarily blotting out the flashes of red. He ducked down, willing his hammering heart to slow and trying to control his breathing. He and Abby had avoided contact with the zombies or crazies or whatever they were so far, and he didn't intend to tempt fate now.

He returned to Abby's side and sat on the floor against the desk. He couldn't fall back to sleep. The adrenaline from the distant explosion he'd heard and the possibility that someone—or something—might be outside their office kept him from nodding off.

His cell phone sat on the surface of his desk, which was still littered with scientific papers he'd printed off and marked up in a bevy of highlights and pen marks. All of it was useless. What good was science in a destroyed world? Navid's doctoral thesis was going to be on delivering drugs to treat neurodegenerative diseases. His twenty-some years of education were worthless now.

He picked up the cell phone and rubbed his thumb over the black screen. Technology was just as useless. The charge in their phones had long since been used up during their desperate efforts to contact their friends and family.

His parents had emigrated from Iran to Canada during the Iranian Revolution. They'd feared the consequences of the burgeoning theocracy. It was almost forty years ago that they had run away for a better life. Now, Navid figured it didn't matter whether they were still in Iran or Canada or anywhere else in the world. There was no running away to safety. He hadn't been able to get a call through to either of his parents or his younger sister, all of whom he prayed were somewhere safe near their Toronto home.

Abby had spent the same fruitless efforts trying to reach her family in Springfield, Illinois. None of her calls had resulted in anything more than a prerecorded message stating, "This number cannot be reached."

As far as they knew, it was just the two of them against the world. Since the outbreak, they'd been sheltering in the small, seven-desk office space alone, surviving on the food and drinks they rationed from the mini-fridge where the graduate students kept their lunches.

Navid's stomach growled.

Abby rolled over and yawned. "You hungry, too, huh?" She pulled herself up next to Navid and laid her head on his shoulder.

"Starving." Navid brushed his hand through her long blond hair.

Another distant explosion sounded. The windows rattled again, and Abby raised herself to the lip of the one nearest them. Navid joined her as they peered into the darkness.

Orange and red flames licked up about a half-mile from their position. Black smoke billowed off the raging fire spreading to the neighboring buildings.

"What the fuck's going on?" Navid muttered.

Abby's eyes remained glued to the conflagration.

A chorus of blood-chilling, animalistic howls rose up. Navid couldn't see the source of the din, but he knew it was the crazies. The flickering light cast by the flames provided enough light for him to make out a few dark silhouettes flitting between low-lying brick buildings. He saw one humanoid shape plunge through the broken window of the Yankee Dock Shop where he and Abby often dropped by for a lobster roll and fries for lunch.

His stomach rumbled again.

"We can't stay here, can we?" Abby asked, turning away from the window.

"I don't think the fire will make it this far."

"No, no, that's not what I mean," she said. "Food. We need food, and all we've got are two moldy cheese sticks and some curdled milk."

Navid sighed. An intense pang of despair stabbed at him. "I know. It's just—"

"We don't have a choice. We have to go out there. We have to risk it."

Navid shook his head. "I just keep praying help is going

to come. Soldiers or policemen or someone is going to come bursting in here and whisk us away."

"The only people I see bursting in here are the goddamned crazies." Abby's chin dropped to her chest. "We should get food and move."

"Where to?" Navid asked.

"Hell if I know, but if we don't risk our asses out there, what chance do we have? We either face the crazies or we starve."

"Not much of a choice." Navid stood. Abby held out a hand, and he pulled her up. Again, he felt a deep-seated pang of despair. Were they the only ones left alive in this hospital? Her eyes locked with his, and he pulled her close. "I love you."

"Love you, too," she said.

Navid gulped, trying to put on a brave face. At least the darkness might shadow the fear coursing through him. But he tried to be strong, tried to be resilient. Because they were alone. They had no one else to depend on. He interlaced his fingers with hers and gave her hand a squeeze before he started pushing the desk away from the office door. "Here we go."

FIVE

———◆~◆◆~◆———

KARA LEVELED HER HANDGUN at the burst-open gym doors. Her pulse raced, and she waited with bated breath for the Skulls to surge through. When the dust settled, she saw someone with familiar blue eyes and light brown, almost sandy hair: her father. With Meredith by his side, Dom rushed to his daughters while training his gun on the scattered bodies of the dead Skulls. A dozen soldiers followed.

Dom hugged Kara and Sadie. "God, am I glad you two are okay. When we saw those things had started coming through the roof…"

Miguel patted Dom's back. "Kara's a hell of a fighter. Skulls didn't stand a chance."

The soldiers flooded into the gym. They encircled the other civilians and began ushering them out the door they'd come through.

"What's going on?" Kara asked.

"The Skulls forced their way over a gate."

"Were they all pushed back?" Miguel asked.

"Not yet," Meredith said. "But the Army just managed to regain control of the gate. A few Skulls may be scattered around the base, and there are still dozens of them around the commissary."

"That's basically next door," Hector said.

"Exactly," Dom said. "We need to move everyone while they're holding the Skulls off."

Medics carried the injured out of the gymnasium, and soldiers hurried the last of the civilians out. The sound of gunfire resounded intermittently outside.

"Last truck's ready to move," a soldier yelled from the gym's entrance.

"Let's go!" Dom said.

Kara followed the Hunters with Maggie and Sadie close on her heels. She stole a final glance at the bodies of the Skulls and for a second considered the tremendous waste of human life. That introspection was short-lived when the rattle of a jeep-mounted M240 greeted their exit from the fitness facility. Dirt and grass kicked up around several bone-plated, snarling Skulls in shredded police uniforms rushing toward the convoy idling on the street. Once enforcers and protectors of the law, the creatures abided only by the law of nature now: kill or be killed. But the beasts soon stumbled and fell as machine gun rounds tore into their flesh.

Dom helped Kara, Sadie, and their dog into the back of a jeep.

"We're good to go," Dom said.

The driver gave a thumbs up, and the vehicle took off. Instead of falling in line with the rest of the convoy carrying the civilians to safety, a Humvee in front of them took off down another street. Their jeep followed.

A voice came over the driver's radio. "South gate secure, commissary clear."

They rumbled over several roads and an open lawn until the two vehicles slowed to a stop outside a building with shattered windows. Kara stared at the rows of lumpy, canvas-draped forms laid out around the building. She knew what must be under those olive-drab sheets.

"Back at the NEC," the man in front said. "Commander Shepherd's going to want a sitrep now."

They piled out of the jeep, and the rest of the Hunters joined them from the Humvee in front of Kara's. Kara helped Maggie down. She filed in behind the group as they entered the NEC building. Winding down the corridors, they passed offices with toppled furniture. Bloodstains still marred the floors and walls.

"Skulls got in here, too?" Kara asked her father.

"Right. This was where the Oni Agent first hit Detrick," he said. "It's the communications hub for the base."

"So that's why we had so much trouble reaching them on our way here, huh?"

Dom nodded solemnly, and the group paused at another set of doors. He knocked, and the doors swung open. The din of radio chatter and voices filled the air. He led them into a space that appeared to be some type of mission control room.

As Kara gazed at the uniformed men and women working at banks of computer systems and communication equipment, she saw a man approaching them with an unmistakable air of authority. She recognized him from when she'd first arrived at the base—Shepherd, the man in charge of Fort Detrick. She felt a sense of unease, as if she shouldn't be in this room. Before the Oni Agent outbreak, a place like this undoubtedly required a certain degree of security clearance. And she, an undergraduate student at a university that probably didn't even exist anymore, stood in this hive of activity.

"Glad to see you all made it safely," Shepherd said. "Thank you for your impromptu service helping protect those inside the shelter. But we don't have time to rest." He motioned to a conference room behind a shield of glass adjoining the comm center. When Kara moved to follow them, Shepherd added, "Your daughters can wait out here."

Kara's unease morphed into frustration. She knew she didn't belong here, but she'd risked her life, she'd been through hell, and she wanted to know what was going on. But the look on her father's face told her that wasn't going to happen.

"Girls, will you be okay?"

Kara patted the handgun Miguel had lent her. "We'll be fine."

Dom surveyed the others seated around the oblong table. Several researchers and brass from Fort Detrick sat across from his team. Jackson gave a quick sitrep regarding the breach and the ongoing efforts to reinforce the defensive barriers around the base's perimeter. Shepherd ordered several patrols to sweep Detrick in an effort to rout out any stubborn Skulls that had evaded their counterattack earlier and to ensure all non-essential personnel on the base remained indoors.

"Now on to the matter of you Hunters." Shepherd laid out a stack of papers before the group. "To recap, Fort Detrick was once in the business of bioweapons, and the Amanojaku Project was one of those studied and developed here. The United States abolished the pursuit of these weapons almost twenty years later. At that time, our records of the Amanojaku Project go dark. All laboratory samples were incinerated along with most paper evidence of the associated work. What we have found are classified records indicating the project was adapted from World War II technology acquired from the Japanese. Specifically from a biological warfare group known as Unit 731. The project abstract we recovered correlates highly with the aggression exhibited by affected individuals. Although several other projects during the 50s and 60s also shared similar goals as the Amanojaku Project, our initial analyses of Oni Agent victims and the intelligence your group reported seem to indicate that, unbeknownst to us, the Amanojaku Project was never entirely scrapped and was instead moved to another organization we have been unable to identify."

Shepherd took a sip of water from a plastic bottle. "Mr. Holland, I believe your group's research has progressed faster than our own. Given our setbacks in restoring power to the base and keeping these so-called Skulls out, we'd benefit greatly by sharing data with your group—and I'll admit freely it's us who might benefit the most."

"I'm happy to do whatever I can," Dom said.

"Then let's get to it," Shepherd said. "I want that science briefing."

Dom was ready to get to work again, but he couldn't help picturing the frightened civilians they'd just rescued from the fitness facility. They'd been lucky to have the Army's protection—but how many outside the base were still hiding and fighting for their lives? "Before we get too heavy into the science, what about rescue operations for those outside Fort Detrick?"

"I'm afraid we don't have the capabilities."

"Why not? You sent fully crewed Black Hawks to save us against a horde of those things. You can't spare any to rescue civilians, even if I offer our assistance?"

Shepherd shook his head. "Truth is, most of the ordnance on this base is borrowed from Fort Bragg. They sent reinforcements to select locations at the height of the outbreak. While they provided enough to help defend what we've got, you've seen how we can barely do that. We can't afford to risk what resources we have left. Our hope is that people follow the advice of the emergency broadcasts and stay inside until we get a handle on the outbreak."

"But even if they stay indoors, we've seen how dogged the Skulls are," Dom said. "Besides, how many Americans have enough food and water stockpiled to survive for weeks—if I'm being optimistic—while they wait for the military to actually do something?"

"I can't answer those questions myself," Shepherd replied. "You'd need to direct them to General Kinsey. He's currently organizing the military's efforts from the Pentagon, and we're scheduled to speak with him later about our scientific developments."

"That would be helpful," Dom said. It was an understatement. "And if he wants to really know what our research team is up to, we should patch them in."

"Agreed," Shepherd said.

Dom directed Adam Galloway, their comm specialist, to help establish a connection with the *Huntress*. While he agreed they needed to move forward on a medical solution to the Oni Agent, he was furious that civilian rescue operations were such a low priority. The military needed to do *something* to help those out there without the means to defend themselves. Even those that were armed and prepared for disaster might be overwhelmed by the sheer ferocity and numbers of the Skulls. If an Army base like Fort Detrick barely stood up to the creatures, how could the average American hope to survive?

SIX

LAUREN SAT BESIDE CHAO LI in the electronics workshop aboard the *Huntress*. This was her chance to finally reach out to other scientists. Maybe they'd have something she could use to combat the neurological changes in the Skulls.

Chao handed her a headset. "Looks like we're linked in to Fort Detrick."

"Hello, this is Dr. Lauren Winters from the *Huntress*. Do you read?"

Dom's voice came across the line. "We hear you loud and clear, Dr. Winters." He introduced the others in the conference room with him at Detrick. "Can you brief us on everything you've found since we last spoke?"

"Aye, aye, Captain," Lauren said. She relayed all her findings since the outbreak: the mode of transmission, the nanobacteria component, and the calcium apatite formation leading to the skeletal mutations.

One of the Detrick researchers spoke up. "What I don't understand is how this leads to the psychological differences."

Lauren drew in a breath. *I'm getting there*, she thought. "More or less, the nanobacteria function like little factories.

They not only pump out the calcium apatite, but it also appears that they produce a complex of infectious proteins."

"Prions," the researcher interrupted again. "And has your group found a way to eliminate them?"

Lauren almost laughed at the irony. "No, I was hoping you all might have something to combat them."

Another researcher spoke up. "I'm afraid not. From what I know, a cure doesn't exist."

Others reaffirmed his statement.

"That's what I figured." Lauren sighed. "The next phase in our research is to identify candidate therapeutics to stop these prion infections and, we hope, reduce the incidence of aggression in those afflicted with the Oni Agent. I'm happy to send along all the data we've collected, if that would help."

"We would appreciate it." Shepherd's voice came over the comm link again. "Likewise, we'll provide continued updates from our research."

"Thank you, sir," Lauren said. "That would be helpful." Another thought sprang to her mind. "Do you have enough samples of the Oni Agent to perform your lab work?"

"A lack of available specimens is not a concern on our end," Shepherd replied. Lauren could sense frustration and grief in the words, and she quickly grasped the implications of his statement. Fort Detrick must have been hit hard. "I do have another question for you, Dr. Winters. Instead of a cure for someone who's already sick with the Oni Agent, why don't we focus our efforts on developing a vaccine, which could theoretically be used to protect everyone from becoming infected in the first place?"

Lauren grappled with his question for a few seconds before answering. Truthfully, she wanted a cure to see if she could help Ivan and Scott. Each day the prions from the Oni Agent were allowed to eat away at their nervous systems meant they were further from any potential recovery. "Most existing research has been performed in the pursuit of prion treatments—not vaccines," she said at last.

"But these cures have mostly failed, right?" Shepherd asked.

"Failed might be too strong of a word," Lauren said. "Every iteration of a marginally functional treatment has brought modern science closer to a molecule or drug with the potential to halt a prion infection."

"And so how does this relate to a vaccine?"

"There has simply been far less research performed on vaccines against prions," Lauren said. "It's my opinion that we may be much closer to finding a treatment to help those that are already suffering from the disease. In fact, if we can start a working relationship with you to accelerate our efforts and build off of the decades of research already out there, we might develop a cure within a few months." She paused for a second and thought better of overpromising these developments. "That is, if we're lucky."

"I appreciate your input, Dr. Winters," Shepherd said. "I'm afraid we have to patch in General Kinsey now, but I look forward to working together."

Lauren took the headset off and handed it back to Chao.

Instead of leaving, she leaned against a nearby desk.

"You really think we'll find a cure?" Chao asked.

"Truthfully, I don't know. I hoped Detrick knew something more than we did." She scoffed. "And if they didn't, I thought they'd at least know who in the United States might have a better idea of how we should deal with the Oni Agent." Lauren pinched the bridge of her nose. "If I'm being realistic, if we don't find someone to help us, I'd say our chances are about as good as the Skulls miraculously recovering on their own."

⌐∿⌐

Dom drummed his fingers on the conference table. The conference phone clicked. He'd watched the faces of the scientists and researchers seated around him when Lauren gave her sitrep regarding the current state of research aboard the *Huntress*. This was the first time he'd heard that prions caused the neurological deterioration leading to the Skulls' destructive instincts. Judging by the expressions of those around him, it was the first any of them had clearly understood what had sent the United States into a perilous nosedive straight to hell.

He had thought rendezvousing with Meredith and his daughters in the middle of Skull-infested Maryland had been an arduous task. The odds had certainly been stacked against him. But that terrifying journey seemed like climbing over the berm in his family's backyard compared to Lauren's Everest-like objective of finding a cure.

"Looks like we have a connection," Jackson said as the clicking finally stopped.

"General Kinsey, sir, do you read?" Shepherd asked.

"I do," Kinsey's baritone voice crackled through the conference phone. "First, I want to thank you all for your service to this country in our time of need, especially as I lead the efforts to organize the United States military in response to this crisis."

"If I may speak freely, what exactly does that mean, sir?" Shepherd asked.

Dom admired the man for his brazen question. He too wanted to know where the hell the military was. When he and the Hunters had flown in from Annapolis, they'd seen only destruction and chaos, pluming smoke and rampant Skulls.

"It means we're ordering anyone we can contact to fall back to defend vital assets such as the Pentagon and high-value targets in metro areas."

"What about civilians, General? Are there any shelters, secure evacuation routes, a response from FEMA?"

"I'm afraid we don't have those kinds of resources," General Kinsey said. "As it stands, we're unable to organize widespread evacuations. We've been performing drone sweeps over populated areas, and so far the visuals are bleak. Spreading our forces too thin is a recipe for certain failure when the entire nation has been turned into a weapon against us."

Dom reeled. He already knew that the situation was desolate out there, but he hadn't considered it in those terms before. The citizens of the United States had become a living, breathing weapon against their homeland. Even as they defeated the Skulls, they annihilated their own people.

"I understand, sir," Shepherd said. "If your priority is bolstering high value installations and targets, when will we receive reinforcements? Our current scientific operations are in jeopardy if we can't keep these things out of our base."

"You already have elements of the 82nd's First Battalion," Kinsey said. "And soon enough, you won't need reinforcements. We're ordering the immediate withdrawal of all armed forces—including your command—from your area with orders to join us in establishing an FOB in Washington."

Dom couldn't restrain himself. "General Kinsey, with all due respect, I fail to see the logic in abandoning Fort Detrick at a time when a biological weapon is wreaking havoc on those you've sworn to protect."

"Who am I speaking with?" Kinsey said with disdain.

Shepherd held a hand up to prevent Dom from speaking up again. "I apologize, sir. I should've explained earlier." He briefly gave an overview on Meredith, Dom, and the Hunters.

"Far be it from me to turn down the sage advice of a government contractor," Kinsey said when Shepherd finished. His voice dripped with derision. "Maybe you should be doing my job."

Dom shared a look with Meredith. Since he'd cut his formal ties with the government long ago, he'd forgotten about the egos driving many of those in power. Even the lowly CIA analysts he'd worked with were staunchly defensive when given any degree of criticism. *Little kings and their little kingdoms*, Dom thought. Still, he decided to try a different tack. "I apologize for my brashness, sir. My crew and I are more than happy to offer our service."

"If you want to help, you can assist in Fort Detrick's evacuation," Kinsey responded.

Dom's face turned hot. He curled his fingers until his knuckles turned white but willed himself to remain calm. He understood the general's difficult position of leading the military forces of a tattered and desperate nation. But he resented the man's stubborn lack of respect.

"Sir, this is Meredith Webb representing the Biological and Chemical Warfare Defense division of the Central Intelligence Agency. My primary interest is in the eradication of this bioweapon and identifying the culprit responsible for its development and subsequent outbreak. Are there currently any plans in development to counteract the bioweapon?"

Meredith had always been the more diplomatic of the two in their working relationships. Dom hoped she might have better luck convincing the man to be more sympathetic toward their cause.

"We do have a plan. As soon as we have reassessed the strength of our military, we will launch an operation to retake our cities one by one."

Commander Shepherd arched an eyebrow. "I'm sorry, sir, what do you mean?"

"I believe our best option for survival is to eradicate each and every one of the infected. We'll kill every single goddamn Skull we find."

SEVEN

D OM WAS NO STRANGER to taking another's life when the need arose, and he had certainly inflicted his share of casualties on the Skulls. But relying solely on the brute force of firepower and soldiers on the field was the wrong way to respond to the outbreak. Such an action would be risking the lives of the men and women in service along with the lives of those civilians caught in the crossfire.

"Your scientific findings confirm the CDC reports I saw before they went dark," General Kinsey said. "When a few head of cattle get Mad Cow Disease, the whole herd must be put down. We need to destroy all hosts of this so-called Oni Agent."

Dom couldn't believe the General's best plan for reestablishing security in the United States was to essentially commit genocide against its people. Yet something else bothered him. "Sir, I have one more question."

General Kinsey's voice seemed to drop an octave, laced in venom. "One more, Captain Holland."

"What happens when the Oni Agent returns? What happens if we don't find the source, the group, or country responsible?"

The line went silent for several seconds.

"When our mission is successful, we'll secure the borders until the disease is eradicated globally," General Kinsey said.

"Excuse my bluntness, but it sounds like you don't have scientific advisers on your staff," Meredith said. "There's a critical problem to your plan."

"Enlighten me."

"You can destroy all the hosts of the Oni Agent, but that will never destroy the bioweapon itself. We eliminated the laboratory where we *think* it was being produced." Meredith shook her head. "But there may be a lab somewhere else producing or storing the Oni Agent. I have reason to believe members of the CIA were responsible for protecting the facility we found, but I have no idea who they were working with. It could be another country, a terrorist group, or an international company for that matter."

"I understand your concern," Kinsey said, only the slightest hint of defeat in his voice. "The idea that there might be a second deployment of the Oni Agent has crossed my mind—which is why we need to secure our cities and borders as soon as we can."

"Right," Meredith said. "But this is why we need more research to combat the Agent on a biological level."

"Your Dr. Lauren Winters has come up with a way to eliminate the nanobacteria. So it sounds to me like we can already treat people if there is another outbreak."

"True, but the nanobacteria are only a vehicle, a vector, for the prions," Meredith said. "And if the technology to produce the Agent still exists, whoever created it could find a new way to infect people. Maybe a different bacteria, a virus, or something completely manmade."

"Then we're back to square one," Dom said, "forced to kill more of our citizens when a *new* outbreak from a *new* biological weapon based on these prions tears through whoever is left after your military operation."

"And according to your assessment of our dwindling resources, we can't handle another outbreak," Commander Shepherd said. "Sir, I understand your need to withdraw forces and concentrate what firepower we have left. But at least grant us enough protection to do our due diligence at Detrick. Let us do what we do best. Let us do the research that will complement your military action and ensure the threat of the Oni Agent is wiped from the face of the earth."

Lauren looked up from her computer when she heard the sound of approaching footsteps.

"How's the research going?" Glenn Walsh asked. Her heart skipped a beat at the sound of his deep voice, and she felt like a lovesick teenager as she admired the muscles rippling along his arms. His large frame took up most of the doorway to the lab. Thomas Hampton, the *Huntress's* second-in-command, sidled up beside Glenn. Lauren forced herself to remember her and Glenn's commitment to prevent their once-passionate relationship from interfering with their duties aboard the *Huntress.*

"The research? It's going...somewhere." She stepped away from the computer monitor. "But I think we're going to need more help than even Detrick can provide."

Glenn folded his arms across his considerable chest. "You mean help from other labs? Like universities and hospitals?"

Lauren nodded. "If any still exist."

"I'd lead a rescue party if we find anyone who can lend a hand," Glenn said.

"Let's not get ahead of ourselves," Thomas said. "I appreciate the enthusiasm, but we'll have to clear any missions like that with Dom."

Lauren gestured to the rest of her medical team. Divya, Sean, and Peter were working beyond the acrylic partition that marked the BSL4 area of the lab. "I take it you two didn't come to enlist as lab assistants."

"I'm afraid this old dog can't learn many more tricks," Thomas said with a smile. The expression quickly vanished. "We just received word from Dom and Meredith that General Kinsey wants to withdraw all forces from Detrick."

"What?" Lauren backed away from the computer terminal. "And does he have some other bioweapons defense group somewhere I don't know about working against the Oni Agent?"

"Apparently medical science wasn't a priority of his," Glenn said.

"But Dom and Meredith sweet-talked the General into keeping Fort Detrick active for another few weeks," Thomas said. "Maybe longer, if they showed progress on finding a cure."

"Is he mad?" Lauren asked. "Does he really think it will take a couple of weeks to come up with a cure that's eluded scientists for decades?"

"Mad or not, that's what we've got to work with," Thomas said. "Dom wanted us to pass along the message and see if there was anything we could do to help expedite the work."

"God, I don't even know how to begin making Kinsey happy on that kind of timetable." Lauren watched as Peter bent over a microscope. Divya and Sean manipulated plastic dishes full of cell samples in a biosafety cabinet. Though her team was working around the clock, Lauren didn't think they'd make enough progress in the next two weeks to satisfy Kinsey. She locked eyes with Glenn. "The only way to realistically speed up our work is if I take you up on your offer."

"Just tell me where to pick up our new scientist friends, and I'll be happy to arrange a ride with Dom," Glenn said.

"I appreciate it," Lauren said. "The only problem is finding researchers that are still alive."

"We've got some work to do, huh?" Thomas asked as he moved toward the exit with Glenn.

"That we do." Lauren nodded a goodbye but thought better of it. "Glenn, could you stick around?"

"Sure thing, Doc."

Lauren started rifling through a drawer. "You haven't had any more luck with Amir, have you?"

Amir was the mechanic they had rescued from the IBSL. The man spoke Farsi, and Glenn was the only crewmember on the *Huntress* who could communicate with him. Amir claimed to have been nothing more than an indentured servant, but they had put him in the ship's brig until they could figure out what to do with him.

"Amir hasn't been very helpful," Glenn said. "Still claims he never knew the Oni Agent even existed until the Skulls started taking over the rig. He seems to be telling the truth, but he's been pretty shady about *why* he got on that rig in the first place. I'm still working on him."

"Good. I know it's silly, but I keep hoping something will come out of his mouth that leads to the magic cure or a vaccine—or maybe to the group responsible for the Agent." She pulled out an individually wrapped sterile syringe and started to undo the packaging. "Mind if we try something?"

Glenn arched one dark eyebrow. "And what are we trying, Doc?" He pulled up a stool and sat next to Lauren.

"When we first treated you for exposure to the Oni Agent, we didn't go over all the side effects of the chelation therapy." Glenn reeled back, and Lauren placed her hand over his broad fingers. The touch of his rough skin against hers sent a tingle through her, and the surprised expression on his faced melted into one of familiar comfort. The momentary intimacy threatened to fluster Lauren, reminding her of everything they'd shared and hadn't quite forgotten, so she rushed to continue. "I'm sure you're fine. I mean, the side effects are rare."

"But?" Glenn asked.

"But there's a possibility you could suffer anything from bone density loss to kidney failure and internal bleeding. I want to start following up with anyone we treated to track any potential side effects."

"Understood." Glenn gestured to the syringe. "And that's for a blood sample?"

"Right." Lauren dabbed at a spot on Glenn's forearm with a cotton swab doused in sterilizing alcohol. "I need to isolate a serum sample from your blood." She inserted the syringe needle into Glenn's skin. "I'm looking for biomarkers—different biochemical molecules that I can use to determine your rate of bone loss to estimate your bone mineral density, or BMD."

"And what happens if you find my BMD is too low?"

Lauren pulled back the plunger on the syringe, and the small plastic cylinder turned red as it filled. "If it's too low, it indicates you're at an abnormally high risk of bone fracture or breakage."

"Weak bones isn't a good trait for a Hunter."

"No, unfortunately, it isn't." She withdrew the needle. "A broken bone in a fight against the Skulls could be a death sentence."

EIGHT

KARA LEANED FORWARD AGAINST HER HARNESS to see out the fuselage window of the chopper as it rose above Frederick. Smoke from the historic downtown billowed up in gray puffs. It seemed like ants crawled through the city streets, over the wrecked and stalled vehicles.

But she knew the creatures moving through the city blocks were nothing as innocuous as insects. The Skulls now inhabited the place where she'd grown up. The Oni Agent had taken hold over the city and crushed it. The memories of getting soft serve at Froggy's Ice Cream, her first hikes through nearby Gambrill State Park with her family, and the thrill of finally being old enough to bike from her house to the riverside walkways downtown felt like stories from a book she'd read long ago. Like something so foreign now, so distant that she could never imagine actually living them.

And the Oni Agent hadn't just taken her hometown. It had also claimed her mother. She imagined her, now a Skull and still trapped in their home's basement, locked up until they returned.

If they ever returned.

They passed over dark green trees, following the highway toward Baltimore. Kara turned to her sister, who'd been silent since Dom had told them they were leaving Fort Detrick. Sadie interlaced her fingers with Kara's as they raced eastward toward the coast. Toward where their father had told them he really worked. The *Huntress*.

Dom wanted to rendezvous with his crew and see if there was any possible way for them to help civilians in the surrounding area while Dr. Winters worked with Fort Detrick on their research. He had told his daughters and crew members he wanted to do what the government wasn't able to: protect those who couldn't protect themselves.

Kara glanced at Dom, but he was busy talking with someone over his comm link. Since they'd been reunited, she hadn't spent much time with him. She wanted to be useful, to help however she could in the fight to contain the Oni Agent, but so far she'd just been told to go here or wait there. *Load up in the helicopter, load out.* She almost wished she'd gotten to stay at Fort Detrick to help guard the facility or at least help protect the families from another Skull onslaught.

The chopper banked near Baltimore. More smoke, more burned-out buildings and abandoned vehicles. More Skulls swarming over the city streets.

Dom finished his conversation over the comm link and leaned forward to look at Kara and Sadie. "You two doing all right?"

They both nodded.

Miguel, seated in another row, piped up, "And your third

daughter's doing just fine, too." He patted Maggie's head, and the golden retriever wiggled while he held her in place. The dog seemed to have taken a special liking to Miguel. *Or maybe it's the other way around*, Kara thought, watching Miguel scratch behind Maggie's ears.

The other Hunters, Meredith included, had their eyes closed, stealing what little sleep they could in the short ride from Frederick to Annapolis. They banked and headed southeast, away from the setting sun.

The chopper shuddered. All the Hunters awoke at once. Sadie gripped Kara's hand, and Maggie stood, her ears perked and eyes wide. Another jolt shook the cabin. An alarm went off, along with a flashing light at the controls.

The pilot, Frank Battaglia, pulled back on the cyclic. "Sorry, folks, looks like we're experiencing a bit of engine failure."

Kara's jaw dropped. A pit opened in her stomach.

"A bit?" Dom asked. "What the hell's going on?" Despite the seriousness of his demand, his voice didn't rise in volume. He was cool and collected in a situation that, to Kara, sounded disastrous.

Frank responded back almost as calmly. "We're losing rotor speed."

Kara watched him mess with the controls. His movements were determined and swift but conveyed no sense of nervousness, like he was dealing with nothing more than a bug splattered on the windshield.

"We're going down," Frank said dryly. "Got to make a

quick pit stop outside Baltimore. I could use a good crab cake."

Adam clicked on his comm link. His voice was not so calm. "*Huntress*, this is Adam. The bird is experiencing engine failure. I repeat, the bird's experiencing engine failure!"

Kara watched him nod as he listened to the incoming transmission. She couldn't hear the other line without a comm link of her own. The Hunters started to tighten their harnesses and check their weapons, and Kara grew more nervous.

She'd seen what lay beneath them. She instinctively patted the pistol she'd stowed in her waistband. Miguel had refused to take the borrowed handgun back from her. He'd told her she needed something to protect herself and her sister. Now she feared his words were about to be proven true.

Lauren scanned the notebook pages of handwritten lists. Each line contained universities, nonprofit research groups, medical companies, and hospitals. Between lab experiments, she and Peter had scoured academic journals and published research conference proceedings to gather names and locations of laboratories that performed prion or neurodegeneration research. They'd tried to narrow down the list to those within reasonable distance from their current location in the Chesapeake Bay outside of Annapolis.

With the notebook under her arm, Lauren left the ship's

medical bay. Her unbuttoned white lab coat billowed out behind her. She prayed *someone* on that list would, by some stroke of luck, be accessible through telephone or radio or email…anything. She rushed through the passageway and burst into the electronics workshop. Normally the room glowed an ethereal blue as Samantha and Chao worked diligently behind their monitors.

Now, the room buzzed with a sense of urgency. Thomas stood beside Chao, speaking rapidly into his headset. Samantha had left her computer station and leaned over a laptop at Chao's station. Glenn spoke with Andris and Jenna, two other Hunters, in one corner. It took only a second of examining their expressions to realize something was wrong.

Tentatively, Lauren approached Chao's side. His computer terminal displayed a map. She recognized the overview of Baltimore. A single flashing dot flew southwest of the city. *The chopper*, she realized. She caught Chao's eyes as he listened to a headset of his own. One nod affirmed her darkest suspicions. The notebook full of research institutions in her hand no longer seemed so important.

"You all hang on," Thomas said. He glanced at Glenn, Jenna, and Andris. "You've got Hunters standing by. Just tell us where to send them."

A canyon of wrinkles formed across Thomas's brow. Chao handed Lauren a headset.

"—not send anyone out to us." *Dom's voice.*

"Can't follow that order, Captain," Thomas said. "We can have a squad of Hunters—"

"It's hell on earth out here," Dom responded. "You can't send any Hunters by land to meet us. There's far too much resistance for one squad to handle a Skull swarm. We barely made it to Detrick as it was, and I won't have anyone losing their lives in a useless effort to save our asses."

"Sir, with all due respect, we can handle ourselves," Glenn said. Jenna and Andris nodded in agreement. "We've seen the Skulls."

"Not like this. Not out here," Dom said. "Listen—" He stopped. The frantic sound of voices on the chopper carried through the line. "We're going to get this bird back up in the air as soon as possible. Night's falling. You don't have any air transport, and you're not making it to our location on foot. Sit tight and help the doctor find a cure."

Thomas audibly exhaled. "Dom, you remember what I told you before you left the ship?"

"I haven't forgotten," Dom said.

"Well, I have no intention of becoming captain of the *Huntress*, and I will get the hell out there myself and haul your ass back if I have to."

"Duly noted," Dom said. "Likewise, I don't want to have to drag *your* ass back to the ship, so save me the work and keep it there."

The readout from the chopper's instrument panel displayed on the bottom of Chao's computer monitor. Chao pointed to the altitude. He put a hand over his microphone and spoke to Lauren. "They're in a controlled descent. All Frank's got is their forward momentum and autorotation of the blades to glide the chopper to a landing."

"Where's he going to put it down without landing in a nest of Skulls?"

Chao pointed to a spot on the map south of Baltimore. "Right about here."

Lauren squinted at the area. "Patapsco State Park." She saw the open parking lot leading to hiking trails through the surrounding forest. How many Skulls were lurking under those trees? She dropped the notebook on Chao's desk. It wouldn't matter if there were any scientists out there waiting for them if they didn't save Dom first.

Navid tiptoed down the stairs. Flashes of red emergency lights illuminated the stairs enough to guide him and Abby down toward the first floor of the hospital building. He nudged open a door with his right hand while holding Abby's hand with his left.

No shadows danced across the walls, but the sterile smell of the hospital had been replaced by one of musty neglect and rot. He strained his ears. No footsteps. No yells. Only the sound of water dripping somewhere unseen.

He nudged the door open wider to reveal a broad hall. An empty gurney speckled with stains lay against one wall. Pieces of crumpled paper and shredded bed sheets lay strewn over the tiled floor.

At the end of the hallway was a set of doors. Splatters of something dark mottled the letters CAFETERIA on the placard above the door. Navid shuddered as the emergency lights flashing in the hallway revealed the same stains all over the floors and wall. He led Abby into the hall, and his suspicions were confirmed when the coppery scent of blood overwhelmed the mustiness he'd smelled from the stairwell.

Navid turned to Abby. He raised his eyebrows and mouthed, *You okay?* With her nose scrunched, she nodded back. Neither said a word while they crept toward the cafeteria's entrance. It struck him as odd that no one else was there. Maybe it was easier for the other survivors to loot the smaller conveniences stores and restaurants lining the streets. Or maybe the cafeteria had already been ransacked. Navid hoped not. It had been frightening enough creeping through the halls between the laboratories and hospital corridors—he didn't want to have to search somewhere else.

He took another step forward. Abby squeezed his hand and pulled him backward. He almost lost his balance, and his heart thudded against ribcage. Abby caught him and pointed at the floor where he had been about to step.

Shards of glass glinted red in the flashing emergency lights. He nodded to her before picking a path around the debris. Even if they hadn't seen anyone or anything yet, crunching that glass would've pierced the silence, attracting any of the crazies within earshot.

He felt almost exhausted from the tension of their slow progress to the cafeteria entrance. By the time they finally made it, sweat trickled down his back. He sucked in a breath of the humid, fetid air. He steeled himself, preparing for whatever lay before them, and nudged the cafeteria door open slightly.

More emergency lights blinked over the tables and toppled chairs. Navid's heart felt like it was climbing into his throat as he stared. Between those empty chairs and tables, humanoid silhouettes staggered slowly back and forth. They moved with no particular urgency, stumbling through the darkness. Navid's arms shook. He slowly drew back from the door and closed it as noiselessly as possible.

Abby cocked her head.

"Crazies," Navid whispered. His stomach grumbled again.

He wanted to run upstairs and hide, but there was no turning back. They needed food and water. Going through the cafeteria was no longer an option. Not with those things meandering about in the shadows.

Abby pointed down another hall and started forward. Navid snuck after. They navigated between empty hospital beds, tipped-over trash cans, and the occasional IV pole. Abby abruptly stopped, and Navid almost ran into her.

Then he saw what had made her freeze.

A body—if Navid could even call it that anymore—lay on the tiles in a puddle of dried blood. Its skin had been shredded, and little remained of its organs. Mostly, Navid saw only the broken bones of someone who apparently had met their end at the hands of the crazies. Abby held her hand over her mouth while she trudged past the person's remains. Navid gingerly stepped over the cracked skull and busted spine.

A shiver raced through his flesh, and a sensation of lightheadedness almost overcame him. He paused for a second, leaning on the handrail on the hospital wall, and waited for the feeling to pass.

Abby pulled him onward until they came to an *Employees Only* sign above a single door. Navid understood where Abby had taken them. Judging by their location in relation to the cafeteria, this must lead to the kitchens.

Abby tightened her fingers around the door handle, but Navid shook his head. He didn't want her to go in first. If there were crazies or violent looters or who-the-hell-knew-what inside, he wanted to be in front of her. He wanted her to have a chance to escape.

She frowned, but he took her place at the door, slowly twisted the handle, and opened it a crack. He held his breath as he peeked inside. The smell of rotting fruit and meat hit him with an almost palpable force. He began to retch but held it in. He forced himself to survey the kitchen. This time, he saw no lingering crazies. Just stainless steel counters littered with utensils, cookware, and spilled food. Heaps of trash and empty tin cans were piled about the floor. Navid ushered Abby inside, and they tiptoed through the wreckage toward the shelves near the rear of the kitchen. Cans and boxes of food, most still undisturbed, were arranged in rows. *Enough food to last Abby and him a year. Maybe even two,* Navid thought.

They gathered as much as they could into two cardboard

boxes, one for each of them to carry. When the boxes were filled, they carefully shuffled back to the door they'd entered through.

Unable to see his feet, Navid kicked something. It pinged against the empty cans resting on the floor. He and Abby froze and stared at what he'd kicked. His stomach turned over as he realized it was a bone—a human bone. He looked down at his feet. A skeletal hand was sticking out from under a rolling cart. Between the empty boxes and rotting produce, he saw a mess of scattered human bones.

He and Abby had been so focused on the prospect of food, and their senses so overwhelmed by the malodor of the spoiled food, that they'd missed the bones, picked clean by the crazies, hidden by the piles of refuse.

A low growl echoed through the kitchen. Navid twisted and saw a humanoid shape come out of the open walk-in cooler at the far end. The red emergency lights flashed over its face. Long hair trailed over its shoulders, and it wore the tattered remains of a line cook's white uniform. Knobby growths jutted out around its scalp, and its fingers seemed to be long and serrated like kitchen knives.

All thoughts of Navid's empty stomach were immediately forgotten. He dropped the box of food and yelled, "Run!"

NINE

———◆❧◆———

D OM PATTED KARA'S KNEE and leaned over to
squeeze Sadie's shoulder. "Don't you two worry.
This type of landing isn't that bad."

"Speak for yourself," Kara said through gritted teeth.
Maggie whined.

"I hear ya, dog." Miguel held the dog close.

Hector and Renee both clutched their weapons as they
watched the ground rise. Long shadows cast by trees and
picnic shelters draped across the mulch and grass surrounding
the state park's entrance. The cars in the parking lot were
rapidly growing larger as the chopper descended.

"We're right on target," Frank said. His eyes remained
straight ahead. "No need to panic, folks. This is one of the
first things they teach you when learning how to operate a bird
like this." Without glancing at his passengers, he shot them a
thumbs up.

"Fuck that, bro," Miguel said, "I don't care if you say it's
easy, we're still going down!"

The Hunters shuffled in their seats, and Dom fought the
fear trickling through him.

"Seriously," Frank said. "This isn't as bad as it looks."

Frank's confidence wasn't as contagious as the pilot must've thought. Dom knew he was telling the truth; an autorotation glide landing wasn't exactly routine, but in some ways it was easier than hovering in place or the other advanced piloting Frank had mastered. But it didn't make him feel any better. He did his best to appear stolid and unworried. In truth, he wasn't too concerned about himself. He glanced at Kara and Sadie again. Kara remained staunchly stone-faced. Sadie seemed to draw from her sister's strength, but her bottom lip still quivered and her eyes remained wide.

Dom pressed his binos to his eyes. He searched along the empty parking lot, lines of trees, and abandoned vehicles. "I don't see any contacts, but be prepared, Hunters."

"Aye, aye, Captain," came the responses.

The trees grew closer, and the leaves and branches no longer appeared as an indistinguishable blur of browns and greens. They skimmed over the forest as those branches scratched the bottom of the chopper.

"Brace yourselves," Frank said.

The chopper hit the asphalt and bounced on its wheels. Frank leaned his weight into the collective and brought it down again. Dom reached for his daughters, holding their hands as the chopper slid toward a minivan. The rotor blades still spun, cutting through the air. With a jerk, the chopper lurched to a stop.

"Everybody okay?" Dom asked.

"Aye, aye, Chief," Miguel said. "Might need a change of pants, but I'll be all right."

"God, I hope you're not serious." Renee wiped the sweat from her forehead with the back of her hand. She undid her harness, as did Hector and Meredith. Each loaded their weapons.

"Frank, how long until you fix this thing?" Dom asked.

"Hard to tell," Frank said. "Based on the loss of rotor speed and the throttle's lack of response, I'm going to say there's something wrong with digital engine control."

"Can you override it?" Dom asked.

"Afraid not. These things are fully automated."

"Then how do you fix it?"

"I'm just the pilot, not the electronics expert."

Adam held up his hands. "Don't look at me."

Dom clicked on his comm link. "Chao, Samantha, do you read?"

"Loud and clear," Samantha responded. "We heard you, and we're ready to troubleshoot the FADEC."

"FA—what?" Adam asked.

"Full authority digital electronics control," Chao said. "We can relay instructions to Adam and Frank if you guys are ready."

The sun had already dropped below the trees. Shafts of orange fought against the encroaching hues of purple and blue. Without daylight, repairing the chopper would be hard.

"Let's do this quick," Dom said.

"Contact spotted," Renee said, her voice cold. "Make that two."

"Skulls?" Meredith asked, crouched and making her way

toward Renee's side of the cabin.

"Definitely," Hector said. "They've got the bony talons to prove it."

Dom's heart sank as he looked at his daughters. He'd thought he was saving them by taking them to Fort Detrick. After Detrick had been compromised, however brief the scuffle had been, he'd thought they would stand a better chance at survival aboard the *Huntress*. He had only taken them from one disaster to another. It seemed there was no escaping the Skulls' reach.

"Everybody, stay low," Dom said.

But it was already too late. The Skulls didn't need to see their faces to be interested in the chopper. The near-crash landing of the AW109 had piqued their curiosity. The two Skulls broke out into a gallop. Their screeching howls pierced the cabin.

"I don't think they realize we don't have room for any more passengers," Miguel said.

Renee hoisted her rifle. "Should we check their boarding passes?"

Dom held up a hand. "How's it going with the computer system?"

Adam shook his head, and Frank opened a panel in the controls.

"It's going to take us a while to diagnose the problem, assuming it's software-related and not hardware," Frank said.

One of the Skulls leapt at the helicopter. Its bony claws scratched at the exterior. Sadie threw her hands over her ears.

"Captain, mind if we take over as TSA?" Renee said. "I think we've got passengers trying to bring aboard unauthorized weapons."

"That depends," Dom said. "Frank, how long 'til we fix this thing? I don't want to attract any more Skulls than we can handle."

The two Skulls scraped at the side of the chopper and continued howling. A third Skull, dressed in a torn mechanic's coverall, broke through the edge of the forest and sprinted toward them.

"Shit," Dom said. "Looks like they're already getting riled up." He nodded to Renee, Hector, Meredith, and Miguel. "Ready?"

"Aye, aye, Captain," the Hunters said again.

Meredith shot him a thumbs up before wrapping her fingers around her rifle.

"Girls, stay back," Dom said to Kara and Sadie.

They moved toward the opposite side of the cabin. Kara held Maggie's collar as the dog growled. A fourth and fifth Skull burst from the foliage. Leaves and branches snagged on the skeletal spikes protruding from their shoulders and elbows. Another three Skulls tore out from the entrance to the hiking trails.

If they were going to do something, they needed to act soon or they risked being overwhelmed. Hector sidled up to Dom, and Renee joined him at his other side.

"Three, two"—Dom slid back the cabin door—"one!"

He planted a boot into the coverall-wearing Skull's chest,

and the creature flew backward. Hector and Renee's rifles barked to life. Blood and bone fragments exploded from the two other Skulls. Their bodies dropped. The one Dom had kicked recovered and stood. With a quick pull of his trigger, Dom sent two bullets through the beast's head. Crimson liquid poured from its wounds. The other Skulls surged. Their claws clicked on the asphalt as they ran. Dom, Hector, and Renee filed out and formed a defensive perimeter around the chopper.

Meredith and Miguel leaped out next. Miguel shut the chopper door as Maggie, Kara, and Sadie watched. He patted the side of the bird before shouldering his rifle.

Muzzle flashes exploded from the Hunters' weapons with each measured shot. One of the charging creatures let out a high-pitched wail. A chorus of other cries, some distant, others sounding considerably closer, joined the beast's frightening song. A spatter of bullets knocked the monster off its feet. For a few seconds, the parking lot was clear of living Skulls. The last throes of the sinking sun cast long shadows over the crumpled bodies and pools of blood.

"Everybody's night vision in working order?" Dom asked.

Meredith flipped down the NVGs she'd borrowed from Adam. "Seems good to me."

The Hunters followed suit. Dom clicked on his NVGs and peered into the now black-and-green landscape. Next to him, Meredith and the Hunters each wore infrared tags on their shoulders. The tags glowed a bright white when viewed through NVGs but were invisible to everyone else. The tags were commonly used by American forces to prevent friendly fire when operating in the cover of darkness.

The vacant vehicles in the parking lot were ghostly apparitions. He played his rifle across the trees. Everything remained silent despite the earlier cries they'd heard.

Dom clicked on his comm link. "Frank, how's my flyboy doing with the FADEC?"

"We managed to use one of Adam's sat link devices so Chao and Samantha could dial into our systems from the *Huntress*. They're troubleshooting now."

"Keep your eyes on my girls for me, will you?"

"You got it, Captain."

A guttural cry escaped the woods to their left. Dom and the Hunters swiveled. A Skull lunged over a fallen tree trunk. It sprinted toward them until a spray of bullets sent it sliding across the grass. Another howl sounded to their right, followed by a series of screams directly in front of them. More Skulls poured from the woods. Like the legendary hydra's heads, each one they took down seemed to be replaced by two more.

"Reloading," Renee called. She jammed a fresh magazine in place and resumed firing.

As soon as she did, Miguel yelled, "Reloading."

Dom took his turn, clicking a new magazine into place.

The incoming Skulls seemed to be swarming them like Dom had kicked a beehive. His thoughts turned toward Kara and Sadie, and he wondered how they were holding up. He prayed the Skulls would never reach the chopper. He squeezed the trigger and sent another skidding, dead, across the asphalt.

Dom realized they were losing ground. There were far too many to hold back. A chorus of howls echoed across the parking lot directly behind them. Dom swallowed hard. He risked a glance over his shoulder. His NVGs lit up in bright flashes of green. A frenzied horde of Skulls scrambled across the lot to the other side of the AW109.

"Frank," Dom said. "I hope to God you're about to tell me the bird's ready to fly."

"That's a negative, Captain," Frank said. "And if these new passengers decide to climb all over the chopper, there's a good chance we're never getting out of here."

The wails of the approaching Skulls grew louder, and Dom's pulse thumped in his ears. Hot adrenaline flooded his vessels. Next to him, his four crew members were clearly visible with their IR tags illuminated in his NVGs. The tags were completely invisible to the Skulls, but the bright flashes of white bursting from the muzzles of their rifles were not. An idea struck him, and he stopped squeezing the trigger. "Hold your fire!"

TEN

———⊰⟡⊱———

WITH ME!" DOM STARTED RUNNING AWAY from the chopper toward a picnic shelter. The others followed. When he reached the shelter, he flipped a picnic table on its side against one of the shelter's support columns. Hector and Miguel turned over another, then Renee and Meredith shoved a third table over. It gave them a meager barricade against the Skulls.

"Why the fuck are we running away from the chopper?" Miguel asked.

Instead of answering, Dom squeezed the trigger and sent off several bursts into the flanks of the Skulls. The beasts swiveled and crashed into each other. Confusion riddled their ranks. Exactly what Dom had hoped.

"This is why!" He fired again. "Open up on 'em!"

The other rifles chattered to life. The oncoming Skulls switched their attention to the muzzle flashes. Howls and calls rending the air anew, the beasts scrambled toward the picnic shelter where Dom and the Hunters had set their firing position. The tide of Skulls shifted away from the chopper.

"What's going on?" Adam's voice broke over the comm link.

"They hunt based on sound and sight," Dom yelled through his mic. "So keep your asses down and work quietly while we draw them away."

Three Skulls in ragged clothing broke away from the pack and came bounding at him. The growling bellows coming from their mouths made them sound like creatures two or three times their size. Dom gritted his teeth and fired. He was rewarded with the gratifying smack of bullets plunging through bone and flesh, and the monsters tumbled into the grass. He shot off another burst, praying his daughters would stay hidden under the fuselage windows of the chopper. The scene reminded him of the attack on Detrick: a seemingly endless stream of Skulls flooding them with no end in sight.

When they'd left the base, Shepherd had only given Dom and his crew enough supplies to tide them over in case of an emergency. He had no idea how long they could last.

He patted his tac vest to confirm what he already knew: one more magazine left. He squeezed his trigger, pumping lead into a Skull with its claws outstretched and its mouth open in a wail. A long mess of dark hair trailed behind it, and a leather belt was still wrapped around its waist, a lingering reminder of its former humanity. Dom's rounds knocked the creature back, and its muscles rippled and writhed under spikes and bony plates as its life ebbed away. Still more creatures came at them.

"How's everybody holding up?" Dom asked.

"Reloading," Miguel said. "Last fucking mag."

"Same," Hector said.

Meredith and Renee continued to fire. When they paused, they confirmed their dwindling ammunition.

"Frank, Adam, when's liftoff?" Dom asked.

"Chao's telling me we're close," Adam said.

A group of Skulls were running near the dark chopper. A six-foot-tall, skinny one still wearing cargo-pocketed hiking pants and a backpack scraped it as he ran. In the background, over Adam's comm link, Dom heard Maggie's frantic barking. The thin Skull paused. Its neck twisted and its mouth gaped as it let out a screeching roar. It tore at the chopper with its claws.

Gunfire continued while the Hunters tried to hold off the Skulls still on the attack. But Dom's attention was drawn to the monster trying to get into the chopper—trying to get at his daughters. Two more of the beasts climbed atop the AW109. Their spiked and mutated arms flailed. They pounded their fists against the fuselage in a rabid frenzy.

Dom had the creatures lined up in his sights, but he hesitated. "How strong is that glass?" he asked Frank over the comm link.

"Strong enough to keep out most small arms fire," Frank said.

Dom lowered the weapon. If his bullets strayed from their target, he risked not only damaging the chopper, but also its passengers. He couldn't take a shot from here. Not with this vantage point. None of them could. He stepped from behind the overturned picnic table.

Meredith grabbed his arm. "Don't. You're not going to

be of much help to your girls if you end up dead."

Another two Skulls joined the assault on the chopper.

Frank's voice came over the comm link again. "We might be able to take some small arms fire, but if they damage the intake or the rotors, it won't much matter. Even if we get the FADEC back on track, none of us will be going anywhere."

Kara had only known Frank for a couple of days, but she could hear the worry in his normally cool voice. Another creature climbed atop the chopper. Its wails resonated through the cabin. Maggie no longer let out her deep, throaty barks. Instead, she whimpered beside Sadie, who crouched in the corner and clung to the dog.

Kara held the pistol in her hands. "We've got to do something."

"You're not doing anything." Adam spun in the copilot's seat. "And I'm not going to let anything happen to you two." He pointed to the gun. "You got another magazine for that?"

Kara shook her head.

Adam climbed over the seat and into the rear of the cabin. He dug through the Hunters' supplies and pulled out two more magazines. "Here. Just in case."

Kara took the magazines and tucked them snugly in her pocket. When Adam continued to search through the supply box, she asked, "What are you doing?"

He gave her a vest complete with body armor plates and handed another to Sadie. "Put these on. If those pieces of shit get in here, I want you two to have some protection."

The Skull on top of the chopper started to throw itself against the cabin's roof. The rotor shuddered, hit by the Skull's violent attacks.

"That thing cannot wreck this bird or we're all fucked," Frank said.

Definitely not as calm and collected as before, Kara thought. His marked change in demeanor told her everything she needed to know about the gravity of the situation, as if it hadn't already been obvious. Her father, Meredith, and the Hunters were still fighting off the wave of Skulls desperately charging the shelter. She doubted they could stop the Skulls assaulting the chopper before the beasts grounded the bird permanently.

More demonic shrieks and cries tore through the night air.

The unmistakable sound of a gun being loaded and cocked echoed in the cabin. Adam closed his eyes and took a deep breath before mumbling a prayer to himself.

"What are you doing?" Kara asked.

"Going to take care of these fuckers," he said. He positioned himself near the cabin door opposite where the Skulls were trying to tear into the chopper.

Kara started to squirm out of her vest. "You take this. You're going to need it."

"Hell, no," Adam said. "It's yours."

He pressed the vest back over her shoulders, its weight

slumping over her again. It felt heavy enough to suffocate her small frame, but she relented.

"I'm coming with you," she said.

"God, no. If I let you do that, your father will kill me if those things don't," Adam said, adjusting his thick-framed glasses.

Kara clenched her fingers tight around her pistol. "You can't do this alone."

"I'm about to." He wrapped his fingers around the door handle. "Slam this thing shut as soon as I clear it. And don't open it for any goddamn reason."

Frank closed the panel on the dash. "Chao tells me the FADEC is working again." The chopper shook. More Skulls rocked against its side, threatening to topple the bird like enraged rioters flipping a car. "Christ, these things are relentless." Frank turned to Adam. "Don't do anything stupid."

"Doing something stupid would be doing nothing at all while they fuck up the chopper!" Adam yanked open the door and rolled out. "Close it!"

Kara had no choice but to do what he said.

Frank's hands dashed across the controls in preparation for takeoff. "Dom, as soon as it's clear, we're good to go. But you're going to have to do something about Adam."

As Frank listened to Dom's reply over the comm, he nodded. Kara pressed her hands to the windows and watched Adam round the chopper toward where the Skulls were slamming their fists and tearing at the fuselage. He shouldered his rifle and let loose a salvo into the pack of monsters. Each bullet tore into their flesh or smashed into the bony plates along their gray skin. He couldn't miss from such a short distance.

The gunfire diverted the Skulls' attention. Adam ran backward, away from the chopper and the pack of Skulls. He moved so his gunfire wasn't directed anywhere near the chopper. Most of the Skulls tumbled to the parking lot, where their pooling blood glimmered in the moonlight. Kara watched Adam continue to fire on the monsters. The orange muzzle bursts reflected off parked cars as he drew the beasts away. Only two Skulls from the pack that had assaulted the chopper remained.

Kara was sure Adam could handle it. She released the breath she'd been holding. More gunfire sounded from the picnic shelter as the Hunters mowed down the other Skulls they'd drawn away. They might actually make it. They might actually live.

Then Adam stopped firing.

What the hell is he doing? Kara thought.

Reloading, he dropped the magazine from his rifle as the two remaining Skulls pounced. While he scrambled backward, he fumbled with the replacement mag. One of the beasts lashed out. Its crooked claws caught Adam's right shoulder. He struck back with the butt of his rifle. It connected with the Skull's jaw, and the creature's head snapped back.

But the other Skull took advantage of the momentary vulnerability. It lunged at Adam, and the two went down hard.

Adam disappeared under a flurry of skeletal limbs. Kara's heart pounded wildly. The weight of the body armor no longer seemed so significant. Her fingers tingled and her nerves sparked as adrenaline surged through her. In her mind's eye, she watched her mother attacked by a Skull—attacked because Kara had hesitated.

She couldn't watch this man die. She tore the cabin door open and slammed it shut before Frank could protest. Sprinting across the lot, she drew up the handgun. The muzzle burst to life with each successive shot. Most of the bullets sank into their targets, plunging into the skeletal beasts before her, but a few smashed against the skeletal plates, sending shards of yellowed bone flying.

One Skull spun around to face her. Blood dripped from its mouth. Patchy hair stuck up around the horns jutting from its forehead. For a moment, it stared hard at Kara before roaring and swiping its talons through the air. Kara ducked and fired. She missed and jumped back from another swinging claw to fire again. This time, blood poured from the cavity in the Skull's face where its nose had once been, and the monster crumpled.

Growling, the second Skull—much smaller than the first—turned away from Adam's body. It dove at her with its cracked lips pulled back and its tongue whipping between its serrated teeth. She fired at its face, but it came at her unexpectedly low, and the shot went wide. She squeezed the trigger again. The slide on her handgun clicked back.

Empty.

She sprinted away and reached for a new magazine. But the Skull was quicker. It crashed into her legs. She dropped the fresh magazine and fought to hold the pistol as she slammed against the asphalt. Pain radiated through her elbow, the back of her head, and her tailbone. The Skull drew back a claw. It snarled, and saliva mixed with Adam's blood dripped onto Kara's face.

She refused to flinch and tightened her grip on her empty pistol. She wouldn't go out without causing some damage to the beast. Its claws stabbed at her chest. The body armor deflected the strike, but the sheer force of the impact resonated in Kara's ribcage. She returned the blow by swinging the handle of her pistol into the creature's face. Cartilage cracked, and its nose burst inward.

Pain didn't stop the beast. It slashed at her again. This time its talons connected with her face. She felt the jolt of electricity through her nerves along with the unreal sensation of the thing's claws tearing into her cheek.

But if pain didn't stop the Skull, she wouldn't let it stop her.

With another determined strike, she crushed the creature's eye socket with the pistol. Her vision clouded with blood. She exchanged more blows with the monster. An image of Sadie flashed through her mind. Then her father. Meredith. The Hunters.

If her sacrifice saved them—saved the team, saved her sister—it was worth it. Maybe they'd find a cure and save her mother, too. The beast's fist connected with the side of her face again, slamming the back of her head into the asphalt.

Kara's world went black.

ELEVEN

M EREDITH WATCHED KARA go down through her NVGs in a nightmarish flurry of flashing greens and blacks. The other Skulls continued to rush the picnic shelter, but she saw an end. Only a dozen or so of the monsters remained. She patted her vest and stood beside Dom. *No more magazines.*

"Hold your position," Dom said. Without further explanation, he dashed toward where his daughter had fallen.

Meredith had no more rounds to provide cover fire. She couldn't help Hector, Renee, and Miguel take down the remaining Skulls. There was only thing she could do: She sprinted after Dom. One of the Skulls haphazardly swung a claw. With the stock her rifle, she bashed its horned face. A second blow to its jaw sent its neck snapping unnaturally backward, and it slumped to the grass. Gunfire continued to chatter behind her.

Miguel's voice broke over the comm link. "We've got you two covered."

It didn't matter whether the Hunters did or not. Meredith knew Dom wasn't going to stop until he reached his daughter, and she wouldn't falter until she was by his side. She saw

Adam bring himself up into a sitting position. His arms shook as he struggled with his rifle, desperate to feed in a fresh magazine.

The Skull on Kara tore at her chest. Meredith's heart climbed into her throat as she and Dom ran. Dom didn't risk shooting the beast yet. Meredith knew he wouldn't fire until he could be sure he wouldn't hit his daughter. They bounded across the grass toward the lot. When they were finally close enough, Dom shouldered his rifle and fired. The beast fell limply across Kara's body.

The girl was still. Meredith couldn't tell if she was breathing or not.

As Dom lifted the Skull's corpse from Kara, another of the creatures rushed him. Meredith slammed her empty rifle's stock into the creature's face. Its arms whipped at her, but she dodged its desperate attacks and landed another debilitating blow. The gunfire from the shelter quieted. The last of the beasts dropped in the grass. Hector, Renee, and Miguel ran toward Meredith and Dom.

Dom dropped his SCAR and knelt next to his daughter.

Meredith ran to Adam. "We need to move. Can you do that?"

Blood seeped from lacerations across his scalp and the torn flesh on his side. He managed a slow nod, and Meredith guided his arm over her shoulder before helping him stand. She escorted him to the chopper's cabin, where Frank had already slung the door open. As she laid him down, Hector and Renee rushed in. They tore into the first-aid kit on the fuselage wall and began applying a compress to Adam's side wounds.

Meredith grabbed a handful of gauze and another compress before running back to Dom. Miguel stood guard over the father and daughter. Dropping beside them, Meredith applied the bandages to the ragged strips of flesh still clinging to the side of Kara's face.

Dom, his hands bloody and shaking, clicked on his comm link. "*Huntress*, do you read?"

"Loud and clear, Captain," Chao responded.

Meredith slid two fingers over Kara's neck, trying to monitor her pulse. A faint throb beat. The girl might yet have a fighting chance, but she was nowhere near being in the clear yet.

"We have two casualties incoming," Dom said, his words rushed, almost panicked. Meredith could sense the inner turmoil raging within him. "Heavy bleeding. They've also been exposed to the Oni Agent. They'll need to start treatment immediately."

"Copy that," Chao said. "Message will be relayed to the medical team. Godspeed."

Meredith admired Dom's ability to hold himself together even while he watched his daughter barely clinging to life. She helped him lift Kara aboard the helicopter then shut the door. The whine of the engines accompanied the Hunters' voices. The rotors spun, and the roar of the chopper attracted a few lingering Skulls from the area. Four sprinted straight at the helicopter, but it lifted past their reach.

Frank pushed the cyclic and the chopper responded, moving forward with it. He adjusted the throttle, and Meredith thought she could see him holding his breath, waiting to see if the repairs to the FADEC had worked. With no ringing alarms or flashing warning lights, they sped off over the forest. Meredith watched Dom's face. His eyes were wide with worry as he pressed the dressings over his daughter's injuries. Meredith undid the straps on Kara's body armor. "Let's get this off so she can breathe."

Dom nodded and pulled his hand away from Kara's face. Meredith quickly removed the vest. After she cleared it over Kara's head, Dom reapplied pressure to the wounds. Blood saturated Kara's shirt. Meredith cut the fabric away and used a cloth to wipe the blood away from her skin. She found no other cuts or wounds. The armor plates had protected Kara's vital organs.

From the first aid kit, Meredith drew another set of bandages to replace the ones over the side of Kara's face. She had sometimes regretted her decision to join the CIA and embark on a life without a family. Occasionally, she had dreamed about what it would have been like if she'd chosen a less tumultuous career and raised a gaggle of children somewhere in suburbia. But as she watched Dom tend to his daughter, as she imagined the parents whose children had succumbed to Skulls or were transformed by the Oni Agent, she thanked God she'd never brought anyone else into this unkind world.

Lauren Winters rushed across the helipad, and the AW109 landed aboard the *Huntress*. Peter, Sean, and Divya followed with two gurneys. When they reached the chopper, the cabin door slid back. A mad rush of voices greeted Lauren, and she helped load their first patient onto a gurney. She took one look at the youthful, unfamiliar face half-covered by bandages and stifled a gasp. The auburn hair was a dead giveaway—she had to be Dom's daughter. Meredith and Dom bounded out beside her. A soft groan escaped the young woman's lips. Her left eye was covered in bandages, but her right eyelid started to flutter open.

"Kara," Dom said. "You're okay. You're going to be okay." He held her hand, and Peter and Lauren took command of the gurney.

"Anything besides the cranial trauma and lacerations?" Lauren asked while the group rushed back into the *Huntress*.

"I didn't notice anything external," Meredith said.

"Okay, thanks," Lauren replied and then spoke to Dom in a measured voice. "We're going to take damn good care of her, Captain."

"I know you will." Dom's fingers slipped from Kara's. Lauren wheeled her into the operating room. He stood outside the small room, separated by an acrylic partition. Lauren and Peter donned surgical masks and gloved up.

Lauren gave him a nod through the window. She peeled back Kara's saturated bandages. "Kara, if you can hear me, we're about to administer an anesthetic. You'll go to sleep, and when you wake up, your father will be back beside you."

A weak, rasping sound escaped Kara's bruised lips. Her eyelid fluttered again but didn't open.

"Pulse is weak, blood pressure's dropping," Peter said.

Lauren inserted an IV needle and connected the line. "She's lost too much blood. We need to make this fast."

Already, the yellow calcified tissue symptomatic of the Oni Agent had formed over her wounds and helped to stanch the bleeding. With a scalpel, Lauren scraped it away and sutured the torn flesh. She and Peter continued this grueling task, removing the mineralized growths and then closing the wounds.

She could feel the hot burn of Dom's gaze on the back of her neck. The sounds of Divya and Sean treating Adam in an adjoining room rang in her ears, but she focused hard on the task at hand. Each loop of the suture and dab at the dried blood brought Kara closer to life again. With the IV pumping fluid into her, Kara's blood pressure stabilized. Her pulse continued its rhythm, steady and slow.

"I didn't notice any significant craniofacial bone trauma," Lauren said when they'd patched Kara up.

"Her cheek was torn up bad enough. Poor girl's going to have wicked scars along the left side of her face."

Lauren nodded. "Let's start her straight on the chelation therapy and antibiotics. We need to eradicate the Oni Agent immediately."

Peter picked up a small glass vial he'd prepared and withdrew the chelation solution with a syringe. He inserted the liquid into Kara's IV line. Lauren followed with a glass bottle of tetracycline—a strong antibiotic to wipe out the stubborn nanobacteria in the Oni Agent. When she finished, they wheeled Kara to the patient area. Adam lay in a neighboring bed, already recovering from his emergency treatment. White gauze, taped in place, covered his right arm and chest. Dom walked over to the side of Kara's bed and brushed back her hair. Meredith laid a hand on his shoulder.

"I know it looks bad, but I think she's going to be okay," Lauren said. "We already started her on the chelation therapy." Holding a button on the side of the bed, Lauren raised the top half until Kara's torso was at a forty-five degree angle. "We stitched up the back of her head, too. Judging by the wound alone, I'm guessing there's a chance she suffered a concussion. Can't really confirm that with any equipment we have on board, so we'll keep her upright to avoid fluid buildup on the brain."

"Thank you," Dom said, caressing his daughter's hand.

A knock at the door drew their attention. Miguel stood in the doorway with a hand around Maggie's collar and his other arm on Sadie's shoulder. "These two have been itching to see their sister. Mind if I let them in?"

"Should be fine," Lauren said. "But the best thing for Kara right now is rest, understand?"

Sadie ran to her sister, and Maggie bounded behind her.

"She's not going to turn into one of those things, is she?" Sadie asked, her eyes wet with tears.

Dom shook his head. "Dr. Winters was the one that found a way to stop the Oni Agent. She already gave it to Kara."

"So she'll be fine?"

Dom locked eyes with Lauren, and a grateful smile spread across his face. "Kara couldn't be in better hands. If Dr. Winters tells me she'll be fine, she'll be fine."

"We've done everything in our power," Lauren said, conscious of Sadie's gaze studying her face for any hint of a comforting lie. "Your sister's strong, too. Every sign points to a healthy recovery."

"Thank you," Dom said. Still holding Kara's hand, he gestured toward the laboratory, where Divya and Sean had busied themselves with their cell cultures. "How's work on the cure for the prion disease coming along?"

Lauren allowed herself a small smile. As soon as Dom had found out his daughter would survive, he wanted to make sure his team was still on task to save the rest of the world. "I'm not sure we can make General Kinsey's deadline. I'm not even sure we're going to find *anything* on our own." She caught Dom up on her and Peter's efforts to identify neurological research labs that might be able to develop a prion disease cure or vaccine. "But we haven't had time to reach out to any of those labs."

"Understood," Dom said. "If you've got a list available, might as well go talk with Chao now to see if you can reach any surviving researchers."

Surviving researchers, Lauren thought. She swallowed the lump in her throat. "We'll be lucky if anyone helpful is even alive, much less able to be contacted."

"Won't know until we try," Dom said.

"I know, I know."

Next to them, Peter recorded Adam's vitals and checked the man's bandages.

"Can you take care of our patients while I talk to Chao?" Lauren asked.

"Surgeon, researcher, lab tech, nurse." Peter smirked. "I'm happy to do your bidding, Dr. Winters." His expression grew serious. "Really, I'll be fine. They'll be fine. Go find us a cure."

TWELVE

———————

L AUREN KNOCKED BEFORE SHE ENTERED the electronics workshop.

"How's Adam?" Samantha asked, jumping up from her workstation and knocking over a pile of empty energy drink cans.

"He's okay. From what Sean and Divya told me, he's probably suffering a couple of broken or fractured ribs, but they dealt with the internal bleeding—"

"Internal bleeding?" Chao perked up from behind his monitors.

"Yes, but they patched him up, and we started him on the chelation therapy." She glanced at the empty computer station where Adam normally worked. His blue Doctor Manhattan figurine was lying on its side, and she righted it. "He'll be back in this seat in no time."

Samantha's face relaxed, and Chao breathed an audible sigh of relief.

Lauren held out a notebook and a small USB flash drive. "Peter and I compiled a list of a few laboratories we hoped you might reach out to. We've included all the contact information we could, too. It's by no means complete, but it should be a good starting point."

"Thanks." Chao took the drive and inserted it into his computer. "We'll do what we can. Email, phone, radio…whatever it takes, we'll find someone out there who can help us."

"I'd appreciate it," Lauren said. "Anything else I can do to help?"

"No, I don't—" Chao stopped. "Actually, we could use some help at Adam's station. It's going to take time just to try all these phone numbers." He pointed to the list that popped up on one of his monitors. "But I don't want to take you from your research or your patients."

"No problem. I'll recruit another crew member or two."

"That'd be perfect."

Lauren left the workshop. As she entered the passageway, she spotted Renee and Glenn speaking near the door of the medical bay.

Glenn waved to her and said, "Dom's girl is a trooper, huh?"

"Certainly is," Lauren replied.

"She saved Adam's life," Renee said. "I mean, she ran straight at the Skulls attacking him. We never would've made it in time, but she—" Renee shook her head. "That girl is cut from the same block as Dom, that's for sure."

Lauren readjusted her white coat. "She's something. I can't even imagine everything those girls went through while waiting for Meredith and Dom...but I've got a favor to ask."

"Anything you want, Doc," Glenn replied.

"You two interested in working as telemarketers?"

Renee arched a skeptical eyebrow, and Glenn's brow furrowed.

Lauren placed a hand on each of their shoulders. "Never too late to realize those dreams."

Dom shifted in his seat while he watched the EKG's endless pattern reporting Kara's heartbeat. Each time he saw the familiar peaks, he felt a sense of relief while simultaneously fearing the line might go flat at any second. He kept telling himself she'd be okay now; she was stabilized and healing.

Sadie had fallen asleep, curled in a chair with Maggie napping between the chair legs. Yes, both his daughters would be okay. He was lucky to have them by his side.

His right leg started to cramp. He had been sitting in the same seat since Kara had been wheeled out of the OR, and he needed to move—loosen his limbs and stretch.

He took a short stroll down the passageway. He walked toward the mess hall. Soft music drifted out of the hatch, and he leaned in as the notes swelled around him. Inside, Owen Hunt, eyes closed and head bobbing, strummed a guitar. The fingers on his left hand climbed up and down its neck as he plucked the strings with the fingers of his right.

Dom lowered himself onto a stool a table away from the seat where the former Ranger from Austin played. Owen continued his melody—some classical acoustic guitar song Dom didn't recognize. The Ranger locked eyes with Dom for a second, and Dom nodded back, a slight gesture to keep Owen playing.

Spencer Barret, another former Ranger, came into the mess hall with an energy drink in hand and sat next to Dom. He leaned over and whispered, "We getting a free concert today?"

"Suppose so," Dom said in a low voice. "You know what he's playing?"

"Yep, it's one of his originals," Spencer whispered. "Can't remember what he calls this one. Something about rolling seas or waves." Dom watched Owen's fingers with each precise movement. No mistakes. No missed notes. Perfect rhythm. Content to admire Owen's talent, he let the music envelop him for a moment. He encouraged all the Hunters to pursue a hobby outside of their duties on the *Huntress*. It kept them sane, gave them an escape from the violent realities they faced on a daily basis.

He reminisced about his own foray into playing guitar. He'd tried to be like Peter Frampton when he was in high school. For a few years after picking the instrument up, he'd played off and on. But once he joined the CIA, his guitar sat in the corner of his living room gathering dust.

That hobby had been replaced by his fervor for work as a covert agent along with a burgeoning love for the ocean. As a kid, besides having dreams of being a rock star, he'd been enamored with sandy beaches along with crashing Atlantic waves and the ships that cruised them. Working in Langley put him just close enough to the ocean that he had learned to sail on his weekends off. It also slowly gave him the skills and connections he needed to take care of larger and larger vessels until he finally acquired the *Huntress.*

Sailing and covert ops. He was good at those things. But he was a hopeless musician.

And he figured that was okay. After all, Dom had long since come to terms with the fact that he couldn't be good at everything. At most, he really only had time to be good at a couple of things. If he tried to master more than that, he ran the risk of being good at nothing instead. He'd made his choices long ago when he'd given up those six strings that he watched Owen manipulate so well now.

His thoughts strayed back to Kara and Sadie sleeping in the medical bay. He hadn't been a good father to them, not for a long time. Maybe even before the divorce. He'd spent most of his life trying to excel, first in the CIA and then as captain of the Hunters, but he'd failed at the one thing that should have mattered most. He hoped to God he had time to make it up to his girls.

Dom left Owen to his impromptu performance. Spencer had laced his hands behind his head and soaked up the song. The man didn't look up when Dom left the mess hall. He went back to the medical bay and sat next to Kara's sleeping form.

Her hand was draped over the side of the bed, and Dom held it. Her fingers seemed so thin and frail in his calloused palm. Yet she had proved time and time again she was anything but frail.

He'd do anything to take back what his daughters had seen and what they'd gone through. But the scariest part of all was that they'd lost their mother. Bethany had been an anchor for them and created a stable home. She'd practically raised them singlehandedly. By God, he didn't blame her for their eventual divorce. She had been acting like a single parent without the benefit of actually being single.

It was up to him to replace her. He had missed Kara's soccer games and Sadie's dance recitals. He hadn't been there to ensure they got to school on time or had dresses for a school dance or to take them to the library to share his favorite books. It had always been Bethany.

And he had to fill that void. On top of everything else Armageddon had piled on him, he had to fill in as both mother and father for the girls. He inhaled deeply. Bethany had played both roles before, so it was his turn now. It was the least he could do to honor Bethany's memory, and he owed it to his daughters.

Sadie yawned, stretching her arms out, and rolled over in the neighboring bed. Her eyes opened slowly. She blinked a few times before looking up at Dom.

"Remember when you used to tell us fairy tales?"

"I do." Dom smiled and spoke in a low voice so as not to disturb Kara. He recalled his method of co-opting movies he'd seen and books he'd read by replacing the characters with knights and princesses and changing the settings to magic forests and castles. It was a lame attempt at storytelling, but it had seemed to work. "Always used to tell you girls one before bed."

"Until Kara decided she was too old for them."

"That's right. And it wasn't long after when you were too old for them."

Sadie frowned. "That's not true. I always wanted to hear more. I didn't care if it was a baby thing. I liked your stories."

Dom felt the heavy weight of regret roll over him. She was right. He realized now she'd never asked him to stop tucking her in or making up silly stories. Kara might've asked. But Sadie never had. He'd been too distant, too detached from his relationship with his daughters to truly appreciate their differences—and truly appreciate *them*. "I'm sorry. You're absolutely right. I can't believe I ever stopped."

"It's all right. You were busy."

"No." Dom shook his head. "No, it's not all right." He squinted, biting his lower lip in concentration. "Now, do you remember the last story I told you? I think we were in…the Kingdom of Atlantica, is that right?"

Sadie laughed. "Real original name. Right when we're near the Atlantic."

"Do I get bonus points for trying?"

"Sure. But just know that I'm on to you."

"Noted. Now do you want me to continue or not?"

"Oh, yes. There's no TV in here, so this is the best I've got." Sadie settled into her pillow.

"Good. Then here it goes."

In a world scarred by the Oni Agent, he might not get another chance to play the guitar as well as Owen. But maybe now he was getting another chance to be a better father.

Meredith followed Jenna down a passageway. On her back, she carried every possession she had left in the world. It wasn't much. Having lost her original pack escaping a Skull horde in Frederick, she had only an extra change of clothes and a pair of shoes she'd received from Fort Detrick. She thought back to everything else she'd left behind. Maybe her house was still standing in Virginia. Maybe there were still people alive and well in her neighborhood. But it didn't matter. She was here now.

She took in the rails along the bulkhead and the dim amber lights lining the passageway. A constant groaning murmured through the ship as it rolled back and forth in the waves. Hunters and other crew members zoomed back and forth past her on their post-mission assignments. Despite working with Dom for the past couple of decades, she'd never actually seen his ship, much less boarded it. She never imagined she'd have to, and she certainly hadn't anticipated becoming a resident of it. Yet now this ship was her new home. Dom's crew were her new neighbors, her new family. Her life would be far different than the one she'd grown accustomed to in Virginia. But then again, she thought, wouldn't that be true of everyone living through the apocalypse?

"The heads are over here." Jenna gestured to a hatch.

"Ship talk for bathrooms, right?"

"Yep."

"Good. Just didn't want to make any mistake there."

Jenna laughed. "No, no you don't." She led Meredith down the passageway and opened another hatch. Beyond it lay a small room with an overhead light and a single porthole. "And here's your quarters."

"Thanks." Meredith lugged her pack onto a chair next to the berth.

"Not exactly a five-star hotel, but at least you've got the ocean to rock you to sleep at night."

"Trust me, I'm not going to complain." Meredith took a seat and removed her boots. "I've gone from living in a rundown apartment hiding out from the CIA to hiking along the Appalachian Trail getting away from Skulls. This is going to suit me just fine."

She unzipped her pack and pulled out a pair of sneakers. Much more comfortable than the boots she'd worn practically nonstop for the past long, several days.

"Anything else you need?" Jenna asked, leaning against the bulkhead with her arms across her chest.

"Think I'm all settled in." She grinned. "It was a lot easier moving in here than my last house. Know what I mean?"

"Wouldn't know. I've been on the move since I joined the Army. Biggest home I'd ever had was this ship."

"Ever miss the land?"

Jenna laughed and pulled a hand through her short, blond hair. "Used to think about it. But now, I'm pretty damn happy with my choice. Hell of a lot nicer to be here than out there with the Skulls."

Meredith wondered how long it would take her to feel at home. She missed the running path that led behind her backyard, the shelves of books in her library, and the kitchen where she'd experimented with different cuisines on nights when she wasn't tied down at the office. But most of all she missed her bed. Exhaustion started to creep through her, beckoning her to lie down. She knew she couldn't yet, though. "I need to check in with Dom and see if there's anything I can do to help with our mission."

"Sounds good. I can take you to him, if you want. Probably still in the medical bay with his girls."

"That would be great." Meredith could practically feel the bags under her eyes. "First things first, though. Is there somewhere I can grab a cup of coffee?"

"We don't exactly have a Starbucks, but the coffee in the galley will do the trick, if you're brave enough to choke it down."

"That bad, huh?"

"Bad enough to wake the dead."

"Then it sounds exactly like what I need."

THIRTEEN

———◆◆◆———

A KNOCK AT THE MEDICAL BAY DOOR drew Dom's attention.

"Can I do anything?" Meredith asked, entering and walking toward Dom. She took a sip from a Styrofoam cup before throwing it away.

Placing his hand on the back of Kara's, Dom shook his head. "Right now, we're stuck in limbo until Lauren's team makes a breakthrough or Chao and Samantha find someone—"

Meredith shook her head with a gentle smile. "I'm not talking about finding a cure right now or convincing General Kinsey to keep Fort Detrick open. I'm talking about you and your family. Anything I can do for you all?" She gestured to Kara. "I mean, the girl did save my life and Adam's."

"I think I'll be okay," Dom said. "Or at least, I'm doing better knowing the girls are safe." He studied his daughter and the bandages wrapping her face.

"She's going to be fine, too," Meredith said.

"I know you're right. She's more stubborn than I am. There's a fire burning in that girl."

"That's for sure. Whenever she's had a chance to lay low,

she went out risking her life to help someone else."

"I've made a huge mistake, haven't I?" Dom asked.

Meredith cocked her head and gave him an inquisitive look.

"I brought her here and expected her to be safe. But there's no way in hell she's going to sit tight aboard the ship. Every time I've told her to stay hidden, stay safe, she's charged right into the fight."

"You need to find a job for her," Meredith said. "Something worthwhile, something impactful."

"She's not going to become a Hunter."

"I'm not implying she should. I've only known her for a short time, but even I can tell she'd argue until her face turned blue to become one."

"She doesn't have any military training."

"Not debating that either," Meredith said. "But you know, I once wasn't that different from her."

"True, it took quite a bit of convincing for the CIA to get you out of the field and back into the offices and labs."

"Exactly. But you know how they tricked me?"

"They convinced you you'd be more valuable managing operatives than being one yourself."

"Right." Meredith chuckled. "So if you want to shield her from this world a little longer, you know what you need to do."

Dom had opened his mouth to respond when heavy footsteps echoed from the corridor and into the medical bay. He stood as Glenn stopped at the entrance.

"Captain, sorry to interrupt, but we've made contact with a vessel and we need your authority to proceed."

"Scientists? Researchers?"

"I'm afraid not," Glenn said. "It's an SOS from a nearby cruise ship."

Dom started to follow Glenn out of the room. He paused. "Meredith, you want to join?"

"I don't want to impose on your operations."

"Not an imposition," Dom replied. "You're no longer sitting in your desk chair in Langley. We need you out here in the field again."

"Well, aye, aye then, Captain."

The trio rushed down the corridor toward the electronics workshop, where Lauren paced near Chao, Samantha, and Thomas. Renee stood behind the empty desk where she'd been on phone duty with Glenn.

Static crackled from the radio at Chao's station. "This is the passenger ship *Queen of the Bay*. Repeat, this is the passenger ship *Queen of the Bay*. We are requesting medical and armed forces support, law enforcement, anybody."

Chao turned to Dom. "Do we engage or not?"

"Go ahead." In those two words, Dom knew he'd set a potentially dangerous precedent. Before he'd left for Fort Detrick, he'd told his crew to remain as ghost-like as possible and avoid too many interactions with civilians. Their armory and medical supplies were limited and would become even more constrained since they could no longer resupply with the same ease as before the outbreak. Each time they reached out to help cost time and resources they could use to solve the larger matter at hand: finding a cure.

"*Queen of the Bay*, this is the *Huntress*. We read you loud and clear. What's your status?" Chao asked.

"*Huntress*, we have—or rather had—over five hundred souls aboard. We lost a hundred or so due to the infected, and we're afraid more are turning."

"Copy that." Chao turned away from the mic. "So what next?"

"Let me talk to them."

Chao handed Dom a headset.

"*Queen of the Bay*, this is the captain of the *Huntress*, Dominic Holland. Have you contained the infected?"

The radio operator hesitated. "We think so, but there may be civilians still trapped with them."

"Can you expand on that?"

"We ordered everyone above deck and closed off the interior decks, but we had to act quickly before the infected killed more." The man's voice grew shaky. "We have men, women, and children aboard. All are civilians we managed to evacuate before Annapolis fell to those monsters. We desperately need your help."

For a moment, Dom considered the thousands of others that probably needed their help somewhere, somehow. He shook the thought away. At least they could help these people here and now. "Okay, *Queen of the Bay*, give me a moment to confer with my crew."

"Copy."

Dom took the headset off. "If they have more than a dozen people that need medical attention, we'll be unable to handle those numbers aboard our ship."

"So you want us to go with?" Lauren asked.

"Yes," Dom replied. "I want Divya, Peter, and Sean to join the boarding party and bring whatever supplies you think we might need. You can stay to take care of the patients and research."

"Captain," Lauren said, "send me instead of Divya."

Dom scrunched his brow. "I need you here. Where it's safe."

"I know, but Divya's still healing. If the ship's compromised and we run into any danger, it could be devastating to her recovery. Plus, Divya's about as good a scientist as me."

"About as good isn't good enough. She's talented, but I'm trying to be pragmatic. We can't lose you."

"How about this: at the first sign of real trouble, I jump in the Zodiac with the rest of my team and hightail it. Promise."

Dom considered her compromise for a second. "I don't like sending you along." He sighed. "But if I do, you better be true to your word. Get your ass back to the *Huntress* if things start to go downhill."

"You got it, Captain."

"All right then. They'll probably also have plenty of people who need the chelation therapy for Oni Agent infections. You think we have enough supplies to go around?"

"Probably not," Lauren said.

"I assumed as much. Gather up everything you can, while leaving us enough supplies to subsist on."

Lauren said nothing and hesitated a beat.

"I know you're worried," Dom said, "but as soon as we do this, we'll do our best to resupply our medical stocks."

Lauren nodded.

"You're going to have to trust me," Dom said.

"Aye, Captain." Lauren started to take off but turned back to Dom. "One more thing before you all run off. Everyone who's had a dose of the chelation therapy needs to undergo a lab workup. I need to keep an eye on any potential side effects before they crop up and make things more dangerous for anyone out in the field."

"You got it," Dom said. "Renee, Glenn." The two Hunters nodded. "You two gather the remaining Hunters." He added up the number in his mind, a painful reminder that he'd already lost one, and two others had been rendered nothing more than aggressive shells of their former selves by the Oni Agent. Renee still wore bandages from their Skull encounters in Frederick. "Make sure you both consult with Lauren. Whoever she clears, we'll meet in the armory for standard boarding equipment."

They saluted and ran out into the corridor with Lauren tailing them.

"Thomas—"

"Stay back and babysit the ship, am I right?" Thomas finished, already chewing on the end of an unlit cigar. It was the only sign Dom needed to tell the man was nervous about this mission.

"You know it," Dom said. "I've got a hot date and I'm not sure when I'll be home tonight, so help yourself to the fridge."

Thomas patted his stomach. "Always do."

"Chao, do we have a precise location for the *Queen*?" Dom asked.

Chao used his mouse to expand an upper-deck camera's view from the *Huntress*. "I've got a visual on them. They didn't make it far from Annapolis."

"Perfect. If all goes well, this will be a short ride in and out, back in time to sleep in our own beds." Dom put on the headset again. "*Queen of the Bay*, the *Huntress* will also be sending a medical team. If you have any medical personnel or passengers with medical education, assemble them at the stern of your ship. We're going to need you to help us help you."

"Understood."

"We'll see you in less than hour. If you should need anything, stay in contact with my communication operators, got it?"

"Copy. Thank you."

Dom handed the headset back to Chao. He wondered how many SOS calls like this they would respond to. How many other people were out there looking for help, especially when that help wouldn't be coming from General Kinsey or the US military?

"While we're on our dinner cruise, I've got something for

you and Samantha."

"Anything for you, boss," Samantha said, cracking her knuckles.

"I like the enthusiasm," Dom said. "General Kinsey ordered the withdrawal of all active duty armed forces from populated areas and has sequestered anyone he can to high-value targets—whatever those may be. But those orders only apply to units with the ability to retreat."

"All right," Chao said, "so what are you getting at?"

"Two things." Dom held up a finger. "First, we've got law enforcement officials in the surrounding areas who may be able to help us with what I've got in mind. Plus we've got the entire Naval Academy in Annapolis. I'm not sure if they've withdrawn yet, but I want you to make contact with them."

"What's the second thing?"

"I want you two to identify an area that's easily defensible, somewhere to direct refugees and evacuees to." If the US military wasn't going to do it, Dom would. "Not everyone's lucky enough to be holding out in a ship like us. And if the *Queen of the Bay* is any indication, we could be busy for days trying to rescue civilians. We need somewhere organized and ready to protect against the Skulls."

"So you want us to assemble a joint operations force and set up a bioweapon-free safe zone," Samantha said. "And I suppose you want that done before you're back from this little errand."

"That's correct. And if we clear the *Queen of the Bay*, that ship will be great for ferrying civilians to the new safe zone."

He held up his index finger. "Ah, one more thing. It would also be nice if you identified a way for us to resupply our medical stock."

"Just medical supplies?" Chao asked.

"It wouldn't hurt to restock the armory, either."

"What about identifying neuro research labs for Lauren's research?" Chao asked.

"Definitely. If you need help, feel free to enlist whoever's left aboard the ship. Tell them it's on my orders."

"Will do." Samantha stretched her tattooed arms.

"And what about me?" Meredith asked.

"If you're ready to get back in the field—and if Lauren clears you—we could use another Hunter."

The crazy sprinted at Navid and Abby. It lost traction on the hospital's kitchen floor and slammed into a counter. Navid used the momentary advantage to run after Abby and out of the kitchen door. As soon as he shut it, they pushed an overturned patient bed in front of it. The door shuddered. The crazy beyond it howled and hissed.

Other chilling voices began to rise up out of the quiet hospital in response.

"Let's go!" Navid said.

They dashed down the hall. Navid's pulse raced as he rounded a corner with Abby by his side. At the other end of the corridor, a large shape burst out of a room. It looked like an overweight man, but the wail that came out of its mouth was anything but human. Navid and Abby spun on their heels and sped in the other direction. They passed by the entrance to the cafeteria.

Hands slapped against the windows of the cafeteria's entrance, and more cries escaped from under the door.

"Outside!" Abby managed between gasping breaths. She directed them toward the front of the hospital.

Navid didn't look back. The sounds of clicking footsteps followed them as they ran toward the lobby. More creatures— many in hospital gowns, others in scrubs—turned toward them when they made it to the atrium. Their hunting cries joined with the yells of the other crazies. At least two dozen blocked their way outside.

Abby's mouth dropped, and her eyes went wide. She froze in horror. The monsters started to run at them.

"Move!" Navid yelled. He dragged her with him toward another hallway and turned left at an intersection. The cacophony of wails and screeches chased after them. His lungs burned. He shoved through a door to another stairwell. This one was bathed in darkness; no emergency lights pierced the shadows. Outside, the crazies churned down the hallway, past where he'd turned left. Maybe they'd lost them.

Navid jumped when a face pressed itself against the window of the stairwell. Two bloodshot eyes stared at him above a crooked nose. The teeth chattered, and the crazy slapped the door.

"Let's go!" Navid and Abby took the stairs two at a time.

"Where?"

Navid racked his mind. There would be no going outside. There would be no going back to the kitchen or cafeteria. The crazies stood between him and the graduate student office.

But there was one other place they could go. The place where they had usually spent over eight hours a day, back when the world wasn't full of twisted abominations.

"The lab!" Navid said. "Let's get to the lab!"

They dashed up the stairs until they came to another landing. Navid slowed. The sounds of the crazy struggling with the door downstairs followed them, but he no longer heard the telltale pounding feet. The hunting cries of the swarm of crazies seemed lost in the distance. They ran up one more flight of stairs, and Navid led them out into another hallway.

This one was empty. No trash strewn about. No lurking crazies. Only silence and darkness. Navid breathed a sigh of relief. They crept toward the door to the Neurodegenerative Drug and Drug Delivery Research lab, where he and Abby worked. He jiggled the door handle, but it didn't open.

"Locked," he said. Abby shot him a worried expression. "No problem. Just a second." He dug into his pocket and took out a keychain. "Still got these."

He unlocked the door, and they went inside. He checked between the lab benches and lab equipment, but no crazies showed themselves.

"It's clear," he reported.

"Good," Abby said. She started shoving a bookshelf in

front of the lab's door. "Let's block this off."

They pushed another shelf to the makeshift barricade and pulled the heavy cart with the liquid nitrogen tank to reinforce the shelves. Any loose, heavy objects soon found themselves stacked against the door. After ten minutes of reinforcing their barricade, Abby slumped next to it and wiped the sweat from her brow.

Navid trudged to one of the lab benches and tentatively twisted one of the handles of the faucet. No water. But he felt a small sense of victory when he saw a squirt bottle full of tap water used to clean lab scoopulas, forceps, and other small tools. Every lab training video and course he had taken advised him not to drink it, but his thirst told him he didn't have a choice.

He took a sip of the room-temperature water and then offered it to Abby.

"Thanks." She gulped down a third of the bottle before handing it back.

Navid dropped to the floor beside her. "Too bad we don't have anything to eat."

Abby smiled and reached into her pocket. She took out a handful of granola bars. "It won't last long, but we got something."

They shared one bar, agreeing to ration the rest while they figured out their next move.

"So what do we do now?" Abby asked.

Navid pulled her close to him, and they sat, sides pressed together. "We wait," he said. "We wait, and we pray."

FOURTEEN

———◦∾◦———

GLENN WATCHED FROM THE CARGO BAY as the Zodiacs sped off. A foamy wake followed the small craft.

The words Lauren had delivered still stung: "You aren't cleared. Your bone density biomarkers are showing abnormally high bone loss."

He felt frail and weak despite the muscles he'd worked so hard to maintain. Beneath them, according to Lauren, his skeletal system had suffered from the chelation therapy.

Thomas sidled up beside Glenn. He stared after Dom and the others. "Tough to see them go while we stay, huh?"

Glenn nodded solemnly.

"Now you know how I feel every time Dom demands I stay here while he plays cowboy." He patted Glenn's back. "You look like you could use a rest. The therapy hit ya that hard?"

"I'm a lab experiment." Glenn shrugged. The Zodiacs turned into small flecks fading into the horizon. "Lauren said since I was one of their first patients, they overestimated the dosage I needed. They thought I'd need an extra-large dose given my size."

"Is it permanent?"

"No, Lauren thinks as long as I continue to exercise moderately, it's just a matter of time." The bay doors started to close with a mechanical grind. Glenn's eyes adjusted to the dim lights of the cargo bay. "I hate sitting on the sidelines like this."

"Join the club." Thomas gave him a knowing grin before exiting through a hatch to the interior decks.

Left alone, Glenn's thoughts returned to the other Hunters. It wasn't just the warriors on this mission; Lauren and her medical team had gone, too. Maybe it was a foolish, antiquated notion, but he wanted to be there to help Lauren. He wanted to protect her if things turned sour—which, with the Skulls, seemed inevitable.

He prayed he was wrong, and he pulled open the hatch Thomas had gone through. He vowed to make himself useful. But if he wasn't going to be cleared to fight in the near future, he needed to find a new job. He could keep talking to Amir down in the brig. The Iranian mechanic might have new tidbits of info to help uncover the mystery of the Oni Agent's outbreak. After all, Amir had been the only worker aboard the IBSL who had been saved from the Skulls and the rig's destruction. He had to know *something*. But each conversation with the man seemed to end with the same response: "I don't know."

As Glenn strode through the empty passageway, he strolled by the medical bay. He knew Lauren was under immense pressure to develop a cure or a vaccine while having her team perform an endless battery of experiments in those occasional moments they weren't trying to save someone's life.

A thought struck him, and he whirled around. He barged into the medical bay and went to a shelf of textbooks near the entrance to the laboratory. He saw Divya working beyond the clear acrylic partition in the lab, but her focus remained on the plastic dishes and tubes on a lab bench.

Maybe it was foolish—maybe he had no business studying a subject he hadn't touched since his undergraduate years. But Glenn picked up one of the books anyway. If he couldn't battle the Skulls with a rifle, maybe he could do battle with the Oni Agent armed with a pipette and lab coat. He couldn't help the grin cutting across his face at the ludicrous idea, but at least it kept his mind from dwelling on the mission underway without him.

<hr />

Sunlight glinted off the whitecaps in the choppy waters. The *Queen of the Bay* was anchored in the middle of the Chesapeake. Around her floated a veritable armada of seacraft, though most paled in size compared to the two-hundred-foot-long dinner cruise ship. Dom had once taken his ex-wife, Bethany, on one of those cruises, though he'd sailed out from Baltimore. It was a romantic way to spend an evening drinking, dancing, and enjoying the sunset while at sea. A far cry from the floating doomsday ship that it was now.

He crouched over the prow of the Zodiac as it bounced on a wave, his fingers tight around the rope tracing the rubber gunwale. The sun climbed into the sky off their starboard bow. Dom found it hard to believe they had been defending the chopper against the Skull onslaught only hours ago, and now they found themselves embarking on yet another rendezvous with the beasts.

It had torn him up to say goodbye to his daughters once again, to leave them on the ship while he went off to fight. Especially when Kara was still lying unconscious and injured. But he had no choice. He had a crew to lead and a mission to accomplish.

Meredith gripped the gunwale beside him. "I won't lie, I have butterflies in my stomach. Have you ever lost that feeling?"

"Not quite," Dom said. "But I think it's different now. Before, when we were still in the Agency, my nerves would be on fire when I thought I might be in danger. Now my concern is for my crew."

Miguel clapped a gloved hand on Dom's shoulder. "And your concern is appreciated, O Captain, my Captain."

"Don't get poetic on me," Dom said, bracing himself as they hit a rolling wave.

"Can't help it, Chief," Miguel said. "On a crisp and clear morning like this, I can practically feel Whitman's ghost in the air."

"Did you break into Lauren's medical supplies and take

something you weren't supposed to?" Dom asked.

Miguel smirked. "The salty sea air is intoxicating enough for me."

"Better take it all in while you can," Dom said as the Zodiac slowed near the *Queen of the Bay*. A gaggle of passengers waved at them. Some wore expressions of relief at seeing a paramilitary group. Other faces seemed green with sickness. Even from their vantage point, Dom could tell the refugees had overloaded the ship's safe capacity. "I have a feeling it's going to smell a lot worse when we're aboard."

Hector steered the Zodiac aft-ward toward the *Queen's* stern. Along the lower deck, empty metal hooks swung behind the ship.

"Shouldn't they have lifeboats?" Hector called out over the gurgle of the Zodiac's motor.

A man in a white steward's uniform waved at them from among a crowd of passengers pressing him into the safety rails. Dom threw a mooring line to him, and the man made quick work of knotting the rope around the rails. Renee followed suit from the second Zodiac after Dom's boat had been secured.

Dom climbed from the Zodiac onto the deck. The steward shook his hand. "Thank you so much. I'm Jeremy Holtz. The captain's up in the pilothouse. He'd greet you himself, but as you can see, it's a bit of a madhouse around here, and he's a bit indisposed."

Voices carried up around them, and Dom struggled to be heard above the din. "No kidding. Has anyone else responded to the SOS?"

Holtz shook his head. "No."

"You said the captain was indisposed. Is he…infected?"

"I'm no medical expert," Holtz said. "But he did come in contact with one of those *things* while we were battening down all the hatches to keep the creatures inside."

"Shit," Dom said. "We heard there are survivors that may still be trapped below deck."

"That's correct, sir." Holtz hung his head low. "We couldn't mount any type of rescue effort. The best we could do was get as many passengers as we could above deck and throw any aggressors overboard."

Dom gazed at the hanging cables from the painted white steel arms where the ship's lifeboats should have been. "And what the hell happened to your lifeboats?"

Holtz's cheeks flushed red, his eyes narrowing as he turned away, looking toward the choppy waves. "A few of the crew abandoned ship. We loaded up the remaining lifeboats, but the passengers were too panicked, too overwhelmed. A couple of boats are out there." He pointed toward the orange vessels floating in the distance, closer to the shore. "But the rest took off underloaded. We have no idea where they went."

"But you and a few others stayed behind to protect the remaining passengers."

Holtz held his head slightly higher and adjusted his white jacket. "Of course. Dinner cruise or not, that's our duty."

"Absolutely." The winds shifted, and the scent of body odor and sickness drifted over Dom. "We don't have any time to waste. What's the best way for us to get below deck?"

Holtz gestured to a glass door behind them. "We haven't seen any activity on this deck, so I can let you in through here."

"Perfect." Dom raised his voice. "Hunters, on me!"

The group, clad in their black tactical vests and body armor, pushed their way through the crowd toward Dom. Lauren, Peter, and Sean continued to lug boxes of medical supplies aboard.

"How do you want to set up triage?" Dom asked Lauren.

She pulled back a strand of hair matted by sweat and sea spray. "There's not enough room down here. How's the top deck?"

"Not any better," Holtz said. "Actually, probably worse up there."

"We'll make do here until you clear the interior lower decks," Lauren said.

"You heard her," Dom said to the Hunters. He motioned for the steward to unlock the door.

Holtz inserted his key into the door then stopped. He reached into another pocket. "Before I forget, take this. It'll be more helpful to you than me."

Dom took the laminated paper. It was a copy of the deck plans. "Thanks."

Nodding, Holtz unlocked the door. Dom and the Hunters rushed in, rifles shouldered. The steward locked the door behind them, shutting out the cacophony of the crowd. Dom took a moment to evaluate his surroundings. An empty buffet bar took up the center of the open room. Chairs lay askew, scattered around dining tables, and white tablecloths and blue napkins were strewn about. The unmistakable scent of decay and death wafted around them, though Dom didn't see an obvious source.

"Smells worse in here than above deck," Meredith said. "Not a good sign, huh?"

"Not at all," Dom replied.

Past the buffet bar, a wide, twisting staircase rose to a second level of the dining area. Expansive windows let sunlight in to illuminate the far wall, which held two doors, presumably leading to the galley. Dom led the group toward the stairs. He scanned the debris with his rifle as they approached, but nothing leapt out at them. When he reached the bottom of the stairs, he held up a fist to signal the rest of the team to stop. He glanced up, but the entrance to the deck above was blocked with a pile of overturned dining tables and chairs. They wouldn't make it through easily without making a considerable amount of noise and potentially attracting whatever Skulls might be milling about. They needed another route.

With another quick flick of his hand, he sent Renee and her squad toward the starboard galley door across the room. He led his squad toward the portside door. His fingers on the door handle, Dom waited for his squad to get in position near the entrance. Mirroring his actions, Renee caught his eye, and they both moved to swing the doors open.

Neither door budged. *Locked*, Dom figured. *So much for a*

quiet entrance. He reared his leg back and slammed the heel of his foot on the door. The lock broke, and the door thumped against the interior bulkhead. The sound of Renee's door bursting open followed an instant later. Their two squads filtered in. Without portholes, the only light penetrating the darkness came in from the dining room.

The Hunters clicked on their barrel-mounted flashlights. Swathes of white light reflected off industrial stainless steel appliances and pans hanging from the ceiling. Broken dishware and cooking utensils littered the floor. A small clatter made Dom swing his barrel toward the noise. His light shone on a large can of beans rolling with the ship's gentle sway.

Dom ignored the can and led his squad down one side of the galley, separated from Renee's squad by a long island of sinks and stovetops. As the squads snuck forward, a thump resounded from the large walk-in refrigerator at the end of the galley. It sounded again. *Thump, thump*. Muffled cries were audible from within. Dom's pulse quickened, beating in his ears. He approached the walk-in, treading as lightly as possible. He took a deep breath and signaled Miguel and Hector to take up positions around the door.

With a steady hand, he slowly peeled the walk-in open so Miguel and Hector could get a better look. The door suddenly burst back, flinging Dom against the galley bulkhead. Screams echoed as something barreled out.

FIFTEEN

H OLD YOUR FIRE!" Miguel's voice rang out.

The three shapes charged past, but without the aid of light, they tripped and fell over the mess of pots, pans, and dishware piled through the galley.

Renee lowered her rifle and took out a second flashlight, shining it on the trio. A man, woman, and child backed themselves against the door of a massive oven.

"It's okay," Dom said, holding up a hand.

The civilians huddled in the shadows, shying away from the beams.

Dom pushed himself up from where he'd fallen and steadied himself, one hand gripping a counter. "We're here to help."

The woman shook her head, long locks of hair waving. She shivered, as did the man and child. The cool air escaping the walk-in made Dom wonder if it was cold alone or fright that contributed to their shaking.

"We're not going to hurt you," Miguel said, lowering his weapon.

"Who–" the man said, his teeth chattering. "Who are you?"

Dom made quick introductions while he shone the light over each of their faces. Their clothes were dirty, but none seemed hurt or injured. Their eyes were still clear of the bloodshot sclera characteristic of the Oni Agent, and their nails were free from the yellow growths signifying an early infection.

"Jenna, Andris, escort them outside," Dom ordered.

"Aye, aye, Captain." Jenna shot him a thumbs up, and Andris stepped over a sideways serving cart toward the family.

"Before you all go," Dom started, "can you tell me where you saw any of the—" He fumbled for words, unsure if they'd seen Skulls or just people who'd only recently been turned by the Oni agent. "Anyone acting overly aggressive?"

"You mean the cannibals?" the woman asked.

"Right," Dom said. "Anyone like that."

She pointed out the exit doors nearest the walk-in refrigerator. "That way, mostly." She nodded to indicate the doors on the opposite end of the galley that led to the dining room. "We tried to escape, but one of them cornered us down here. We couldn't get away, so we holed up in there."

"Okay, thank you," Dom said. He scanned the walk-in to ensure no one—or nothing—else lay inside, and then turned back to the family. "Do you know where any other survivors might be?"

The man shook his head solemnly.

"Go warm yourselves up outside, away from this place."

Jenna and Andris led the family out of the galley and into the dining room.

"They said they saw one down here," Meredith said, "but where the hell did it go? I didn't think Skulls were too bright."

The Hunters played their lights around the galley.

"There," Hector said. His barrel-mounted flashlight illuminated an open ventilation shaft near the top of one wall. Its grating had fallen to the floor. It was wide enough for a thin individual to slip through. He pointed toward scratches along the metal lip. "Something climbed in."

Miguel shone his flashlight into the recesses of the shaft, but the beam of light revealed only the metal ribs of the empty passage. After a little under a minute, Jenna and Andris returned and reported they'd delivered the family safely outside.

"Time to go up," Dom said, moving toward the end of the galley. "If Skulls are in the ventilation shafts, keep your eyes open."

A set of swinging double doors next to the walk-in each contained a round porthole. Like the galley, the space beyond the doors was bathed in darkness. Dom shone his light through to reveal a black steel staircase going up to the next deck.

"Ready?" He asked the Hunters.

They nodded in unison.

He nudged one of the doors to make sure it was unlocked. It gave way with the gentle push, and Dom shot another quick hand signal. With his shoulder, he leaned into the door and shoved through. He quickly moved to a corner in the stairwell as the others poured out and took up positions.

Waiting with bated breath, he listened for any growls, cries, or scratching claws, but no sounds gave away the presence of any Skulls. The flashlight beams from the Hunters cast haunting shadows against the bulkhead.

Dom gestured for Renee to take point.

She placed a boot on the first step and played the barrel of her gun up, directing the flashlight toward the next deck. "No contacts." She started up the stairs.

The other Hunters lined up behind her, rifles at the ready. They crept up to the next landing. Once there, Dom shone his flashlight through the small porthole in the door. The meager beam reflected off a stainless steel table and whitewashed tile floors. Two sinks and a soda fountain were on a counter that glinted as the light played across it.

"Looks like a food staging area or something for the mid-deck dining room," Dom whispered. He rotated the flashlight beam to scan every corner before moving in. "I don't see—"

A hand slapped across the glass, its fingers leaving a trail of blood. A croaking, gurgling sound escaped from under the door.

"What the fuck?" Renee said.

Meredith readjusted her rifle against her shoulder. "That doesn't sound like the Skulls I'm used to."

"Could be an injured passenger," Dom said. "Cover me."

Dom pushed on the door, but the body the hand belonged to blocked it from opening all the way. He slipped through the crack and aimed his flashlight at the person. The light illuminated her bloodstained face. Her mouth opened and closed, blood bubbling and popping from it as the gargling continued.

"Holy shit," Miguel said, sliding in after Dom. Meredith and the other Hunters filled up the rest of the food staging area and secured the next set of doors.

"The smell…" Jenna gagged.

Dom knelt next to the woman. He played the light across the rest of her body. What he saw made him stagger. "Fuck."

There was hardly anything left below her torso. Her left leg was nothing but ribbons of flesh. Her right leg, apparently still strong enough to stand on, was covered in dried blood and the scratch marks characteristic of a Skull attack. One arm hung limp by her side, chunks of flesh gnawed to the bone. The woman reached out with her one good arm and dragged herself up by lacing her fingers into the door handle. Her body shook with the effort to stand. Her nails, long and talon-like, clicked against the metal, and bone-like spikes burst from her skin near her elbow.

"She's a goddamn Skull," Renee said. She leveled her rifle at the woman's face.

Lurching forward, the Skull fell and crashed against the floor. She tried to rise again, lashing out toward Dom. He stepped back and, with one hand, pushed Renee's barrel down. "No firing. We don't know what else is out there."

Slinging his SCAR-H over his shoulder, he drew a knife from the sheath strapped to his thigh. He bent next to the woman, and her bloodshot eyes locked with his. He expected to see hate and anger radiating from her pupils, but he instead saw only a sad, desperate hunger. Animalistic instinct, nothing more.

With a quick flick of his blade, he slit her carotid, and she slumped backward. Blood pumped from the severed artery, spilling across the floor and adding to the already strong ferrous scent and odor of decay permeating the space. Her arm shot out in one final attempt to reach her prey. But Dom merely stepped back again and watched the life flow from the cruel atrocity that had once been a human being.

"Good lord," Andris said, his Eastern European accent coming in strong. "Skull or not, how was she even alive?"

Meredith pointed to the tourniquets near her shredded appendages. "Looks like someone tried to help her after she was attacked."

"Man, she wasn't coming back from that," Miguel said.

Dom stepped over the remains of the Skull and held up a fist for silence. "We're moving." He edged across the food staging area toward another set of doors. He nudged one open. The room beyond was bathed in darkness. In an effort to shield themselves from the Skulls, the crew must have dropped the curtains on the windows. Dom mentally commended the crew member who had thought to cut off the Skulls' line of sight.

"Flashlights off. NVGs on," he said in a low voice.

His vision went dark for a moment until the NVGs clicked into place. The food staging area lit up in a sea of blacks and greens. He glanced at his Hunters, who gazed back at him with their own NVGs secured and IR markers shining.

They were all tensed with weapons at the ready. He pointed to Miguel to take point. The Hunter crept up to the door. Dom held up three fingers and counted down.

When his last finger curled toward his palms, Dom followed Miguel out through the door. The odor of rotten meat mixed with a coppery scent threatened to overwhelm his senses. His pulse throbbed in his ears, and he struggled to make sense of his surroundings. Pools of blood seemed to shimmer through his NVGs' lenses between the scattered remains of what once must've been humans. A man on the floor nearest Dom was now nothing more than a length of vertebrae, a fractured skull, and the torn remains of a tuxedo. A wall of tipped-over tables, broken dishware, and jumbled chairs blocked the path toward a wide dance floor.

Fuck, Dom thought. Bodies filled the dance floor. No, it would be generous to even call them bodies. Much like the remnants of the man nearest him, what remained of the cruise ship passengers was now nothing more than broken and pitted bones, chewed on and discarded by the Skulls.

The sounds of scraping and scratching caused Dom to swivel. He pressed the stock of his rifle to his shoulder and peered down the sights. Low growls and the sounds of flesh smacking flesh echoed across the macabre dance floor. A pack of Skulls jostled with each other, fighting to be the first to get at something at the opposite end of the room. Between their bodies, Dom could make out a door. It shook each time the Skulls threw themselves at it. There must have been someone behind it. Maybe more survivors. He used two fingers to point to his eyes, then at the half-dozen Skulls climbing over each other and grunting. The rest of the Hunters nodded and trained their gun barrels on the pack.

If there were survivors beyond the door, Dom didn't want to unwittingly take them out with a stray bullet. He signaled for the team to spread out in two clusters. Miguel, Jenna, and Andris took starboard while Dom, Meredith, Jenna, and Hector took port.

They crept along the sides of the room until they established clear firing lanes. Making a fist, Dom held up a hand and approached a column near an overturned dining table. The other Hunters followed.

The clatter of the Skulls crashing at the door and the scratch of their bony claws against the walls echoed throughout the room. The beasts continued to snarl and shove each other as they beat at the door. The Oni Agent had left its inevitable mark on them, evidenced by the coils of bony plates protecting their vital organs and the hooked claws growing from their fingers.

Dom prayed someone beyond that door was still alive. Whoever had barricaded themselves behind it was hopefully in better shape than the shredded corpses scattered around the dance floor.

As Dom shouldered his rifle, the Hunters mirrored his movements. Their labored breaths echoed over his comm link. He imagined the rivulets of nervous sweat streaming down their foreheads under their helmets and behind their NVGs. He held up three fingers against the forestock of his rifle. It was an almost imperceptible gesture, but the Hunters were well trained. He could practically feel their gazes as he counted down.

Three.

The others shouldered their rifles.

Two.

Dom inhaled sharply.

O—

The loud crash of broken ceramic sounded behind them before they even got a shot off. Several busted chairs flew as a beastly shape hurtled through the shadows toward the Hunters. Its overgrown shoulder blades stuck out like shark's fins. And this shark was headed straight toward live meat.

Another burst of clattering dishware and crumpling tables echoed as a second, then a third and fourth Skull fell from a broken tile in the ceiling. The four Skulls charged, and the half-dozen Skulls that had been clamoring at the door on the other side of the ballroom swiveled. Each bellowed, their earsplitting voices a chorus straight from the darkest of hells.

Dom aimed at the first Skull barreling toward him and squeezed his trigger. He missed. The beast ducked low, and the bullets tore into a table instead, sending a shower of splinters into the air. The Skull disappeared beyond a bar near the shattered dining furniture. Another salvo erupted from Dom's weapon, joining the bark of rifles and the screams of Skulls. The rounds smashed into the few bottles of liquor still remaining. Glass shards exploded, and alcohol poured from the shelves.

The Skull appeared from behind the bar unscathed and leapt at Dom. He drew a bead on the beast, but a hand tugged him hard on the shoulder, pulling him backward. He lost his aim. Another Skull swiped, barely missing his head. Whoever had grabbed his shoulder had helped him avoid the skeletal claws cutting through the air in front of his face now.

Meredith stepped forward, her gun chattering at the Skull that had attempted the attack from behind. At point-blank range, she couldn't miss. Dom gave her a quick nod. No time to thank her for saving his ass. The Skull that had attacked from behind the bar scrambled back to its feet. Its bony appendages scraped against the floor and clattered against each other. Long, stringy hair flowed from its head, and it reared back in a howl.

The creature charged again, and Dom squeezed the rifle's trigger. A volley of bullets slammed against the Skull's ribcage. Each round smashed against the organic body armor, staggering the Skull but not stopping it. The beast drew back a taloned hand. It was close enough for Dom to see the spittle fly from between its serrated teeth. Another squeeze of the trigger, and the bullets plunged into the creature's face. Its body, carried forward by inertia, tumbled and crashed against a tangle of dining chairs.

More gunfire and shrieks hit Dom's eardrums like a rogue wave. The scent of blood and gunfire permeated the air. Hunters battled against Skulls; all order and organization was lost.

The beasts dropped from the ventilation shafts and

broken ceiling. Another Skull burst into the room, rendering the door nothing but broken splinters. It appeared even more brutish and ogre-like than its brethren, huffing as it ran at Dom. Its bulbous muscles throbbed and flexed under the skeletal plates. It surpassed the size of any Skull Dom had ever seen, and it tossed aside tables and chairs as if they were toys. There was only one word Dom could use to accurately describe it: Goliath.

Dom fired at the Goliath until his slide locked back. The beast's footsteps shook the floor, and its bellows rattled Dom's bones. He barely had time to jump to the side when the brute barreled past.

As Dom rolled and took a knee, he reloaded his rifle, drawing his sights on the giant monster. He expected the creature to skid to a stop and attempt a second charge. But it made no such effort. Instead, it continued toward another Hunter focused on bringing down a smaller Skull.

"Hector!" Dom yelled and lunged, shooting. He hurdled over a chair.

Hector turned and saw the Goliath. But it was too late.

SIXTEEN

K ARA PAUSED AT THE BASEMENT DOOR. She'd heard
something just beyond it, and she leaned against the
wooden door to see if she could catch it again.

Scratch. Scratch. Scratch.

Maybe it was a mouse. She smiled to herself,
remembering the mouse she'd found in a flowerpot on the
back deck when she was eight. She never understood how
other people could be so frightened of such a tiny, furry little
animal with its sad-looking black eyes and round Dumbo ears.
She'd run inside the house and grabbed a slice of bread. Each
time she'd tossed a breadcrumb into the pot, the mouse had
scooped it up in its little paws and gnawed at it until it
disappeared. The little critter had licked its paws clean and
looked at her, anxiously awaiting the next morsel. Kara had
giggled, which had caused the mouse to jump then freeze in
place underneath the tangle of perennials.

Scratch. Scratch. Scratch.

The memories scattered from Kara's mind. The wood felt
cool on her ear. She pressed it closer and concentrated on the
sound. The scratching was louder. Too loud for a mouse.
What was it?

"Kara…"

She shot back from the door. The hairs on the back of her neck stood on end, and a slow shiver traced its way down her spine. The voice seemed familiar. But there was something off about it. She couldn't quite place it, but she knew she didn't like it.

Scratch. Scratch. Scratch. Louder, closer. *Scratch.*

"Kara…"

She backed away, her eyes wide and heart pounding. Something slammed against the door, and she jumped.

"Kara!"

The door exploded in a spray of splinters, and a shape bounded forward. Kara fell and landed on her tailbone, pain radiating up her back. She tried to crawl away, but something strode out from the basement. Something almost human—but definitely not.

It prowled, its arms tensed. Long talons splayed from its hands. Knobs twisted from its brow like small horns, and crooked yellowish growths sprouted from its joints as if its bones had broken and torn from its skin. It stepped closer, its bloodshot eyes locking with Kara's. And in that gaze, beyond the curtain of hair snarled in the mass of grotesque skeletal protrusions, Kara recognized the creature's bright eyes. The ones that had once looked down on her in sympathy when she'd fractured her wrist snowboarding, that had offered her comfort when her first boyfriend had dumped her after a middle school dance, that had shown pure joy when she found out she'd earned a full-ride scholarship to the University of

Maryland to study biology. Now those eyes were filled with unfamiliar hunger and hate.

The Skull's mouth opened, and its tongue flicked between jagged teeth. Hot breath rolled over her as it spoke. "Kara…"

It was her mother's voice, but this monster was no longer her mother.

"No, no, no, no." Kara wanted to run, wanted to flee, but she couldn't. Her muscles were locked, and she couldn't take her eyes off the body that once belonged to her mother but was now owned by the Oni Agent.

"Kara!" The Skull lunged with claws spread, its mouth opened wide, ready to bite into warm flesh. Kara closed her eyes and waited for it all to be over.

But she never felt the teeth sink into her skin. Instead, she felt only numb paralysis.

"Kara?" This voice was different. Still familiar but younger, softer.

Kara tried to open her eyes. The world was a bright mess around her, blinding her instantly. It was as though someone were shining a spotlight into her face. She realized she could only see out of one eye. Something was wrong. Her pulse raced and panic swelled. She tried to reach up to her eyes. But her arm felt too heavy to move.

"Kara, are you awake?" That voice again.

Her one good pupil adjusted to the surroundings. She was in a hospital. At least it looked like one and certainly smelled like one. But she swore she could feel the whole room swaying.

Oh, God, was she going insane? Moving from one nightmare to the next?

It all rushed back to her. Her mother infected and trapped in their basement. Reuniting with her father and flying into Fort Detrick. The chopper crash, the Skull attack. And now…now she must be on her father's ship.

Her breathing started to slow, her pace settling. It was starting to make sense. She'd been injured when the Skulls had surrounded the downed chopper. And then somehow she'd made it here.

"Kara, are you awake?" the voice asked again. Sadie. Her sister.

Kara tried to twist her neck to see Sadie, but the effort was too much. "I…" she began before coughing. Her tongue, dry and bloated, stuck to the roof of her mouth. She heard the patter of feet on the tiled floor and caught sight of Sadie racing around the other side of the bed.

"Is that better?"

Kara smiled at her sister. At least, she tried to smile. Her lips felt numb, and she wasn't sure what kind of ghastly expression she was actually making. "Yeah," she managed. "Wh… Wh…"

"Shhh, you're okay," Sadie said. "I'm going to get Divya."

Footsteps raced away. Something wet and slobbery tickled the back of Kara's hand. She strained her right eye and saw Maggie's snout poking up over the edge of the bed. The dog's tail waved like a golden, furry fan. Kara wanted to pet her but still couldn't find the strength. The sound of two pairs of footsteps greeted her. A woman with short dark hair and brown eyes approached her bedside.

"I'm Divya," the woman said, adjusting her white coat. "I'm one of the doctors. How are you feeling?"

"Thir… Thirsty," Kara got out.

Divya nodded and held a Styrofoam cup with a straw near Kara's mouth. She inserted the straw between Kara's lips. The cool water trickled over her tongue. Another few sips and her tongue felt normal again. Or at least closer to normal.

After pulling over a stool, Divya sat beside Kara. "Do you remember what happened?"

"I was attacked by a Skull," Kara said. "It's all a blur, but that's the last thing I remember."

"That's right."

Kara's nightmare returned to her. She pictured her mother's transformation. "Am I going to become a Skull, too?"

A slight, pitying smile cracked across Divya's face. "I don't think so. We developed some antibody assays—you know what those are?"

Kara nodded, recalling the term from her bio classes. "You found an antibody for the Oni Agent?"

"We did," Divya said. "We can tell if your body is producing the antibody in reaction to the presence of the Oni Agent. Your levels have dropped dramatically since you were first brought in, which we think means the Agent is no longer in your system."

"Divya said you were brought here just in time," Sadie

added with a grin.

"That's right," Divya said. "We started the treatment right away. I believe you'll rebound in no time from the Oni Agent." The doctor's face dropped slightly before she recovered her smile.

"But?" Kara asked, knowing there must be something else.

"Well, I want you to understand we're just a small medical bay on a ship. We don't have all the equipment a normal hospital might."

"No need to sugarcoat it." Kara tried to sound stern even as dread filled her. The doctor claimed she wouldn't be turning into a Skull, so what could possibly be worse?

"The damage to your face was substantial, and we did the best we could with the supplies we had, but there's going to be some scarring."

"That's it?" Kara asked.

Divya cocked her head, nonplussed. "Well, your eye's been scratched up pretty badly, too, but I think your vision should recover."

"But I'm not turning into a Skull?"

"I don't want to lie to you and tell you I'm one hundred percent sure you're free and clear, but all signs point to no."

Kara sighed. "Okay. Scars I can deal with. But Skulls…" She tried to lift her arm again. A new fear struck her. "Am I going to be paralyzed?"

Divya shook her head. "No, no. You should be fine. The side effects of the treatment can leave you feeling extremely weak for a day or so. Unfortunately, we may have overestimated your dosage of the therapy since you're the smallest patient we've had. I think that's why your body's reacting especially strongly to the drugs. That means your bones are extremely vulnerable right now, so you'll need bed rest for a while."

"But I'll keep you company!" Sadie said. "And Maggie will, too!"

Kara forced a smile, but another thought nagged at her. "Where's Dad?"

Sadie's face lost its joy as quickly as a puddle evaporating in the desert. She turned away, leaving Divya to answer the question.

"Your dad's on another mission," Divya said.

Kara stared at Sadie. Her sister wouldn't look her in the eye, but Kara could see the tears brimming. She should tell Sadie their dad would be okay, that he'd be back soon. Offer her vague reassurances that she couldn't even believe herself.

But she knew what her sister was feeling. They'd already lost one parent to the Skulls. They couldn't lose another.

SEVENTEEN

"DOC, MY STOMACH FEELS like it's turning inside out and my skin's hot and my head hurts and I've got these shivers," a potbellied passenger with a half-crown of brown hair said to Lauren. He grabbed her shoulder while she tried to give a shot of antibiotics to a ten-year-old girl with a scraped arm on the crowded deck of the *Queen of the Bay*. "Come on, Doc. I don't want to turn into one of those *monsters!*"

"Calm down, sir!" Lauren said. "Holtz, can you please help me out?"

Sweat beaded on Holtz's head. He tried to pull the middle-aged man back into the crowd of passengers waiting their turn for Lauren and the medical crew to examine them.

Lauren had tried to organize some sort of triage on the exterior decks while Dom and the Hunters cleared the ship, but the people pressing against each other on the meager deck space hadn't made the task easy. The heat of the crowd was suffocating. Passengers jostled for positions along the gunwale. A woman bent over the side of the ship, her retching and gagging audible to Lauren amid the desperate passengers. An elderly woman elbowed past a couple in their mid-thirties as she shoved her way to the front of the crowd. A baby wailed as her father tried desperately to calm the infant.

"Patience, people, patience!" Sean yelled, his voice cracking. The wiry epidemiologist's command did nothing to quiet the passengers.

Lauren patted the young girl's arm after she finished administering the shot. She put a fresh bandage on it to match the one she'd placed over the scratches. "All better!"

She willed herself to appear confident and smiled. She patted the girl's arm. The girl had claimed to be unsure where the small cuts on her arm had come from. No doubt the girl's memory had been compromised by shock. Her face was still ghost-white.

Lauren hoped the girl's scratches hadn't been from Skulls—hoped the girl wouldn't turn into one of *them*—but there was nothing more she could do besides give the child a minimal dose of the chelation treatment. She watched the girl's parents take her back into the crowd, sucked away beyond the wall of passengers.

"Next!" Lauren called.

An elderly man, his back hunched by age, was practically shoved forward. Lauren caught him and helped lower him to a step near the temporary medical station she'd established with her team.

"How are you feeling, sir?" Lauren asked, already checking over his skin for abrasions and cuts. "Any scratches or scrapes from…from the Skulls?" She still felt strange about referring to the monsters as if she were asking her patient if they'd been bitten by a dog without a leash. Rabies, frightening enough before the Oni Agent, now seemed like a much kinder disease.

The man's face was ashen. He wasn't sweating either.

"Skulls…my skull hurts." He put a veiny hand up to his head and pulled at a wisp of white hair. "My head is pounding."

The potbellied, balding man watching stepped back, and his eyes went wide. He was no longer desperate to be near Lauren and her medical team. "He's one of them! He's one of them! He's got a headache! That's a symptom, isn't it, Doc?"

More voices rose up among the passengers. A scream rang out.

"Stop!" Lauren yelled. "Stop, goddamnit!"

The people surged forward then backward, shoving each other, frantic to get away from the old man they suspected might've contracted the Oni Agent. Holtz waved his hands. He cried out into the crowd, saying something to get them to stop, but his words were drowned out.

Lauren willed all the professional calm she could muster while her nerves ran cold and adrenaline pumped through her vessels. She wouldn't let the crowd drive her wild, and she continued to examine the man's skin. "So, no scratches or scrapes?" she asked again, finding none herself.

"I'm getting—" The man's eyes started to roll back, and he slumped into Lauren's arms.

The crowd roiled in response. More voices. More limbs in the air, people shoving, people rushing back and forth with nowhere to go.

"Peter, help me!" Lauren said, trying as best she could to gently lay the man down. Her heart thrashed against her ribcage while she waited for him to complete the psychological changes of becoming a Skull, and she anticipated an upcoming violent outburst. But as she sat him down with Peter cradling the man's neck and head, she saw the old man's eyes remained closed. *Was he dead?*

She felt for a pulse, relieved to feel the weak throb. She pushed aside the primal fear coursing through her, the innate evolutionary response to potential danger that had kept humans alive for eons. Fear would do nothing but distract her now. She pressed the back of her hand against his head. "He's suffering from heat stroke! Get him water!"

Sean bounded toward a cooler and took out a bottle of water. He tossed it her way, and Lauren caught it with one hand. She pressed the cool bottle against the man's head. After unscrewing the cap, she did her best to coax him to take a sip.

"He needs to be out of the sun," Lauren said. "All the children, all the elderly need to be out of the sun." Her throat scratching, she yelled above the passengers' din at Holtz. "Otherwise we're going to be dealing with more of these cases!"

"I know, I know," Holtz said, his skin flushed red from heat and his failed attempts to quell the crowd's panic. "But we don't have anywhere to go until your crew gives us the all-clear."

Lauren doused a cloth in cold water and pressed it against the elderly man's head.

Peter stood and yelled into the crowd. "He's not one of them. It's heat stroke. Heat stroke!"

The passengers were too bitten by paranoia. They carried on, raucous and wild, nearing complete anarchy. Lauren hoped Dom would clear out the rest of the ship soon. They needed somewhere to house these people. She stole a glance at the waters around them, dotted with other ships. All these people with nowhere to go, their situations growing more desperate each day. They needed to establish a shelter, somewhere with food, water. Somewhere more amenable for their long-term survival.

The potbellied man shoved a woman with a baby in her arms. She almost lost the infant and screamed. Another man, appearing to be her partner or husband, swung a fist at Potbelly. The crowd erupted into more yells and shoving while Lauren focused on the old man before her.

She fought the anxiety welling up in her, the worry that these crazed people might riot, might send themselves into the ocean, might trample her. She wondered if they would kill themselves, kill her, before the Skulls did.

Gunfire resounded from within the ship. The Skull's wails, though muffled by the bulkhead, pierced the din of the passengers. A few people screamed; others went quiet, frozen by fear. The old man opened his eyes slightly, actively drinking from the bottle of water now. Lauren might've saved his life for the time being, but it was up to Dom and the Hunters to save the rest of the ship.

❦

Dom unleashed round after round on the Goliath running at Hector. Its massive frame rocked side to side as it raced, unperturbed by the lead that crumpled against its skeletal armor. The *thing* didn't even bother leaping at Hector. It simply bowled into him like a steamroller. Hector flew when the beast hit him and landed on his back, crushing a dining chair and scattering strewn silverware. Forks and knives clinked against the floor. Hector's rifle fell from his grip and hit a busser's discarded plastic bin.

The Goliath shuddered to a stop and punched a massive fist at Hector. Its fingers looked like fossilized daggers slicing through the air. The Navy SEAL rolled to his left, and the claws plunged into the floor. The monster slammed its other fist down. Hector barely dodged it. As the Goliath lifted its hand for another blow, Dom could see the crater the beast left.

More gunfire chattered around Dom; more Skulls screamed. But Dom focused on Hector. He could already see the hot blood coursing from Hector's scalp. Dom took aim at the Goliath's head, which appeared small atop its colossal body. He squeezed the trigger until his slide clicked back. *Empty.* The Goliath brought up both fists, ready for another attack.

A second, smaller Skull came at Dom. Hair tangled between the horns crowning its head. Long shreds of fabric billowed from its body—the remains of a cocktail dress. It snarled and swung its arms wildly. Dom deflected its blows with his rifle, and its claws scratched against the gun. He parried attack after attack until he smashed the stock of his rifle into the bridge of its nose. The Skull stumbled backward, and he bashed the weapon into the creature's face again. The crunch of cartilage and bone rang out, and it crumpled.

Dom turned to help Hector fight the Goliath, but another Skull pounced and knocked the rifle from his hands. This one wore a flowery Hawaiian shirt. Dom might've thought the creature's appearance was comical if he wasn't holding the creature's wrists as it bore down on him. It shrieked a high-pitched, angry wail—a far cry from a friendly "aloha." Dom twisted the Skull's arm back until he heard a snap and then pulled a knife from his thigh-sheath. He plunged the blade into the creature's open mouth, driving the weapon into its brain until it stopped trying to chew the knife. He planted a boot on the creature's chest, kicked it, and pulled out his knife.

He continued on to Hector. The Navy SEAL was crawling away from the Goliath. Each downward strike from the creature sent shudders through the deck. Hector scrambled to regain his footing, but the beast landed a blow on Hector's leg. He let out a yell filled with agony, rising above the cries and screams of the bloodthirsty Skulls.

"No!" Dom sprinted and leapt onto the Goliath's back.

The creature hardly seemed to notice him. Its talons tore into Hector's legs while Dom wrapped an arm around the creature's neck, careful to avoid puncturing his own skin on the razor-sharp shoulder blades. The Goliath lunged, snapping at Hector, its teeth gnashing. Hector tried to stand on his good leg, but the beast lashed out and knocked him off his feet.

"We need some help over here!" Dom yelled, his throat mic picking his voice up.

"Pinned down!"

"I'm fucking trying!"

The Hunters' voices came back in a flurry of curses and yells. Meredith was fighting off a trio of Skulls while Miguel thrashed out at another pair, the concealed blade flashing out from his prosthetic arm and impaling one. Jenna, Andris, and Renee were backed into a corner, firing at a wave of Skulls.

Dom and Hector were on their own.

"Motherfucker!" Dom swung his knife around, connecting with the side of the Goliath's face. But the blade glanced off the monster's bony forehead. The monster bucked, whirling its arms around wildly, blindly reaching for Dom. Hector retreated, dragging his injured leg.

Dom clung to the brute. He had at least distracted it, even if his attempt to bring it down had done little more than enrage it. He tried to strike with the blade again, but the beast kept thrashing its head about, and he almost lost his grip around its neck. His knife scraped against the bony collar lining the creature's neck while he probed for a weak spot.

He felt it. *Soft flesh*. He pulled with all his might to slice at the chink in the Skull's armor. Warm blood gushed over Dom's hand and saturated his gloves. But he didn't relent, driving the blade into the flesh. The creature fought back, shaking violently and twisting. Its claws tore into itself as it tried to impale Dom.

Dom dodged the clumsy blows. Gradually, as the blood drained, the giant's movements slowed. Its impassioned fury trickled away and it lolled, letting out a grunt before it fell.

A feeling of victory flooded through Dom, and he leapt off the fallen creature. He turned, preparing to run toward Hector and help the poor Hunter off the battlefield, but another Skull, no more than five feet high, was prowling across the grisly dance floor toward Hector.

"Hector, look out!" Dom called.

The Navy SEAL was losing blood fast from his shredded leg, and a trail of crimson liquid followed him as he crab-crawled away. His mind, too, must've been fading. Dom glanced at the smaller Skull, then at his own empty rifle. No more mags. He wouldn't make it to Hector in time.

A thought struck him. *Hector's rifle.*

Dom scooped up the SCAR-H, pressed the stock against his shoulder, and squeezed off a burst of fire, praying that the bullets would find their target. But his prayers went unanswered. The creature pounced, and its claws stabbed Hector's shoulders. The SEAL tried to push the Skull off, but he was too weak to put up a decent fight.

"No, no, no!" Dom bellowed. He charged, firing more

rounds into the creature. But even this small Skull's organic armor was enough to thwart the bullets. The rifle was empty before Dom reached the monster, and he tossed the weapon aside. He ripped the Skull off Hector with one gloved hand and plunged his knife into the vulnerable flesh with his other hand. The Skull didn't even let out so much as a shriek as its life flowed out with its blood. Its body went limp, and Dom dropped the fresh corpse.

His eyes caught the gaping wound in Hector's neck and traced down the SEAL's mangled legs. Everything seemed to go on in slow motion. The crack of gunfire. The Skulls' bellows. The scratch and scrape of their claws and skeletal appendages. He dove next to Hector, glancing around to see if any other Skulls were preparing to attack. The remnants of the creatures seemed to be focused on the other Hunters, attracted by the flashes from the gun muzzles and constant chatter of the weapons.

Dom pressed his hand against Hector's neck to stem his bleeding. But he felt the warm liquid ooze through his fingers. Hector's mouth opened, his tongue pushed against the roof of his mouth. He appeared to be trying to say something.

"Stay with me, buddy. You're going to make it." Dom didn't believe it, though. And he knew Hector didn't. But he said it anyway, because, fuck, what else do you say to a man bleeding out in your arms? A man who'd been a friend, a brother? A man who'd sacrificed himself like this? "We're going to get you out of here, Hector. I promise."

And that *was* true. Dead or alive, Dom wouldn't leave the

Hunter behind.

Hector's head turned to the side. His mouth hung open. Dom could almost feel the man's spirit leave his body. Hector was gone—but the fight wasn't over. He took a couple of fresh mags from Hector's tac vest and then retrieved the rifle he'd dropped. He stood and twisted toward the nearest Skull, a six-foot-tall, lanky beast reaching for Meredith with outstretched arms.

"Son of a bitch!" Dom clicked the selector toward Automatic, jammed one of the mags into Hector's rifle, and sent a volley into the creature's side. The Skull turned and ran at Dom.

But Dom never let his finger off the trigger, plugging rounds into the creature until it crashed forward, dead. Unadulterated rage coursed through him, battling with the calculated coldness and discipline ingrained through his years as a covert operative and combat specialist. He knew he shouldn't be acting like a cowboy, but his crew was faltering, backed into corners, clinging to what little ground they had left. He wouldn't stop until every last one of the fucking Skulls was dead.

EIGHTEEN

K ARA HELD HER HAND OUT and stretched her fingers. She clenched them into a fist before waving each one individually. She could feel the strength returning to her muscles, slowly replacing the fatigue that had overwhelmed her since waking up.

Her sister was sleeping in a neighboring hospital bed with Maggie curled around her. The faint beep of the EKG and, if she listened closely, the waves slapping against the side of the ship's hull filled the otherwise silent room.

And she hated it. She hated sitting here in silence while everyone else made themselves useful. She hated being stuck in bed while the rest of the world burned. She hated knowing she couldn't help anyone outside this little medical bay on a ship stuck in the Chesapeake. She couldn't help her dad, her mom.

She glanced at Sadie's sleeping form. The girl's chest rose in slow breaths. At least she was safe. At least she wasn't going anywhere.

And beside the thoughts nagging at Kara as she sat in silence, as she sat listless from the drugs and useless from her injuries, the healing skin under her bandages itched with an intensity as hot as the summer sun. She desperately wanted to scratch at the gauze, but Divya had told her not to mess with it lest she disturb the stitches.

She couldn't help anyone. She couldn't even relieve her own itching.

The door to the infirmary opened, and an older man peered in. Deep lines etched his face. His gray eyes met Kara's, and he smiled. Each one of his long wrinkles seemed to grin, too.

"Kara! You're awake." He hustled into the room and offered her his hand when he reached her bed. "I'm"—he paused when he saw Sadie sleeping and lowered his voice— "I'm Thomas Hampton, your dad's second-in-command. How are you feeling?"

How are you feeling? Kara disliked the question. She was feeling useless. She was feeling angry. She was feeling hate for the goddamned Skulls. But all she said was, "Fine."

"I've heard so much about you. It's great to finally put a face to the name. Have you seen Divya?"

"Not in a while. I think she went back to the lab."

Thomas's face dropped in a frown, and he glanced away. "You'll have to excuse me."

As he turned toward the lab, Divya burst into the room. "I'm sorry. I was so focused on my work I didn't see your message. But I'll have everything prepped for their return."

"Lauren said it's worse than she expected. She barely had time to radio Chao."

Kara cocked her head, glancing between the doctor and

the grizzled first mate.

Thomas looked at her and then ushered Divya into the corridor to speak privately. Kara could still hear their voices under the door. They sounded hurried and frantic.

When the door opened again, Divya rushed toward a supply closet and started rifling through the plastic bottles and sterile packages of gauze. She piled supplies on a cart.

Thomas poked his head back into the room. "Anything else I can do to help?"

"I'll radio you if I need something, but I can handle the prep work. The best thing you can do is keep tabs on potential casualties for me."

Casualties. Kara sat upright in bed. Her heart dropped. "Is my dad okay?"

Thomas pushed the door open all the way and padded across the floor to her side. "Your dad's fine."

"Doesn't sound like it. What the hell's going on?"

Thomas checked his watch. "He's currently in a hot zone on a dinner cruise ship packed with civilians. Our initial estimate of how many people were on that ship was a little low, so Dr. Winters radioed in and told us we need to up our preparations. Just in case, okay?"

Kara pursed her lips but didn't say anything. It was clear she wouldn't get much more from this man.

"Right now," Thomas continued, "the Hunters are clearing the Skulls out of the ship and rescuing the passengers trapped inside."

"Why's he risking his life on *that* ship?"

"Lots of people need our help there. Plus, if we can get the ship back in working order, she'll help us ferry people to safety. We're going to set up an outpost somewhere. Probably in a protected park or something as a safe zone away from the cities."

"Away from the Skulls."

"Right," Thomas said. "So what your dad is doing is extremely important. And I promise he's going to be back safe."

Kara wanted to believe him, but she found doubt weighed heavier on her mind than optimism.

"Any other questions, Miss? I've got to get back to Chao and the rest of the comm team."

"Yes." Kara couldn't stand letting her dad risk his life for people he didn't even know while she sat in this bed idling away the time. "What can I do to help?"

"Help? You just focus on getting better." Thomas patted the bed's rail and turned to walk out.

"No way. I can't just do that. Let me do something."

Thomas looked back at her over his shoulder, his brows carved in deep, sad creases.

"Please. Anything." Kara's bottom lip trembled slightly as she thought about her father facing those monsters. "I need something to take my mind off what's going on with my dad. Just give me something easy to do if you have to. Whatever you want." The injuries under her bandages began to itch again. "Anything I can do to help."

Thomas pulled his hand through his gray hair. "I'll talk to

the comm team and see if they've got any ideas." His eyes narrowed. "The apple really doesn't fall far from the tree, does it?"

After Thomas left, Divya pushed the cart of medical supplies toward the exit. "Press the call button if you need anything."

Kara nodded and watched the doctor leave. She was left alone with Maggie and Sadie once more. She wondered if Thomas would actually return with something for her to do. Or, for better or for worse, with news of her father.

The sound of the door opening interrupted Kara's brief nap. She jolted upright. Sweat along her back made the thin hospital gown cling to her skin. She whipped her head around and immediately saw Sadie and Maggie were missing. Her heart pounded in worry, and she looked toward the open passageway.

A familiar—although bruised and bandaged—face with black-rimmed glasses and a thick beard came through the door. Adam. His face was white, and he gulped when he locked eyes with her. He ushered in Sadie and Maggie. Sadie looked defeated, and the dog wagged her tail, completely unaware that they were apparently in trouble.

"We can't just be locked in here like prisoners." Sadie huffed and folded her thin arms across her chest.

"I know, I know," Adam said. "But things are a bit tense right now. I'm going to need you to watch your sister and, well, stay out of the way."

"Yeah, but Dad said—"

"Come on, Sadie," Kara said. "What's going on?" She didn't expect an answer given how Thomas had evaded her before, but she couldn't help herself.

Adam stepped toward her bed with a laptop under his right arm. "Thomas gave you the rundown, right?"

Kara nodded.

"There's been a little more resistance than expected on the passenger ship. More Skulls."

"Is my—"

"He's still fine."

Kara let out a breath. "Why do you look so frazzled?"

"Don't worry about me."

Kara hated the way he too was avoiding straight answers. She was an adult now. She could handle whatever he wasn't saying.

Adam held out the laptop. "Heard you wanted to help."

"I do." Kara grabbed it. The computer felt heavy—much heavier than the Mac she'd taken to college. Her arms almost trembled with the effort, reminding her how weak the Oni Agent treatment had made her. Weak and helpless. She couldn't wait until she could get out of this damn bed.

"Okay, so here's the deal: It's not much, but Dom gave Chao, Samantha, and I several tasks to complete. Between keeping tabs on him and the Hunters, trying to find a place to resupply, and somehow locating a safe zone, we haven't had time to identify the best neurological disease laboratories to search for, but Lauren and Peter already started a list of potential places to check out nearby."

"So what do you need me for?"

"You can help us by adding other places around the United States with research interests that might more closely align with our goal of finding a cure or vaccine or something for the Oni Agent."

"And then what?" Kara asked.

"We'll try and see if any of them are still functional. Or better yet, find out if any of their scientists or research staff are still around."

"Still alive, you mean?"

Adam nodded. "I know it's not much, but if you can do this, once the mission's over, our team will start trying to establish contact with the labs."

Kara thought of her mother, trapped in the basement, driven mad by the Oni Agent. "And you'll try to recruit them to help find a *real* cure for the Oni Agent? Like something that can heal the brain damage for people who didn't get Lauren's treatment on time?"

"Exactly," Adam said. "I've got to get back to the workshop." He turned and powered out of the room before Kara could say thanks.

"Wait, how are you supposed to connect to the internet? Aren't all the cell networks down?" Sadie asked, squeezing into the bed beside Kara.

"I'm assuming they have a satellite connection." Kara booted up the laptop. "As long as there are servers live somewhere, I think they can access most of the net." She paused and waited for the desktop to appear on the screen. "I think one of my engineering friends at school told me something about archived sites too. Like, saved or downloaded versions of sites or something when their hosts are down."

"Whatever," Sadie said. "So are we going to help them or what?"

"We are." Kara's fingers danced across the keyboard, typing search terms on the web browser. She created a text document and started listing results she found from an inquiry for neurological disease laboratories.

She found labs belonging to the National Institutes of Health in Bethesda and a lab at Stanford with a bevy of scientists, academics, post-docs, and grad students. Research institutions at universities all across the United States popped up, along with others around the world. There was no shortage of scientists interested in neurodegenerative diseases and other neurological topics. But she wondered how many of them were still alive—and whether any of them could actually help find a cure for the Oni Agent, for her mother.

NINETEEN

———❦———

NAVID HID BEHIND THE LABORATORY BENCH and peered between the empty glass beakers and flasks. Screams filtered in under the door to the room where Navid and his fellow graduate students had once run experiments. Silhouettes raced past the window in the door, their shadows playing across the lab. Furious red emergency lights flashed along the corridor.

He ducked. His bottom lip trembled, and his shirt clung to his sweat-soaked back.

"What the hell are we going to do?" Abby asked, sitting on the floor next to him. Her knees were tucked against her chest, and her arms were wrapped around her thin legs. Navid crouched next to her. He looked into her blue eyes, willing any courage that might still be hiding in him to show itself now. By the still-frightened look on Abby's face, he could tell there wasn't much of it left.

"We'll be okay," he said. "We just need to stay hidden. Help's on its way."

"It's not, Navid. It's really not. We've been sitting in here for…God, I don't even know how long. No more food. Just people screaming out there. And it keeps getting worse."

THE TIDE: BREAKWATER

"I know, I know."

When the initial Code Disaster had been called over the hospital intercoms, Navid had hoped it was a mistake.

But now he knew it wasn't. He knew what it meant, but he didn't want to believe it. The crazy people had spread to Boston. He and Abby had seen it with their own eyes and barely lived through the experience. A place once meant for healing, Mass Gen had been hit hard and fast when all these people infected with the virus or bacteria or whatever it was started coming here for help.

"We can't stay here," Abby said, drawing into a crouch. She placed a hand on the black laboratory bench and peeked at the door.

The chairs and the heavy liquid nitrogen tank still braced the door along with all the boxes and shelves they could pile there. But the intense howls and shrieks echoing throughout the hospital made Navid wonder if that would be enough.

Abby lifted her head higher. Something smacked into the door.

Navid grabbed Abby's shoulder and pulled her down next to him. He wrapped one arm around her. His heart hammered, and he could practically hear hers pounding away too.

Another crash against the door sent a shiver down Navid's spine. He pressed himself closer to the metal drawers beneath the lab bench. Abby clung to him, one hand clenching his arm tight enough to hurt. He closed his eyes when the door shook again, and a chair crashed onto the tile floor. He

167

bit his bottom lip to stop himself from crying out.

God, he knew he was a coward, but he felt so helpless. So pitiful. Those people out there were crazy, demented. And he'd seen their shapes in the darkened hallway. The glimpses through the window were enough for him to tell they were something more than people, something monstrous. Their limbs were grotesquely deformed and misshapen. Small horns protruded from their heads and fins grew from their shoulder blades along with spikes along their spines.

And one of those things was trying to get in the door.

Another loud thwack of something against the door, a scream—a human scream—followed by the sound of tearing and chewing. Like flesh being ripped and eaten, Navid realized. There was a grunt, and the distinct sound of clicking against the tiled hall floor faded into the distance.

Silence again.

Navid let out a deep breath, and Abby shivered in his arms. They'd been lucky this time. The shadows of the dark lab had hidden them. The door had held. But it had sounded as if someone out there hadn't been so fortunate.

Maybe Abby was right. Maybe they needed to get out of here. But where could they possibly go? And how would they get there?

He tiptoed to a window that overlooked Cambridge Street. Smoldering cars filled the street along with a mess of corpses. People ran between the lines of abandoned vehicles and overturned trashcans. It was hard to tell from this floor, but it looked as if most of them ran half hunched over. Many of them seemed to have the same strange growths and protrusions as the silhouetted people he'd seen throughout the hospital.

Fear and worry and hunger and nausea seemed to grip Navid all at once. His stomach lurched, and he threw his hand over his mouth. He gagged but refrained from letting the contents of his belly spill over the floor.

"Navid, are you okay?"

He pinched his eyes closed for a second and recomposed himself. "I'm fine."

"We can't stay here. We have to find help."

"I know, I know…"

Something crashed against the door again, emphasizing the point. Navid and Abby ducked and waited for almost five minutes before daring to peek around the lab benches. No more footsteps in the hall. No more screams.

At least for now.

Navid hesitantly stood and gazed about the room. There was a sink in one corner with an eyewash station and an overhead shower in case of chemical emergencies. A fire extinguisher was secured to the wall next to a shelf full of glassware, beakers, and flasks. Two lab benches took up most of the room, and each of them held a bevy of equipment ranging from thermocyclers to microscopes. Normally, the room was hot with all the machines running and a chorus of beeps and buzzes filling the air.

But right now there was nothing but a chill in the air and lonely silence.

Navid turned to Abby. "You really want to go out and search for someone else again? You heard those things out there. It doesn't take much to imagine what they do to the people they find."

Abby slowly stood, her arms wrapped around herself, shivering. "I know, but if we stay here…then what? We starve to death? We die of thirst? We wait until they break in? We're no better off now than when we were in the grad student office."

Navid's eyes traced the floor. He had no good answer for her. Working in a research lab associated with a hospital, he'd been trained for disasters ranging from a wild gunman to a missing child to an earthquake, as unlikely as that was in Boston.

But he'd never been prepared for when some kind of zombie virus turned everyone in the hospital, everyone in the city, into bloodthirsty monsters.

"Whether we stay or not, we at least need weapons," he said. He pulled out a few of the drawers and then moved aside boxes full of nitrile examination gloves and plastic pipette tips. Most of the tools they had here were for dealing with things like neurons or the nanoparticles and drug carriers they used to administer therapeutic molecules. All those things were microscopic, and the tools used to handle them were not meant to defend against zombies.

"What about these?" Abby took out one of the ring stands from a chemical fume hood. The long, metal pole was attached to a heavy steel base. "Maybe you can use it stab or"—she held the rod in her hand so the base was in the air, like a golf club ready for a swing—"you can use it like this."

"Maybe," Navid said. But even that seemed horribly inadequate compared to what he'd seen. "What about—"

Something slammed against the door, rattling it on its hinges. Navid and Abby froze. They locked eyes but didn't say a word. Maybe, like all those times before, the zombie-thing wouldn't notice them and would keep on moving, keep on looking for someone else to attack.

The door rattled again. A dark shape slapped against the window. It blotted out the red emergency lights from the hall. A low growl sounded, and the crazy thing pressed itself against the door. It hammered away with its fists.

The lock's got to hold, Navid thought. And if that failed, at least there was all the refuse they'd pile up to help bolster the door.

Another creature crashed against the door. It seemed to push the first out of its way. The door shuddered again and again as more crazies piled up outside. The din became almost unbearable. Abby's face turned red, tears streaming out of her eyes. She barely held the ring stand now.

Navid realized she must have known how useless the makeshift weapon would be against the assembling horde. He cursed inwardly. In their search for finding a weapon to defend themselves, they must've been too loud and attracted the crazy zombies' attention.

And now they'd be after him. They'd be after Abby.

"What do we do?" she asked.

"I don't—" Navid stopped and stared at the heavy steel door separating the lab from its walk-in cooler. Normally, they kept cell media, antibodies, and a host of other supplies for their experiments in there. With the power out, all those supplies would be ruined. Some of the perishables had also spoiled, making the place smell rotten. But it might offer them a final place of protection.

Abby followed his eyes and shook her head. "Even if we hide in there, how long before they tear us out?"

The creatures pounded on the door, hitting so hard the walls shook. A tile fell from the ceiling. The wood groaned, and the doorframe was starting to peel from the wall. Dust and paint chips rained down.

Abby was right. Hiding would only delay the inevitable. There had to be another way. Navid ran to the window. It was a three-story drop. No fire escape. No ladder. Hardly a ledge to get his fingers around.

He tried to pry the window open, but it wouldn't budge. The safety locks on the windows prevented grad students from making a rash decision when the long and lonely hours of their research got to them.

But he needed to make a rash decision now. Abby ran over to him with the fire extinguisher. She hefted the heavy red cylinder as if preparing to throw it through the window.

The sight of the device sparked another idea. "Wait!"

Abby paused, the extinguisher held above her head.

"Get in the cooler. I'll take care of those monsters."

"What—"

The door shuddered.

"There's no time! Just get in!"

Abby did but kept the bulky metal door propped open and watched Navid.

"Close the door until I come in!" Navid said.

He ran around and twisted all the knobs on the gas nozzles. Normally meant for use with items like Bunsen burners, with nothing attached, natural gas hissed and filled the lab. The pungent odorant added to the gas overwhelmed Navid's sense of smell, and he started getting lightheaded. He wasn't sure if it was the gas, the fear coursing through his nerves, or some combination of the two contributing to his dizziness.

The door cracked. Two of the crazies pushed their arms through. Their heads squeezed through next. They had bloodshot eyes and gray faces lined with horn-like growths. Their howls intensified when they caught sight of Navid.

But Navid didn't let that get to him. And he couldn't let them get to Abby. He ran to the flammable acids storage and tore open the metal door. He pulled out a brown glass bottle of nitric acid, normally used as an analytical agent.

He ran to another metal cabinet of biohazardous reagents and yanked out a small glass bottle of toxic hydrazine. The two chemicals were kept on opposite sides for a reason, and Navid hoped to take advantage of it now. He sprinted to the walk-in cooler door. One of the monsters pushed through the gap. The boxes and shelves clattered and fell. The door flew open, and four of the monsters rushed in.

Navid only had one shot to do this right. He opened the cooler door, tossed the two glass bottles of chemicals into the air, and squeezed into the walk-in. Then he engaged the internally releasable lock, rushed to the opposite side of the small space, and threw his body over Abby's.

The crash of shattering glass sounded, followed by a crackling explosion as the chemicals reacted violently. A deafening whoosh rattled the door. The air in the lab, filled with natural gas, had ignited. Heat radiated through the door, despite its thermal protective properties. The creatures outside didn't even have time to shriek before the explosion took them.

A few seconds later, it was over.

"Are they...dead?" Abby asked.

"I don't know what could've survived that. But we can't stay here. If there are more out there, they would've heard that blast, and they might be on their way." He inched open the door. "Let's move."

Shattered glass and pieces of shelving were strewn about. Several chemical bottles had spilled. Their contents pooled across the floor. Navid didn't want to stick around to find out if there would be a second explosion or a reaction causing a toxic gas.

As he opened the door wider, he caught sight of the dead monsters. The explosions had charred their skin and blackened their bones. Skeletal talons curled from the remains of their hands, and grotesque spikes jutted from what appeared to be their vertebrae, which now looked like burned-out coal. Horns grew from their heads, sticking out from their brows and the crisp skin over what was left of their gaunt faces. Faces Navid knew would haunt him for the rest of his life.

But there was no time to worry about nightmares yet to come. He was living in one now.

"Come on!" He tried to guide Abby past the grisly tableau so she wouldn't have enough time to soak in the barbecued monsters.

"Oh, my God!" She froze, staring at them. "Navid, what did you do?"

For a moment, Navid hesitated. Where would they go now? He thought about the roving packs of creatures in the streets. They'd go up. Up and see whoever else was left alive. Up where there might be fewer creatures and less danger. Up to the roof, where they could make a sign or an SOS for a military rescue.

Good God, where was the military? How long would they be alone? Two grad students in a hospital overrun by murderous creatures. In a city destroyed. In a nation falling.

Navid and Abby's feet pounded against the stairs, echoing in the narrow shaft as they raced upstairs. A howl followed them. Footsteps clicked and clacked. *The monsters.* He and Abby were no longer alone after all.

TWENTY

MEREDITH WATCHED IN HORROR. The three Skulls stalked toward her. Her whole world was lit up in splotches of green flashes and black shadows. The Hunters' NVGs gave them an advantage over the Skulls, who relied primarily on sight. However, the Skulls also lashed out at anything that made a sound. Gunfire. Footsteps. Breathing. Even a goddamned heartbeat seemed enough to attract their attention.

Desperate to reload her rifle, she fumbled with a magazine. One of the Skulls, fatter and rounder than the others, leapt past an overturned dining table. The magazine clicked into place, and the Skull homed in on the sound. It rushed Meredith, and she brought the muzzle of the rifle back up. The creature flew through the air in spite of its non-athletic appearance, slashing with its hooked, bony claws. Meredith squeezed the trigger, but she could already tell her shots were going to go wide. She sidestepped to avoid the monster.

A loud rattle of gunfire from her left assaulted her eardrums. The Skull's head snapped back even as its body flew forward. The thing skidded to a stop, leaving a trail of blood.

Dom stood beside Meredith with the barrel of his gun aimed at the Skull in case it decided death didn't suit it. But when he saw it didn't move, he moved on to the next target, careful to stay out of the way of his Hunters while bringing down Skull after Skull.

He seemed to be in a sort of trance. He shouldered his rifle, killed a monster, and then sprinted to his next firing position. A final Skull, thin and limber, dashed across the corpse-filled dance floor. Meredith watched Dom kneel and fire once. The beast stopped, its head rolled back, and its body crumpled among its fallen comrades.

"On me!" Dom commanded.

Meredith followed the others as they circled around Dom. Their guns bristled, facing outward from the small formation.

"We lost Hector," Dom said, his voice stern, a dam against the inner turmoil he must be feeling. The Hunters looked stricken by the news, but they retained their sense of professionalism. The battle wasn't over yet. But at least now Meredith could understand the sheer coldness with which Dom had dispatched the Skulls. "We still need to keep moving and find the captain and any other survivors." He pulled out the map of the ship that Holtz had given him. "Behind that door, there should be another short passageway leading to the pilothouse. Once we've rounded up any other survivors, we're going to lead them onto the deck. There, we'll start ferrying passengers from this ship to a quarantine zone as soon as Chao tells us we've got someplace to take these people."

177

"Permission to speak freely, Captain," Miguel said.

"Be quick."

"Just to be clear, I thought the plan was to retake the pilothouse and set up triage on the lower decks."

"That *was* the plan. But those things poured through the ventilation shafts and ceiling. We can't risk the possibility that even one of them is prowling around in there. This whole ship has to be abandoned."

"Understood."

"For now, Hector's staying here. But we will not leave him. He comes with us after we clear the pilothouse." Dom gestured toward Miguel. "Take point. Renee, you're on rearguard. And everyone, watch your backs, watch your front, your sides. We can't let those goddamn things take us by surprise again."

The Hunters surged forward like a silent wave, rolling toward the opposite side of the dining room. Meredith fell in beside Dom. She wished she could offer him some form of comfort, but she knew him well enough to realize that he would not accept it. While his people were still in danger, he wouldn't let himself show weakness when they needed him to be strong.

Miguel paused by the door to the passageway and looked back at Dom for further instructions. Dom gave him a slight nod, indicating for him to try the door. Meredith held her breath as she watched the Hunter give the handle a slight pull. It didn't give.

Dom approached the door, his face pinched in

determination. He rapped on it with the back of his hand. "This is Dominic Holland, captain of the *Huntress*. I'm with a group of trained military contractors, and we're here to rescue you. Please, open up."

No response.

Again Dom knocked and repeated the statement. Still there was no response.

Meredith hated to acknowledge the thought now drifting through her mind, but she asked anyway. "What if Skulls already got to these people?"

Dom gave her a nod but didn't say a word. He sent Renee and Miguel a series of hand signals. They positioned themselves at the sides of the door. Dom tried the handle once more, took a step back, and smashed into the door with his shoulder. The wood shattered, sending a spray of splinters into the passageway beyond.

Meredith caught herself holding her breath and let it out. She peered down the sights of her rifle, waiting for Skulls to come charging out of the shadows. But none came.

"Jenna, Andris, Miguel, you take the portside," Dom said in a low voice. "Meredith, Renee, on me. Go!"

The Hunters padded down the passage. They checked the two doors on their way to the pilothouse, but the rooms were clear. The tension in the air as they approached the last was almost palpable. Meredith could feel a trickle of sweat drip down her neck, and she readjusted her hold on her rifle.

Like before, Dom approached the door. He knocked on it and repeated the same words he'd said prior to breaching the passageway.

This time there was a response. But instead of relieved voices, all that came back was the guttural growl of a Skull.

Meredith's heart sank. They'd been charged with rescuing the passengers and returning the ship back to its service as a temporary shelter. It looked like they'd failed at both directives.

Dom gestured to the Hunters, and they organized themselves as before. He threw himself against the door, and it slapped against the bulkhead of the pilothouse. The force of it knocked back a person—no, a Skull—onto the helm. The Skull promptly stood, wielding its claws before its plated chest and grinding its teeth together. Dom wasted no time in putting a bullet through the creature's face. It slumped, its body limp, and smacked against the deck.

No other Skulls appeared. But as Meredith gazed around, she saw the tattered remains of several crewmen's uniforms clinging to bloodied bones.

Dom kicked the Skull's corpse. "This was the goddamned captain."

Holtz had said the captain was sick—and now it looked as if he'd killed his crew.

"Fuck." Dom punched a fist against the bulkhead, causing Meredith to jump. He shot her a look. A look she could tell at once wasn't meant for her, but was rather an unintentional view into his thoughts. She could see the anger, the frustration, and the sorrow over losing Hector.

And she knew why. After all, what had they gained on

this mission other than to reaffirm their knowledge that the Skulls were dangerous?

She didn't envy Dom's position. It must have felt to him as if the responsibility of saving the world rested on his shoulders. General Kinsey had been reluctant to support further scientific efforts that might thwart the Oni Agent, and the man hadn't ordered any active rescue efforts, instead choosing to withdraw his forces and reorganize. To what end, they couldn't be sure.

As the Hunters scoured the pilothouse, Meredith reminded herself she'd been the first to put Dom in this terrible position. She'd sent him to the IBSL and unwittingly mired him in the resulting mess.

She trudged up to Dom. "What now?"

"We get Hector and we get the hell off this ship. We get *everyone* off this ship." Dom pressed his finger over his earpiece. "*Huntress*, this is Alpha team. Can I get a sitrep on the safe zone efforts?"

"Alpha, *Huntress*." Chao's voice rang out over the public comm link line in Meredith's ear. "We've got a potential site to establish a more permanent shelter, and we think we've identified targets to help defend the location."

"Thank God," Dom said. "I'm going to need you to open comms with your potential reinforcement targets. I need boats on the water to ferry these people off this ship."

"Copy that, Captain. We'll do the best we can, but I think we're going to need the Hunters to do a little work to help our new recruits."

"And why's that?"

"They're currently surrounded by Skulls. But according to our satellite imagery, they seem to be holding out."

"Kill it with the suspense, Chao," Dom said. "Who are we talking about?"

"The Academy."

"The midshipmen at the Annapolis Naval Academy?" Miguel asked. "They're practically kids."

"From what I've found, the Academy has a modest supply of weapons and ammo they use for firearms practice," Chao said. "And a lot of it's outdated. MP5s, some old M11s."

"So they might not last long," Dom said. "Hunters, hear that? We're moving out immediately. Miguel, Andris, grab Hector." He started toward the door, shouldering his rifle.

"One more thing, Dom. They've got boats. Sailboats and yard patrol craft. That small fleet should work for ferrying the passengers."

"Good to know," Dom said. "We're headed your way immediately to resupply. Prep all the intelligence you've got, because we're going to need it for Annapolis."

Meredith followed Dom into the passageway. The Hunters covered each other, advancing through the bloody, gory remnants of the previous battle. They stepped over the Skulls' broken bodies and the bones of passengers and crew members whose flesh had been mauled and devoured. Miguel and Andris hoisted Hector between them, and the Hunters retraced their steps until they were on the first deck near where they had entered this tomb of a ship. They made it out of the lower decks without incident.

A wave of relief washed through Meredith. She turned off her NVGs and headed outside into sunlight. That brief respite was quickly replaced by the chaos of the shouting passengers. People wanted answers regarding where they were going, what would happen to them. She saw their faces turning red and their fists shaking in the air. Children crying, adults shouting.

A hand grabbed her arm and she spun. Lauren faced her, hair matted by sweat and her skin sporting a red hue, no doubt a combination of sun and stress.

"What's going on?" Lauren asked. "Is Hector—"

Meredith nodded. "He's gone."

Dom rounded up the Hunters around Lauren's medical team. "We're leaving the ship. There's no way we can guarantee people's safety inside that shithole. It's best to leave all the hatches and doors secured and make sure no one, or no *thing*, gets in or out."

"You're leaving us?" a middle-aged woman asked. "We'll die out here."

Dom whipped around to face her. "The best thing we can do for you is leave." He cupped his hands together and yelled at the passengers. "I need quiet. Quiet!"

Their voices only carried higher and louder, crashing like waves against rock. Meredith waited for him to fire his gun into the air to silence the crowd. But Dom did no such thing. Even fueled by rage against the Skulls and pity for his fallen Hunter, he maintained a relatively cool head. "Hunters, med team, back to the Zodiacs!"

"And leave these people?" Lauren asked, closing up her medical kit.

"I'm not losing anyone to a mob of civilians. We'll be back with help, whether they believe it or not."

The medical team hopped into the Zodiacs first. Dom helped keep back the passengers threatening to trample each other and force themselves on the small craft. The other Hunters boarded the Zodiacs. Meredith moved to follow Renee down the ladder when someone squeezed her shoulder. She looked up to see Holtz, the ship's steward.

"The captain's dead, isn't he?"

Meredith nodded.

Holtz's brow creased in wrinkles. "You can't leave us stranded."

"We'll be back. But there's nothing we can do now."

Holtz turned away. "I hope to God you aren't lying."

Meredith knew there was nothing she could say to convince him otherwise. "Take care of these people, and we'll make good on our word."

Meredith descended the ladder. Dom jumped into the Zodiac. "Go, go, go!"

The crowd pressed against the gunwale, almost spilling over into the bay. The nimble Zodiacs raced into the open water to the *Huntress*. People yelled as they were trampled by their fellow passengers. There was nothing Meredith could do to help them except pray that they really would be able to liberate the Academy and come back to save these desperate souls. So desperate for escape, for deliverance, that they'd fight among themselves and stampede over each other to get off the cruise ship.

Since the Oni Agent outbreak, Meredith had quickly learned how dangerous Skulls could be. But she'd neglected to consider the danger that even healthy humans now posed. She turned away from the ship as it became an indistinguishable white blob on the horizon.

Dom had wrapped an arm around Hector to ensure he didn't fall over the side of the craft as it bounced over rolling waves. Meredith sidled up next to him. She kept one hand on the gunwale and placed the other on his shoulder in a reassuring gesture. She expected him to shrug her off, to hide behind a wall of stoic determination.

But instead he reached up and placed one gloved hand over hers. He left it there, and in that moment Meredith realized something. As the world went to hell, as humanity devoured itself—literally and figuratively—there was no one's team she'd rather be on than Dom's. A formidable and compassionate leader, a daring and intelligent captain, a dependable and selfless friend. She knew he'd do anything in his power to help his family, his friends, and his crew. And now Meredith knew that she'd follow him to the ends of the earth, to hell itself and back, if that was where he needed her to go.

TWENTY-ONE

———◦◦◦◦◦———

DOM ENTERED THE MEDICAL BAY with Meredith at his heels. She hadn't left him since they'd gotten off the Zodiacs, but he found he didn't mind. Her presence gave him stability and comfort. He wasn't used to those feelings, bouncing from mission to mission, never knowing what covert op he faced next. The threat of the Skulls, the constant disorientation of a world turned upside down and an enemy that could hardly be considered human, had made his job of being the steadfast captain of the ship harder. But Meredith made that burden a little easier to bear.

"Dad!" Sadie said, jumping off a patient bed. She sprinted to him and wrapped her arms around his waist. Maggie pressed her furry body against his legs and whined. Her tail thrashed all the while.

He saw Kara awake and alert. Fresh bandages covered most of the left side of her face. His mind was at once overwhelmed by a combination of intense joy to see her alive intermingled with a father's pain of seeing her bedridden and injured. He locked his gaze on her uncovered eye, expecting her to be equally relieved at his return. Instead, he was met with a stare colder than Medusa's.

"You can't just leave us without telling us what's going

on," Kara said.

He was taken aback by his daughter's annoyance. "Glad to see you're doing better." He stepped forward and took her hand. "You were completely out of it when I left. I'm sorry."

"So do you have some time now to talk? Maybe fill me in on where you've been for the past couple of decades? Catch me up on your life outside of Frederick?"

Dom turned away for a moment. Meredith was speaking with Sadie and scratching Maggie's head. "I would," he said, "but I just came to check on you. I've got to get moving again. Another mission to prepare for."

"I guess the end of the world waits for no one, right? But at least this time you were nice enough to make sure I knew you were leaving." The steel in her gaze vanished, replaced by a younger version of Kara, the one Dom had tucked in at night and assured no monsters lay in wait for her in the closet. And here came the veiled emotions, the ones Kara tried to hide with a toughened exterior—not so different from him, really. "Come back soon, okay?"

"I promise." But Dom's thoughts turned back to Hector. Lost in what should've been a relatively straightforward mission. He had no delusions that this mission would be any easier.

Meredith placed a hand on Dom's shoulder. "I'll make sure he gets his ass back aboard this ship."

Kara smiled and looked up at Meredith. "I've seen her in action. I trust her."

Dom squeezed Kara's hand. She wrapped her thin fingers

around his. "I won't fail you or your sister."

"Or Maggie," Sadie added, forcing a slight grin as she ruffled the dog's ears.

"Or Maggie." Dom stood straight again and let go of Kara's hand. He hated feeling her fingers slip from his. But there were lives—so many lives—depending on him and the Hunters. "I'll be back soon. Love you both."

"Love you, too," Sadie and Kara echoed.

"I mean what I said, Dom," Meredith said. "I'm making sure you get back to your daughters if it's the last thing I do."

"I appreciate it." And he did. But he steeled himself for what he knew was the right thing to say, the right thing to do in a position with his responsibilities. "But remember, the mission's got to come first. There's a whole ship full of people and who knows how many survivors in Annapolis depending on our success."

Meredith looked like she was about to protest but nodded instead. She narrowed her eyes slightly and scrunched her brow. It was the look she'd given him a thousand times, dating back to the days they'd worked in the CIA together. It meant: *You can trust me.* And he knew he could.

Dom placed his hand on the door to the electronics workshop. He paused before opening it. His thoughts turned to Hector. Another man gone, another Hunter killed by the Skulls. And his crew wouldn't even have time to mourn before he shipped them off on their next mission. He prayed they wouldn't lose anyone else before they saw the end of this nightmare.

"Something up?" Meredith asked.

"You don't need to go to Annapolis."

"I'm not sitting on the sidelines."

"Things are only going to get more dangerous," Dom said. "When was the last time you were really out in the field?"

"I can handle myself just fine." Meredith glared for a second, and then her expression turned questioning. "What's this really about, Dom?"

Dom let out a deep exhalation and wrapped a hand around Meredith's. "I don't want to be responsible for you getting hurt out there." He shook his head, finding it hard to find the right words. "I couldn't bear that."

"You won't be responsible. I'm volunteering for this of my own free will." She shook her head, her long red hair flowing over her shoulders. "If I would've taken my discovery of the IBSL straight to the top of the CIA rather than doing my own investigation…Dom, I've got to do this." She jabbed a finger at his chest. "And you aren't responsible for my choices."

Dom gritted his teeth. She wasn't understanding what he was trying to say. Hell, he didn't quite understand it. He looked down the passageway to make sure it was still empty. "Meredith, it's just…I don't want to lose you."

Meredith looked up at him, and her eyes softened. "Dom…"

He let go of her and pushed open the door to the workshop. He'd already said too much, and they didn't have time to untangle the complexities of their relationship in the bowels of a covert-ops ship. It was time for work. For action. He and Meredith joined Thomas, Miguel, and Renee at a table. Chao and Samantha sat on the other side.

"What do you have for me, Chao?" Dom asked as he settled into a seat next to Meredith. He felt her hot gaze leave him. She too must know their emotions had to wait. They'd figure things out later.

If there was a later.

Dom watched the comm specialist run his finger along a touchpad. The glass tabletop lit up and projected a map of the Chesapeake Bay. Chao pinched his fingers on the pad, and the map zoomed in on a large island between Annapolis and the Eastern Shore of Maryland. "Kent Island. Largest island in the Chesapeake. Connected to the mainland via US 50."

"So this is your proposed safe haven?" Dom asked. "An island seems like a good idea in practice, and Kent Island might be big enough for evacuating nearby survivors. But even assuming the Skulls can't swim well, what's to stop them from following US 50? We'll need to take out the bridge to truly isolate the place."

"Right." Chao tapped on the touchpad, and the high-res satellite imagery moved to part of the Chesapeake Bay Bridge leading to Kent Island. A two-hundred-yard section of the bridge was simply gone. Several large columns rose out of the water where the toll road had been, but they had nothing to support. All across the rest of the four-mile bridge lay the charred and oftentimes still smoking remains of cars. The images were detailed enough to show bodies littering the span of the bridge. "As you can see, half the job's done for us. Samantha did a bit of digging and found out the Air Force ordered a strike. Maryland's National Guard couldn't keep people in Annapolis and Baltimore inside the quarantine zone after the initial outbreak. Destroying the bridge was a last resort. Looks like the same thing happened at several metropolitan locations around the US, but that's beside the point."

Chao gestured to the eastern side of the bridge. Once again, the image shifted. This time it focused on a line of police cars and civilian vehicles. They appeared orderly, as if they'd all been intentionally and meticulously parked along the bridge over Kent Island. At the end of the row, sandbags had been placed behind a series of makeshift walls. Scores of people seemed to be milling about near these barriers.

"Kent Island isn't too densely populated," Chao said, "but it looks like the locals took to defending their turf."

"Hopefully that means the towns on the island haven't been hit too hard by the Skulls," Dom said. "But either way, that small force won't stand up to a Skull horde like the ones we saw in Frederick. We need to reinforce them if we're going to secure this island for use as a safe zone. Which leads me to my next question: What's the situation at the Naval Academy?"

Chao's fingers drummed along the pad once more. A new map popped up. This time it displayed the crisp green lawns, verdant trees, and orderly, rectangular buildings of the United States Naval Academy. Time-lapse satellite imagery showed enough detail to reveal that a tide of Skulls had swept through the campus. They'd rolled through the parade grounds and out to the Dewey Seawall. Packs of them had roved along Santee Basin where the academy's seacraft were docked.

"Here's the latest images," Chao said. "More time-lapse photos."

The new view showed dozens of Skulls outside Halsey Field House. Yet the mass of monsters wasn't moving.

"They look like they're all taking a nap," Miguel said. "I thought you said this was time-lapse imagery."

"It is," Dom said, understanding immediately. "These Skulls are dead, aren't they?"

Samantha nodded, taking over for Chao. "That's right. I ran the images through an anomaly detection algorithm I wrote."

Dom raised his eyebrows, his oft-used gesture to get Samantha to speak in layman's terms.

"Basically, we know the Skulls like to move. Even when they're tired and hungry, they keep moving. Slowly, maybe, but they keep going." She pointed to the tabletop image. "In this sequence, the Skulls aren't moving, even while other packs are roaming through the city."

"So maybe these Skulls are dead tired?" Miguel offered.

"Or just plain dead," Samantha said.

"They didn't just drop dead for no reason." Dom leaned over the table to get a better view of the scene. He pointed at the field house around where Samantha claimed the Skulls had died. "This is where the academy's survivors are organizing their resistance."

Thomas sidled up to Dom and squinted at the projected satellite photography. "It looks like they've still got plenty of sea craft in the basin. Why didn't they just make an escape?"

It was a valid question, but Dom figured the midshipmen and officers alive at the academy had far more honor than that. He used a finger to indicate the field house's location again. "That building is right near the visitor's entrance and the pedestrian gate into the Academy. If I were to guess, those men and women are housing civilians, and they're not about to abandon their guard."

"Right," Meredith said. "And they're isolated in the field house. Even if they could ferry the civilians out in shifts, they'd have no idea where to take them."

"Exactly," Dom said. "Which is why our mission will be doubly crucial. Here's how we kill two birds with one stone: We'll liberate the survivors in the field house and help them establish a secure ferry line between Annapolis and Kent Island. Once we've evacuated all the survivors, we can direct any armed midshipmen, officers, or local law enforcement we rescue to help keep the barricade safe on the Bay Bridge to Kent."

He considered the plight of the *Queen of the Bay*. After losing Hector and managing only to save a single family from within the depths of that hellish ship, he'd ordered his team to leave the rest of the passengers, giving the poor survivors little more than a rain check for their rescue. At best, the mission remained incomplete. At worst—if he neglected the ship—it would be an utter failure.

"When Kent is secure," Dom continued, "we go back for the *Queen of the Bay* and any other passenger vessels still in need of dry land." He used the Chesapeake Bay map to indicate the flotilla of ships. "Lauren and her team can set up a triage to ensure all survivors are free and clear of the Oni Agent and administer the chelation therapy to anyone who was recently infected." He turned toward Miguel and Renee. "Have all Hunters prep their gear. Meet in the cargo bay at 1400 hours for a briefing and immediate departure."

"Aye, aye, Captain," Miguel and Renee said in unison. They jogged out into the passageway together.

When the door shut behind them, Meredith bit her bottom lip. Dom knew that expression well. "What's on your mind?"

"Just because the Skulls outside the field house are dead, how do we know that living ones didn't make it inside?"

Dom understood the unspoken implications. Maybe there weren't any survivors. Maybe this entire mission and everything that hinged on it was a wasteful risk. He gulped, not wanting to believe the possibility.

"Take a look at this." Chao directed the satellite images to focus on a section of flat roof on the field house. An inverted American flag flew from a pole, a historical signal of maritime distress. "According to our images, this was added to the field house no more than an hour ago."

An hour. Dom knew how much could change in an hour when Skulls were involved. He thought back to Hector being impaled by the sneaking, lithe Skull. A lot could change in minutes—or seconds.

Could he expend more of the *Huntress's* depleting resources on another high-risk mission? And what would he do if he lost another Hunter?

He shook those thoughts away.

His priority when he'd joined the CIA, started his covert ops organization, and now surviving in what might very well be the apocalypse had always been clear in his mind: to save as many lives as he could.

Meredith was still looking at him, waiting for his decision.

"We're going in today," Dom said, "and we're going to find survivors."

TWENTY-TWO

D OM SCANNED THE MAP OF THE ACADEMY a final time. "Good work, techies."

Thomas brushed a hand through his thinning gray hair. "You guys"—Samantha glared at him—"and gal deserve a commendation for accomplishing all this in such a short time."

"Definitely," Dom said. "But there were two other things I asked before we left."

"We didn't forget." Adam opened his laptop and placed it on the electronic glass table. He adjusted his glasses over the bandages he still wore and then tapped his keys. The small image from his screen took the place of the academy map. It showed a chart of the United States coast with glowing white dots. "I know you're probably getting tired of looking at maps, but I've indicated all likely locations where we can obtain a resupply. These are active military bases and supply depots— or at least they were active before the outbreak."

"Good, very good," Dom said. He recognized many of the locations, ranging from Brunswick, Maine, to Key West, Florida.

"Should we try opening lines of communication?"

"Not yet," Dom said. "Last time I spoke with General Kinsey, he didn't seem too supportive of our efforts. My guess is we'll get one shot to convince him to help us establish a resupply." He could see the gears turning behind Samantha's eyes as he spoke.

"And you want us to wait until"—Samantha held up a finger—"we get to the final task you gave us. Once we identify a neuro lab with surviving scientists we can recruit to help Lauren's team, then you'll contact Kinsey."

"Exactly. It would be better if we have a direct plan of action, and I don't have to be wishy-washy with the details. We can organize a resupply while we make our way to a lab. Kinsey doesn't have a lot of time, and he has even less patience. So have you found any potential labs?"

Adam tugged at his beard. "Yes, actually, we're investigating a number of possibilities. You can thank your daughter for her help, too."

"Kara?"

"That's right," Adam said. "She wanted something to do, so I had her help me expand our candidate list of neuroscience and neurodegenerative disease researchers and labs in the United States and beyond. I think it's pretty extensive. Now it's just a matter of finding which ones actually have survivors."

"Thanks for keeping her busy. I know she hates sitting still. Bed rest to her is like being put in the brig."

"You got it, Captain."

"One final thing," Dom said. "While we get ready, I want

you three to put Lauren in contact with Detrick. See if they have any updates on the research front, because I know we sure as hell haven't had time for any."

"Will do," Samantha said, already picking up a handset. "I'll call her in now."

"Keep up the good work." Dom left the workshop, trailed by Meredith and Thomas. They walked down the passageway now churning with Hunters running back and forth with equipment and weapons. The sounds of their voices, stern and curt, echoed off the bulkhead. They dodged Dom as they flew past on whatever urgent errand needed to be completed before the next mission.

"I take it I'm on ship-babysitting duty again," Thomas said.

Dom clapped the man's shoulder. "That you are. I'll have you bring the *Huntress* as close as you can to the basin at the academy. Keep tabs on the comms in case we need to set up an evac."

"Aye, aye, Captain. If you need a quick getaway or if things get hairy out there, I'll be waiting for you." Thomas jogged down the passageway toward the ladders to the pilothouse. The Hunters dashing between the armory and the cargo bay had since departed.

That left Meredith alone with Dom once again. "You going to finish that thought from earlier?" she asked.

"About?"

"Don't play coy." She brushed her hand against the back of his, a gesture imperceptible to anyone who might happen to glance in their direction. But the touch of her skin against his sent a warm feeling through Dom. "You were never one to express your emotions well, but I've known you for over twenty years. You might fool everyone else, but you can't lie to me."

Dom sighed. There were so many objectives in the upcoming missions, so many demands on him as he did his best to fight the Oni Agent outbreak. "Look, Meredith, back when we were in Frederick, when you were unconscious after the bus crash…" He met her gaze. "I won't lie to you. It almost killed me to see you like that. And it seems casualties follow me. My own daughter, for God's sake…" He turned away.

"I'm sorry, Dom."

"Nothing for you to be sorry about. These people—my crew, you, and my family—all trust me. I'm supposed to lead everyone in a world where all the rules have changed." He leaned in. "I won't tell my crew this, but I'm making this shit up as I go. There's no training, no handbook, no special-forces boot camp that prepares you to kill hordes of sick civilians infected with a biological agent that turns them into monsters."

"I'm not arguing with you there."

"So the thing is, my crew is in this fight with me. It's what they signed up to do. But you and my girls—you didn't choose this. You didn't sign a contract to be a covert mercenary or do battle with the Skulls."

"But I did choose to join the CIA. I took an oath to

protect others without so much as a public thank you."

"That's true," Dom said. "And if I'm being honest with you, it's more than who took what oath. I don't want to see you or my daughters end up dead." He thought of his ex-wife again, trapped in their old house, her body mutated by the Oni Agent. He imagined that fate for Meredith, and he shuddered. "Or worse, see any of you turned into a Skull."

Meredith counted her magazines one more time before cinching up her tactical vest. She readjusted it to sit evenly on her shoulders and fit snugly on her natural waistline before joining up with the rest of the Hunters. They stood in the brightly lit cargo bay as the ship's engineers prepped the Zodiacs for departure. The ship rocked back and forth slowly, and the slap of the waves against its hull echoed softly in the cavernous hold.

Near her, Owen inserted his last magazine into a pocket. The slim but muscular former Ranger was about young enough to be Meredith's son. It was a stark reminder that she was about to embark on a mission where she had an extra ten to twenty years on most of her teammates.

"You feeling okay?" Owen said to Meredith in a lowered voice.

She must've been letting her nerves get the better of her, so she quickly steeled herself. "I'm fine," she said. But her thoughts lingered around the mess that was their last mission. She'd managed to keep pace with the team and prayed she could do so again.

Owen flashed a smile. "I saw the feeds from the *Queen of the Bay*. Didn't seem like you had a problem jumping back in the saddle." But his smile faded, and Meredith guessed what he was thinking. Although she had lived, Hector, a more experienced Hunter and former SEAL, had not.

Meredith strapped on her thigh holster. She watched Owen's face turn contemplative as his eyes stared at some point only he could see. She had been around field operatives long enough to know what that expression meant. And she knew if someone didn't intervene, Owen would soon be spiraling into a dark abyss of "what if" and "it should've been me on that mission."

"We're going to kick some Skull ass," she said, forcing a wry grin. "For Hector."

Owen locked eyes with Meredith, the low-burning embers of a fire returning to life in his pupils. "For Hector," he agreed.

"I can only imagine he'd be damn proud we're saving his Navy brothers and sisters."

"Goddamned right," Owen said. The Ranger pounded his chest with one fist. "This land grunt's going to save some fucking squids."

Spencer, another fellow Ranger, turned, evidently overhearing the conversation. "Ain't that always the story, bro? Army saving Navy?"

Terrence, another SEAL, crossed his arms and stared them both down. "You fucking bullet sponges think you're the shit, huh? We'll see who's saving who when you're pissing your pants."

"No problem, bro," Spencer said with a shit-eating grin. "I brought my goddamned Depends."

Meredith couldn't help but laugh even as she admired the trio. Professional soldiers and operatives on the battlefield, they maintained enough of their humanity in the face of despair to partake in a bit of good-natured ribbing.

As Spencer and Terrence turned away, Meredith noticed Owen's expression turn vacant and moody again. Now it was Meredith's turn to ask him the question that had started this conversation: "You feeling okay?"

Owen's face flushed. "Yeah, yeah, I'm doing fine."

Meredith arched an eyebrow. "What's the look for?"

"Sounds corny"—Owen brushed a hand over his head and then left it on the back of his neck—"but I'm thinking I ought to write a song to commemorate Hector and Brett. Maybe Ivan and Scott, too. All the casualties of the fight against the Oni Agent."

Meredith nodded, remembering Dom had mentioned to her before that Owen was a talented guitarist. "Not corny at all. You should do it." She wanted to say more, but Dom started clapping his hands to get their attention.

"All right, Hunters. This is our second rescue mission op for the day, and this one is going to be one-hundred-fucking-percent successful." Dom paced in front of a map of the

Naval Academy overlaid with one of Chao's satellite images. "We believe the survivors are here." He pointed to the Halsey Field House. "We need to clear a path to here." He indicated the Santee Basin. "We're going to separate into three teams. Alpha will start at the basin and clear out all hostiles there. Bravo is going to land on the shore by the field house and immediately secure the survivors." He paused for a moment.

Meredith scanned the Hunters. The crew consisted of a more or less ragtag band of men and women from all walks of life and various military organizations. Their ears were glued to Dom, and they stood at rapt attention. They banded together under him and melded into one cohesive unit despite their differences. And here they were, once again, ready to fight, placing their full trust in Dom.

"Charlie team's going to have it hard," Dom said. "The goal of this mission is to get the survivors out—midshipmen, officers, civilians—without running into the Skulls. That means we need to attract as little attention as possible. And moving hundreds of people is going to pique the Skulls' interest." He stared at his Hunters, meeting each of their eyes. Meeting Meredith's eyes. She gulped. "We need a distraction. I need two wily-ass volunteers who will fly with Frank, drop down to the Academy's chapel, and make those bells ring to the high heavens. I want every goddamn Skull on Academy grounds to head to church like it's Easter Day and they're the most God-fearing creatures put on this green earth."

"I'm in, Chief." Miguel raised his prosthetic without hesitation.

Meredith thought about what Dom had said earlier. She couldn't help reminding herself of how she'd felt about him. Back when they were partners, back before he'd married Bethany. Hell, even after he married Bethany. But she had never let her selfish emotions get in the way of her professional activities. She thought about raising her hand. After all, out of sight, out of mind. If she and Dom weren't on the same team, they wouldn't be constantly worrying about each other. Right?

But before she could, Andris stood a little straighter and spoke out with his slight Eastern European accent. "Put me in for Charlie." He elbowed Miguel. "Someone's got to keep an eye on this crazy mother—"

"You've got it." Dom cut him off. "You two, head up to Frank. You'll hear more from me when we're moving out."

The two Hunters saluted and padded out of the cargo bay side by side.

"Renee, you'll lead Bravo. Terrence, Meredith, you're with Renee. Jenna, Owen, Spencer, you're on Alpha with me."

Meredith met Dom's eyes for a second. So he *was* on the same wavelength as her. *Out of sight, out of mind*, she thought. Or maybe he thought he was keeping her safer by sending her on the team to the field house rather than with his group that would fight for control of the basin.

"Here's how it's going to go down. Charlie will hit the chapel and ring the bells. Once the Skulls start moving, that's when Bravo gets on land to the field house. Alpha will strike if and only if Bravo confirms we've found survivors. And this goes for all of you: Do not be afraid to retreat. Do not be afraid to call Frank or Thomas for an immediate evac. It's better to live and fight another day than to end up on the ends of those monsters' claws."

A low murmur of agreement answered back from the Hunters.

"Hunters, load up and move out!" Dom's voice boomed, bouncing off the bulkhead.

The cargo bay doors slid apart. Brilliant white sunlight poured in from the crisp blue sky. A gentle sea breeze whirled in with it as the whitecaps crashed and swelled.

Meredith hopped into a Zodiac with the rest of Bravo and gripped the gunwale when they were hoisted out over the Chesapeake. The cables lowered them down, and the craft splashed into the water. Low waves splashed against the Zodiac and sifted into the boat, puddling at their feet while she and Terrence worked to unlatch the craft.

"Engineering, this is Bravo. We're free," Renee said over the comm link when Meredith and Terrence had finished.

Terrence took the tiller and directed the Zodiac out from the shadow of the *Huntress*. The motor chugged. A fine mist of salty spray beaded on Meredith's face, and the boat curled toward Annapolis.

She shielded her eyes from the intense sun and surveyed the bay. A flotilla of small craft, mostly leisure sailboats and motorboats, drifted around them. Dom's boat with Alpha team dropped into the water shortly after. The two Zodiacs cruised northeast, winding between the civilian seacraft.

From one twenty-footer, two men waved at them with both hands, clearly wanting the Hunters' help for something. But Meredith knew they couldn't stop at every single boat along their way to the Academy. The delay could be disastrous for the survivors waiting on land. At least the people on the open water were relatively safe from Skull attacks. And she reckoned they'd be even safer once the Hunters liberated the Academy and used the people there to help secure Kent Island.

But of course, those waiting in the civilian seacraft had no idea. Families, looking haggard or sick, waited on the decks of their respective boats. Some waved; some yelled. Some watched with a lack of interest that said they'd already given up hope. Meredith hated seeing their sometimes desperate, sometimes disheartened faces as the Zodiac sped by. She wished she could tell them they'd all be safe soon, to just hold tight.

The Zodiac bounced over another wave, and Meredith tightened her grip on the gunwale. She leaned forward, peering into the distance where the colorful buildings of Annapolis came into focus. The thrum of rotors beat loudly, and the AW109 thundered overhead.

"Bravo, Dom speaking. Frank will be taking Miguel and Andris to the chapel before we get there. They'll use the position to scout threats and will be waiting on us to signal whether or not we need them to set the bells off."

"Copy that, and roger," Renee said. Hunched over, using one hand to follow the rope looped along the gunwale, she made her way to the bow of the craft with Meredith. "You ready for this?"

Meredith reflected on their last mission on the *Queen of the Bay*. She had always spent time at the firing range to preserve her firearms skills, worked out regularly to maintain her physical fitness, and kept her mind fresh by running through training exercises with the covert ops divisions of the Biological and Chemical Warfare Defense division back in Langley. She considered herself strong and tough, but would that be enough in a world gone to hell? Renee's words echoed in her head. *Ready for this?* Probably not. But truthfully, was anyone ever ready to face the Skulls?

"Ready as I possibly can be," Meredith finally answered. And she figured that was how everyone else on Dom's team felt. No one could ever be completely prepared to face the apocalypse. But they didn't have a choice.

"That's all any of us can ask." Renee squinted toward the white, square buildings of the Naval Academy. "Now let's kick some Skull ass. And, who knows, maybe save some lives."

"Sounds like a decent plan," Meredith said. The Zodiac made its final approach toward the shore near Halsey Field House. "Always wanted to visit the campus, but never had a chance before."

"Lucky day for you." Renee reached out to moor the Zodiac. She winked, and a sly grin formed across her face. "And even luckier for the Skulls."

TWENTY-THREE

L AUREN WATCHED CHAO'S MONITOR in the electronics workshop. The dot labeled Charlie blew past Alpha and Bravo on the screen. It wouldn't be long before all three dots were hovering near the academy.

Chao gave her a handset and scooped up a set of headphones for himself. He called up the contact information they'd saved on the ship's intranet for Commander Shepherd's direct line. His index finger punched down on the Enter key, and the line began ringing.

"*Huntress*, this is Shepherd."

"Commander, this is Dr. Lauren Winters. I'm calling to give you a sitrep from our end and hoped to get one from your research team."

"I've got about five minutes, Dr. Winters. You go first."

Lauren gave him as brief a rundown as she could regarding the *Queen of the Bay* incident and their almost nonexistent medical supplies. She told him they'd been eking by on their research, but they desperately needed to find a neuroscientist or biochemist or anybody specializing in neurodegenerative diseases before they'd make any progress. "So we're still seeking out potential surviving researchers while the Hunters establish a safe haven on Kent."

"Good idea on the safe haven," Shepherd said. "Because I'm afraid I don't have good news. Kinsey's ordering half the troops sent from Fort Bragg back."

"Didn't he agree—"

"He did. The situation in Washington has gone from hell on Earth to…goddamnit, I can't think of anything worse right now. But you get the picture. We're scraping by out here, and frankly, I don't know how much longer we're going to hold on."

Lauren clenched her fingers until her knuckles turned white. Why was Kinsey so obstinate, so determined to hamper their medical research efforts? Was protecting a bunch of overpaid Congressmen more important than discovering the origin—and maybe even the cure—for the Oni Agent?

"However, we did have one breakthrough," Shepherd continued. "Two of my computer boys unearthed something. If you'll open a data link, I can send you the historical documents we've found. We're not sure if they'll lead anywhere, but it's at least worth a look."

Samantha shot a thumbs up from behind her computer monitor to say *I'm on it*. Lauren flashed a brief smile to indicate her thanks.

"I'll look them over as soon as we receive them," Lauren said.

"Glad to hear it, Dr. Winters. Now I've got to go deal with a perimeter check. Need anything else?"

There were a million things she needed. More lab techs.

More servers to run biocomputational analyses. Supplies—and more labs—to run all the experiments she had planned. But Shepherd wasn't in a position to provide any of that right now. "That should do it. Thank you, Commander."

"And send my thanks to Captain Holland and the crew. Keep fighting the good fight. We'll be in touch soon. Over."

The line went dead. Lauren hoped Shepherd would report back soon with a real breakthrough on the origin of the Oni Agent, maybe even a potential vaccine candidate. But while Shepherd's researchers toiled in the lab, General Kinsey had called for a tactical retreat, weakening Fort Detrick's chances of surviving a resurgence of the Skull horde.

Lauren's blood ran cold, and she inhaled sharply. If Detrick was lost, finding a vaccine or some way to stop the prion component of the Oni Agent would be up to her and her meager floating laboratory.

"You okay?" Chao asked. "Looks like you just saw a ghost."

"Just thinking about what's in store for us if we lose Detrick." She gave him back the handset, still wet with sweat from her clammy hands. "We're going to need all the help we can find."

The howls bounced off the walls and seemed to grow in intensity. Navid's lungs burned, and his leg muscles cramped.

He cursed himself for spending so much time in the lab. He should've gotten outside to run a little. He wasn't fat, but he definitely wasn't fit.

"Come on, Navid!" Abby said.

Unlike him, Abby *was* a runner, putting in three miles every day before she checked on her ongoing nerve regeneration experiments. She'd asked him to start running with her. He should've taken that invitation.

The click and clack of claws against the stairs below urged him to fight against his physiological limits. *Mind over matter. Come on, Navid.*

Abby turned back, fear etched across her face. Her eyes were wide. "Let's check this hall." She peeked through the wire-reinforced window. "No crazies."

She pushed open the door. They poured through. Navid gasped for air, his hands on his thighs. He couldn't breathe enough fresh oxygen.

"Where should we…" Abby's voice trailed off.

Navid forced himself to look up. Nondescript doors led off both sides of the hall. A myriad of offices and laboratories lay before them. But would any be safer than the labs they'd just fled?

"Just…pick…one…" he managed between wheezes.

Abby didn't give him a chance to catch his breath and kept moving. She tried the first door to their right. It didn't budge. Navid tried his hand at the next three doors but was met with the same result. They needed a janitor's closet, an open office, anything where they could hunker down and prepare themselves for the next move.

But trying to search for an open door in a highly secured research facility was proving to be futile. The echoes of the creatures' yells in the stairwell sifted out into the hall.

Abby whimpered as she tried another door, then another. Navid's pulse throbbed in his ears. Frustration welled up in him. He yanked another door handle uselessly. He tried a different tactic. Lowering his shoulder, he backed up and then slammed against the door. It shuddered slightly but didn't budge. Pain radiated across his shoulder. He tried again. *No use*, he thought.

"We've got to keep moving. Got to find somewhere else." He ran to the end of the dark hall and sped around the corner. His feet slipped on the polished tile, and he almost lost his balance. As he recovered and stood straight, Abby froze alongside him.

"Navid…" The fear in her voice sent a shiver down his spine.

He looked up, peering into the shadows to see what had alarmed her. A dark shape lumbered. Malicious red emergency lights flashed over it. The thing twisted to look at them, cocking its horn-crowned head. A tattered white lab coat hung off the monster. Spikes and plates stuck out of its spine, and its fingers ended in sharp hooks. They clicked together, its hands tensing and relaxing. A low growl escaped its mouth as it approached.

Navid backed up, pressing himself flat against the wall. The creature's eyes went wide, and it let out a wild howl. The noise was deafening. It bent forward slightly and then sprinted, the lab coat fluttering.

"Go! Go! Go!" Navid yelled, adrenaline forcing aside his exhaustion. He ran toward the stairs, where the other crazies were. He didn't know where else to go, but he did know they wouldn't make it past the beast in the hall.

The creature chasing them slammed into the wall, carried by momentum as it tried to round the corner they'd just left. Navid risked a glance. The thing picked itself up. It stood straight enough that sunlight poured over its face from a window. Crimson liquid dripped from its lips. And by the way the red chunks of flesh and blood were patterned around the creature's mouth, Navid could tell the creature wasn't injured; rather, it had been feeding on something—or someone.

The crazy beast bellowed. As it charged again, red spittle flying from between its serrated teeth, a chorus of distant howls echoed in response. The creature had called its brethren to the hunt.

Abby stopped, and Navid ran into her. She wrapped her arms around him and buried her face into his chest. He opened his mouth to urge her on, but saw why she'd stopped.

Why she'd given up.

Another crazy stood at the opposite end of the hall, its body as twisted and grotesque as the first, marred by strange bony formations. Its flesh appeared gray under the plates and spines and spikes. In its eyes, a pure red fury pulsated.

Then another crazy tore out of the stairwell, followed by a second and third, shoving each other when they caught sight of Navid and Abby. The crazy behind them yelled again, sprinting down the hall. The others at the stairwell joined in, their screams and wails crashing against Navid like a tidal wave.

He thought these would be the last sounds he'd ever hear. Paralyzed by fear and clinging to each other, he and Abby would die, torn apart by these creatures.

No, Navid thought. *No fucking way am I going out like this.*

He reared back, tensing every muscle in his body, and threw himself at a door in a last-ditch effort to find an escape. The impact rattled his teeth. Agony radiated down his right arm.

The creatures were drawing closer. He imagined their hot breath washing over him and Abby as they were devoured alive. Navid ignored the throbbing pain in his shoulder and threw himself at the door again.

But the frame didn't so much as crack. The door didn't budge.

This was it.

TWENTY-FOUR

———◆❧◆———

MIGUEL HELD THE RAIL ABOVE HIS HEAD with his prosthetic. The helicopter hit a nasty headwind and shuddered. His heart leapt, but he kept his mouth straight and jaw clenched. A bead of sweat trickled from under his helmet and down his cheek. He stole a glance at Andris to see if the man had noticed.

But Andris was seemingly too enamored with the azure waves hundreds of feet below them to worry about Miguel.

"Sorry about the rough ride, gentlemen." Frank's voice echoed over the comm link. The pilot pulled up slightly on the cyclic. The AW109 steadied itself. "Windy day."

Miguel pressed his tongue to the roof of his mouth. It was dry, a visceral reaction to the shaking of the vehicle. He'd always tried to put on a brave face, but he couldn't help the instinctual reactions to a vehicle that seemed ready to explode.

He'd rather face a roomful of Skulls than ride in another Humvee over Al Qaeda territory, waiting for another IED to go off under his feet.

The memories before the explosion that day in the godforsaken dry heat of Afghanistan were hazy at best. Routine escort mission. Convoy over a dirt road followed by overwhelming heat. A blinding flash of tearing metal and licking tongues of flame. Air sucked out of his lungs. The left side of his body hurt for a moment then went numb. He'd later learned that third-degree burns had charred his nerves.

The next thing he remembered, he was waking up at a military hospital in Germany. He'd passed in and out of consciousness for a while, doped up on pain meds.

He remembered the intense itching on his ribs. He had moved his arm to scratch it, but his arm had felt lighter than usual. A strange, ghostly sensation. His arm had definitely hurt. Healing burns, he'd thought. He had tried to crane his neck to see what was going on. The small movement had strained his tight muscles and caused more pain than he expected. Then he had seen why he couldn't get his fingers at the bandages to relieve the itching.

He had no goddamn fingers to scratch with. Nothing past his elbow. His stomach had twisted, and he'd almost vomited all over the crisp white sheets and bandages. But he'd fought the rising panic and controlled his breathing.

A nurse had wandered by to check on him with a chart in her hands. "Awake again. How's the pain?"

Miguel had struggled to speak, swallowing hard to clear his mouth. His breath had felt hot and tasted sour. "Not…bad," he had rasped.

"Good. Just hit this little guy if things get worse." She had held up a white plastic button with a cord attached to his IV. He had almost reached for it with his left hand. His left stump, now. She had given him a pitying look, as if she had sensed his mistake.

He couldn't stand the pity. Couldn't stand the *oh, poor soldier* look she'd given him. She'd probably seen worse. Guys with all four limbs missing. Guys with their guts spilling out, their brains oozing out their skull. And what did he have? Burns up his side, mostly just on his ribs, and a stump arm.

He was alive, damn it. He was fucking alive.

"Need anything else?" the nurse had asked.

"Actually, I do have a request." He'd tried to adopt a serious expression, but wasn't sure, in the haze of the pain meds, what the hell he had looked like. "I seem to be missing an arm, so if you see it around, will you let me know?"

The nurse's sorrowful blue eyes had lit up slightly. The corners of her lips had trembled ever so much. A tiny smirk. Miguel had grinned back, and the nurse looked at him with a hint of relief. Maybe a bit of joy that this grunt hadn't come back angry, hadn't lashed out at her for the injuries he'd sustained from some goddamn Al Qaeda bastard.

She had turned and walked away, but not before flashing him another small smile. "Let me know if you need anything, soldier. But between you and me, I think you're going to do just fine."

Long after he'd left the hospital, he never figured out what she'd meant by those last words. Had she meant he would recover physically? Or had she meant he was going to be one of the few guys who weren't tormented by PTSD? Either way, he wasn't sure she had turned out to be right.

The chopper jostled again, and Miguel cringed. The ghost

pains in his prosthetic arm lit up, sending an electric wave through the ends of his stunted nerves. "Shit, Frank. You learn how to fly yesterday?"

"Nah, buddy. But they did take my pilot's license away last week for landing on an old lady's car." The pilot shot Miguel a half-smirk before returning his eyes back to the land drawing nearer.

Miguel turned away from the bay and surveyed the almost empty chopper. Just him, Frank, and Andris. Alpha, Bravo, and Charlie teams were all drawn from a smaller pool this mission, too. It was a stinging reminder of the brothers he'd lost in the fight against the Oni Agent. The meager amount of humor he'd mustered to hide his physical and mental scars fled. Guilt replaced the void in his mind, as it had in the hospital.

Back at the hospital, as soon as he had quipped about his missing arm, he'd realized that he had no idea what had happened to the others in his squad. It turned out Philips, Vasquez, and Abbas wouldn't have to worry about missing limbs or scars. None of them had made it home.

But he had to live with the fact that somehow fortune had favored *him*.

The AW109 passed over the Zodiacs, skimming the water's surface. If he squinted, he could make out the tiny forms on the crafts. Aboard them was all that was left of the Hunters. They'd lost Henry and Brett. Glenn and Renee had at least recovered from their confrontations with the Oni Agent, but Miguel doubted Ivan and Scott ever would. Once again he was left wondering why fate had chosen him to live and taken others.

"There it is, boys," Frank said. The Naval Academy appeared among a scattering of trees near the edge of downtown Annapolis. A few shapes meandered there, roaming in seemingly random paths. Skulls, no doubt.

The two Zodiacs trailed behind the chopper now. They would land well after Miguel and Andris had a chance to scout out the area from the sky. The chopper shuddered again, steel shaking against steel. Miguel's arm tensed. He felt the muscles and nerves in his missing limb tense as well. A ghost of the past, never to leave him, always to remind him of everything and everyone he'd lost.

"ETA five minutes," Frank said.

Miguel nodded and tightened the grip on his SCAR-H. He vowed that he wouldn't let death take another Hunter today. Not a single goddamn one. If he died atop the chapel, ringing that bell and attracting every fucking Skull in the state of Maryland, at least he would die a hero.

***

"Charlie, this is Alpha. What's it look like on the ground?" Dom waited. The static in his earpiece settled.

"Copy, Alpha. This is Charlie," Miguel replied. "We're not seeing much. Scattered Skulls, most looking like lazy sons of bitches."

"Can't be too careful, Charlie." Dom readjusted his position between Jenna and Owen in the Zodiac so he could better see the AW109 making its rounds over the Academy. "Remember how quickly they forget their lethargy when they see fresh meat."

"Roger that."

Spencer slowed the throttle, and the Zodiac sputtered. The motor noise lessened to a low gurgle in their approach to the basin. The docks were lined with yard patrol craft and sailboats. Their masts stood tall and bare as trees in the winter. Only four slips lay empty. At least someone might've escaped from the Academy, but judging by the sheer number of remaining boats, most people hadn't been so lucky.

Dom held his binos to his face to better survey the area around the basin. A line of trees obscured the view of most of the campus. A few white buildings peeked out between the dense trunks. Shapes moved, shadowed by the leaves and branches. And though they remained largely in the shade of the trees, Dom could see enough of their ghastly silhouettes to tell they were Skulls.

Two long barriers sheltered the basin, leaving only a single way for seacraft to enter and exit. The Zodiac drifted toward it now.

"Bravo, Alpha. Do you copy?" Dom asked.

"Copy, Alpha," Renee replied. "We're mooring now."

"As soon as you make contact with the survivors, you can give us the go-ahead. We're in position now."

"Aye, aye, Captain."

The Zodiac started to drift into the entrance of the basin, carried by the choppy waves.

"Bring her back a bit, Spence," Dom said.

Spencer nodded and rotated the throttle. The motor's gurgle kicked up in volume as the Zodiac twisted away from the basin.

A growl echoed over the water in response. Dom turned, shouldering his rifle. A Skull burst through the trees. When it caught sight of them, it tilted its head back and let out a deafening bellow. More Skulls poured from between the trees and raced over the docks.

"Move, move, move!" Dom yelled.

There was no use in keeping the motor quiet now. Spencer gunned it, and the Zodiac kicked up a spray of water. They started to put distance between themselves and the charging Skulls. But not before one leapt from the end of the dock. Its clawed hands pinwheeled, and its mouth opened. An earsplitting shriek escaped from between its cracked lips. The beast caught the gunwale while its body splashed into the water.

Spencer kept the Zodiac pointed straight toward the bay and away from the basin. The Skull hoisted itself up, water sluicing off its skeletal growths and the rippling muscles that peeked out between the plates and spikes. It was a full six feet in height and wore the remains of a biker's leather jacket, making it all the more menacing. Jenna and Owen adjusted their aim, but their rifles proved unwieldy at such a close distance. The beast sprang at Dom.

Dom dropped his rifle and grabbed the Skull's forearms. It snapped at him, spittle flying from between its teeth. The Skull let out another frustrated scream. Dom wrestled it away from his face, careful not to cut himself on the jagged bones climbing out of its flesh. He planted his boot on the creature's chest and kicked it backward.

The Skull tripped over the side of the Zodiac and fell into the churning water. It tangled one of its twisted hands in the rope around the gunwale. The Zodiac, still racing, dragged the creature. The Skull bounced against the craft and screamed, its eyes filled with hatred and hunger. Dom steadied his rifle, took aim, and planted two bullets into those eyes. Blood and gore splattered from the gunshot wounds. The creature's arm went slack. It lost its grip and slipped under the dark waters.

Dom's earpiece crackled. *Renee's voice.* "Alpha, this is Bravo. We're in position."

"Copy," Dom replied. "Charlie, do you read?"

"Charlie here," Miguel replied. "Still in the sky. Alpha, you trying to take our job of distracting the Skulls? Seems like they all ran your way, Chief."

Dom scanned the basin, and Spencer curled the Zodiac around to face it once again. A horde of Skulls clambered along the docks. Some leapt into the water, disappearing beneath its surface. Others let out frustrated howls, jostling each other for position.

"Charlie, you got a better view than me on these guys?" Dom asked. "Can you tell me how many contacts we have on the docks?"

"Eh, a good fifty, sixty, maybe," Miguel replied. "You want us to ring that bell?"

"Negative, Charlie." He held up a hand to signal Spencer to slow the Zodiac once more. They floated a couple of dozen yards from the basin. Just enough to keep the Skulls riled up, but not close enough that they would attempt another stunt like the one Dom had dispatched. "This is going to cause a slight change in plans. But I told you Alpha would secure the docks, and that's just what we'll do. This might be easier than I thought."

He knelt at the stern of the Zodiac and signaled Jenna and Owen to shoulder their rifles.

"Bring us in a little closer, Spence," Dom said.

The Zodiac gurgled forward.

Jenna leaned her head forward slightly to see through her optics. "Captain, there aren't sharks in the bay, right?"

"No idea. Why? You don't think they'd like to feed on Skull meat?"

"Nah, it's just that we're about to chum the water with blood. We've got Skulls on dry land; I don't want to deal with sharks, too."

"Easy solution for that." Dom took aim. "Don't fall off the boat. Fire at will!"

The Hunters let loose. Skulls dropped to the docks, their heads snapped back by gunfire. Bodies slipped into the water; others fell across the bobbing sailboats. Even as their twisted kin fell to the Hunters' trained aim, the Skulls climbed over each other, still desperate to get at live prey.

The crew continued their barrage until the docks were void of the Skulls' shrieks and howls. Only bodies and a slick layer of blood were left when Dom held up his hand to signal for the Hunters to hold their fire. Picking the Skulls off at a distance had been too easy. The grotesque shooting gallery meant his Hunters got to stay out of harm's way. They waited a few minutes, the Zodiac bobbing in the basin, to see if any more Skulls would arrive late to the party.

But no more showed. Maybe the unexpected attack had made the mission easier for the rest of his team, too, and for that, Dom was thankful.

"How we looking from the air, Charlie?" Dom asked.

"Pretty damn clear around the Academy. You got a half-dozen Skulls to the northwest, maybe three or four to the northeast. Otherwise, you made our job pretty pointless."

"Copy that, Charlie. Bravo, what's your position?"

"Alpha, the doors to the field house are locked," Renee said. "Windows are barred. Might be able to gain entrance through an emergency exit on the east side. Permission to force entry, Captain?"

"Permission granted. Watch out for civvies."

"Copy that."

Dom signaled Spencer to bring the Zodiac into one of the empty slips at the docks. Jenna and Owen immediately tied a couple of mooring lines to the bollards.

"Alpha, this is Bravo," Renee said. "We've gained entry." A pause. "Not much to see. Just a hall. Going to check out the arena."

Dom climbed out onto the dock. His boot slipped in the mix of blood and saltwater. He steadied himself by grabbing the top of a piling. He offered a hand to Jenna and Owen. Spencer killed the motor and hopped up next to them.

The slow, muffled breathing of the Bravo team members sifted through the comm link. Dom signaled Jenna to take point as they secured the dock and headed toward the Academy.

"So far, no—" Renee stopped.

Dom waited a tic and then asked, "Bravo, do you copy?"

A loud roar echoed over the mic. Dom and the rest of the Alpha team Hunters flinched. A single word, a single syllable came through the din. "Skulls!"

TWENTY-FIVE

———◆◆◆◆◆———

MEREDITH SHOULDERED HER RIFLE, covering Renee and Terrence. They chose their steps carefully, avoiding the ring of dead Skulls littering the lawn and sidewalks. She'd known what to expect from the satellite imagery, but the smell of death and the macabre scene still made her retch. She took a deep breath to settle her nerves, and they inched toward Halsey Field House. Its central roof bulged like a surfacing whale. Underneath that dome lay the main arena, where she expected they'd find the survivors hunkered down.

"Alpha, the doors to the field house are locked," Renee said. "Windows are barred. Might be able to gain entrance through an emergency exit on the eastside. Permission to force entry, Captain?"

"Permission granted," Dom's voice came back over the comm link. "Watch out for civvies."

"Copy that."

They made their way to the emergency exit. It was one of the few doors that hadn't been boarded up.

"Here we go." Renee heaved the butt of her weapon into the wire-reinforced glass. It cracked, and she struck it again.

She picked away at the glass and then pulled out her multi-tool to cut the wire. Each wire snapped and coiled until she had enough room to reach her gloved hand through and push the door out from inside. It cracked open, and Renee stuck her boot in the door.

"Alpha, this is Bravo. We've gained entry." Renee signaled for Terrence and Meredith to enter.

Meredith followed Terrence's hulking frame into the doorway. Plywood covered most of the windows. She blinked as her eyes adjusted to the darkness. A series of heavy doors lined the hall, presumably leading to the main arena. The floor seemed clear of debris and clutter—no signs of life anywhere. Meredith listened closely but could only hear the sound of her and the other two Hunters breathing.

"Not much to see," Renee said in a low voice, reporting to Dom again. "Just a hall. Going to check out the arena."

She indicated one of the heavy sets of doors with a nod, and Terrence took point.

He leaned into one of the doors, a hand on the handle and the other holding his rifle. He pressed lightly on the handle. "Locked," he said. "Want me to break it down?"

"Hold up. Don't know who we've got hiding behind those doors, so watch your fire. Don't want any civilians harmed." Renee gave the door a single rap with the back of her knuckles. "This is Renee Boland, crew member of the *Huntress*. We're here on a search and rescue."

Meredith waited with bated breath, but no response came from within. She could see the gears turning behind Renee's eyes. No doubt the squad leader was wondering whether there were actually survivors behind those doors.

Renee knocked on the door again. "This is Renee Boland." She spoke louder, repeating her words, and waited another twenty seconds. "I think I hear footsteps. Terrence, crack it open."

The Hunter did as commanded by swinging the stock of his rifle down on the lock. Renee pushed the door open slightly. Meredith couldn't see past her, and the squad leader quickly drew back and closed the door. Her face was ashen and her eyes went wide. "Skulls," she whispered. "Maybe they didn't—"

Something slammed against the door, knocking Terrence back. He fell, sliding on the polished wood floor. His rifle clattered beside him. "Fuck!"

Meredith watched in horror. Something crashed against the door again, knocking it open all the way this time. In that brief moment she saw into the arena. Like she'd expected, it had served as a shelter. Boxes of MREs and canned food lined one side of the old basketball court. Cots were strewn about the center.

But instead of the survivors—midshipmen, officers, and civilians—she'd expected to find sheltering there, a horde of Skulls filled the room. Hundreds of them. Mangled appendages, bones jutting through their skin, heads crowned in horns. A massive roar echoed. The creatures' hunting cries grew louder, a sound so great it threatened to shake the air out of Meredith's lungs.

The one that had burst through the door rapidly scanned Renee, then Meredith, then Terrence. Its muscles coiled, and it sprang into the air. Meredith fired a quick burst. The rounds smashed against the Skull's side, knocking it off its trajectory. It landed inches from Terrence.

As the other Hunter recovered his rifle, Meredith fired two rounds into the Skull's face. The impacts shattered the creature's cheekbones. Blood pooled out onto the floor.

"Skulls!" Renee yelled into her comm link. The screams and wails of the Skulls reverberated through the hallway while she helped Terrence stand.

Meredith shot off a volley to cover them. Two more Skulls charged through the open door. One of the beasts was cut down by the bullets, but the second continued forward. It was no more than four feet tall, scrambling on all fours, its clawed feet slipping on the polished wood floor.

"Watch out!" Meredith yelled.

The small Skull dashed at Renee and Terrence. Terrence drew his rifle up and fired. The monster fell face-first, its arms and legs going placid.

"Move!" Renee said. "Go, go, go!"

"What the fuck is going on?" Dom's voice cracked over the comm link.

The trio took off down the dark hall. Skulls poured from the arena.

"Fucking Skulls," Terrence said. "Hundreds of 'em."

The beasts stampeded, crashing against each other and the walls. Their snarls and howls and claws clicking against the floor chased after the Hunters. The beasts quickly filled in the hall, blocking the emergency exit. There was no going back out from where they came.

Meredith could practically feel the creatures' body heat and their breath on her neck. There was no way they could outrun the Skulls.

Terrence unclipped a grenade from his tac vest when they reached a wide corner. "Frag out!"

He tossed the grenade. Meredith didn't bother turning to see the results of the Hunter's counterattack. Her quads burned, but she pushed forward, following Renee and Terrence. An explosion went off after they cleared the corner. Heat rushed through the hall. For a moment, Meredith thought the Skulls' cries had been quieted, that they'd been defeated by the grenade.

Then the ringing in her ears started. She'd been temporarily deafened. Now she risked a quick glance back. The Skulls surged, spilling over the scattered corpses and torn limbs of their comrades.

"There!" Renee pointed toward another exit door. Only a single folding table was pushed up against it.

Adrenaline gushed through Meredith. She fired a spray of bullets into the wave of Skulls. She saw one, two, maybe three monsters falter. Their bodies were quickly trampled by the rest of the horde.

Terrence, too, fired off a barrage. But Meredith saw the pathetic impact of their attempts to fight back. She knew they didn't stand a chance. Their only hope lay in that door. Ten yards away. Five now.

The din of the Skulls grew louder, a cacophony straight from hell. Renee reached the exit first. She shoved aside the folding table and threw her weight against the door. It opened outward. Meredith followed the other two Hunters out. They spilled into the harsh afternoon sun.

"Barricade the door!" Terrence yelled. "Got to find something—"

But the door gave way before the words came out.

Renee shouldered her rifle, and her weapon chattered away. Meredith and Terrence joined in. The bark of their guns accompanied the thud of Skulls falling to the wall of lead. The single door funneled them through one or two at a time, slowing the Skulls' progress enough for the Hunters to catch their breath. Bodies piled up at the exit.

"Changing!" Terrence called.

Meredith performed a speed reload next, followed by Renee.

"Bravo, let's rendezvous," Dom called. "Abort mission and head north toward Alpha's position. Charlie, provide air support!"

"Got it," Renee said, backing away while still firing.

Meredith continued to squeeze the trigger, letting the automatic fire hose a stream of bullets over the hungry Skulls. But soon four of the creatures escaped the exit. They rushed across the lawn, leaping over the dead ones piled around them. As Terrence and Meredith adjusted their aim to take out the closest ones, more of the beasts rushed from the field house.

"Retreat, retreat!" Renee yelled. She waved Terrence and Meredith onward.

Meredith fired off a final three shots. Her rifle clicked. Empty again. She pushed out the mag and jammed in a fresh one as she ran. Terrence led the way, barreling between trees and over another sidewalk.

"Shit!" Renee called out.

Meredith spun to see Renee had fallen. Her rifle fell across the concrete, skittering away from her grasp. A thin Skull with shoulder blades like small skeletal wings wrapped its fingers around Renee's ankles. She kicked at its bony face, knocking it back slightly. The rest of the Skulls would be on top of Renee in seconds.

Dread filled Meredith. She tried to sight the monster attacking Renee through her optics, but she wasn't confident enough that she wouldn't accidentally hit Renee. Terrence sprinted straight at their squad leader, probably sharing the same thoughts. The only way they could save Renee was by running back to her, back to the oncoming horde. Another Skull bounded ahead of the pack, a bloodied naval officer's uniform whipping around it.

Meredith cursed. Renee tried to shove the Skull back again. Terrence was on his way, but she saw he'd never make it in time.

TWENTY-SIX

L AUREN GLANCED OVER the historical documents Commander Shepherd had sent her. Most told her things they had already found out on their own. The Oni Agent had been developed by Japanese scientists during World War II. No surprises there. But she did find one interesting aspect: a short abstract on the early project claimed the complex came from livestock-derived proteins. It still didn't provide a molecular or chemical structure for these early iterations of the Oni Agent, and she wondered how much had changed in the half-century between its development and now, when the Oni Agent had spread across the earth and left its debilitating, mutating marks on the human population.

She shuddered and put those documents aside.

Next she scanned the extended candidate list of neurological labs that Kara had come up with. She saw several names she recognized from scientific manuscripts. She'd found those papers while searching through the medical literature to see what potential cures might be waiting in research labs for her to adapt, like she'd done with the chelation therapy.

But she found only drugs with ameliorative effects. They would slow the progress of different forms of spongiform encephalopathy, but they never fully cured the disease. Nor did they restore lost neurological function.

She thought of the millions—maybe billions—of infected roaming the world. Their minds were destroyed by the prions pumped out by the nefarious Oni Agent nanobacteria. She found herself wondering what researcher or scientist could possibly have pursued this technology. Who would've approved of this and worked so hard to use their genetic engineering prowess for such a despicable act?

But cursing the guilty individual or organization responsible wouldn't find Lauren a cure. She shook aside these thoughts and focused once more on the scientific papers on her computer monitor. There had to be an answer somewhere.

The longer she searched, her thoughts turned increasingly negative. Maybe there wasn't an answer. Maybe there was nothing she could do about the Oni Agent. No way to develop a cure to help those who'd had it far too long for the chelation therapy to work. No way to develop a vaccine that would prevent those who hadn't yet succumbed from turning into a Skull.

An alarm went off from the patient's ward, jolting Lauren from her ruminations. She jumped from the stool and dashed to the lab's exit, where she pushed through the door. Ivan and Scott were still in medically induced comas in the isolation ward, their breathing slow and their EKG readings normal.

Lauren burst into the infirmary where Sadie and Maggie waited anxiously beside Kara's bed. Sweat poured over Kara's forehead. Her mouth drooped open, and her skin was a sickeningly pale white.

"What's wrong with her?" Sadie said.

"I need some room," Lauren said, squeezing past the girl.

Sadie backed away and pulled Maggie with her. The dog let out a whimper. Divya and Peter ran in from the passageway.

Lauren checked the screen on the blood pressure monitor. "BP's dropping fast."

"EKG's reporting tachycardia," Divya said.

"Must be a side effect of the Oni Agent therapy," Peter said.

Sadie piped up again. "Is she going to be okay?"

"I need her out." Lauren pointed at Divya to take Kara's sister out into the passageway. She didn't need the distraction right now. She thought briefly of telling Divya to relay a message to Dom. But that would be stupid. There was no way she would risk his life and the lives of his team by distracting him. She had no intention of letting the captain return to find his daughter near death. She racked her mind, desperate to identify the cause of Kara's drop in blood pressure and the simultaneous rapid heart rate. Possible causes scrolled through her thoughts as she tried to stabilize Kara. She doubted it was a coronary artery blockage—the girl didn't fit the typical heart attack victim. Maybe it was an infection, but she guessed the antibiotics used to treat the Oni Agent would have knocked out any other bacteria in her system. Still, it could be a possibility.

Divya returned from the passageway. "Thomas is watching Sadie."

"What do you want us to do?" Peter asked, his face scrunched in worry. The team had dealt with battlefield injuries, and they'd overcome the challenges of treating patients with Oni Agent infections, but now they were faced with something entirely different: a young woman presenting signs of heart failure.

Lauren found herself wishing they had a more extensive radiological imaging suite to get a better idea of what was going in Kara's body. But wishes didn't heal sick patients. So she called for the next best thing: "Grab the ultrasound."

Divya nodded and sprinted to a corner of the ward. She moved past an empty patient bed and pushed out a cart containing the ultrasound monitor and probe. The device didn't provide the highest resolution medical images, but it was reliable and could be stowed away easily on a smaller ship like the *Huntress*. The doctor applied a cool gel to the probe, and Lauren pulled aside Kara's hospital gown. Mottled bruises covered the girl's ribs—evidence of her bout with the Skulls.

Most concerning to Lauren was the slight bulge near Kara's stomach. Her heart dropped as she felt the spot with her fingers.

"Ultrasound ready." Divya held up the probe and turned on the monitor. "Where do you want it?"

"Here," Lauren said, pointing to the suspicious spot. She

feared she already knew what the answer to Kara's steadily dropping blood pressure was.

Divya maneuvered the probe. A puddle of dark shadows showed across the grainy image.

"Oh, God," Lauren said. "Peter, prep the OR."

The surgeon ran toward the OR and started scrubbing his hands.

"Divya, get her set up on anesthetics."

The other doctor nodded and ran toward a locked cabinet full of medical supplies. She started to dig through the bottles, and Lauren unlocked the wheels to Kara's hospital bed. After she unhooked Kara's IV drip from its stand and mounted it to the bed, she pushed Kara to the OR.

If what Lauren suspected was true, then her attempt to save Kara from the Oni Agent might be the reason the girl was dying now.

The cries of the crazies grew louder and bounced off the walls of Mass Gen. The monsters were close. Just steps away. Navid had one more chance. With everything he could muster, he ran at the door, leading with his shoulder. He crashed into it, and more pain seared through his bones and muscle. But the door didn't give.

"Oh God!" Abby screamed when one of the crazies lashed out at her.

By some miracle, the laboratory door opened a crack. "Quick!"

Navid didn't hesitate. He kicked the crazy reaching for Abby and simultaneously pulled her through the door. The crazy gripped Abby and didn't let go. It howled louder as its mutated brethren drew closer. Navid sensed other people in the room, but his eyes were glued to Abby and the grotesque thing trying to drag her back into the hallway.

Someone sliced down with a heavy steel pipe. The improvised weapon hit the crazy's forearm, and the bony plates snapped. Its wrist went limp, and its grip loosened. Navid gathered Abby into his arms, and they tumbled backward onto coarse green carpeting.

Another person slammed the door shut. He had a crown of gray hair and a bevy of wrinkles lining his face. The man pushed a tall bookcase filled with medical texts in front of the door. He grunted as another man, dropping the steel pipe, joined in. This man wore a set of navy coveralls drenched in dried blood. As they pushed another bookcase in place, a woman in slacks and a collared shirt dragged a large conference table toward the door. All the while, the growls and thuds of the crazies trying to get in resonated through the small conference room.

Navid joined the trio and bolstered the makeshift barricade with all the remaining chairs, bookcases, and trashcans. The three older individuals took a moment to catch their breath.

"Thank you," Navid said. "Thank you so much."

The man with gray hair scowled and adjusted a set of chairs. The crazies continued throwing themselves at the door.

The man in the coveralls, a custodian Navid vaguely recognized, gave him a slight nod. "It was only right." He narrowed his eyes and stared at the man with gray hair. "Told you we could do it."

Gray Hair snapped, "Are you kidding? Are you joking?" He held his hands out in exasperation. "We're stuck in here, worse than before, and now we've got all those goddamned monsters breathing down our necks. And for what?" He held out a hand to indicate Navid and Abby. "For a couple of kids? What the hell can they do for us?"

"Relax." The woman placed a hand on Gray Hair's shoulder. "Come on, James."

"Oh, come on, Sandra!" James said, his voice rising to mock Sandra.

"She's right," the custodian said. "You need to relax. I saved your ass. You wouldn't be here if I hadn't helped."

Navid cowered next to Abby, who still hadn't gotten up from their fall. He put an arm around her shoulder, and she whimpered. Her face remained ghost-white.

"Don't pretend you were being a hero," James said. "You ran in here to hide!"

"I trusted fate," the custodian said, "and you should, too. If I hadn't, you'd be dead."

James stepped toward the custodian, but Sandra jumped between them and put her arms out to hold the two apart. "You boys both need to cool it. What's done is done, and there's no use arguing about it. Instead of fighting with each other, we're going to need to figure out how to avoid fighting those things." She gestured toward the door hidden behind the jumble of furniture. The books on the shelves shook each time the crazies slammed into the door.

"She's right," Navid said. "Those things won't stop for anything. I had to...I had to burn a whole group of them just to get away earlier."

"Didn't burn enough of 'em, did you?" James said, folding his arms across his collared blue shirt.

"Ignore this asshole. He's still sour because he has to share his office with a dirty janitor." The custodian held out his hand. "I'm Geraldo."

Navid took his hand. "Navid, and this is Abby."

Abby's face contorted in pain. "I...I think I'm hurt."

Navid immediately let Geraldo's hand go and knelt by Abby. "What's wrong?"

"She's going to turn!" James said. "Just like Kaitlyn. I told you this was a mistake." He took the heavy steel pipe Geraldo had picked up and cranked it back like a batter ready to swing.

"My ankle...I think I twisted it," Abby said.

"No!" Navid yelled at James.

"Move out of the way." James shoved Navid back. The steel pipe was still cocked over his shoulder.

Geraldo grabbed the pipe and yanked. "Stop!"

Sandra threw herself between James and Abby. Rage filled Navid. His heart thumped almost as fast it had when he'd run from the crazies. He stood and pushed James backward. The older man tripped and fell on his tailbone. Geraldo stole the pipe from his loosened grip.

Sandra stood over James, her hands on her hips. "Her ankle, James. She wasn't bitten. She wasn't scratched."

James's face went red as he took the scolding. "I couldn't risk her turning… she'd kill us!"

"But she won't turn because of a twisted ankle," Sandra said.

"Kaitlyn came to my office with a broken arm…then"— he pointed at Geraldo—"you saw what she became!"

Geraldo's eyes dropped for a second, his hand with the pipe falling to his side. "I didn't like doing it, but it had to be done. I saw too many of them in the first couple of days…changing and going crazy because of a scratch or a bite." He shook his head, and Sandra placed a hand on his shoulder.

"See?" James asked. "You can't blame me for wanting to protect us."

"There's no 'us' about it," Sandra said. "You wanted to save your own ass."

Abby whimpered. "God, I could really use some ice."

The barricade shuddered. The crazies' growls and cries filtered under the door.

Geraldo jolted toward another door in the back corner of the conference room. He started to open it, and Navid cringed. "Don't worry—it just goes to James's office." He came back out a moment later with a first aid kit. "Brought this along with me. Thought it'd be useful."

He tossed it. Navid caught it and unzipped the small red canvas bag. He tore through the gauze, antibiotic spray, and bandages until he found a sealed foil package with ibuprofen tablets. It wouldn't be much, but the pain relievers would have to do. He ripped open the package and gave the pills to Abby.

"Anybody got water?" Navid asked.

The others shook their heads.

"You can do this," Navid said to Abby.

She nodded and dry-swallowed the two red pills.

"I'll be okay." She scooted back against the wall under a wide window. Sunlight filtered in around her, making her look almost angelic. For a moment, Navid realized how lucky he'd been and how close he had come to losing her. He couldn't help the slight wet sheen forming in his eyes and looked away to hide what he thought was a sign of weakness. He rubbed his eyes with the back of his hands before rejoining James, Sandra, and Geraldo.

"Shouldn't we leave?" Navid asked as the crazies continued their assault.

"And go where?" James held out his hands in an exasperated gesture. "Jump out a window? Let those things devour us?"

Geraldo shook his head. "Until we come up with something better, the best we can do is pray that barricade holds."

"Can someone please explain what the hell is going on?" Navid asked.

"I'll do the best I can," Geraldo said. "I first came across a man down in the basement, traveling between the test animal facilities and one of those imaging labs. He came at me, growling like a rabid dog, and tried to bite me. I punched the guy out cold, but I knew I couldn't leave him there. He needed help.

"So I picked him up"—Geraldo mimed putting the man in a fireman's carry—"and dragged his sorry butt to the emergency room."

"So he was a crazy, right?" Navid asked.

"Right as rain, he was. Only I didn't know it…until I got to the ER. Whole damn place was full of people biting and scratching and clawing." He shook his head. "It was awful. Bloody, violent. I ain't proud, but I ran from there fast as I could. Tried to go outside, but it was even worse. Streets were filled with crashed cars, fights and mobs. I ran back inside like the chicken I am and went straight up the stairs 'til I got to one of these research floors."

"This one?" Abby asked, her voice still strained. Navid squeezed her hand to reassure her it was all right and hoped Geraldo's story would at least distract her until the meds kicked in.

"Nope. I found another one." He gestured to the blood-soaked coveralls. "But it wasn't as safe as I thought. Fought until the last crazy died."

Navid imagined the strength of this man. He seemed so full of humility, yet the way he described it, the custodian had survived a veritable bloodbath and come out unscathed. At least, physically unscathed. Navid shivered at what the man must've done and seen in order to get here.

"So I went to hide again, heard the screaming from in here, and found that woman—"

"Kaitlyn," Sandra offered.

"Well, she was trying to eat these two." He indicated Sandra and James with an open hand. "And I did what I learned I had to do."

"You killed her," Abby said.

"I don't like it when you say it like that. Whatever is causing these people to turn into those zombies took the human out of 'em. I felt like I didn't have a choice." Geraldo shrugged. "That's how I see it anyway."

"So you don't know what's making these people turn?"

Geraldo shook his head.

"What about you two? You're a professor, right?" Navid asked James.

"I am, but I couldn't tell you a damn thing about these raging lunatics running around Boston."

Sandra pulled a hand through her long hair and left it at the back of her neck. "Besides, once the emergency announcement came around the hospital, we stayed put. We were having a meeting with Kaitlyn O'Connor—we're all on an NIH grant together—and decided it'd be safer to stay in here a little while."

"A 'little while' turned out to be a goddamned long time," James said.

"Certainly longer than we expected," Sandra added. "We only followed what was going on by listening to the radio and peeking out the windows when we were brave enough." She shivered. "God, it's just awful."

"And against our advice, Kaitlyn heard someone scream and just had to help. She got attacked and came running back. Somehow escaped the zombie that had tried to eat her, and then, after a while, she turned into one."

"Which is when I showed up," Geraldo added.

The barricade shook again as the crazies pounded against the door. It seemed the monsters wouldn't give up. Abby shrank back against the wall and wrapped her arms around her knees.

Navid glanced at the door to the office. "Can we go in there? Does your office lead somewhere else?"

"It just goes right into the hall with those *things*. And besides, Kaitlyn's in there."

"I thought you said she was dead." Navid was nonplussed.

"She is. It's just her body there," Geraldo said. "But those bony growths kept on showing up all over her long after she died, and the radio said not to touch 'em or you might get infected and turn into one of 'em. All it takes is a poke, a scrape, or a bite, and bam—you're gone."

Abby whimpered, and Navid interlaced his fingers in hers. "It's going to be okay. I won't let those things near you again."

The door shook, and several books thumped onto the floor.

"Maybe joining Kaitlyn isn't such a bad idea right now,"

Geraldo said. "If those things come through *that* door, at least we'll have the other door to delay 'em."

"Agreed. Gives us time to think of something else." Sandra turned to Navid and Abby. "Try to keep your eyes on the desk. It's pretty…gruesome in there."

"Gruesome is a goddamned understatement." James stomped into the office.

Sandra followed after with Geraldo. The custodian waited at the entrance a moment before asking, "Do you two need help?"

Navid shook his head, putting his arm under Abby's shoulder to help her to her feet. "I got it."

Abby whimpered again.

"It hurts that bad?"

A tear rolled down her cheek as her head twisted slowly left, then right. "No… it's not my ankle."

She revealed her wrist to him, letting him see where the crazy had grabbed her earlier. It felt like a semi-truck hit him, going full throttle, and blew his heart out. He stared at the delicate skin he'd caressed so many times since he'd fallen in love with her during their first year in grad school together.

A couple of scratches, red and only freshly scabbed over, traced their way along Abby's flesh. Small scrapes—nothing to bat an eye about normally. Only now, Navid knew those tiny injuries were not normal.

He hugged her, running his hands through her hair, kissing her cheek, her lips. How long would it be before she became one of *them*?

TWENTY-SEVEN

T HE SKULLS WERE EVERYWHERE. They swarmed out of
the field house like bees defending their hive. Miguel
gulped hard and peeled back the door to the AW109.
The wind and rotor wash rushed around him, threatening to
blow him out of the chopper. His body remembered what it
felt like to be thrown out of a vehicle and left to die. But the
harness around his torso held him secure, and he reminded
himself that other lives depended on him. He wouldn't be
frozen by fear.

"Think the chapel bells are still going to distract these
fuckers?" Andris asked.

Miguel watched the wave of Skulls. There was no way
Renee, Terrence, and Meredith could possibly fight them off.
"We don't have time. And even if we did, those Skulls are too
focused on prey. They wouldn't give a shit about some bells."
He wrapped his fingers tight around his rifle. "Get us as close
as you can!" He yelled into his mic. "We've got to get them
cover fire!"

"Will do!" Frank replied.

The chopper banked hard and descended toward the
thronging mass of Skulls. One of the creatures was already on

Renee. She fought the skinny thing, kicking it and trying to bash its face with her rifle.

Miguel wanted desperately to help, but he couldn't get a clean shot from a moving chopper. The rest of the Skulls were closing in, pouring from the field house and rushing over the lawn. Their screams and wails reached Miguel's ears even through the beat of the chopper rotors.

"We aren't going to help from here," Andris said.

"He's right," Miguel said. "Frank, bring us down right behind Renee. Put us between Bravo and the Skulls."

"You got it!"

The AW109 began a rapid descent, the grass and trees reaching toward them. Wheels hit the lawn. Bravo team lay on the opposite side of the chopper, and Miguel and Andris faced the oncoming horde. The rotors still went full speed, ready to lift off at a moment's notice. Miguel aimed his rifle at the nearest Skull. It was close enough for him to make out red eyes between the jutting cheekbones and demonic horns. He squeezed the trigger, and the Skull's face exploded in a gory mess. He picked out a second target. Andris did the same. Their rifles chattered as they chose marks and fired.

"There's no fucking way we're taking 'em all on," Andris said between bursts of gunfire. "Reloading!"

"Just hold 'em until Renee's moving again."

Gunfire exploded from behind Miguel. He stole a quick glance to see through the chopper window that Terrence had blasted the Skull attacking Renee. Meredith helped Renee up, and they began running north again toward Alpha and the basin.

The scent of gunpowder and blood permeated the air. Miguel and Andris sprayed into the mass of Skulls. An especially lithe Skull ran low to the ground, dodging Miguel's shots. The rounds that did connect glanced off its organic body armor. Miguel realized they'd overstayed their welcome. He unclipped a grenade from his tac vest, pulled the pin, and lobbed it into the crowd.

"Frag out!" He slapped the cabin wall of the chopper. "Frank, take us up!"

"Lifting off!"

The chopper jolted and then began its ascent. An explosion rocked through the Skulls. The metal shards tore through the monsters, cracking their bony plates and tearing apart their limbs. A geyser of blood and bone shot into the air.

The beasts that weren't hit by the blast continued their mad rush. The skinny Skull that Miguel had failed to bring down leapt and twisted through the air. It caught one of the static landing wheels on the AW109 and swung itself up into the fuselage.

Miguel tried to readjust his aim, but the Skull pounced on Andris before he could get a shot off. The man went down hard. He managed to grab the creature's forearms, preventing it from flaying him alive with its hooked claws. Saliva flew from the creature's mouth. Its howl filled the fuselage.

"Hey, asshole!" Miguel yelled and brought his rifle back.

He smashed the creature's face with the butt of his gun. The Skull's nose flattened inward, and flecks of blood sprayed a window. A growl escaped its dry, scaly lips, and it coiled back. It sprang at him, and he dodged. The creature crashed against a passenger seat. Its muscles twitched and flexed, preparing for another attack.

But Miguel didn't give it another chance. He was too close to the Skull to bring his rifle around, but his prosthetic was in perfect striking distance. He twisted his wrist, and the concealed blade flashed out, impaling the creature straight through its damaged nasal cavity. The monster went slack, and Miguel kicked it in the chest, knocking the thin Skull out the open door.

He watched the beast fall to the earth and smash into four of the enraged monsters still running after Bravo. The small distraction Miguel, Andris, and Frank had provided had hardly stemmed the flow of creatures. Yet all three members of Bravo were still alive, and for that, Miguel was thankful.

Frank circled the chopper so the two Hunters could take potshots at the swarm of monsters. It seemed each one they took down led to another three charging out of the field house. The building was like some twisted clown car spewing creatures straight from hell.

"Charlie, Alpha here," Dom's voice came over the comm link. "Nice job, boys. Keep up the cover fire."

"Aye, aye, Captain," Miguel and Andris said in unison.

"We're aborting this mission and will reconvene at the *Huntress*."

"Copy," Renee said, sounding out of breath.

Miguel couldn't help but feel disappointed. They'd had a

decent plan, but they'd been too late. The Oni Agent had found the survivors before the Hunters did. He watched Bravo pass the huge Bancroft Hall dormitory. The team looked small compared to the massive hall with its towering columns.

A sudden burst of gunfire pierced the air. Miguel could see Renee, Meredith, and Terrence still running; none of them had taken a shot. More gunfire exploded around Bancroft, and Miguel watched a line of Skulls fall.

"Alpha, Charlie. Are you firing on these guys?" Miguel asked.

"Negative," Dom replied.

Miguel pressed his binos to his eyes. More gunfire resounded over the Academy. He spotted rifles brimming from the windows of the dorm. "Holy shit! We've got survivors."

"Charlie, repeat that?" Dom said.

"Survivors, Dom. They're holing up in Bancroft, firing down into the Skulls."

As quickly as hope had appeared, it began to fade. A pack of Skulls still chased Bravo, but the gunfire had drawn the interest of the main contingent. The creatures began to roil and climb over each other to get at the gunners. They used their claws to scale the building, easily gripping the sculpted flourishes along the great hall.

Miguel lowered the binos and spoke into his mic again. "Chief, those people aren't going to survive long if we don't do something."

—◆◆◆—

Gunfire resounded from across the academy and echoed over the basin. Dom's heart stopped. "Charlie, repeat that?"

"Survivors, Dom. They're holing up in Bancroft, firing down into the Skulls."

Shit. Jenna, Spencer, and Owen looked at him, awaiting orders. They'd come to save these survivors, but now he wasn't sure they could rescue them without sacrificing themselves. Whose lives would he save today? The Hunters or the people hiding in Bancroft?

"Charlie, are the survivors fortified enough that they'll be fine on their own while we regroup?"

"Negative, that's definitely a fucking negative!" Miguel yelled back. "One of the Skulls punched through a window. I think they got him, but it ain't going to be pretty if we don't do *something*, Chief."

"Copy." Dom racked his mind for a solution. Engaging in a suicidal firefight wasn't going to save his Hunters or the survivors. From what his Hunters reported, they wouldn't be able to put up much of a resistance against the monsters out in the open. But if they routed the Skulls somehow… "Charlie, get to the chapel and go with the original plan. On my signal, ring that damn bell and cause as much of a racket as you can."

Shots erupted south of Alpha's position, and Bravo came running. They sprinted along a brick pathway. A small pack of

Skulls followed.

"Alpha, let's move out!" Dom yelled, leading the charge to meet Bravo. The two Hunter teams rendezvoused in the field near the basin. But there wasn't time for hellos. "Fire, fire, fire!"

Dom shouldered his rifle. Each shot kicked his shoulder as he picked his targets. First, a lanky Skull with spikes jutting from its joints. Another Skull with considerable body mass followed, covered more in plates than spikes. Each time Dom fired, bony fragments and flesh sprayed off the beasts. The chatter of gunfire around him continued as the Skulls sprinted across the field. The Hunters mowed them down, and their screams and wails dissipated. Bodies littered the grass, and the smell of spilled blood intermingled with the salty breeze from the bay. The last Skull fell forward and tumbled in a heap of limbs.

"Alpha, Bravo, on me!" Dom held up a fist. The Hunters surrounded him. They scanned the field for signs of more Skulls. Distant cries from the monsters called, and gunfire sounded off in response. Dom concentrated, focusing on the map he'd studied of the Academy.

"We aren't going to take these things outside. It'd be suicide," Dom said, "but Bancroft is attached to McDonough and Luce through enclosed walkways." He pointed at the two buildings. "We're going to get inside, find the survivors, and then get them back to the boats. We'll secure their exit, making sure every fucking person gets out of here and onto Kent Island. Understood?"

"Aye, aye, Captain," the Hunters replied.

"Renee, take point, and let's go!"

Renee ran to the front of the group. They spread out, covering each other while sprinting across the field. They reached Luce Hall, and Dom could plainly see the boards covering and reinforcing the doors along the building's entrance.

"Andris, get a breaching charge ready!" Dom ran up the stairs toward a heavy wooden door with wire-reinforced glass. Plywood boards blocked his view of the inside. He rapped the back of his gloved hand against the door and then cupped his hands over his mouth as he yelled, "If anyone can hear me, stand away from the door. I repeat, stand away from the door."

As he'd expected, he didn't get a response and moved for Andris to place the small explosive. Dom backed away and joined the rest of the Hunters. They pressed themselves flat against the wall in anticipation of the blast.

"Fire in the hole!" Andris dashed away.

A few seconds later, the door exploded inward with a crash of splintering wood and tongues of flame. Dom signaled his team to move. They plunged through the settling dust and over the bits of plywood scattered in the hallway. Renee maintained her point position, and they secured a four-way intersection.

"Charlie," Dom barked into his mic. "Can you tell me what floor you saw the survivors on?"

"Gunshots were coming from the fourth floor, mostly

from the second wing," Miguel replied.

"Copy," Dom replied. The bark of the survivors' weapons and the howls of the Skulls continued. At least the humans were still putting up a fight. The Hunters might yet have a chance at rescuing them. "Are you positioned at the chapel?"

"We are. Want us to start playing 'Hell's Bells'?"

Dom considered it, but he wanted to prolong the distraction as long as possible. Get to the survivors then divert the Skulls' attention while the Hunters brought them to the ships. "Hold off until my orders. Over."

"Copy, Chief."

The Hunters ran down the halls and followed the signs for Bancroft posted on the walls. Their feet pounded against the marble floors. When an ornate, engraved placard announced they'd made it to Bancroft, they took a corner toward a flight of stairs.

The gunfire started to sound closer. It echoed throughout the building.

"We're almost there!" Dom said.

Other sounds started to permeate through the din of the resisting survivors and the chorus of Skulls outside. A high-pitched screaming. This was no cry of pain, though. It was one of fear or hunger, maybe. It was a baby.

"This way!" Renee yelled back to the group and then turned down a hallway. Dom sprinted to catch up and almost ran into her.

She'd stopped, her gun lowered to her side. All along the

hallway, doors cracked open. Scared faces peered out. The cry of the baby sounded from one of those dorms.

"Mama, Mama, the soldiers are here to help!" a young boy said and rushed out. He ran to Renee and Dom. His mother chased after. The boy smiled and tugged on Dom's sleeve.

Dom flashed the child a quick, reassuring smile, but there was no time to waste. "Bravo, start rounding people up. Find out if there are other floors with survivors and get them on those boats!"

"Aye, aye!" Renee responded.

The mother of the young boy grabbed her son and pressed herself flat against the wall to make room for the Hunters.

"Where are the midshipmen? The gunners?" Dom asked her.

The woman pointed further down the hall. "That way."

"Thanks." Dom started to jog between the curious and frightened people now starting to fill the halls. "Alpha, on me. Civilians, out of our way. Move, move!"

Several shell-shocked people still stood frozen in place. Dom shouldered his way through the crowd. He thought these people were practically acting like zombies themselves. They'd lost their homes, maybe the people they loved. And now he was about to tell them they needed to move again, that they needed to make one final run for freedom to escape the monsters banging down their doors.

Dom ran toward another intersection and took a left

toward the sound of gunfire. He tore open a door and barreled through. A young woman in a sweat-stained white t-shirt and jeans spun, surprised, and almost brought her MP5 around to bear on him. A line of men and women around the same age aimed a menagerie of weapons out the windows to fire at the onslaught of Skulls.

"Whoa!" Dom held up a hand and pointed his rifle toward the floor. "We're on your side."

Sweat matted the young woman's dark hair down over her face. She lowered the MP5. "Who are you?"

"Dominic Holland, captain of the *Huntress*, a private covert contracting ship."

"Guns for hire?"

"Something like that. Who's in charge here?"

The young woman laughed hysterically. "Who's in charge? I don't have a damn clue."

"Hunters, take positions and reinforce these men and women," Dom said. "Is no one organizing your defenses?"

"Right now?" the woman looked at him, her blue eyes wide, an almost crazed grin on her face. "I hold rank. Midshipman First Class Rachel Kaufman."

"No officers?"

She shook her head. "Most died when the field house got attacked. Those monsters, those, those…"

"Skulls," Dom offered.

"Sure, we tried to rescue the civilians, shelter them, but they started turning into those Skulls, and then, pardon my bluntness, Captain, but we were fucked."

"Understood," Dom said. "Are there other survivors anywhere else on campus?"

"That's a negative," Kaufman said. "We're it."

The gunfire became almost deafening. Skulls were making it farther up the side of Bancroft before falling under the hail of bullets.

"Round up your men and women," Dom said, "because we're getting out of here. We've secured the basin and plan to ferry everyone out. Can you all handle that?"

"There are no more of these...Skulls...at the basin?"

Dom shook his head. "We took care of 'em. The only ones we've got left on campus are the ones trying to get through the fucking windows."

"Understood." Kaufman turned to her fellow midshipmen. "These people are getting us out of here, so be ready to move!"

A few midshipmen, covered in sweat, dirt, and blood, gave assenting nods. Most still fired at the Skulls. One reloaded, and a Hunter covered for the cadet.

"Bravo, are the survivors ready to go?" Dom asked over the comm link.

"Affirmative," Renee said. "We're good to go when you are."

"Charlie, let's hear that music!"

"Roger," Miguel replied. "Here's a little AC/DC for you!"

The chapel bells began to make a clashing din, ringing across the campus. The disharmonious clang of the bells drowned out the sounds of the Skulls. Many of the creatures began sprinting toward the source of the sound.

Yet those that had already started climbing the wall continued their ascent. One of the midshipmen shot a spray of bullets that knocked a Skull to the grass. Dom estimated a little under a hundred of the beasts still focused on Bancroft and were determined to get to their besieged prey.

"Bravo team, go!" Dom called. "Midshipmen, Alpha, hold your positions!"

The civilians, burdened by children, would move slower than the trained Hunters and midshipmen. Dom wanted them to get on their way while his team held off the Skulls as long as possible.

"We're moving!" Renee called back.

The Skulls reinitiated their attack in earnest, climbing like spiders up the wall of Bancroft. One smaller Skull, barely five feet tall, dodged the incoming rounds. It climbed over the windowsill and lashed out with one clawed hand at a midshipman. The claws connected with the young man and stabbed into his side.

Kaufman whipped her MP5 around and let loose a burst that caught the side of the Skull. But each bullet pinged off the bony armor harmlessly, serving only to knock the creature back a bit. The Skull's mouth tore open, and it let loose a blood-curdling scream. Its bloodshot eyes locked on Kaufman.

Dom aimed at the Skull still holding on to the now-dead midshipman. He squeezed the trigger once, and the Skull's hateful face exploded in a spray of red and white. It fell back out the window, and its bodyweight dragged the midshipman out with it.

"Oh, God," Kaufman said. Her face blanched, and she stared at the spot where the other midshipman used to be. Dom thought for a moment that she was going to freeze. But she shuddered and then turned back to her own post. "Bastards!"

"Bravo, give me your location," Dom said, desperate to fall back.

"We're in McDonough, almost to Luce."

"Copy. Alpha, midshipmen, let's move! Close every fucking door behind you, make it hard for them to follow us!"

The midshipmen hopped up from their positions and filed down the hall toward Dom and Kaufman. The Hunters brought up the rear, guarding the cadets. A sudden crash of glass caught their attention, and a Skull plunged through another window. It barreled toward the group and pounced before anyone could get a clear shot.

Sounds of ripping flesh and spilling blood filled the hall along with the yells and screams of the other midshipman. Dom kicked the Skull off a fallen cadet and smashed its face with the heel of his boot. "Move, move, move!"

More broken glass clattered against the floor as Skulls poured into the hallway. The click of their claws on the floor chased after the Hunters. Dom fired a spray of bullets into the mass of creatures. "Jenna, take point, lead them out. The rest of you, stay back with me and cover the midshipmen."

Their volleys brought down the monsters leading the

pack. Skeletal bodies crumpled, blood pouring out of gunshot wounds. Frenzied by the hunt, more climbed over the dead ones.

Dom slammed a door shut behind them when they rounded another corner. The Skulls threw themselves at the obstacle until it burst from its frame. One broke its arm in the attempt, yet the injured limb did nothing to distract it from its singular mission to kill and devour.

"Reloading!" Dom called. Jenna and Owen laid down covering fire. Three more Skulls went down, and their bodies were quickly trampled by their brethren.

A bellow echoed down the hall, louder than the others, louder than the gunfire. The floor shook. A Skull, its muscles swollen and bulging, towered above the rest. It threw the normal-sized creatures out of its way like a child tossing aside dolls. The smaller beasts splattered against the walls as the giant Skull rushed toward Dom. Somehow, it was even bigger than the mutated monster he'd fought aboard the *Queen of the Bay*.

"A Goliath!" he called. "Go, go, go!"

"Goliath?" Jenna asked, turned around, and then caught sight of the gargantuan abomination. "Holy shit!"

Dom sprayed gunfire into the creature's chest, its neck, and its face. Nothing perturbed it. The creature's cheekbones jutted out. Overgrown fangs stuck out from beneath its lips. Even its nose was shielded by a cage of bone. Squeezing the trigger again, Dom hoped to see a bullet pierce one of the giant's beady eyes, the only weak spot he could catch in his sights.

The beast continued onward, the skeletal plates on its shoulder blades scraping against the walls and ceiling. Dom unclipped a grenade from his vest. Not a choice he liked to make in an enclosed space like this. But the Goliath gave him few options.

Dom caught sight of a small sign saying they'd made it to McDonough. They were almost there, almost out. He couldn't let this creature stop them.

He lobbed the grenade when the midshipmen and his rescue party turned another corner. "Frag out!"

The grenade hit the Skull on its chest. The beast paid about as much attention to it as a charging rhino does to a pebble thrown at its thick hide. The grenade exploded, a flash of light and heat overwhelming Dom. The blast sent him sprawling, his ears ringing and pain lancing up his side. He scrambled to his feet, reaching to recover his rifle.

Behind him, the roof caved in. Dust, pipes, and tiles fell across the body of the Goliath. The only benefit of the enormous Skull was its ability to block the hallway.

Dom exhaled slowly then continued jogging after the Hunters guarding the midshipmen's rear. The frustrated cries of the Skulls could be heard behind the wall of broken cinder blocks and fallen rafters. They weren't going to get through.

The rubble shook. Debris shifted as the body of the Goliath moved. Not just moved—stood up. The gargantuan monster was covered in gray dust. Its chest, caved in and mangled, wept blood. Several ribs were busted and torn outward, pointing at Dom. The Goliath's head snapped back, and it let out another fearsome bellow.

It began to charge.

TWENTY-EIGHT

L AUREN WATCHED PETER make the first incision in Kara's abdomen. Sean and Divya waited in the OR, patiently making themselves available in case things took a turn for the worse.

A million worries burned through Lauren as she watched the scalpel cut into the bruised flesh. In her mind's eye, she saw Dom landing in Annapolis and then ushering the survivors onto boats in which they would sail off to Kent. A surge of guilt flooded her. Dom had left Kara in her team's hands twice already while he risked his life fighting Skulls. Now it looked like she might have failed in her duty to protect the captain's daughter.

Dom would never forgive her if Kara died on her watch.

"Be ready with the hemostat," Peter said, his voice measured and calm. He cut into a small space beneath Kara's ribcage.

"Got it," Lauren said. She might've been the lead on the medical team, but Peter's specialty was surgery. She had no problem letting him take charge when the stakes were as high as they were now.

"Through the peritoneum now," Peter said. The scalpel

sliced the thin membrane. "Divya, clean it up for me."

Divya took a plastic hose used to suction the excess blood and inserted it where Peter pointed. The blood drained, but more pooled in its place.

"You were right," Peter said, pointing to another small, purplish organ. "She's got renal hemorrhaging." He indicated another vessel. "Internal bleeding. Hemostat."

Lauren clipped the hemostat in place. She'd recognized the shadows she'd seen on the ultrasound. And given the location, she'd guessed it was a combination of kidney damage and internal bleeding caused by the chelation therapy to combat the Oni Agent in Kara's body. She couldn't shake the fact that she'd been the one to develop the therapy. She'd even argued with Peter and Sean that the side effects of the therapy were definitely no worse than letting someone suffer from the Oni Agent. But now Kara was bleeding out, and it was all Lauren's fault.

She desperately wanted to fix her mistake, but it was up to Peter now. His fingers worked, delicately suturing a torn vessel. "Suction."

Divya responded by placing the suction tube back into Kara's abdominal cavity. This time it took longer for the blood to fill the volume. The bleeding was slowing.

"Hemostatic gel," Peter said.

Sean tore open the sterile packaging. He handed the open packet to Peter. The surgeon sprinkled the small, clear particles from within it over the ruptured vessels and kidney. Blood around these particles immediately coagulated in response to the chemical factors within the gel.

"Suction."

Again, Divya removed the blood. Far less flowed in. Peter probed the site of Kara's internal injuries with a laparoscope. He exhaled slowly behind his surgical mask. "I think we got it."

Lauren watched Kara's blood pressure rise to a normal level. The EKG reported her pulse had returned to an acceptable rhythm. Peter began to stitch the wound with precise, small loops. When he finished, he laid his tools on a surgical tray and caught Lauren's eye.

She waited for him to say, *I told you so. I told you the therapy was dangerous.*

Instead, the expression in his eyes turned warm. "I think she's going to be fine. We caught the bleed in time."

"Right," Lauren said. "We'll need to watch if there's any permanent renal damage."

"Definitely, but with your quick thinking, we identified the problem soon enough that I think her kidneys are going to be okay."

Lauren nodded. All at once the physical and emotional toll of the past few days seemed to catch up to her as Divya and Sean wheeled Kara out of the OR and back to the patient room. Lauren followed Peter out of the OR, and they removed their masks and gloves.

Peter looked hard at her while he washed his hands. "You think you're responsible for what just happened, don't you?"

"Of course," Lauren replied. "It was my therapy. You

warned us about the side effects, and Kara proved you right."

"I know what I said, but you were the one that was right. If we wasted our time and never tried the chelation treatment, Glenn would be a Skull right now. Divya would be a Skull right now. Kara would be a Skull." Peter started to dry off his hands. "Lauren, you were right. We didn't lose Kara, and we *won't* lose her. And it's because of your work. It's because you convinced me."

Lauren stood, silent for a moment, and then "Thanks, Peter. I appreciate it."

"You got it, boss."

Lauren shook her head. She peeked into the patient room to see Divya holding back Maggie as Sean told Sadie that her sister would be okay. She knew her presence wasn't needed there, so she went to see a former patient she'd neglected over the past few days.

She made her way to the crew quarters. She should have been checking with Chao to see their progress in identifying viable neuro research labs. But she also needed to take care of herself; she needed a breather, a respite from the demands of helping save the world.

The door she was looking for was ajar. She knocked on the frame and nudged the door open.

Sitting on his bed, Glenn looked at her from behind a thick textbook. His lips cracked in a wide smile. "Howdy, Doc." His grin evaporated. "You look like you've come to deliver bad news. Got something to tell me?"

"No, you're doing fine." Lauren sat at the foot of his bed.

"I'm betting you'll be fully recovered from the chelation treatment and good to go on your next mission."

"And is that what the glum face is about?" He swung his legs over the side of the bed and sidled up next to her with the textbook in his lap.

"Not exactly." Lauren brushed a hand through her hair before catching sight of the book. "Molecular bio? Where did you get that, and why are you reading it?"

Lauren thought she detected the former Green Beret's dark skin turn a hushed shade of red. He was always full of surprises, always thirsting to learn something new. It was one of the reasons she admired him—why she'd always enjoyed his company.

"The book's from the medical library," Glenn said.

"Didn't realize you had joined my team."

Glenn grinned again. "Lauren, you know I've always been on your team."

"Too much, Glenn, too much." Lauren patted his knee. It was corny, but she admitted she liked hearing him say it. She left her hand on his knee. "But what are you really doing with it?"

"I wasn't sure how long I'd be out of commission as a Hunter. I wanted to make myself useful, so I was trying to see if I could learn anything to help you out in the lab. Maybe I could just wash petri dishes." He put his hand on hers. "If there's anything I can do, I want to be there for you."

Lauren knew she should pull away. After all, they'd agreed not to pursue a relationship. They worked in too close of quarters on the *Huntress*. Neither wanted their mutual feelings to get in the way of their professional duties.

But did any of that matter? Skulls roaming landside, governments falling, science turned upside down. Screw convention and professionalism. Tomorrow was no longer a guarantee. All they had, all that was certain in their lives, was this moment. This *now*.

She didn't say a word to Glenn but leaned in close, pressing against him and laying her head on his thick shoulder. He wrapped an arm around her.

"Lauren…" he started.

She didn't let him finish. Instead, her lips met his. She pushed the hulking man back into his bed and kicked his door shut in one motion. He pulled one hand through her hair, something he knew she loved, something he clearly hadn't forgotten.

A brief worry flashed through Lauren's mind. Maybe they should go slowly. Maybe they should let the dying embers of their previous relationship ease back into the flames they once were.

But as her flesh pressed against his, as their tongues met and she traced one hand over the muscles bulging across his chest and abdomen, she knew their feelings for each other had never died. They still burned for each other, and there was nothing she could do to stop it.

She slipped her shirt over her head and then pulled his off. He tossed aside their clothes. With Glenn, she could let herself relax into the warmth and passion they shared. It was a release she needed more than she could ever imagine. Each passing second gave her a break from the grim realities that would face her once she left his bed.

His hand traced down her back, pulling her closer, reminding her to leave her thoughts behind, to give in to the moment and let the world outside slip away.

TWENTY-NINE

———◦◦◦———

NAVID SQUEEZED ABBY'S HAND and then brushed away the tear rolling down her cheek. He glanced at the scratches on her wrist again. "You'll be okay. It's small, and we'll find help, all right?"

She bobbed her head. He could see she wanted to believe him, but her expressive blue eyes told him she wasn't hopeful.

"Come on, kids," James said, peeking back out into the conference room. "We don't have all goddamn day."

The door and the makeshift barricade shook. The crazies' growls sounded just as loud as when Navid and Abby had first sought refuge here.

"We're coming." Navid stood and held out his hand to help Abby. She took it, hoisted herself up, and wrapped one arm around his shoulder. "We're going to be fine. Just got to make it until help gets here."

Again, she nodded, her long blond locks bouncing on her shoulders. She hobbled forward; her sprained ankle clearly still bothered her.

"If I do turn," she whispered, "promise you won't kill me, okay?"

Navid pulled her into a hug. "Never, never, never." He

pulled her against his chest and brushed the back of her head.

The voices of Sandra, James, and Geraldo from the office were growing louder and more anxious.

"Let's get out of here," Navid said.

As they made their way to the office, he spotted the first aid kit that they'd used earlier to find pain medication. An idea struck him, and he tore through its contents. He poured the gauze and pills and bandages out until he found the antibiotic spray. *Maybe...*

He took Abby's wrist and sprayed the antibiotics over the wound. The spray hit the scratches, and she winced.

"Just in case," he said. "Want to make sure the scratches are clean, right?"

"Right."

Navid slipped the spray into his pocket, and they entered the office. Geraldo and James were moving a heavy desk from the door leading to the hallway. Sandra moved a few boxes full of books. The smell of ripe meat and copper hit Navid, and he almost gagged.

In the corner, a curtain had been torn off one of the windows and placed over something. It wasn't until Navid saw the speckles of blood on the wall that he realized exactly what was causing the smell. It was Kaitlyn, the woman the other three had talked about—the one who had gone crazy. He resisted the strange urge to peel back the curtain and make sure she was actually dead.

"Come on, kid," James said. "Help us out here."

"Sorry," Navid said. He helped Abby into a chair so she

could rest her ankle. "What do you need me to do?"

"Get this shit away from the door so we can make an escape if we have to," James said. "And if we're running for it, you can help your little girlfriend. We aren't slowing down because she's hurt."

Geraldo frowned. "Speak for yourself, James. We ain't leaving anyone behind."

"Christ," Sandra said. "Let's just get this done and talk about our next plan."

They heaved the office furniture out of the way. With no air conditioning, the small room quickly grew humid and hot, adding to the putrid odor of death hanging in the air. Navid was almost ready to leave with Abby due to the oppressive smell and temperature alone. Certainly, without water, they wouldn't last much longer anyway.

"We need to get the hell out of here," James said.

Sandra rolled her eyes. "That much is obvious. You got a way to do that without getting devoured by those things?"

James huffed and folded his arms across his chest but said nothing else.

"I got an idea." Geraldo picked up his pipe, the only weapon among the group. "We run upstairs. Head to the roof. There's a heavy steel door up there. Hard to tear down."

"How the hell do you know that?" James asked.

Geraldo's face flushed red. "During the day, I need a smoke break."

"And you're too good to join all the nurses with their cigarettes out by the dumpsters?"

"No, it's just that…I'm not smoking cigarettes."

"Christ!" James said.

"Come on," Sandra said. "Focus, focus."

"I think Geraldo has a point," Navid said.

"And what do we do on the roof? Jump off? End it all on our own terms?" James looked incredulous.

"No," Navid said. "We call for help. Like, make an SOS sign or something."

"Bull—"

Geraldo cut him off with a stern look. "Boy's right. They were doing work on the sixteenth floor. Painting some new offices. We grab a can, bring it to the roof, and then we paint our SOS."

Sandra sighed and leaned against the wall. "That's a nice thought, but what if no one sees it? You're banking on a flyover or someone paying attention to some satellite imagery or something. That's a big gamble. What do we do if no one shows up to rescue us?"

Geraldo shrugged and then looked at James. "I guess if you really want to jump, you can jump."

"Great, this is just great." James started to pace.

Navid rubbed Abby's hand. He let his mind wander back toward a Friday two weeks past when she'd suggested they take a weekend trip together. She'd said they needed it. They'd been working too hard in the labs, spending too much time on their research and not enough time together. She'd even pulled together a list of places in Vermont they could visit. Bed-and-breakfasts, lodges near pristine hiking trails. Just a quick escape, she'd promised. Work can wait.

But he'd been stubborn, adamant that work was what was important right now. After they graduated, after they got a post-doc or industry job and did that for a bit, then they could afford to spend time and money on weekend trips.

Now he realized how foolish he'd been. He kissed her cheek. "I'm sorry. You were right."

She shot him a puzzled look.

"We should be in Vermont right now. Hiding out in a cabin together, far away from this madness."

Her lips trembled before she spoke. "Maybe next weekend. Promise me, when this blows over, we'll do that?"

"We'll go all over the US. I've never been to Portland. Maybe we'll go there. And then after that, Seattle." He could feel a wet sheen form over his eyes. "The Redwoods in California. Always wanted to see them. South Dakota, the Needle Mountains. Heard pretty things about the Black Hills, too. We're going somewhere every weekend, Abby. I promise."

She interlaced her fingers in his. Her touch was cold, clammy. "I can't wait."

"Time's ticking away," James said. "If you don't give us something to work with, you won't see any of those places. We're all going to starve to death in here."

Geraldo and Sandra lifted their shoulders noncommittally. The banging against the conference room door persisted, and Navid shut the office door to muffle the noise. An idea came to him.

"Okay, I've got something. The only way back to the stairs is straight down the hallway."

"Right," Geraldo said.

"And if we go out there now, those crazies will come after us," Navid continued. "So, I need you all to hear me out for a second. Let's get them into the conference room. While they're all in there, we escape through this door." He pointed to the office door.

"Just how do you propose we get all those monsters into the conference room?" James asked.

"They want *us*," Navid said, "so let's give them what they want."

THIRTY

D OM RAN WHILE FIRING at the Goliath's chest. Rounds punched into bulging muscle where the grenade had shattered its skeletal body armor. But that only slowed the beast down, jerking it from side to side, its flesh absorbing the rounds. Wailing in a voice that assaulted Dom's ears, the monster continued its charge.

Several swifter Skulls dodged under the lumbering beast and ran toward Dom, the Hunters, and the midshipmen. One of these Skulls leapt, and Dom hammered the stock of his rifle into its face. The creature fell, and the Goliath trampled it. The small Skull's body crunched under its heavy footsteps.

The Hunters and Dom brought down the other Skulls, but the barrage of bullets did nothing to sway the Goliath. It forced its way forward. Its spikes and blades tore into the ceiling and knocked down paintings as it went. Dom watched the beast tear off a placard announcing they'd entered Luce Hall. They were almost out of the dorm complex and into the field near the basin.

"Bravo, what's the status on the boats?" Dom said, gasping.

He could barely hear Renee's reply over the behemoth's

bellows. "Alpha, we're loading people as fast as we can. Got about half of the survivors on boats, but only four boats to sea."

"Faster!" Dom said between breaths. "Got to go faster!"

He twisted and fired another salvo at the Goliath. The monster flinched, turning its head away. For a second, he thought he'd gotten a shot through the thing's eye and ended it. The glimmer of hope that he'd delivered a fatal blow dissipated as it hurtled forward and let out a guttural roar. One of its bent ribs caught on a doorway and snapped off, tearing with it a chunk of flesh.

The midshipmen ahead spilled out of Luce and ran toward the field. A brief image flashed through his mind of the slaughter that would unfold if Dom led the Goliath and the pack of Skulls directly to the survivors.

"Bravo, keep loading. Alpha, on me!"

The Hunters obeyed, turning away from the midshipmen exiting the building, and stayed on Dom. They just needed to buy Bravo time. They didn't have to kill the Goliath, just—

The Goliath swiped at a squawking smaller Skull. He grabbed it by the back of its neck and tossed it.

The rattle of bones whistled over Dom's head as he ducked, and the creature smashed against the wall with a crunch. Dom raised his rifle and fired a short burst at the Goliath.

"Come and get it, you fuck!" Dom shouted.

The beast roared, staring in his direction. Dom shut the exit door the midshipmen had run out of.

Jenna shouldered her rifle and fired at the mammoth creature, but her shots were no more effective than Dom's. Owen and Spencer let loose a salvo to the same effect. The rounds chipped away at its armor, but what they needed was a solid eyeshot that would hit soft tissue and, with luck, the brain.

"Head up the stairs!" Dom pointed to a stairwell.

The Hunters sprinted, and Dom fired another blast to ensure he had the Goliath's full attention. The monster ran past the closed exit door, hot on Dom's trail. He hoped the normal-sized Skulls would follow and not stray out that door and straight into Bravo and the survivors. But with the Goliath's bellows and its bulky frame blocking the view, Dom couldn't see whether or not his plan was working.

The Hunters hit the stairs and started taking the steps two, then three at a time. Dom ran after with the Goliath following. The beast made it to the bottom of the stairs. Its hulking frame and the horns and hooks jutting out of its body got it stuck on the support beams surrounding the entrance to the stairwell. Smaller, swifter Skulls leapt and climbed around the banisters.

The Hunters opened up on the gaining Skulls. Round casings pinged off the stairs. Gore sprayed against the walls, and the creatures' howls echoed in the space. All the while the Goliath struggled, caught in place by its own bulk.

"Keep moving!" Dom yelled. He pulled the pin on another grenade and lobbed it. "Frag out!"

He and the Hunters made it up another flight. Fire and

fragments of Skulls and marble flew through the air. The scent of explosives and charred flesh wafted up. Yet more of the creatures leapt and pounded up the destroyed stairs. At least half a dozen Skulls were gaining on the Hunters when they reached the fourth floor.

A Skull with patches of short-cropped hair and bumpy horns along its scalp pounced at Dom. He juked, and the Skull hit the floor hard. Dom took advantage of the creature's momentary confusion and smashed the stock of his rifle into the back of its head with a sickening crack. He jumped past the injured beast.

"Where the fuck are we going?" Jenna called.

"Keep running!" Dom had no concrete plan. He only knew he couldn't lead the Skulls to the survivors and Bravo. "*Huntress*, do you copy?"

"Copy, Alpha," Chao responded. "The fuck is going on?"

"No time to explain." Dom pointed down the hall and directed the Hunters to take a left at the intersection.

A roar sounded behind them. The Goliath had somehow freed itself and made it to the top of the stairs. But this hall was narrower than the ground floor. Progress for the huge creature became more difficult as it struggled to free the hulking shoulder blades and spikes from the walls and ceiling where they kept getting stuck. It roared in frustration, and its plight gave the Hunters a precious few extra seconds.

"How the hell do we get to the roof?" Dom asked Chao. "We're in Luce Hall now."

"Oh, God," Chao said. "Give me a minute to find the

architect—"

"We don't have a fucking minute!"

"Working on it!"

"Oh shit!" Spencer yelled. He skidded to a halt, and Dom, Jenna, and Owen stopped beside him. "Contacts dead ahead!"

Ahead of them, a dozen Skulls charged. Several wore the white, short-sleeved, button-down shirts characteristic of the Academy's midshipmen uniforms. Those shirts were now covered in dried blood and ripped where the creatures' sharp growths poked through the fabric. Dom and the Hunters let loose a barrage of gunfire. Bullets ricocheted off the walls, and the sound of barking rifles became deafening. Blood poured from the first several Skulls knocked back, their bodies a tangled mess.

Yet more creatures surged up the stairs on the opposite end of the hall to replace those that had fallen. Their claws clacked along the floor and their bones rattled. Dom's pulse pounded in his ears, his heart hammered against his ribcage, and adrenaline poured through him.

In front of them, Skulls ran at the hail of gunfire. Behind them, the Goliath tore through the building, drawing ever closer, its angry bellows and footsteps resonating. The Hunters were surrounded by the beasts with nowhere to go and no way to possibly fight them all off.

Dom had tried to save the survivors and Bravo, but now he might have led Alpha to their end.

But he wouldn't give up. No matter what, he was

determined to save his team.

"Grenades out!" Dom yelled.

Jenna, Spencer, and Owen tossed their grenades into the oncoming Skulls, both in front and behind. Dom shouldered through a door, and his team followed. Explosions rumbled through the hall. Dom's ears rang with an unholy pain at the deafening din. He slammed the door shut and found himself in some kind of shared office space.

He knew his Hunters would have been similarly deafened, so he grabbed each of their shoulders, one at a time, and signaled for them to barricade the door with the heavy oak desks and bookcases lining the room. They worked quickly to build the extra layer of protection. Dom had no doubt the Goliath had survived their last round of grenade blasts and knew the feeble defenses wouldn't last once the enormous Skull made it to the doorway. If they were lucky, it would buy them enough time for Chao to tell them how to get out of there.

The ringing in Dom's ears began to subside, and he heard a voice calling for him. "Alpha, do you read? Dom, are you there? Come on, guys!"

"Copy, Chao. Alpha here," Dom replied. His voice still sounded muddled to his recovering hearing.

"I recovered the blueprints. There's roof access from the service elevator shaft. Elevator doesn't go all the way up, but there's a ladder that does."

"Great, where is it?"

"Hold on."

The door and barricade shook as the Skulls slammed against it. Glass shattered when they broke through the thin, wire-reinforced window in the door. Their spindly arms stuck through, and claws raked the furniture set up to keep them out. Jenna, Owen, and Spencer aimed their rifles at the blockade. Dom saw the sweat trickling across their skin and the worried expressions on their faces.

"Elevator's near the south stairwell," Chao said.

"Shit. Copy." Back where they'd come from. Straight past the Goliath and the horde of Skulls in its wake. "Any other ways to the roof?"

A sharp crack sounded. The wood of the doorframe split and bowed inward.

"Negative," Chao said.

"Sure?"

"Affirmative. Don't see any other way."

"Charlie, this is Alpha," Dom said into his throat mic.

"Copy, Chief," Miguel said.

"I need you above Luce Hall. We need a quick exit."

"Roger that. Ride's on its way."

One of the bookcases toppled sideways, and the desks shook.

"What now?" Jenna asked.

Dom searched the office space as if it held the answer to her question. He spotted the windows on the far side. He sprinted to one and smashed through it with the stock of his rifle. Craning his neck out, he scanned the wall. But only the lips of the neighboring window ledges stuck out. There was no easy way to scale the exterior to the roof—and the only way down was a fall.

Maybe there was something they could use as a makeshift grappling hook and cable. He took one quick glance around the room before realizing the next best escape.

"Up!" Dom called. He stepped onto one of the desks, still shuddering as the Skulls roiled to get in. He could smell them, the distinct fermentation stink of the nanobacteria chewing through their flesh and remodeling their bones, like a bad batch of home-brewed beer spiced with sediment from a landfill.

Dom ignored the odor assaulting his nostrils. He reached up and slid a ceiling tile to the side. "Get up!"

Jenna hopped on the desk first. Dom cupped his hands under one of her feet and boosted her up.

"Plenty of solid support beams up here!" she said.

Jenna reached from the ceiling to guide Spencer up next, followed by Owen. Dom strapped his rifle over his back, and the three other Hunters helped hoist him into the space. He replaced the ceiling tile and then pulled out a flashlight to pierce the darkness. The Hunters crouched, their helmets brushing against the rafters. Below, the Skulls' cries and their banging against the door grew louder.

"That way!" Dom shone the flashlight toward the other end of the cramped space. It illuminated floating dust motes and a lattice of support beams and crossbeams, punctuated by pipes and ventilation shafts. "Quiet as we can."

Jenna, Owen, and Spencer clicked on their flashlights. An

enormous crash sounded from below. The splintering of wood and the din of falling bookcases rattled through the ceiling. There was no turning back now.

They made their way slowly toward the far end of the crawlspace. Dom took measured, crouched steps, ensuring his boots fell only on solid footing. He tried to control his heavy breathing while fighting to catch his breath from their flight. Any mistake now could attract the Skulls.

The team made their way forward. Cobwebs stuck to Dom's face. He tried to ignore the mass of writhing creatures separated from him by only a few flimsy ceiling tiles. But it wasn't an easy task. The wails of the monsters continued.

Jenna climbed through a V-shaped lattice, carefully guiding herself on the solid support beams. She helped Owen and Spencer over, and Dom followed last. He wiped a bead of sweat from his face and pointed his flashlight toward a metal panel a few yards from their position. It appeared to be in the right location leading to the service elevator.

The Hunters nodded to acknowledge Dom's direction, and they started along the rafters again. Something slammed against the wall below them. The impact sent dust falling from rafters. Owen lost his footing, and one boot slipped off a support beam. He flailed his arms and tried to grab a rafter. Jenna leaned forward, one hand outstretched to steady him, and Spencer reached to help. Jenna managed to grab Owen before he fell.

But Spencer lost his grip on his rifle. The weapon smacked into the ceiling tile. Dom's heart leapt into his throat as he watched, waiting to see the gun break through the flimsy tile. It held, but the Hunters all froze. Dom didn't notice any changes in the growls and shrieks of the Skulls below to make him think that they'd heard the gun drop.

Clamminess coated the insides of his gloves as he pulled his rifle up. Spencer tentatively reached out to retrieve his dropped gun. A massive fist tore through the tile and wrapped its claws around the weapon. The Goliath's hand drew back, and pieces of the ceiling tile fell away.

A swathe of Skulls tensed below. Their bloodshot eyes all gazed toward the fresh opening, and their muscles coiled. The Goliath's deep voice thundered, and the Skulls frenzied, jumping and climbing for the hole in the ceiling.

"Go, go, go!" Dom yelled.

The Hunters moved as fast as they could toward the service elevator. A rumbling growl from below preceded another upward punch from the Goliath. This time its claws snagged on Spencer's fatigues. The Hunter started to fall backward, but Dom grabbed him. Jenna took out a knife and cut the fabric around where the Goliath's claws had pierced Spencer's jacket. The fist pulled away with nothing but the scrap of fabric in its grip.

Dom let the Hunter move past him and breathed a sigh of relief when he saw the white shirt Spencer wore beneath his fatigues was free of blood. The Goliath hadn't injured him. And now the Hunters were only a yard away from the metal panel, close to the shaft, close to the roof and freedom.

Dom's relief was short-lived when the gigantic claw burst

through the ceiling again. This time the serrated talons were true to their mark. Owen screamed out in agony. The skeletal appendages tore through his leg. The Goliath's other hand eviscerated Owen, and a cloud of blood sprayed in the air. Dom fired blindly, desperate to hit the Goliath. Each bullet punctured the tiles. A few Skulls screamed in defeat, but Dom knew it was hopeless.

The Goliath drew back its arms, pulling Owen through the ceiling and tearing a larger hole between the rafters.

"No!" Dom yelled. The other two Hunters joined in the desperate barrage of gunfire to take down the huge monster and its cohort anxiously jumping for the fresh prey. Blood poured from Owen's mouth, his screams coming out in gargles. The Goliath tore him in half and threw the pieces into the crowd of Skulls. The monsters shoved each other to get at Owen's remains. There would be no way for Dom to ensure every Hunter, dead or alive, made it back to the *Huntress* now.

"Let's go!" Dom said. He grabbed Spencer's shoulder to get the shocked Hunter moving.

Jenna was already climbing toward the metal panel again. As she reached to open it, a Skull burst through the ceiling. It reared back, its teeth chattering and the bony plates on its back scraping together as it prepared to attack.

Dom wouldn't let the creatures stop them. Not now. Not when they were so close to escape. He shouldered his rifle, and the creature pounced. Without time to aim, Dom let loose a spray of gunfire.

THIRTY-ONE

---◦◦◦---

L AUREN BROKE INTO A JOG when she heard the commotion from the electronics workshop. Adam had paged that she was needed immediately, and she'd been lying naked with Glenn in his quarters instead. Something was going on, and she'd done exactly what she'd tried to avoid—let a personal relationship get in the way of duty. She threw open the door to see Thomas next to Adam, standing in front of his comm station. The serious expressions on their faces contrasted sharply with the figurines from *Watchmen* that Adam had set on the desk.

At another station, Samantha and Chao were intently staring at a screen displaying a live stream from Dom's mission. The two specialists didn't even look up to greet Lauren, and she didn't blame them as she made her way to Thomas and Adam.

Thomas had a handset pressed to his ear. "You've got to be kidding me." The wrinkles along his forehead became even sharper when he scowled. "Kinsey isn't even leaving you with a goddamn Black Hawk?"

His cheeks were flushed red, and Lauren guessed he was talking to Shepherd about the latest developments at Fort

Detrick. She stood behind him with her arms crossed. Adam handed her a handset so she could listen.

"There's nothing I can do," Shepherd said. "I wish I could spare a truck or something to help Captain Holland, but it's impossible. I'm already risking my people's lives by staying here. Detrick's going to be vastly understaffed and unsecure."

"Christ." Thomas slammed a fist on the comm console. A computer monitor shook, and Adam had to steady it. "If there's nothing you can do, I'm out." He threw the handset down.

"Lauren." Adam adjusted his glasses. "Shepherd's still on the line, and he said his team found something you might be interested in."

Lauren put a hand over the mouthpiece of the handset. "What the hell's going on?"

"Dom's team is up shit creek, and we can't get any reinforcements from Detrick." Thomas said, pulling a cigar from his pocket. "Don't waste too much time on Shepherd, because I have no doubt we're going to be keeping your medical team busy once we rendezvous with Alpha, Bravo, and Charlie."

"Understood."

Thomas stomped away.

Lauren held the handset up again. "Commander Shepherd, this is Dr. Lauren Winters speaking. You have news for us?"

"I do. I'm not sure if it's of any immediate use, but my team sequenced the prion component of the Oni Agent. We can send you our data on its primary structure."

"Yes, yes." Lauren already began running through ideas in her mind. If they knew the primary structure—all the amino acids, the building blocks, making up the prion—they might have a better chance at identifying small molecules or existing drugs that would interact with it. She'd have Sean and Divya start the molecular simulations as soon as possible. "Anything else?"

"No, I'm afraid that's all we've got right now." He paused. "I'm honestly not sure how long Kinsey is going to let us stick it out at Detrick. Sounds like the Skulls are threatening to overwhelm DC *and* Fort Bragg already. I don't know how we've survived out here this long."

"But if we lose Detrick, we lose access to the research and production facilities that are going to be crucial to manufacturing any cure or vaccine."

"Right," Shepherd said. "You and I both know that. Captain Holland knows it, too, I think. We've got a whole host of classified files and encrypted data. And we may not get time to delve into it. So as a safety measure, I've opened a remote data transfer with your comm specialists."

Adam's head bobbed, his thick-framed glasses bouncing on his nose to confirm what Shepherd was saying. This didn't just sound like a safety measure to Lauren; it sounded like the desperate final actions of a man standing before the inevitable fall of Detrick.

"Your people can try digging up whatever might be of use," Shepherd continued. "We don't have many of our good cyber people left, unfortunately, so you all might uncover something we haven't. Maybe it'll lead you to whoever started this outbreak. At the very least, I just hope your researchers can find something useful."

"Understood," Lauren said. "Our team will do their best." Adam gave her a thumbs up. "And I'll make sure we continue the research, no matter what. You all need to stay strong."

Shepherd laughed. It sounded forced and hollow. "Lab techs and scientists don't make good soldiers, and that's almost all Kinsey is leaving us with."

Lauren soaked in those words for a moment. She thought of the people that had been sheltered at the base. Dom's neighbors, the kid Dom rescued, and the young couple Meredith found on the Appalachian Trail. "What about all the civilians? Did Kinsey escort them out?"

"Afraid not. They're stuck with us."

"Good God." Lauren couldn't imagine how Shepherd was holding the base together. It made Dom's mission to establish a safe zone on Kent Island even more urgent. There needed to be somewhere for all these people to go. "Is there anything we can do?"

For a moment, the line was silent. Lauren realized they both knew her question was nothing more than a kind gesture. There was nothing she could really do now, and Dom and the Hunters were preoccupied at the Naval Academy.

"Just stay alive, Dr. Winters. That's all you can do. That's all *we* can hope to do."

They ended the call, and Lauren joined Thomas. His eyes were now glued to the screen showing the live action streaming from Dom's helmet-mounted camera. Chao and Samantha each waited in silence, their hands hovering over the keyboards, ready to do whatever they could to support the Hunter teams.

Lauren gasped when Dom and the team ran into the office space for shelter. She couldn't see how they'd get themselves out of this mess, especially with no incoming help from the Army.

Creases formed across Chao's brow. It appeared he was listening intently to an incoming transmission. He pulled up a set of blueprints and zoomed in on a section of the building called Luce Hall.

"Elevator's near the south stairwell," he said.

Another beat as Dom's mounted cam swung around to view the shaking makeshift barricade he and the Hunters had constructed.

"Negative," Chao said.

A shorter pause.

"Affirmative. Don't see any other way."

Samantha's face was whiter than normal. Lauren looked to her for an explanation. "They're trapped. Going to the roof for a rescue."

Lauren nodded and watched in rapt attention as the scene unfolded on the screen. The Hunters climbing into the ceiling. Spencer dropping his gun. Massive claws plunging through the ceiling. Owen…torn in half.

A skilled medical professional, Lauren thought she was prepared for the worst. But nothing could have prepared her for Owen's grisly death. She turned from the screen, her hand over her mouth, and shuddered. Chao gasped. Samantha cursed. Thomas threw down his cigar, and Adam clenched his eyes closed.

None of them were ready for what Dom was seeing firsthand.

Lauren shook herself. "I need to prep the medical team!" She ran from the room, hearing more gasps from the others. But she didn't have time to figure out what they'd seen now. She only knew she couldn't be distracted anymore.

Shepherd had given her a tremendous gift by providing the prion sequencing results, but she didn't have time for research or science. In her mind's eye, she watched Owen ripped to shreds by that humongous Skull once more. There was nothing her team could do for him, but she anticipated— she prayed—the others would be returning. And she needed to be ready to help when they did.

THIRTY-TWO

———⟡———

N AVID INHALED SHARPLY, afraid of what he was about to propose to the group. "We have to find some way to distract those bastards out there."

"That's pretty damn obvious," James said.

Sandra ignored him. "Go on, Navid. You have an idea?"

He squeezed Abby's hand. "One of us gets the crazies' attention and draws them into the conference room while everyone else runs out the office for the stairs."

James laughed, resting his arms over his potbelly. "Kid, you're as crazy as them."

"Nah, I think he's got a point," Geraldo said.

"I'm not going to distract those freaks," James said.

Sandra shot him an angry look.

"Look, one of us just needs to open that door and get them to file into the conference room," Navid said. "Then that person can run to the office, shut this door, and follow the others out to the stairs."

"The zombies seem stupid enough to fall for it," Sandra said. "It might work."

"Might work?" Geraldo asked. "Guess we don't have much of a choice. They're going to tear that other door down eventually anyway."

Sweat dripped down Abby's forehead, and her face appeared whiter than before. Navid hoped the others still thought the symptoms were from the pain in her ankle injury. He hoped that was what the symptoms were from. But each time he tried to convince her she was going to be okay, he couldn't shake the image of the tiny scratches on her wrist.

They didn't have much time. If Abby stood any chance of getting out alive, they needed to move fast. Maybe someone out there knew how to treat the crazy virus or whatever it was. Either way, Navid knew he was doing Abby no favors by waiting it out in this office.

"I'll do it," he said. "I'll distract them."

"Confirmed. You *are* one of those crazies," James said. "But that's fucking fine by me." He pointed at Abby. Navid's blood ran cold. Maybe James knew what was going through Navid's mind. "I'm not helping her, though."

Navid almost breathed a sigh of relief. But he realized if he was the one to distract the crazies and stood any chance of escape, he couldn't be Abby's crutch.

"I'll do it," Sandra said. "I'll help the girl."

"Thanks," Navid said.

Geraldo put a hand on Navid's shoulder. "I'll stay in the office, wait by the door here." He stomped his foot to indicate exactly where he planned to be. "You just run through this door, and I'll slam it shut. It'll be easier than you having to slow down and mess with it. Slide in here like you're running home on a ground ball, okay?"

Navid nodded. The reality of what he'd volunteered for started to sink in. He imagined the crazies sinking their claws into him, tearing at his flesh with their teeth, ripping into his gut.

Abby caressed his hand. "You don't have to do this."

"I do," Navid said. "We can't wait here to die. We have to move."

James started muttering to himself and tore open a desk drawer. He started pulling water bottles from it and loading them in a backpack.

Sandra glared. "I thought you said you didn't have any food or water."

"Didn't want to share if I didn't have to," James said without meeting her eyes.

"Asshole," Sandra said.

Navid felt anger flood through him, but he couldn't let his emotions rule him now. Abby needed him. "Let's just get this over with."

Abby placed her fingers on Navid's arm. Her touch sent tingles through his skin. "You don't have to do this," she repeated. "Please."

"You heard the boy. What the hell are we waiting for?" James asked. "Let's do this before the girl convinces him his plan isn't going to work."

Geraldo picked up his pipe. Sandra helped Abby to her feet and stood by the office door. James waited, backpack on and his hand gripping the doorknob, ready to sprint.

Shivers snuck down Navid's spine. He crept toward the

conference room door, where the crazies were relentless in their assault. Another bookshelf clattered to the floor. Navid jumped. He took a deep breath then pushed aside one of the desks. He pulled away another bookshelf. It dragged along the floor then toppled, spilling hardcover books.

The crazies outside howled louder, and the door bent inward. Navid reached out, slowly, his hand shaking when he touched the cool metal handle and twisted it. He pulled the door open only a fraction of an inch before the crazies finished the job for him.

"Run!" he yelled to the others. The crazies spilled in, climbing over the furniture still in their way. Navid charged toward the office and ran inside. Geraldo slammed the door shut, and the crazies immediately began pounding and scratching at it.

Geraldo and Navid ran through the office door into the hall. Navid could hear the crash of the inner conference room door while the crazies shredded it. He and Geraldo caught up to Abby, Sandra, and James as they breached the stairwell. Their footsteps rang out. Abby hobbled along with Sandra supporting her. Navid bounded up the stairs to help.

"Which floor?" James asked, panting.

"Two more!" Geraldo yelled. "Take an immediate right. The lab is the second door on your left."

One of the crazies broke through the stairwell door. It clawed its way up the stairs. Geraldo let loose with the pipe. The impact dented the crazy's skull, but it didn't stop the monster. It growled and pounced. Geraldo dodged the creature and swung the pipe at the back of its head. This time blood and bony fragments sprayed across the stairwell wall. Two more crazies came in.

"I can't...it hurts." Abby's head lolled to the side, and she leaned on Navid.

"Come on, Abby," Navid said. "You can do this."

Sandra gasped for air on Abby's other side. "You've got to help us help you."

Geraldo beat another crazy with the pipe. He cocked the makeshift weapon back to hit another and then let loose. But the creature ducked under the arcing pipe and tackled Geraldo.

The pipe fell from Geraldo's hands and clanged on the stairs. Navid didn't hesitate. He let Sandra bear the brunt of Abby's weight and dove toward the pipe. He picked it up, and the crazy reared back. Its arm tensed, and the muscles under its bony plates rippled. The claws came down in one fluid motion headed straight for Geraldo's face.

Navid took a step forward and swung the pipe as hard as he could. It connected with the creature's arm before glancing off. But it was enough to knock the crazy's hand away from Geraldo.

"Thanks," Geraldo said, scrambling to his feet. He kicked the crazy hard in the face, and Navid followed up with the pipe, catching the crazy under its chin. The thing's head snapped back, and it tumbled down the stairs.

Navid handed the weapon back to Geraldo, and they sprinted to catch up to the others.

"Can you help me with her again?" Sandra asked.

"Of course." Navid slid Abby's left arm over his shoulder.

"This the one?" James asked, far ahead of the rest of the group. He stood in front of a door on a landing.

"That's it!" Geraldo said.

James disappeared beyond the door, not waiting for the others. A loud crash sounded from below. More of the crazies shoved each other, desperate to join the fray in the stairwell. They sniffed and grunted, catching sight of their dead kin. It didn't take them long to look up, their interests piqued by Navid and the others.

"All right, guys, I don't think I can take 'em all," Geraldo said. "Let's move!"

Navid's muscles burned, and he pushed himself up. He couldn't imagine Sandra felt much better. The adrenaline that had been fueling them seemed to be fading—at least, he felt that way. Only fear and his determination to help Abby carried him on. He took the steps quicker. Just a half-dozen to the top.

A smaller crazy wearing a soiled hospital gown decorated with teddy bears separated from the pack. It leapt up on the handrail and then jumped to the rails nearest Sandra. It lashed out with a claw, catching Sandra's shoulder. She yelped in pain.

Geraldo used the pipe to push the crazy off. Its misshapen body fell into the void in the center of the spiraling staircase. The sound of its head hitting the handrails as it plummeted echoed up, joining the growls and cries of the others surging up the stairs.

Navid pulled open the door where James had disappeared. Abby, Sandra, and Geraldo spilled in. He looked around the hall for something to hold back the horde. Geraldo seemed to sense the dilemma and immediately thrust the heavy steel pipe through the door handle. At least if the crazies pulled on the door from the other side, the pipe should hold, giving them a little extra time.

"James?" Geraldo asked. No voice returned his call, but the door shook when one of the crazies hit it. "All right, follow me."

Geraldo led them to their right, then down another hall connecting various research labs. He opened the door to the lab he'd said was under construction. Two windows allowed daylight to filter into the space. Three black lab benches stretched across the center. Power equipment lay on top of them, and white sheets were draped on the floor. Several cans of white paint, a few roller brushes, and two paint pans lay in one corner. James's backpack sat next to them, but the old professor was nowhere in sight.

"Y'all okay?" Geraldo asked.

Abby groaned, her face still pale and her eyelids fluttering. Sandra nodded weakly, holding the wound on her arm.

"Did…did one of them get you?" Geraldo reached out to her.

She didn't answer.

"It's okay," Geraldo said. "I'm not going to…don't think

about Kaitlyn." He took a rag one of the painters had left behind and dabbed at the wound. "Here, we'll just clean it up. It ain't nothing. Just a little scratch. Maybe it don't mean anything."

Sandra's head bobbed, but Navid could tell she didn't believe him. Navid saw what was happening to Abby, knowing she'd had only a tiny cut. Sandra's shoulder had been lacerated. Three long streaks of blood and torn tissue showed from the ripped fabric of her shirt.

"Christ, what took you four so long?" James asked, cradling something in his right arm and coming in from a back door in the lab. He used his left hand to gesture to the doorway behind him. "That lab's being demolished, so they got all kinds of great weapons for us. You all need to grab one."

They ignored him.

He stepped closer to the group. "What's with the mood?"

Geraldo looked up at him, holding the rag to Sandra's arm. Blood saturated it.

James's eyes narrowed. "What happened?"

Navid's heart skipped a beat. No one responded.

"What happened?" James's asked louder. "Did one of those things do this? She's going to turn!"

Abby held her hands over her ears and clenched her eyes closed.

Navid wrapped his arms around her. "Settle down, James. Sandra's going to be fine."

"The fuck she is." James hoisted the object in his arm

back. An ax. He cocked it back. "I saw what happened to Kaitlyn. We can't risk that."

"No, James! Don't!" Geraldo yelled. He stepped in front of Sandra.

James butted Geraldo with the handle of the ax. The janitor fell back, and James took another step. Sandra held up her arm as James swung the weapon. It connected with her hand, and she shrieked.

"Stop!" Navid yelled, his stomach turning over. Abby shook in his arms and cried.

"No!" Geraldo jumped up, but James knocked him in the teeth with the ax handle. Geraldo fell back again.

James took another swing and cut into Sandra's arm. She yelled, high-pitched and grating. James swung again and again until her screaming stopped. The clean white sheets that had been laid out for the lab's repainting were soaked in red.

James's chest heaved, and he caught his breath. He wiped a strand of hair back that had come loose from his comb-over. He pointed the ax at Geraldo, then Navid, then Abby. Abby cowered in Navid's arms, and he squeezed her tighter.

"We can't let our goddamn guard down," James said, his tone menacing. "What I did was the right thing. Don't you forget it. There wasn't anything we could do for her, and you all know that. Better one dies than all of us."

Geraldo stood, his legs shaking. He spit blood. "But—"

James gestured at him with the ax. "There are no buts. This is black and white. They die"—he pointed at Sandra's limp body and the puddle of blood around it—"or we do.

Make your goddamn choice."

Abby looked up at Navid. She said nothing, but he saw the fear in her eyes as she covered the small cut in her wrist with her other hand.

THIRTY-THREE

———◄══✺══►———

BULLETS LANCED INTO THE SKULL from Dom's gun. The spray of gunfire knocked the creature off its trajectory, and it crumpled, falling across a support beam.

"Thanks," Jenna said, already moving forward.

There was no time to enjoy the fleeting sense of victory at saving Jenna's life. Two Skulls, no taller or bigger than Dom, climbed through the beams and rafters. One wore filthy, torn ACUs. Once a soldier, probably one that had tried to beat back the Oni Agent outbreak, it now stalked Dom. Clumps of gray hair hung from the other Skull's head, tangled in between its crooked horns. The two creatures snarled, their bloodshot eyes burning with hatred. But Dom put an end to that hatred with three-round bursts into each of their heads.

He gave a final glance at the spot where Owen had disappeared, the man's life literally torn apart before his eyes, and he started after Jenna and Spencer. He crawled over a set of water pipes. Jenna and Spencer were prying at the metal panel with their multi-tools.

"You positive this is the right place?" Jenn said, grunting as she pushed the corner of the panel open.

"Nope," Dom said. "But we don't have a fucking choice."

The Goliath howled, still stuck below the beams and rafters. It struck out with one arm, but the Hunters were now far beyond its reach. Another guttural yell escaped its gray lips. It grabbed a pipe and pulled it back until it burst. Water sprayed from the pipe, splashing on the floor and turning crimson.

Three more Skulls leaped past the Goliath. A fourth pushed its way through one of the holes the Goliath had made in the ceiling. Dom fired on the Skulls slinking through the lattice of pipes, ventilation shafts, and beams. Rounds pierced the first two, knocking them backward. Bullets smashed into the third, but none broke through the skeletal plates protecting its graying flesh. Dom adjusted his aim and put several bullets through its face.

"Get that panel open!" he yelled and drew a bead on the fourth. He pulled the trigger, but his slide locked back. The Skull dodged under an air duct. Dom dropped the rifle to his side and pulled his HK45C from its holster. He fired off four shots in quick succession as the Skull cleared the duct.

Holes formed in the duct, and air hissed out. But the Skull was too quick and avoided the gunfire. It swung out and grabbed Dom's boot, pulling his leg out from under him. Dom's hand flew out. He tried to catch himself, and he lost his sidearm.

The Skull bit into Dom's boot, but its teeth cracked on the steel toes. A salvo of deafening gunshots rang out. His ears rang, but the Skull went limp, blood pouring out of the fresh wounds in its head.

"Thanks," Dom said, recovering his pistol.

Spencer gave him a quick nod and then holstered his sidearm. He and Jenna pulled together on the metal panel, and it finally released from the wall. The resulting hole led into a gaping void.

"That's gotta be it!" Jenna said, shining her flashlight into the shaft.

"Let's go!" Dom said as he reloaded his SCAR-H.

Jenna's flashlight caught on ladder rungs. But the steel ladder was on the opposite wall. "We're going to need to jump!"

"Then jump!" Dom said. Another six Skulls crept in. They prowled toward the Hunters.

"Help me with the light!" Jenna said to Spencer.

"You got it." He shone his flashlight on the ladder, and Jenna put hers back on her vest.

Jenna's legs coiled and she shot into the air. For a moment, her body disappeared into the darkness. Dom's heart caught in his throat until he heard the ring of her boots hitting the steel rungs of the ladder.

"Down here!" Jenna's voice called. Spencer adjusted the light while she sprang up the rungs. "Who's next?"

A loud growl made Dom swivel. He shouldered his rifle, squeezed the trigger, and shot a burst of fire at the approaching Skulls. Even as he brought them down, more trickled past the frustrated Goliath. They wormed their way between the burgeoning piles of corpses, and Dom worked to cut them down.

"Go, Spence!" Dom called through gritted teeth.

Spencer fumbled with his flashlight, tucking it in his pocket. "Aye, aye," he said, his tone unenthusiastic.

Dom put another three-round burst into a Skull's head. "Jump, or deal with the Skulls!"

Jenna scaled the ladder and shone her flashlight down. The beam caused the rungs to cast long, ghastly shadows along the elevator shaft. "Come on!"

Spencer strapped his rifle across his back, crossed himself, and then jumped. His arms wheeled while he flew through space. He hadn't propelled himself as well as Jenna, and fell almost fifteen feet before one hand hit a rung. It connected briefly, but his gloved hand slipped.

"No!" Jenna cried out.

Dom couldn't watch, turning away momentarily to fend off the onslaught of Skulls. He clenched his jaw, and the rifle kicked against his shoulder. Each recoil shuddered through his torso. The flash from the muzzle illuminated the narrow space above the ceiling like precise, malicious lightning strikes. He watched the Skulls tumble over each other, dead and bleeding. *For Hector. For Owen…For Spenc—*

"Shit!" A deep voice echoed from within the elevator shaft.

"Are you okay?" Jenna called down.

"Fuck no. But I'm alive." The rhythmic clang of Spencer climbing the ladder resounded against the shaft walls.

A fleeting wave of relief flowed through Dom. "Get your ass up here!"

The slide on his SCAR-H locked back. *Out of ammo. Again.* He released the magazine and jammed in a fresh one. A Skull burst out from under a ventilation duct.

Dom had no time to raise his weapon. He jumped backward into the elevator shaft, twisting in the air. He flailed for a rung with his left hand, heart leaping as he came up empty. He tried with his right hand, his fingers slipping down the first, but connecting with the second. The jolt pulled on his arm socket, pain lancing down his side. Wincing, he reached with his left hand and anchored both in place. Momentum carried the rest of his body forward, and his chest slammed against the ladder. The collision knocked the air out of him.

"Captain, you okay?" Jenna called out from above, her voice echoing.

"Fine…I'm fine."

The screams of the Skulls pierced the elevator shaft. The resulting din deafened Dom. He fought through his burning nerves and propelled himself up the ladder to Jenna and Spencer.

Something crashed into the wall on his left. He swiveled in time to see a Skull crumple and plummet. It flailed its sinewy, plated arms as it fell, dimly illuminated by Jenna's flashlight.

"They're coming in, Captain!" Spencer called.

"Don't I know it!" Dom picked up his pace, desperate to

climb above the panel he and the Hunters had leapt from moments ago.

Another Skull smashed against the wall, followed by a second and third. They leapt with abandon, fueled by the hunt, by hunger. Fear of the dark unknown or of heights evidently meant nothing to them.

The wails and earsplitting screams continued. Another hit the ladder below Dom. Its claws fought for purchase. This one didn't disappear into the murky darkness like the others. It grabbed hold of the ladder and began climbing.

Dom snatched his HK45C from its holster with one hand. He used his other hand to grip the ladder, and he leaned back enough to let loose three rounds into the Skull. One of the bullets connected with the beast and knocked it backward, its grip on the ladder lost. Its cry of rage whined away as it disappeared.

"Made it!" Jenna yelled. A sudden square of blinding white light burst from above. The bright sunlight silhouetted her, and she exited onto the roof.

A brief howl caught Dom's attention. Another Skull, short but with long, skinny limbs, leapt into the darkness. He watched it disappear, guessing it too had fallen to its death.

Spencer followed close behind Jenna. Dom found himself envying the spryness of the younger Hunters. His palms burned, his arms shook, and his legs felt like they were giving out from under him. He was too old for this shit.

Just when the feeling was coming back in his legs, a bony apparition reached up and grabbed his boot. The beast hung off the ladder below. Dom kicked the creature in its face. It growled and snapped, its serrated teeth crunching together. Dom brought his leg up. He smashed his boot into its face again, and the Skull cartwheeled backward.

With the sun streaming inside, he watched the creature fall onto a growing pile of Skulls at the bottom of the shaft, like a portal to hell. Above, there was salvation, clouds rolling across a blue sky.

The salty air drifting in washed away the scent of death. Sweat dripping down his forehead, he squinted and climbed toward the sunshine, ignoring the clatter of the Skulls below.

Jenna and Spencer offered their hands and yanked him from the tunnel, locking the panel back into place as soon as he was on the roof. The sweet thrum of chopper blades beating the air masked the screeches of the beasts pounding on the hatch.

"Alpha, we're coming down," Frank's voice sounded over the comm.

"Copy." Dom motioned to Jenna and Spencer to follow him across the roof to where the AW109 was descending. The chopper sent waves of dust and air undulating over them. "Bravo, this is Alpha. What's your sitrep?"

"All aboard and safely out to sea, Captain," Renee's voice answered.

"Well done, Bravo."

Dom stole a glance toward the basin where the sailboats and the yard patrol craft were churning the water. The *Huntress* waited in the bay, ready to guide the boats toward Kent Island.

They were so close to escape, so close to establishing a safe zone.

The side door of the chopper burst open when its wheels touched down.

Miguel and Andris stood at the opening, their hands outstretched and ready to help Alpha. Jenna jumped aboard, followed by Spencer. Dom reached to grab Miguel's hand, but a sudden rumble and shaking of the roof caused him to fall flat. He picked himself up and wondered briefly if they were experiencing an earthquake. A terrifying bellow sounded from behind. Turning his head, he saw the Goliath break through the service elevator shaft. Brick and masonry scattered. The beast pummeled its way out of the building. Blood still seeped down its chest and graying skin. The skeletal plates along its limbs appeared an even sicklier yellow once exposed to the unadulterated sunlight. Its bloodshot eyes locked on Dom, and it roared, its howl rising above the thump of the blades.

As it extricated itself from the ruins of the elevator shaft, the other Skulls spilled out around it like demonic ants, relentless and starving. Dom picked himself back up and leapt aboard the AW109. His hands met Miguel's and his boots hit the floor of the chopper. The Goliath barreled forward.

Dom slapped the side of the fuselage. "Let's go!"

The chopper started to lift, dust kicking up over the oncoming wave of Skulls led by the Goliath. Frank pulled back on the cyclic, and the chopper banked away from the roof, toward the bay, toward safety.

There was a moment of calm, too soon ripped away as

the Goliath leapt from the roof, its thick fingers stretching for the side door. The chopper jerked, but the creature's dagger-like claws crunched onto the lip of the door. It held onto the side of the chopper, hanging with one hand and pounding on the side with the other. More Skulls leapt off the roof, jumping like lemmings. Most fell short, splattering against the ground six stories below. Four latched onto the Goliath, climbing its jagged back as the beast smashed its fist against the bird's fuselage.

The chopper tilted, listing to the port with the uneven weight of the monsters. A red light flashed on Frank's display panel, and alarms echoed through the cabin.

"We're going down!" Frank called. "Brace yourselves!"

But Dom didn't brace himself. He wouldn't let the rest of his team go down in flames. He wouldn't lose another Hunter.

He knew what he had to do. He tore open the side door, and the wind beat against his body.

"Chief, what the hell are you doing?" Miguel yelled.

"Captain!" Andris called.

Dom ignored them and took a deep breath. The chopper shuddered, losing its battle against the excess weight. The Goliath stared at Dom and let out another thundering roar. Spittle and blood flew from its mouth. Its tongue whipped against its jagged teeth. The smaller Skulls swarmed around the Goliath's shoulders and head, leaping at the open door.

But Dom was ready for them.

THIRTY-FOUR

⸺⟊⟊⸺

ANYTHING ELSE I CAN DO TO HELP?" Glenn asked.

Lauren gazed around the medical bay. She ran through the inventory list for the OR and the triage they'd set up. "No, I think we're ready."

"God, I hope so," Thomas said. He'd joined the medical team to help them prepare for whatever happened with the apparently botched rescue attempt at the Naval Academy. He pulled a cigar from his pocket and chewed the end.

The rest of the medical team finished setting up their stations with gauze, antibiotics, and chelation therapeutics.

"Need anything else, Lauren?" Peter asked.

"Just be on standby," she said. She paced between the empty patient beds and wondered how many of them would soon be filled. Thoughts of their diminishing inventory troubled her. Even if they had the beds, even if they could hold the midshipmen and any survivors from the rescue, would they have enough supplies? They still needed to restock from their stymied trip to help the *Queen of the Bay*.

"While we've got some time, can I show you something?" Sean asked Lauren, interrupting her ruminating.

"Make it quick." Lauren stopped her pacing and stood in

front of the lanky epidemiologist. He wore a worried expression.

"Of course." He motioned her over to a computer station. The other scientists, Glenn, and Thomas followed. "So I know it was a while ago that you asked me to do some pattern analysis on the Oni Agent outbreak, but we've been a little busy."

Lauren thought that was an understatement, but she gestured for Sean to continue.

"I managed to finish the simulation based on all the data I got from news reports and everything Samantha, Chao, and Adam passed on to me from the electronics workshop." He pulled up a map of the globe. "And here are the results." He clicked on it, and a bevy of red circles appeared across the continents. "These are where I tracked down our patient zeros."

"Wait, hold up," Thomas said, the cigar poking out of his mouth. "Zeros? You mean like multiple? I'm no scientist, but I thought there's only supposed to be a single patient zero."

"Right," Sean said. "That would be the case in a naturally occurring outbreak. But we know the Oni Agent isn't natural."

Lauren pointed to each of the red circles on the map in turn. Washington, Sydney, Moscow, Beijing, Berlin, London...the list went on. "This was some kind of coordinated effort?"

"Looks like it, huh?" Sean said.

"So the IBSL's failure wasn't the sole cause of the outbreak," Glenn said. "Someone or something else was behind it."

"That would be my guess," Sean said. "The IBSL might have been part of its spread, but it was probably just a small cog in the machine."

"Christ," Thomas said. "Any other major findings? I want to get this to Chao and send what we have to Detrick."

"I've created a time-lapse simulation tracking the Oni Agent's worldwide spread." He saved a file to a flash drive and handed the drive to Thomas. "But I don't have anything else concrete. Just remember to tell Detrick these are all projections and simulations based on the data I have. It might not be a hundred percent accurate."

Thomas nodded and pocketed his unlit cigar along with the flash drive. "Will do. Good work, Sean." He left the medical bay.

"I'll get out of your hair now, too," Glenn said. His gaze lingered on Lauren, and she returned a knowing nod, his touch still hot in her memory. "Let me know if you need me later for anything." He smiled at her. "And I do mean anything."

"Thanks," Lauren said. "Will do."

She watched him leave with his characteristic swagger. His defined back muscles flexed and undulated against his tight T-shirt, and she imagined her hand caressing his skin once more. She shook the thoughts from her mind and turned back to the display with Sean's results.

"Keep on this when you have time," she said. "And let's see if you can dig a bit deeper. Find out not just where these outbreak epicenters happened, but *how*. I want to know why no government had any idea what was going on until it was too late."

"You got it, Doc." Sean turned back to the computer to adjust his simulation software.

Peter and Divya were already working at another computer terminal. She'd trained her team well. Even knowing the Hunters would return within the hour, the medical team used every spare minute to push their research forward. They knew they didn't have time to waste when it came to finding a cure or vaccine to combat the prion component of the Oni Agent.

She stepped up to the screen where Peter and Divya worked. A list of three-lettered abbreviations appeared across the screen. She recognized what the letters represented—each symbolized an amino acid, one of the building blocks of a protein. "Are these the sequences Detrick gave us on the prions?"

"That's right." Peter brushed a hand through his dark hair and left it on his neck. "And we got some strange results running this through our bioinformatics software."

Lauren's brow creased. She leaned toward the screen. "How so?"

"The results indicate the prions consist of sequences similar to those found in sheep and goats." Divya moused over to the bottom of the results report. "But not a significant match with bovine-derived prions."

For a moment, Lauren considered this fact. The media

had made mad cow disease—or bovine spongiform encephalopathy—seem like an enormous threat to human health over the past several years. "You're surprised that the prion isn't more similar to those found in mad cows?"

"Right," Divya replied.

"Thing is, Chao and his team told us the protein complex—what we now know as a prion—came from World War II-era technology in Japan," Lauren said.

Peter fidgeted with a button on his white coat. "Okay, right, but I'm not sure I follow how that relates to cows. Does it have something to do with the Japanese agricultural industry?"

"It could." Lauren lifted her shoulders in a noncommittal gesture. "But I think the more likely answer is the simplest. Scientists and researchers didn't actually identify mad cow disease until the 1980s. However, prion disease in sheep has been documented for centuries, and goat scrapie was identified sometime before the war."

"Ah," Divya said. "So the Japanese scientists selected those animals knowing some protein—or chemical or something—was causing them to go mad."

"Then they isolated it and modified it to work in humans," Peter said. "Insane. And while the media has been focused on a mad cow disease outbreak, someone was working to make mad sheep or goat disease a reality, huh?"

"Looks that way," Lauren said. "So does that inspire any great ideas from either of you on how we stop the prions?"

Divya and Peter looked at each other, then Lauren. They

both wore defeated expressions.

"I know, I know," Lauren said. "We aren't going to have a magic bullet, but keep these new findings in the back of your mind while we dig through more science papers on the subject."

"Of course." Peter nodded before turning back to the screen.

The comm panel beside the hatch to the medical bay buzzed, and a small light shone, glaring red. Lauren ran to it and picked up the attached handset. "Medical, this is Lauren."

"Chao here. All survivors have been evacuated and are en route. ETA to the ship fifteen, maybe twenty minutes. Is the quarantine station prepped?"

Lauren glanced around the medical bay once more. Soon the chamber would be filled with civilians and midshipmen. Those that were free from injury and passed the diagnostic assays the medical team had developed would reboard their boats and head directly to Kent Island. But those that weren't so lucky would become residents here until they were cured of the Oni Agent—or, if it was too late, succumbed to it. Her team stood at attention, all eyes glued on her, and she pressed the handset to her ear.

"Yes," Lauren said. "We're ready for the survivors." She swallowed hard. Another thought percolated through her mind. "What about the Hunters?"

"Bravo team will be arriving with the survivors."

"And Alpha? Charlie?"

"They're...experiencing some difficulties right now. I'm

not sure when they'll make it in."

"Copy," Lauren said with cold, professional detachment. "Anything else?"

"No, but I'll call again when the first boats arrive."

"Understood." Lauren hung up the handset. Images of the triage they'd attempted to set up on the *Queen of the Bay* flashed through her mind. All her team's planning and preparation had been almost useless when the panicked passengers threatened to mob them. Most passengers thought *they* should be treated next; *they* were more important than whoever Lauren happened to be examining at the time. People who weren't even affected by the Oni Agent had been driven mad simply from paranoia.

She took a deep breath and mentally steeled herself for the chaos she knew would soon erupt. Her resolve would be tested, and people's lives would be relying on her ability to stay calm under pressure. A bead of sweat rolled down her forehead, and she wiped it away with the back of her hand. "Everybody ready to go?"

Peter snorted, his tell that he was as ready as he was going to be.

Lauren led them toward the cargo bay where the Naval Academy survivors would arrive. "Let's roll out."

THIRTY-FIVE

⬥⬥⬥

"TIME TO GO!" JAMES SAID, swinging the bloodied ax.

Navid shivered, holding Abby's hand. The old professor paced the lab like a caged, rabid dog. He picked up a sledgehammer in his free hand and walked over to Navid and Abby. He stood in front of them, the ax over one shoulder and the hammer over the other.

"What...what..." Abby stammered.

"Spit it out, girl." James glared at her, his face smeared with blood he'd half-heartedly tried to wipe off. "We don't have all goddamned day."

Abby only stared back and shrank into Navid's embrace. Navid wrapped his arms tighter around her and prayed James didn't see the tiny scratches on her arm. He couldn't stand the thought of the man trying to butcher his girlfriend like he'd done to Sandra. He glanced at the poor woman's bloodied corpse. Nausea gripped his stomach, and he gagged, urging himself not to vomit.

"What's the matter, boy? Can't stand what this world's come to?" His eyes darted between Abby and Navid. They lingered on Abby for a moment, and Navid positioned her behind him. He stood in front of James. "Ah, so your morning sickness passed, did it?"

James dropped the sledgehammer at Navid's feet.

"What the—" Navid started.

"Take it." He pointed at Abby. "She doesn't look like she can hold a toothbrush, much less a weapon."

"What about him?" Navid tilted his head toward Geraldo, who was wiping blood from his cracked lips.

"Dumbass can get his own weapon. Don't know if he'll use it anymore though. Seems to have developed a soft spot for those creatures."

"Sandra wasn't one of 'em yet!" Geraldo yelled.

"Yet!" James countered, mocking Geraldo's accent. "Yet! Yet! Yet! Ain't that a pretty modifier, ya dumb piece of trash. She would've been soon enough, and it's better we took care of her now than when she turned into a monster we couldn't handle."

Geraldo rubbed his jaw and glared at James. He pushed himself up to his knees then stood.

"You can be pissed at me all you want"—James gestured to the cans of white paint—"or you can help us get the hell out of here."

Geraldo's eyes never left James's while the custodian trudged to the paint cans. He pocketed a few paintbrushes and stowed one of the paint rollers in his coverall. One can in each hand, he returned to the entrance of the lab. "You struck her down before we even knew if she was going to turn. You're playing God, deciding who lives and dies."

"I'm not playing God." James shouldered his ax over his

right shoulder and put his left hand over his heart. "I'm as much of a pawn as you are. Only I'm not going to be sacrificed like one."

Abby squeezed Navid's hand. He caressed her forearm and locked eyes with her. Hers were covered in spiderwebs of red vessels. Sweat dripped down her forehead. She opened her mouth as if to talk, but no words came out.

Navid put a finger up to her lips. "It's okay. Once we're out of here, maybe we can go to the Bahamas. A nice Jamaican resort maybe." He forced a smile. "How about San Francisco? I've never been."

The corners of Abby's mouth twitched, and she managed a weak smile. Her fingers interlaced with his, and a tear rolled out of one of her eyes. Navid wiped it with the back of his hand. He felt a presence standing above him.

James had one hand on his hip and the other on the ax handle. "Enough crying. We'll have plenty of time for that when we get a rescue party's attention, and the only way that's happening is if we get to the damn roof." He waited a second. "That means move, son!"

"Right, right." Navid helped Abby to her feet.

She still favored the ankle she'd hurt earlier, but he could tell the injured joint wasn't the only thing bothering her. James sauntered over to the corner where he'd left his backpack of supplies and picked it up. While he wasn't looking, Navid applied another dose of antibiotics over Abby's scrapes. The little scratches were yellowed, and the skin had turned red and inflamed around them. His mind returned to what had become of Kaitlyn and Sandra and all the crazies in the hospital. Maybe Abby had just picked up an infection. All kinds of nasty antibiotic-resistant bugs were known to make a home for themselves in hospitals. Just because she and Navid had worked on a research floor of Mass Gen didn't mean they weren't exposed to them.

He tried to tell himself that maybe she had MRSA, and that was what was making her so sick and weak. The antibiotic-resistant bacteria responsible for those terrible infections seemed better than the alternative.

"We don't have all day!" James yelled. "Let's move!" He ran out the lab door.

Navid stowed the sledgehammer in his belt and struggled to help Abby out. Geraldo shot him a look filled with pity as he followed.

At the end of the hall, near a stairwell, James waited with the ax at the ready. He pressed his ear against the door.

"Don't hear any of those assholes," he said in a low voice.

Navid gave him a nod, straining to hold Abby. He hadn't realized how out of shape he was until the world seemed to fall apart around him. He positioned his arm a little tighter around Abby to help her limp along.

She was the runner, the athlete. She should have been the one in good health and good spirits. She'd always taken care of herself and chided Navid for not doing the same. Whenever he came down with the flu or a cold and she remained healthy, she told him it was because she exercised regularly and ate healthy—something he claimed not to have time to do.

Things will change, he thought. *If we make it out of this, we'll go all over the world together, running and hiking.*

He vowed to minimize his time being cramped up in a little lab, moving liquids from one plastic container to the next, hoping to see some machine spit out a meaningless result reporting a change in RNA expression or relative fluorescence level of some conjugated antibody.

It was all meaningless now. None of those words or numbers mattered. Only Abby did.

"Geraldo, you're leading," James said, pressing a hand against the door.

"Me? You've got the weapon."

James shrugged. "I'm an old man. You're faster."

Geraldo shook his head but took point anyway.

Navid knew what he was thinking, and James didn't even try to make his lie sound convincing. When James wanted to run, he could—and had. He'd left the group behind, and he'd do it again if it meant saving his own ass.

James pushed the door, and it flew open with a smack. Geraldo rushed into the stairwell and began pounding up the steps. James followed, not bothering to hold the door open for Navid and Abby.

Navid threw his shoulder into it. "Come on, Abby. We got this."

Abby's head bobbed, but her eyelids fluttered as if she was ready to fall asleep standing.

"Stay with me!" Navid pushed up the stairs, his muscles burning, still not recovered from their previous flight from the crazies.

The footsteps from James and Geraldo echoed overhead. They were already a full floor above Navid and Abby.

"Three more to go," Geraldo called down. "Come on, guys!"

Three more floors. Navid gasped for breath. He was practically dragging Abby up the stairs. He wasn't sure if he could—

Abby went limp in his arms. Navid tried to catch her, but she slipped from his grip and crumpled down the stairs. Her body slammed onto the landing.

"Help!" Navid said.

"No, don't!" James's voice answered.

But Navid could hear footsteps coming down. He rushed to Abby's side and picked her up. Warm blood dripped from her scalp onto his fingers.

"Abby, Abby, can you hear me?"

Her head rolled to the side and her mouth moved, but no words came out.

"Come on, Abby."

The footsteps from upstairs grew closer. "Navid, she okay? You okay?"

But Geraldo's voice wasn't the only one now echoing in the stairwell. Below them the cries of the crazies sounded once more. A shudder tore down Navid's spine. Their nightmare wasn't over.

"Come on, let's get her up." Geraldo bent down and wrapped an arm around Abby. He still managed both paint cans. "Let's move!"

With the load lightened, Navid continued up once more. Abby's head lolled, and she started murmuring. Navid couldn't hear her words over the growing cacophony below.

A brief flash of white light above caught Navid's eyes. *The sun.* He watched James's silhouette flit out to the roof. The door closed behind him.

Two more floors. Navid huffed. His lungs strained for air. Geraldo's face was turning red with the effort. The custodian appeared as out of shape as Navid. Maybe worse. But the man hadn't for a second hesitated in helping Navid and Abby.

"Thanks," Navid said between breaths.

Geraldo looked at him as they moved up another set of stairs. "Ain't got anything to thank me for yet. We ain't"—he wheezed—"we ain't clear of 'em."

The crazies' bellows grew louder. The click and scratch of their claws on the stairs and walls added to the relentless din. Navid's heart thumped, his pulse racing from a combination of fear and physical exertion.

"Come on, come on," Geraldo said. "We're almost there...almost..."

An inhuman shriek called out from behind. Navid turned. A crazy with flame-red hair streaming behind it jumped with outstretched hands. Its crooked, clawed fingers sliced through the air, and Geraldo pivoted in time to swing one of the paint cans at the crazy's head. Two more climbed over its body and charged forward. They screamed, their pale tongues whipping between yellowed, fanged teeth.

"You go!" Geraldo said, letting Navid bear Abby's full weight.

Navid stopped and pulled out his sledgehammer while still holding onto Abby. He couldn't let Geraldo take these monsters alone.

"No! Go!" Geraldo clenched his jaw. Dried blood still traced his bottom lip from the blow James had delivered back in the lab. "Go!"

Navid nodded and started up the stairs. He heard the smack of the paint can against another crazy's head, but he didn't dare turn back. He was too close, too close to the door, too close to getting Abby to safety. The growl of another monster sounded, followed by a scream of agony that sounded all too human.

Navid didn't look back. He ran up the last stairs and shoved open the door to daylight.

James stood before him, ax at the ready. "Good, good, just you and the girl. None of those beasts. Where the hell is Geraldo with the paint?"

Navid set Abby down and fell to his knees. His pulse still pounded in his ears as he recovered his breath. "Down…down there."

"Down there? Still? With those *things*?" James paced, appearing almost as crazy as the monsters. "You got to go back there, get the paint. Without it, how the hell do we signal a chopper or plane or satellite or drone? Huh?"

The old professor's eyes were wide. He made an imploring gesture, the ax precariously balanced in his right hand.

"You go…you go get Geraldo," Navid managed.

"Me?" James's bushy eyebrows lifted as he scowled. "Not a chance." He raised the ax above Abby. "You. Go."

"No, don't." Navid's heart stopped, his blood running cold. They'd made it this far and finally had a chance to flag down some elusive rescue squad that might or might not exist. And James was going to cut down his hopes right here. "Please."

"Then go!"

Navid pulled his sledgehammer from his belt. He wielded it in both hands and wondered if maybe he shouldn't end James's life first.

The old man's eyes narrowed as if he could tell what Navid was thinking. "You make one step toward me and she's gone. Now go. Go get the paint."

Navid tore open the door. His vision swam, muddled by rage and exhaustion, as he ran down the stairs where he'd left Geraldo. He saw two crazies huddled over the stairs, digging at something. *Geraldo.* The custodian was sprawled out on the stairs, and the monsters were attacking him.

One plunged its hand into Geraldo's stomach and tore the skin back. The glistening red of Geraldo's innards shone in the dim emergency lights. The crazy abruptly flew backward. Geraldo's arm had shot out once more, shoving the beast. He swung a paint can at the other, but missed.

Navid reached Geraldo and slammed the sledgehammer into the attacker's head. It connected with a sickening thud.

The creature staggered but recovered. Its lips drew back in a snarl. Navid smashed the hammer into the creature's face. Its teeth cracked, and blood poured from its glistening lips. He swung again and again, until the creature's skull caved in and it fell.

"Come on, Geraldo. We've got to go." Navid hated saying the words as he watched the life ebb out of Geraldo's body. He knew the man would never make it; there was no use in even pretending. But he had sacrificed himself to save them. How could he abandon him, even in these last moments? He wished it was James dying in a pool of blood.

"Move, kid. You gotta go." Geraldo held up a paint can.

Navid took it reluctantly.

More of the crazies' wails sounded. Another cornered the landing, followed by a second, a third, and a fourth. The group snarled and growled, their muscles tensing under their skeletal plated bodies.

Geraldo gripped the handrail with one hand and pulled himself upright. His legs shook as he stood, and blood poured from the wound in his abdomen. A visceral yell escaped his lips, and he threw himself at the crazies.

Navid sprinted up the stairs. The sounds of ripping and chewing and screaming chased him. He burst back through the heavy metal door and onto the roof. James grabbed the door before it closed and clicked the internal lock so it was secured from the inside when he slammed it shut.

"Those things aren't smart enough to unlock it," James said. "Door should be strong enough to hold them."

"And…and what do we do? How do we get back in?"

James nodded toward the paint can. "Better hope help arrives soon."

Navid set the paint can down and gazed across the flat roof. Two other square structures dotted the otherwise flat, gravelly space. A pit formed in his stomach. "Where's Abby? What'd you do to her?"

A chortle escaped James's lips. "God, boy, how cruel do you think I am?" He pointed to one of the structures with a metal door. "She's behind that one. She was complaining about the sun being too hot and bright or something. Couldn't get her ass up, so I dragged her over there."

Navid glared at the old man.

"You could at least say thank you. She certainly didn't."

A cool breeze rustled over them. James soaked it up for a second, closing his eyes and stretching.

"God, fresh air. No more smell of death." He opened his eyes again. "Geraldo didn't make it, did he?"

Navid shook his head and dropped the paint can. He lowered his head. "No, no he didn't." Remorse flowed through him, and he wondered how he'd ever be able to honor the man's memory. But now he had a more pressing concern. He ran to Abby.

He found her lying against the brick wall in the shade. At least James had shown a modicum of humanity was buried somewhere in his rock-hard soul. Navid kneeled by Abby's side and combed the hair out of her eyes with his hand. He used the other to caress her forearm near the injury. The skin appeared puffier, redder than before, and the yellow scabs were more prominent. He noticed her nails were growing tawny and long. His bottom lip quivered.

Footsteps crunched behind him. "See, she's okay." James put a hand on Navid's shoulder. The gesture felt strange coming from him. "She's going to need help, isn't she? Looks like she's sick. Hurt more than her ankle, huh?"

"Uh, yes," Navid said. "Maybe…maybe all the stress is killing her immune system. Or maybe it was a chemical in the lab explosion."

"Explosion?"

"You know, it was how we escaped those monsters and came to you…and Geraldo…and Sandra."

"Uh-huh," James said. "Right, right. Well, she's not getting any better, so it's in her best interest to get that SOS painted and get some attention, isn't it?"

"Yeah, yeah." Navid didn't trust James's compassion, but the man was right. They needed to get Abby help—probably more help than James realized. He stood and walked back to the more open area on the roof.

James followed. "Let's get to it. We've got a lot of ground to cover." He bent to pick up the paint can, but stopped, groaning, and held his lower back. "I'm not sure I've got it in me, kid. Can't bend down like you."

Navid shot him a distrustful look but started painting the first S on the roof. It needed to get done whether James was going to help or not. He ensured the S was plenty big enough to be seen overhead and moved to begin the O. James unscrewed a cap on a water bottle, took a sip, then deposited it back in his backpack.

"Can I have some?" Navid asked.

"When you're done," James said.

Navid glared. He hated feeling used, but arguing with James wouldn't get the task at hand finished any faster. His thoughts turned to Abby as he painted. He reassured himself that the sooner he got this SOS up, the sooner a chopper would see them, and the sooner they'd be off this roof and away from James. A gust of wind rustled over his back, providing a brief respite from the heat of the sun. It tickled his neck. The cries of crazies sounded from the city streets below like the distant howls of wolves hunting unseen in the forest.

A crick formed in his back from hunching over. He stood and stretched before moving on to the last S.

"Almost there," James said. He placed a hand above his brow to shield his eyes from the sun. "Haven't seen a damn chopper since we've been up here, much less a plane or something."

"Yeah," Navid said. "I remember hearing more when the outbreak first happened, but it's been a while." He thought of the pallor taking over Abby's face. "I hope they haven't abandoned the rescue efforts."

"You got that right, kid."

Navid's back ached as he bent, painting the last S. The three letters stretched across the massive roof of the hospital, and he figured they were big enough they could damn well be seen from space. Maybe that was an exaggeration, but he half hoped it was true. As James had observed, they hadn't heard or seen any signs of aircraft in the past few hours. Maybe the government had given up on Boston. Maybe he'd die up here, alone with Abby and James.

He finished the last brush stroke on the S. The paint can was almost dry, and he felt fortunate he'd rationed it out just right. He stretched his arms out and cracked his neck.

"It's done," he said.

No response from James.

He looked to where James had been sitting, but the man was gone. A sick feeling grabbed at Navid, and he rushed around the structure where Abby had been earlier. His heart caught in his throat when he saw James standing over her with the ax raised.

THIRTY-SIX

———◦〜◦———

THE ROTOR WASH BEAT AROUND DOM. He watched the Goliath readjust its grip on the chopper. The smaller Skulls let out wails to rival the noise from the AW109's engines.

Dom fired at the smaller Skulls. Their heads blew back, flesh spraying from the exit wounds. Their corpses plummeted to the earth, where the chopper would soon be if Dom didn't do something about the Goliath. He shot at the giant beast, but it lowered its head, presenting only the thick, knotting horns. It pulled itself up, clung to the AW109 with one hand, and swung the other to ward off its attacker. Dom ducked inside, narrowly avoiding the claws. No amount of shooting or stabbing would penetrate the overgrown skeletal plates protecting the creature's malformed head.

Not even his last, desperate shots into the creature's face seemed to perturb the Goliath. Now the beast appeared intelligent enough to shield its face entirely to prevent an easy kill. But Dom knew one way to bring the creature down. One method he'd learned aboard the *Queen of the Bay*. He realized how lucky he'd been to take that first Goliath down, and now he needed to employ that lesson to kill this one.

"We're losing altitude fast," Frank said.

But the pilot didn't need to tell Dom. He could see the ground rising up, along with the hungry Skulls waiting below. He dropped his rifle in the cabin, near where the others were strapped in. He grabbed a rescue harness, cinched it in place, then attached it to the chopper's pulley system.

"What the hell are you doing?" Miguel asked, unbuckling and rising from his seat.

Jenna unbuckled and joined Dom at the entrance. She unloaded a magazine on the Goliath. Instead of fighting her off, it dug both claws deeper into the fuselage and shook back and forth. The AW109 listed dangerously. Jenna started to fall, and Spencer grabbed her to prevent her from tumbling out.

"Careful, you fools!" Andris yelled.

"Shit!" Frank said. "Someone needs to do something about this fucker!"

"I'm not letting this bird go down." Dom pulled his blade from his thigh sheath and took a deep breath. The Goliath swiped at him again, and he ducked under the blow. The massive fist scraped against the open chopper door and left a series of claw marks in the paint.

Dom jumped from the fuselage and landed on the creature's shoulder. The Goliath shook, and for a second Dom hoped the beast would let go and drop to the ground. The Goliath would fall while the rescue harness and cable held Dom in the air.

But he had no such luck. The Goliath kept one claw firmly embedded in the chopper as it thrashed. Spencer fired directly at the beast's hand in an attempt to loosen its grip. Chips of the monster's armor flew, but it still didn't release. Pain and physical trauma seemed to be no obstacle to this raging creature.

"Come on, fucker!" Spencer withdrew a knife and stabbed it downward into the creature's hand, but the blade glanced off the beast's plating.

Dom held tight to the Goliath's neck but was careful not to let any of the creature's skeletal growths pierce his skin. He pressed one of his boots against the wing-like shoulder blades to brace himself.

The Goliath let out a frustrated howl and pivoted, trying to knock Dom off its back. The chopper tilted with the creature's movement. Dom could still hear the alarms going off from the AW109's emergency system.

Miguel and Jenna hovered near the open door, ready to lend a hand, but the expressions on their faces showed they weren't sure how they could help. He was alone in taking down this tremendous monster. The beast shook again, and Dom lost his grip. He fell several yards before the cable caught and the harness dug into his sides and legs.

"Chief!" Miguel activated the winch, and the cable pulled Dom upward.

With his knife, Spencer sawed at the creature's hand still gripping the fuselage. "Come on, come on, come on!"

Andris joined him, desperately hacking away at the monster's claws.

The Goliath turned its head and licked its cracked lips. It

kicked out, and Dom did his best to dodge the attacks. But with nothing to push off against or to hold on to, he had limited mobility.

One of the creature's feet connected with his chest. It knocked the air out of him, and deep pangs of agony coursed up his side. His sides screamed in pain as he gasped for air. No stranger to injuries, he could tell he'd broken at least one rib.

"Chief, you okay?" Miguel's voice rang out in his ear through the comm link.

Dom flashed him a thumbs up with his free hand. "Let me finish that bastard!"

"You got it." Miguel moved back into the fuselage to start the winch.

The Goliath kicked again. This time Dom grabbed the beast's foot. He could feel one of the dagger-like toenails dig into his skin, drawing blood. That would have to be dealt with later, but for now he focused on climbing the creature's leg. It bucked and thrashed, struggling to throw him off.

Dom gritted his teeth, every muscle in his body straining against the Goliath's efforts. The chopper shuddered and started to bank.

"Captain, we're going down hard now," Frank said. "Don't have much time."

And Dom didn't have time to reply. He gathered every bit of strength left in his injured body to reach the creature's back. He grabbed one of the grotesque shoulder blades with a free hand. One of the blade's sharp edges bit into his flesh, but he didn't let go. He swung himself atop the Goliath's shoulder and then stabbed his knife into the one weak spot he knew this monstrosity would have.

The knife met the soft flesh between the skeletal plates in the creature's neck. Dom dragged it back and forth like a saw, tearing through sinew, blood vessels, and flesh. The Goliath flailed more aggressively, and the AW109 rocked back and forth, Frank clearly struggling to jockey the chopper against the monster's impressive weight.

The Goliath's jostling knocked Dom's knife hand away. He lost his footing, but hung onto the creature with one hand. The Goliath rasped for air while clinging to the chopper.

Dom hoisted himself up again and repositioned himself over the creature's shoulder to deliver the killing blow. He plunged the blade into the Goliath's injured neck and tore through its airway. The monster roiled, beating at Dom, but its movements slowed, and its head started to roll back. Its grip on the chopper loosened.

"Bring me up!" Dom yelled.

"On it, Chief," Miguel replied. He started the pulley system.

The cable grew taut, and Dom started to rise from the Goliath's shoulder. He reached out to grab the bottom lip of the open fuselage. Jenna stretched to lend a hand once he was in range.

A low growl escaped the Skull, and its body tilted away. Its pale eyelids fluttered over glassy eyes. Dom watched the life bleed out of the gargantuan monstrosity.

For a moment he wondered how this thing had come to be. So many other people had turned to Skulls, explainable from the medical team's research. But this *thing* was not so well understood, and it was the second he'd come across. He hoped it would be the last.

Dom strained his arms for the open side door, ready to be back in the AW109.

Jenna's fingers met Dom's. "Got you, Captain!"

The Goliath's eyes opened once more. Its free hand shot up one last time, firing at Dom with a singular purpose: kill.

Dom twisted, and Jenna lost contact with him.

"No!" Spencer yelled, leaning out as far as he could without tumbling. He flung out an arm to grab Dom, but he couldn't reach him.

The monster's claws scraped against Dom's chest, reigniting the pain in his already inflamed ribs. The creature pulled back its fist and knocked Dom's hold loose. He fell, and the rescue harness and cable caught him once more.

But the creature's final thrashing didn't stop. Its serrated claws cut into the cable attached to Dom's harness. The cable snapped, and Dom plunged. The other end of the cable flew back into the AW109.

"Chief!" Miguel leaned out of the chopper with Jenna and Andris by his side.

Dom landed on the Goliath's chest. He dropped his blade, and it glinted in the sunlight as it fell toward the masses of Skulls below. The Goliath's eyes closed, no longer struggling to stay open, and its maw gaped. Its fingers finally released from the side of the chopper.

The beast started to plummet. Dom scrambled up its skeletal plates. His lungs burned, and fire tore through his busted ribs.

"No, Dom!" Jenna yelled.

The other Hunters watched in horror. Dom felt his body start to accelerate downward with the Goliath. The torn cable whipped uselessly by his side. His thoughts flitted to Meredith and the words he'd left unsaid between them. To the Hunters, those who had valiantly fought to protect the survivors of this horrendous outbreak and those who'd already made the ultimate sacrifice. To Kara aboard the *Huntress*, recovering from the Oni Agent. To Sadie, waiting loyally by her sister's side.

He couldn't fail them now.

Using up every bit of strength, every bit of hope and perseverance he had left, he coiled his legs and then shot up, away from the falling Goliath and into the air, no safety cable to help him, nothing beneath his feet. This was his last chance.

He stretched his gloved fingers out in a desperate attempt to grab the chopper. He watched, almost as if in slow motion, as gravity pulled back. He wasn't going to make it. This was it.

His fingers grabbed nothing but empty air.

THIRTY-SEVEN

NAVID THREW HIMSELF at the gray-haired professor. They skidded across the roof together, tumbling in a mass of flailing limbs. The ax slipped from James's grip.

James hit Navid with a left hook, and his head snapped sideways.

"You think I didn't notice what was going on with her?" James kicked Navid in the ribs.

Navid's vision went red, then black. He gasped for air and recoiled when James's foot connected with his side again.

"You think I'd let her turn?"

A foot in the head left Navid's teeth chattering. He could taste blood, and pain radiated through his skull.

"No way, kid."

Another blow to his stomach. Nausea and pain welled up in him. Navid heaved and vomited in response.

"You and the girl can both go straight to hell as far as I'm concerned."

No more kicks. No more blows. Footsteps moving away from him. Navid shook his head, trying to get rid of the dizziness and his muddled vision. The footsteps returned.

Through the blur, he could make out James. There was something in his right hand. He lugged it over his head.

"No way," James repeated. "No way am I sharing my supplies with you."

Navid rolled away. The air whooshed by his head, and the ax smashed down inches from his body. Struggling against his disorientation, he stood. He spread his arms out to stabilize himself and blinked rapidly to clear the mixture of sweat and blood trickling into his eyes.

Abby lay beyond James. She remained unmoving, pale and sick. James hadn't gotten to her yet. The man charged and let out a primal scream. Navid ducked, braced himself, and tackled James. The bottom of the ax handle crashed against the back of his skull as James brought it down.

Tears of pain welled in Navid's eyes, and he fought the unyielding urge to let go. But he didn't relent. He pushed the man over and kneed him in the groin. Once again the ax clattered to the side.

"You bastard!" Navid yelled. "You bastard!"

He kneed James again. The professor yelped. Navid pummeled the man, landing blow after blow until blood seeped down James's face. The man spit crimson saliva from his mouth and suddenly surged upward, head-butting Navid. James stood above Navid and stomped on his hands. Bones crunched when James ground his foot down.

The adrenaline flowing though his vessels wasn't enough to assuage the intense agony. Navid howled.

"You think that hurts, you little asshole?" James spat out

a tooth and wiped his mouth with the back of his hand. "Wait 'til I feed you to those damn zombies."

Navid's vision swam again. His world started to turn black; the pain in his hand was too intense. He glanced at the broken fingers. They twitched when he tried to move them. Useless.

James grabbed Navid's hand and tightened his grip around the mess of shattered bones and flesh. Navid cried out in anguish. The professor pulled him toward the side of the roof. He kicked Navid's body against the lip that traced the roof's perimeter.

Waves of pain washed over Navid, and his stomach twisted. He wanted to die; he wanted to give up. He heard the moans of the crazies below. Could they hear him? Could they see him? Did they know he'd soon be their next meal?

His weight shifted over the edge as James pressed one foot into the side of his body.

"Bye bye, you piece of shit. Won't be long 'til your little girlfriend joins you."

His pulse pounded in his ears. His vision turned clear, lucid for a moment. Navid gritted his teeth and jumped up, swinging his good hand at James's face. His knuckles connected with James's nose. Intense pain shot up his arm when bone connected against bone, but it was nothing compared to what James had done to his left hand.

James started to recover from the blow. Blood trickled from his nostrils, and his eyes narrowed. He grimaced and bent to tackle Navid.

But Navid was no longer fighting for his own survival. He didn't care whether he lived or died. He was fighting for Abby. He kicked with his right leg, knocking out James's shin as the man charged.

The professor fell flat, and Navid brought his foot down against the back of the man's head. He heard a sickening crunch, the sound of a broken jaw. Still James forced himself up, his face covered in red. The man's eyes smoldered with a vile intensity, a window straight to the selfish hatred the man harbored.

James tried to say something, but it came out as incomprehensible blubbering through his busted lips and jaw. Navid didn't care to give the man a second chance at being understood. He shoved with all his might, using both hands, one good, one bad. The back of the man's legs caught on the lip of the roof where Navid had been dangling moments ago.

The hatred in James's eyes flickered out, replaced by pure fear as his arms pinwheeled. He tried to right himself, but his efforts were futile. Navid planted a solid kick into James's abdomen, and the man fell into empty space. His gurgling cries, loud at first, grew faint in his plummet toward the street.

Navid didn't bother watching the man splatter against the ground. He imagined the remains would be quickly devoured by the crazies, and he thought of no fate the despicable man deserved more.

But now that the fight was over, he had neither time nor interest in wasting a single thought more on James. He cradled his mangled hand and rushed to Abby's side. He felt a different ache when he looked at the hair matted to her forehead and the pained expression on her face. This aching was as visceral as the agony in his hand, but he knew it wasn't physical. It was fear, it was injustice; it was knowing that she was affected by whatever agent had turned the people on the streets into crazies.

And there was nothing he could do about it.

His bottom lip quivered, and he tried to mentally keep his pain in check. He brushed Abby's hair back and pressed his palm against her cheek.

"I love you, Abby. I love you."

He thought he saw her eyelids flutter. Maybe the corners of her lips had twitched. Maybe they'd parted slightly as she tried to mouth the words back to him.

God, she can't go like this. Please, don't let this be it. Please.

"Abby, I'm so sorry."

He hugged her close to his chest. Her warm skin pressed against him, the heat radiating through his shirt. Her sweat soaked into the fabric and intermingled with his.

The sun beat down on him, and the cries of the crazies echoed from below. He prayed they were satisfied with his offering of James, prayed that they didn't know he and Abby were stuck up here.

Prayed that Abby wouldn't become one of them.

"I'll take you anywhere you want when we get through this," he said. "We can go to Wyoming, to Tokyo. Maybe to Iceland and watch the Aurora Borealis. Wouldn't that be beautiful, Abby? Wouldn't that be amazing?"

He combed his fingers through her damp hair and kissed her forehead.

"I promise I'll never take you for granted again. I'll never forget to make time for us."

Tears blurred his vision. He knew it wasn't just from the pain.

"We can go to Barbados. What about South Africa? A safari, maybe. I know how you love animals."

He gently rocked her head. His good hand moved down her arm, caressing her, holding her.

"Abby, can you hear me? I'll go anywhere you want." He kissed her forehead again, then her cheek, then her dry lips. But he knew no kiss would save her. He was no prince breathing life back into a fairytale princess.

Her eyelids started to open. He stared into them. Red vessels mottled her sclera, but he thought he saw understanding in her expression.

"Abby." He forced a smile. It felt like the hardest thing he'd ever done in his life, smiling when he knew what was going to happen next. "We'll go wherever you want in the world. Wherever you want."

She didn't smile back. Her lips moved like she was trying to say something. No words came out. Her tongue seemed stuck to the roof of her mouth.

Navid leaned in close. "What's that, Abby? I can't hear you." He lowered his ear above her mouth. Her warm breath tickled across his skin.

"Home," she muttered. "I just...I just want to go home,

Navid."

Her eyes shut again. Sweat trickled down her forehead, and hot tears streamed from Navid's eyes. He held her with his good hand and with his bad hand. He didn't care. He just wanted to keep her as close and tight as he could. No amount of pain convinced him otherwise.

His bottom lip quivered again, and he sniffled. He couldn't lose her like this; he couldn't make it this far with her to watch the life evaporate out of her now.

She shuddered and went still. Then her eyes opened again. He stopped crying, stopped stroking her hair.

"Abby…"

But when her gaze locked with his, when her lips drew back in a snarl, he knew she was no longer Abby. There was no love, no compassion in her stare.

There was only hunger.

THIRTY-EIGHT

———⦁∾⦁———

MIGUEL DIDN'T HESITATE FOR A SECOND. He wrapped the rescue cable around his prosthetic hand and forced the artificial fingers to clasp it as tight as mechanically possible. Letting his captain—no, his brother—splatter ignobly on the ground next to the goddamned Skulls was not going to happen. The wind rushed past him, and he leapt out of the chopper.

Wide-eyed, Dom's fingers still grasped at the air. His body started to descend like the Goliath's as Miguel swan-dived straight at him. The Hunter met Dom, their bodies colliding, and he wrapped his flesh-and-blood arm around Dom's waist. Dom threw his arms around Miguel.

The rescue cable grew taut and pulled on Miguel's prosthetic. He prayed the interface between the mechanized arm and his body would hold. His nerves burned with the strain. Below, the Goliath's body crashed into the ground.

"Hold on!" Miguel said.

Dom ground his teeth, his face flushed red.

"Get your asses back in here!" Jenna yelled and started the winch.

The cable retracted and pulled them back up to safety.

When their feet hit the cabin floor, Dom slumped into a seat. Sweat poured from under his helmet. He held his side with one hand.

"Thanks," Dom grunted. He opened his mouth as if to say something more then settled on the single word again. "Thanks."

Miguel unwound the rescue cable from around his prosthetic. The friction between his arm and the cable had torn his fatigues. He shook out his arm. All along the nerves stretching to the neuro-electrical interfaces with the prosthetic, he felt a sensation like needles piercing his muscles. He shook the limb again, hoping to alleviate the painful sensation, and sat next to Dom.

"No need to thank me," he said between gasping breaths. "It's nothing you wouldn't have done for me, Chief."

Dom stared hard at him for a moment and then patted his shoulder with one gloved hand. "Doesn't matter who would've done what. You saved my ass."

"Thank God we've got ya back, Captain." Frank's voice came over the comm link. "Everyone ready to get the hell out of here?"

Miguel glanced at Andris then at Jenna, Spencer, and Dom. They'd made it. They'd actually made it. Adrenaline still pumped through his veins, but he pressed himself into his seat, urging his body to calm. For now, they were safe; for now, he and the other Hunters were okay.

"Take us home," Dom said. He spoke into his throat mic. "Bravo, this is Alpha. Sitrep?"

"All Academy ships are clear of the basin," Renee called back. "No more casualties."

No more casualties. Miguel let the words repeat in his head. The unsaid implications rang out loud and clear. Hector had died. Owen had died. Many of the midshipmen had died during the rescue attempt. And how many had died before the Hunters got here? How many other people were trying desperately to fend for their lives out there in a world that had become overrun by monsters practically overnight?

Miguel watched the flotilla of small craft sail for the *Huntress.* The boats left trails of frothy white wakes as they cut through the gleaming waves. He surveyed the ships, full of young midshipmen and frightened civilians, and wondered what would become of them once they made it to Kent Island. The government had abandoned these people, this small but sturdy pocket of resistance. And if everything that Shepherd had told them from Detrick was true, General Kinsey and his cohort weren't trying to rescue the average joe or his family.

They were in the midst of a tactical retreat. Miguel didn't know what the general was planning, but the man seemed more concerned about protecting a bunch of fat politicians rather than saving the people who made this country worth protecting.

But what the hell did Miguel know? He was a grunt.

Dom patted Miguel's prosthetic and broke Miguel's reverie. "Seriously, I owe you, buddy. I owe you big time. I don't know how I can thank you enough."

"Damn it, Chief. You don't owe me anything." Miguel thought about the times Dom had saved him, how Dom had given him a second chance to serve when the Army honorably discharged him. Dom had become family. He thought about saying all these things but instead let a wide grin form across his face. "Now, if you want to give me a big fat bonus on my next paycheck, I'll take it. 'Bout time for me to afford one of those fancy cigars Thomas is always rolling around." Miguel put his prosthetic arm behind his head as if he was daydreaming. "Maybe I'll blow it all at our next port o' call. Rounds for everyone at the bar, on me."

"You find an open bar out there, I'll give you a goddamned bonus like you never dreamed."

"You got it, Chief."

After the chopper had landed, Dom received an immediate batch of the chelation therapy. Lauren had personally seen to the scrapes and gashes in his chest from the fight with the Goliath. She'd noticed him flinch when she touched his bruised ribs.

"Think you broke something else?"

Dom nodded. "Think so."

"I'll patch it up later," Lauren said. "For now, you go wait there." She pointed to the part of the medical bay where her team was triaging patients with less urgent injuries.

351

"You got it, Doc." Dom joined the crowd of other civilians. A couple of midshipmen talked quietly in one corner. He gave them a solemn nod before heading toward the far end of the bay. A hand grabbed his shoulder, and he spun.

"Sir, I want to thank you." It was Midshipman Rachel Kaufman. The fire and desperation Dom had seen in her eyes when they were at the academy had been replaced by a stoic calm. "You saved us, and you saved the people we were protecting."

Dom shook his head, remembering those that had died during the rescue attempt. But there was no use voicing his reservations. If Kaufman was half as good a leader as he suspected her to be, she would feel the pains of their deaths for the rest of her life. She, like him, would spend long nights awake, replaying the action in her head to see what she'd missed, what she could do better next time. How she could prevent others from making the ultimate sacrifice.

"*You* saved those people," Dom said, shaking her hand. "You deserve the commendation. If it weren't for your efforts, there wouldn't have been anyone for us to find at the academy."

Kaufman's brow furrowed as if she were going to protest. She didn't seem to like receiving praise, and Dom noted that on his mental list of what it took to be a humble, selfless leader.

"What's happened to this country…it's horrific," she said. "I don't want to stand by and watch everything fall apart. Can I join your crew?"

Dom thought about it for a second. They'd lost two more Hunters. The space those Hunters had left was like a bleeding wound on his team—and in his mind. He could certainly use someone like Midshipman Kaufman. But he knew others that needed her more.

"Kent Island could use some strong leaders," Dom said. "And the men and women from the academy already trust you. I can't take you away from them."

"Defending a civilian stronghold? That's all you want me to do?"

"I don't think it's going to be as easy as you think," Dom said. "I can't spread my crew any thinner, and I need someone on Kent I can trust. Someone who's faced those Skulls and lived to tell about it. You're that person, Kaufman."

She chewed her bottom lip, straightened her posture, and nodded. "I understand. And you're right. My responsibility to my fellow midshipmen isn't through. And neither is my responsibility for the survivors we promised to protect." Her expression grew serious once again. "I'll do it, Captain."

"And you'll do a damn fine job of it," Dom said. Kaufman was young, still wet behind the ears, but what choice did he have? She would need to work with the local law enforcement officials and makeshift civilian militia that had already done their part to set up defenses around Kent. But her midshipmen and even those civilians would benefit from working with someone like Kaufman who had some military training under her belt, despite her age. Skulls wouldn't be the only challenge Kaufman faced when it came to negotiating

353

how the island should be defended, but he would do his best to support her and ensure Kent remained a habitable shelter for the time being. He made a mental note to have Chao set her up with a radio and sat-phone so she'd have access to the Hunters whenever she needed it.

Another civilian bumped into his side as he made his way through the people awaiting triage. The slight touch sent undulating waves of fire through his ribs. But he hardly gave the pain a second thought when he saw his daughters. Maggie, her tail wagging, jumped when she reached Dom. He patted the dog's head and headed to Kara and Sadie.

Sadie wrapped her thin arms around him, squeezing his sides. He ignored the pain from his injuries and embraced her.

"You're back," she said, burying her face against his chest.

"I told you I would be," Dom replied.

Kara's lips parted in a wide smile as she lay in one of the medical beds.

"I kept my promise, didn't I?" he asked.

"You did," she said. "You did."

He bent over her, and she draped her arms around his neck. Even in that small gesture, he could tell she was weaker than before.

"How are you doing?" he asked.

"Been better," Kara said. "But Lauren and her crew took care of me. Going to have a couple of bad scars, but"—she shrugged—"I'm alive."

Dom put his hand over hers. "That's right." He gave her

a gentle squeeze. "And I'll always be thankful for that."

"I'll tell you one thing," Kara said. "I'm ready for some fresh air. I've been cramped up here for too long."

"We'll have to talk to the doc about that. But right now, she's got her hands full."

"Totally understand. Wish there was something I could do to help."

Dom let out a half-laugh.

"I'm serious."

"I know you are," Dom said. "You came off treatment for the Oni Agent. Your injuries haven't even had a chance to heal. And the one thing bothering you is wondering how you can help." He put one hand on her shoulder and the other on Sadie's. "I love you, girls." Maggie whined and pressed her body up against his legs. "You, too."

The dog's tail beat the air faster, and for a moment Dom could almost forget about the hell around them. He still had his family. He wondered how many others in the world were left that could count themselves as lucky as him. He doubted the tally was high.

But even now, he didn't have much time to enjoy with his family. He had a job to perform, and the *Huntress* needed its captain. He had only a couple of hours, waiting for Lauren and her team to process the civilians and midshipmen, with Kara and Sadie. They spent that time recalling camping trips and hikes and vacations to the Florida Keys. He had to comfort his daughters when those stories brought up memories of Bethany. This time, they didn't ask whether or not she'd be okay. They must've seen enough, as he had, to know the Oni Agent would've had plenty of time to complete her transformation into a Skull.

He tried to guide their conversations away from their lost mother. But he found he couldn't sincerely tell them everything would be okay. He feared the world had changed far too much to make such promises. He thought of the debriefings he needed to have with his crew and the tremendous task of setting up Kent Island. Then he pushed those thoughts aside. He'd almost died. He'd almost failed his daughters. He sat beside them, holding Kara's hand. Sadie nestled into his chair, and Maggie lay at his feet.

All he could do was enjoy this moment. He would relish every goddamned minute he got with them more than he ever had before, starting now. They laughed over shared memories, like the time Kara caught a ten-pound largemouth bass with a pink kiddie fishing pole. Back when they first brought Maggie home after adopting her, Sadie, only five at the time, was so scared of the fuzzy, golden puppy that she cried whenever Maggie came close.

"But I got over that quick," Sadie said, brushing her hands through Maggie's fur.

"That you did," Dom agreed.

Soon enough, the medical bay was empty except for the few midshipmen and survivors with more serious injuries that needed prolonged monitoring.

Lauren walked toward Dom and his daughters. "You ready? You're our last patient of the day."

"Fix me up, Doc," Dom said.

Lauren finished the job she'd started earlier, applying fresh bandages and giving Dom a second dose of the chelation treatment to treat the Oni Agent before it took hold. He found he wasn't scared of the possibility. He trusted Lauren. He trusted his crew. And he'd seen their determination and skill in the face of an almost unknowable enemy. One that faced them on land, manifesting itself as Skulls, and just as easily faced them in the microbiological realms in their bloodstreams. Yet he knew the men and women aboard the *Huntress* were prepared to vanquish the Oni Agent wherever it appeared.

When his bandages were changed and the injections done, Lauren gave him a few pills. "For the pain. Not much else we can do for those ribs now. I'd tell you bed rest is what you need, what with the chelation therapy potentially weakening your bones, but I know you're not going to listen."

"You got that right." Dom popped the pills and washed them back with water from a paper cup Lauren handed him. He paced toward the isolation ward and peered into the window. Scott and Ivan still lay in induced comas. The Oni Agent might've been eliminated from their bodies, but its effects had still damaged their brains. "You think we'll ever find something to help them?"

"I don't know," Lauren said. "I hope so, but I'm afraid the damage has taken its toll. The best we can do…" She paused, her voice trailing off. "The best we can do is keep their bodies alive. But I don't know that they'll ever get their minds back."

Dom sighed. He turned away from the invalid Hunters and faced Lauren. "Can your team take care of the patients here?"

Lauren nodded.

"I'm going to need you at a roundtable." He checked his watch. "We'll meet in forty."

"Aye, aye, Captain. I'll go inform the medical staff." She went back toward the patient exam beds, her white coat trailing behind her.

Dom returned to Kara and Sadie. "I've got work to do—"

Kara cut him off. "You always do." Her eyes appeared to well up for a moment before she wiped them with the back of her hand.

Tears streamed openly down Sadie's face, and her bottom lip trembled.

"I know, I know," Dom said. "But I'll be back soon."

"You always say that, too," Kara said.

"I haven't broken that promise."

"Not yet," Kara agreed.

He hugged both girls again. "You two mean the world to me. Don't ever forget that, okay?" He used his thumb to brush a tear away on Sadie's face then kissed her forehead. "As soon as our meeting's over, I'll be back here. Got it?"

They both nodded.

"Love you." He hugged them again before leaving the medical bay.

The passageways were still filled with his Hunters

unloading gear and helping resupply and ready the civilian flotilla for their short journey to Kent Island. He knocked on the door to the electronics workshop and told Chao to gather the Hunters, Thomas, and the comm specialists to the mess hall for the upcoming roundtable.

Dom had ten minutes before the meeting, and he needed the time to mentally prepare himself for everything they'd have to face: organizing the burials at seas for Hector, Owen, and Brett; finding their resupply depot; going over the new information Lauren's medical team had uncovered on the Oni Agent's spread and its biological origins; and determining where they'd travel to next to see if they could find any researchers or resources to help them combat the Oni Agent's prion disease components.

He found himself traversing the ladders to the upper deck and pushing out of a hatch. The breeze over the bay sprayed a salty mist over his face as the *Huntress* cut through the crystalline waves. He approached the bow and wrapped his fingers around the steel rails. He closed his eyes for a moment, soaking in the air and the warmth of the sun.

"Dom?" A voice broke his momentary reverie.

He turned to see Meredith.

Dom stared hard at her. It was the first time he'd seen her since the academy rescue operation. And he found himself damn glad to see her here. He pulled her into an embrace, and she wrapped her arms around him, her own grip strong and hardened.

They pulled away from each other for a second, and Dom

held her elbows. Her red hair whipped around her face, still smeared with a combination of dirt and dust and dried blood. She evidently hadn't spent a second to herself since reboarding the ship—probably helping the survivors and ensuring everyone else was accounted for and taken care of.

Typical Meredith, he thought. He admired her selflessness, her dedication to others. It was what had drawn them to each other in the first place.

"Dom, I need to know—"

Dom pulled her close. The sight of her before him like this crushed all the mental barricades he'd constructed to contain his emotions. His lips met hers for a moment. One small but significant moment. It wasn't a long kiss, but it was enough to make his skin tingle. Meredith interlaced her fingers with his, and he wrapped an arm around hers. Together, they faced the open water. She pressed herself close to him and laid her head on his shoulder.

"This has been a long time coming, hasn't it?" he said. "Too bad we had to go through hell first to get here."

"And there's no one I'd rather go through hell with," Meredith said.

"I'm not going to stop until we eradicate the Oni Agent," he warned.

Meredith chuckled. "You say that as if you think *I'd* give up."

Dom pulled a hand through her hair and kissed her forehead. "Let's get to it, shall we?"

"Aye, aye, Captain."

Together, they walked hand in hand back to the hatch. They shared a final kiss, alone above deck.

When their lips parted, Meredith let go of his hand and opened the hatch. "After you, Captain."

He nodded and climbed down the ladder, back into the noisy passageway. A thousand nagging thoughts plagued his mind as he rejoined his crew. But as the chatter of those traveling through the passageway filled the air around him and he caught sight of Meredith flashing him a grin through the crowd, he at least knew one thing about the coming days and the immense challenges before him.

He would not face them alone.

EPILOGUE

THE ORANGES AND REDS OF THE SETTING SUN bled across the docile sky. Eastward, the first sparkling stars were like pinpricks in a blanket wrapping the earth. Even the gulls seemed to have quieted as the *Huntress* idled in the Atlantic.

At the roundtable two days ago, Dom had been apprised of Sean's findings that the Oni Agent had originated at many different sites around the world. That seemed to support the idea that some deliberate act had led to the Oni Agent outbreak.

They'd also discussed setting up the final preparations to make Kent Island a habitable stronghold. Chao's team had been assigned to radio all nearby ships and direct them toward Kent. They'd guided the civilian and Academy flotilla to the island and anchored off the coast for a little over a day. Lauren had helped set up a landside triage center for the processing of new survivors, with Midshipman Kaufman's help and the aid of the island locals, who'd agreed to take on responsibility for protecting their little piece of earth against the Skulls. They'd even managed to hail the *Queen of the Bay* and ensured the ship could be towed safely to the island. Dom felt grateful to fulfill a promise he hadn't been certain he could keep.

After departing the island, they'd stopped briefly at an abandoned Army Supply Depot to reload their munitions. Given the depot's remote location, there'd been few Skulls to contend with, and the mission had been fortunately short and painless.

Their new mission was anything but. They'd sailed out into the Atlantic, far enough from shore to hold a much-deserved burial at sea for the Hunters who'd given everything.

Dom glanced across the deck filled with the men and women who served him. Miguel gave him a knowing nod as he stood behind Kara in her wheelchair. Maggie sat next to the Hunter, and Sadie stood beside her.

Before Dom lay the remains of Brett and Hector, their bodies wrapped in weighted shrouds. A third weighted shroud flapped in the wind, devoid of a body and filled only with a few symbolic belongings of Owen's. The guitar, the one Dom had seen Owen play only a few days ago, was one of them.

"These men gave their lives so that we may continue to fight for those who are defenseless," Dom said. "They fearlessly faced an enemy none of us could've imagined, that none of us were prepared for. They died so that we may live another day, so that we may pursue the promise of a better tomorrow, a brighter future. Today, we honor their service as Hunters. Firing party, present arms."

Several Hunters stepped forward, their rifles shouldered. Glenn, Andris, and Thomas tilted the platform with the fallen Hunters. The bodies and shrouds slid into the Atlantic. They quickly sank below the crashing, hungry waves, and the firing party shot off their three-volley salute while Jenna played "Taps" on a bugle.

Dom felt the mixture of pride for those Hunters who remained and the deep pangs of remorse for those they'd just buried. As the last notes of "Taps" echoed hauntingly over the ocean, Dom dismissed the crew. Meredith caught his gaze and gave him a reassuring, sympathetic smile. A small sign to let him know she was there.

"Captain," another voice called to him. Chao rushed between the others on deck. "I'm sorry, Captain, but I've got some urgent news."

"What is it?"

"We might have found a lab with the facilities and research experience we've been looking for."

"You mean a lab with surviving scientists?"

"Potentially," Chao replied. He led Dom back through the departing crew and into the electronics workshop. A series of satellite images were displayed on the monitors.

"What is this?" Dom asked.

"We've been doing everything we can to seek out any neurological labs that might be able to help us with the Oni Agent. Needless to say, it's been hard to find any signs of life. The pictures I'm showing you were taken from various satellite images we obtained during the past week over Boston Mass General Hospital, where the Center for Neurodegenerative Diseases is housed. Some world-renowned researchers work—er, worked—there."

"Okay. And what makes you think anyone is alive?"

"This." Chao flipped through the images. The first showed an empty roof over the hospital. Nothing special about it. It was time-stamped almost a week ago. He flipped to a more recent image. A large white SOS had been painted on the roof.

Dom's heart climbed into his throat. Someone was alive. Or at least, they had been. "So there might be someone there who can either help us with our research—or more likely, they're just someone who knows their way around the hospital."

"Is that good enough for you? Or do you want us to keep searching?"

Dom mulled it over a moment. "If someone can simply get us to the labs, we might be able to find research or even materials for Lauren's team. Why not get Lauren in here to see if she thinks it's worth it?"

They paged the doctor, and she arrived a few minutes later. "God, yes," she said once they'd updated her on Chao's discovery. "The papers my crew and I have been reading...well, plenty of the research I'd love to get my hands on happened at Mass Gen."

"Good, good," Dom said. Still, he was reluctant to risk his Hunters' lives after the losses they'd already suffered. "Is there any other evidence we'll find someone alive? Someone who can help us make the trip worthwhile?"

"I think so," Chao said. He moused over the image and zoomed in on a section of the hospital's roof.

Dom's blood ran cold at the image. A man, looking to be in his mid-twenties, sat against the lip of the roof. He had a backpack near him along with a couple of empty plastic bottles. The man wasn't alone. A woman, looking to be in the first stages of Skull transformation, lay beside him. The way her limbs were splayed, she seemed to have died.

And by the man's body language, the way he appeared to be staring at her, Dom could tell there was more to the story than this grainy satellite image alone could tell.

"Call up Detrick," Dom said, knowing Commander Shepherd would want to know where the *Huntress* was headed and what they'd discovered. "Let them know we're going to Boston."

THANK YOU FOR READING

I sincerely hope you enjoyed this second volume in *The Tide* series. Would you like to know when *Salvage*, Book 3 of the *Tide* series comes out? Check out my mailing list. You'll be able to stay updated on all my new releases. Plus, I give away ebooks, paperbacks, and audiobooks to readers on the list. Not a bad deal, I hope! Sign up here: **http://bit.ly/ajmlist**

I love to hear from readers, too! Don't be afraid to contact me through any of the following methods.

Facebook: **www.facebook.com/anthonyjmelchiorri**
Email: **ajm@anthonyjmelchiorri.com**
Website: **http://www.anthonyjmelchiorri.com**

ABOUT THE AUTHOR

Anthony J Melchiorri is a writer and biomedical engineer living in Maryland. He spends most of his time developing cardiovascular devices for tissue engineering to treat children with congenital heart defects when he isn't writing or reading.

Read more at **http://anthonyjmelchiorri.com** and sign up for his mailing list at **http://bit.ly/ajmlist** to hear about his latest releases and news.

Made in United States
North Haven, CT
23 November 2022

27165562R10226